Berkley Sensation Titles by Maureen McKade

TO FIND YOU AGAIN
AROUSE SUSPICION
CONVICTIONS
A REASON TO LIVE
A REASON TO BELIEVE
A REASON TO SIN

Anthologies

HOW TO LASSO A COWBOY
(with Jodie Thomas, Patricia Potter, and Emily Carmichael)

A Reason To Sin

Maureen McKade

BERKLEY SENSATION, NEW YORK

THE BERKLEY PUBLISHING GROUP
Published by the Penguin Group
Penguin Group (USA) Inc.
375 Hudson Street, New York, New York 10014, USA

Penguin Group (Canada), 90 Eglinton Avenue East, Suite 700, Toronto, Ontario M4P 2Y3, Canada
(a division of Pearson Penguin Canada Inc.)
Penguin Books Ltd., 80 Strand, London WC2R 0RL, England
Penguin Group Ireland, 25 St. Stephen's Green, Dublin 2, Ireland (a division of Penguin Books Ltd.)
Penguin Group (Australia), 250 Camberwell Road, Camberwell, Victoria 3124, Australia
(a division of Pearson Australia Group Pty. Ltd.)
Penguin Books India Pvt. Ltd., 11 Community Centre, Panchsheel Park, New Delhi—110 017, India
Penguin Group (NZ), 67 Apollo Drive, Rosedale, North Shore 0632, New Zealand
(a division of Pearson New Zealand Ltd.)
Penguin Books (South Africa) (Pty.) Ltd., 24 Sturdee Avenue, Rosebank, Johannesburg 2196,
South Africa

Penguin Books Ltd., Registered Offices: 80 Strand, London WC2R 0RL, England

A REASON TO SIN

A Berkley Sensation Book / published by arrangement with the author

PRINTING HISTORY
Berkley Sensation mass-market edition / March 2008

Copyright © 2008 by Maureen Webster.
Excerpt from *Where There's Fire* copyright © 2008 by Maureen Webster.
Cover art by Jim Griffin.
Cover design by George Long.
Hand lettering by Ron Zinn.
Interior text design by Kristin del Rosario.

ISBN: 978-0-425-22059-7

BERKLEY® SENSATION
Berkley Sensation Books are published by The Berkley Publishing Group,
a division of Penguin Group (USA) Inc.,
375 Hudson Street, New York, New York 10014.
BERKLEY SENSATION and the "B" design are trademarks belonging to Penguin Group (USA) Inc.

PRINTED IN THE UNITED STATES OF AMERICA

10 9 8 7 6 5 4 3 2 1

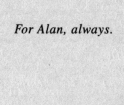
For Alan, always.

$\mathcal{O}$NE

MARCH 1868

REBECCA Glory Bowen Colfax was out of options. Her worn-out shoes muddy and her cheeks nearly numb, she paused at the corner of the street and brushed back a drooping tendril of hair from her face. Nobody needed a clerk or a waitress or even a laundress, which left few alternatives.

Rebecca studied the handful of false-fronted buildings interspersed with large canvas tents that lay across the invisible line separating the respectable from the disreputable. Although it was only two in the afternoon, numerous horses were tied to hitching posts and men wearing battered hats and noisy spurs milled in and out of the saloons. A piano's off-key notes spilled down the street along with the occasional raucous laughter. Rebecca had already experienced many frontier towns in Kansas, but this one was by far the biggest and wildest.

The sound of gunfire startled her, and she lifted her head sharply. Five men raced down the street, their horses' hooves tossing mud clumps in their wake. She covered her ears as more shots rang out and was shocked to see that few people gave the rowdy men more than a passing glance. The ruffians halted in front of one of the numerous drinking establishments and went inside, shoving and pushing each other like children.

Rebecca's courage wavered, and she started back the way she'd come. However, the gravity of her predicament stopped her, reminding her she had no choice. With her heart in her throat, she took a deep breath. Squaring her shoulders, she turned and marched back, crossing the invisible line that would no doubt lead to hell. But she'd made a promise a month ago, and even damnation couldn't stop her from fulfilling it.

Rebecca held her head high as she sidestepped a grizzled drunk who staggered out of one of the tent saloons.

"Hey, missy, wanna wet my whistle?" he slurred as he rubbed his crotch.

She swallowed back the bile that rose in her throat and scurried past him. If she stopped to think about what she was about to do, her courage would desert her.

She arrived at her destination and stopped to stare at the hanging wooden sign that displayed a rendition of a woman's shapely thigh encircled with a red garter. The Scarlet Garter. A scandalous name, but Rebecca had been impressed by the owner, or as impressed as she could be by a man who ran such an establishment.

The double doors taunted Rebecca, dared her to cross the threshold. She smoothed her gloved hands down the front of her once-fashionable skirt. Her heart thudded in her breast, and sweat dampened her palms and underarms. Closing her eyes, she pictured him, her reason for living and doing what she never in her worst nightmares dreamed of doing. The image strengthened her resolve and she opened her eyes. She extended her arm and pushed through the door, stepping onto a layer of fresh sawdust covering the wood floor.

Inside, it smelled of stale alcohol and caustic tobacco, overlaid with sour body odor. Rebecca fought the urge to press a handkerchief to her nose, and breathed through her mouth. Yet she knew the Scarlet Garter had a less offensive odor than most saloons.

Her eyes adjusted to the relative dimness, and she sent

her gaze around the room. Although there were a couple of dozen tables, only a few were in use. At one table two burly men drank beer and talked in low voices, and at the second, a thin man balanced a fancy lady on his lap while she whispered in his ear.

Could she do the same if she had to? Rebecca Bowen couldn't, but Rebecca Colfax had no choice.

At a third table a dark-haired man sat alone with his back to the wall, shuffling a deck of cards, then fanning them across the tabletop. Although he wasn't looking at her, she suspected he'd already cataloged her presence.

She dragged her attention away from the gambler and searched for the owner, but he wasn't in sight. Drawing her shoulders back, she crossed to the bar, her skirt hem brushing aside the sawdust.

"What may I get you, madam?" the bartender asked.

Startled, Rebecca stared at the man, whose body was disproportionately small compared to his head.

He wiped a towel across the bartop with a short, stubby hand and smiled. "Haven't you ever espied a dwarf?"

She snapped her mouth shut and shook her head. "No."

"Come closer."

Reluctant but curious, Rebecca neared the bar and spotted the plank the dwarf stood upon. He was perhaps three feet tall. "Have you always been this way?"

His eyes twinkled. "When I was eighteen, a barn roof fell upon me." Her eyes widened, and he shook his head sadly. "It was a very tragic day, indeed."

Rebecca suspected he wasn't speaking the truth, but it would be rude to accuse him of lying.

Suddenly he laughed. "I'm sorry for confounding you, madam. Yes, I have always been short of stature."

Eased by his sense of humor, Rebecca smiled. "No, I'm sorry for being so ill-mannered." She sobered. "I'd like to speak with the owner."

He eyed her, and Rebecca had the impression he could see more than most people. "I shall get him for you." The dwarf hopped onto the floor and disappeared through a doorway that probably led to a back office.

Rebecca's gaze lit on a nearly life-size portrait of a voluptuous nude hanging on the wall, and her cheeks burned. How could she even consider working in such a wicked place? Yet she couldn't afford to be embarrassed, not with so much riding on her finding Benjamin. And to continue her search, she needed money. Badly.

The owner followed the bartender through the doorway. He was as she remembered him, a man of medium height with thick, steel gray hair. His white ruffled shirt and black pinstriped suit were of high quality, the quality she'd seen in places like Chicago and New York.

"Mr. Andrew Kearny, owner of the Scarlet Garter," the bartender announced.

"Thank you, Dante," Kearny said to the small man before turning to Rebecca. The owner's brown eyes surveyed her from head to toe, and there was a hint of a leer in them. "I didn't expect to see you again," he said with a faint Southern drawl.

"I didn't expect to be here again," she retorted, hiding her apprehension behind a facade of brashness.

He came out from behind the bar and leaned against it, loosely clasping his hands across his waist. "I still haven't seen the man you're looking for."

Although she hadn't expected anything else, disappointment rolled through her. Two days ago she'd shown Benjamin's picture around in the saloons, but no one had seen him. She buried her frustration. "I'm here to inquire about a position." He continued to stare at her. "I'm in need of a job."

"Perhaps you should try the other side of town."

She fought back impatience. "I did." She glanced down, afraid the moisture stinging her eyes would form tears. "Nobody has anything."

"What can you do?" he asked.

She blinked and brought her head back up to meet his shrewd gaze. No matter what, she couldn't allow him to see her desperate fear. "I can read and write. I can also play the piano."

"I already have a piano player. Can you dance?"

Rebecca felt a twinge of indignation. Back in St. Louis,

she had learned everything a young woman of means needed to know. "Of course. I also sing."

He canted an eyebrow. "Well, well. I could use a singer, but it would only be for the busier nights. What I really need are more hurdy-gurdy girls."

Rebecca had never heard of a hurdy-gurdy girl. Was it simply another name for a lady of the evening? "What does a hurdy-gurdy girl do?" she asked warily.

"They wear short dresses, smile pretty, and dance with the clientele to get them to buy drinks," Kearny replied matter-of-factly. "The girls make a nickel for every drink the men buy for them."

Although she had her doubts about the short dress, Rebecca could dance and paste on a smile. However, she'd never touched alcohol other than the occasional glass of wine. "Do I have to drink whiskey?"

Kearny grinned, revealing a gold tooth. "No. The girls drink weak tea that comes out of a champagne bottle."

It was cheating plain and simple, but Rebecca wasn't in a position to argue. "Would I be expected to do more than sing and dance?"

The man shrugged. "It's not required, but some make extra money on their backs."

The crude expression sounded odd with his easy drawl, and the image his words invoked brought burning heat to her face. Although she was willing to do what she had to, the thought of lying beneath a panting, foul-breathed man made her stomach churn with revulsion. "I—" Her voice broke, and she cleared her throat. "I'd prefer to simply sing and dance, Mr. Kearny."

A knowing smile touched his lips. "That's fine. Do you have a name?"

Rebecca's tongue stuck to the roof of her mouth. "Glory Bowen."

"When can you start, Miss Glory?"

"Tomorrow night?"

He nodded. "That'd be fine. There's one empty room upstairs—fifty cents a night, and it'll come out of your pay. Do you want it?"

Relief made Rebecca dizzy. "Yes, I would. When can I move in?"

"Today, if you'd like."

"Thank you." Suddenly uncertain, Rebecca toyed with the strings of her reticule. "What do I need—for work, I mean?"

"Each girl supplies her own black stockings and shoes, and of course, underthings." His eyes glittered with amusement.

Rebecca wondered if she'd ever stop blushing. "What about dresses?"

"There's a room upstairs where we keep dancing dresses. I'm sure some will fit you." Kearny eyed her modest neckline. "You'll want cleavage. A man wants to see a woman's flesh when he dances with her. Each girl is required to wear a red garter, too."

Her face burned and she glanced away, only to have her gaze fall on the giggling whore still on the man's lap. Her yellow dress was hiked up high enough that the red garter was plainly visible on her thigh, and her bosom threatened to spill out of the low décolletage.

Rebecca quickly turned away. She couldn't imagine herself acting so brazen, yet wasn't that what she'd just agreed to do?

"Are you sure you want to do this?"

At his softly worded question, Rebecca looked up at Kearny. For a moment, she was tempted to confess everything, but her pride and apprehension kept her silent. Her stomach queasy, she nodded. "Yes."

He shrugged. "If you're moving in today, you can meet some of the girls this evening. They can answer any questions you have."

"When do I start singing?"

"How about Saturday night? That'll give you and Simon time to go over some songs."

Rebecca's gaze slid to the empty piano seat.

"He'll be here in a couple of hours. You can talk to him before it gets busy."

"All right."

"I'll show you out the back door. You can use that to come and go."

"Thank you."

"Don't thank me yet. Wait until tomorrow night, after your feet have been stomped on a few dozen times." He extended an arm. "I'll walk you out."

Projecting a coolness she didn't feel, Rebecca allowed him to guide her through the back doorway, past an office and a flight of stairs.

"These stairs take you to your room. You'll have number three," Kearny said.

Three. It used to be her favorite number. Her mouth paper dry, Rebecca nodded.

Kearny opened the door which led into an alley behind the building. "Last chance. Are you certain you can work in a place like this?"

No!

She ignored the silent scream and met his appraising gaze with her own steady one. "I'm certain, Mr. Kearny."

He held out his hand and, after a moment's hesitation, she gripped it. "Welcome to the Scarlet Garter, Miss Glory."

Not knowing what else to say, Rebecca walked out. The door closed behind her and she stood silently, the damp cold seeping into her. Her breath misted as she fought tears of helplessness, anger, and panic.

What have I done?

You did what you had to, for your baby.

In order to get her infant child out of the orphanage, she had to find her husband and tell him about the son he didn't know he had. But would Benjamin Colfax, who had gambled away her entire inheritance, even care?

SLATER Forrester shuffled the deck, the motions as familiar to him as shaving. He laid the cards facedown, fanned them across the table, then lifted the end one and brought them back together in his hands. Another shuffle, and he dealt four cards faceup. All were aces, just as he expected. He smiled to himself.

You haven't lost your touch, Forrester.

He heard the approach of someone and tensed, but immediately relaxed when he recognized the familiar footfalls. Andrew set a cup of steaming coffee down in front of him, then pulled out a chair and sat down.

"Thanks," Slater said.

Andrew took a sip from his own coffee, then deliberately looked down at the aces. "I thought you didn't deal a crooked game anymore."

"I don't, but it doesn't hurt to stay in practice."

Andrew laughed shortly. "Did you see her?"

Slater doubted he'd forget her light blonde hair and almost painfully straight backbone. When he'd first seen her enter the saloon, he thought she was lost. But then she'd pulled back her shoulders, displaying a fine set of breasts, and marched right up to the bar. An odd combination of admiration and protectiveness had rolled through him, but he kept his voice indifferent. "Couldn't miss her. Dresses nicer than most whores."

"According to her, she doesn't do that."

"Then why was she here?" Slater picked up his cup and leaned back in his chair, curious despite himself.

"She wanted a job. Says she can sing and dance."

Slater snorted, recalling her shapely figure. "I give her a week before she's on her back upstairs."

Andrew shook his head, his expression concerned. "You never used to be so cynical, Slater."

Slater quirked his lips upward in a caricature of a smile. "Sure I was. You were just too busy fleecing the sheep to notice."

The older man shrugged. "I was young and foolish. I never thought I'd end up running a straight house."

"We both ended up doing things we never thought we'd be doing." Slater stared into the distance, his thoughts detouring to Andersonville. For a moment, he could hear the endless groans and smell the blood, piss, and misery. His left hand trembled, spilling coffee onto his trouser leg. He set the cup down hastily and shook his head to dislodge the too-real memory.

"You more than me, my friend," Andrew said, compassion in his eyes.

Slater gnashed his teeth, hating the sympathy. "Yeah, well, like you always told me, a man makes his own bed." He grinned lecherously. "Unless he's got a soft woman to make it for him."

"Women, cards, and danger, and not necessarily in that order." Andrew quoted the description he'd pegged Slater with years ago.

Slater gathered the cards he'd laid on the table and shuffled them, relieved to see his left hand had stopped shaking.

"Is that"—Andrew gestured toward his hand—"going to get in the way of dealing?"

Slater fought down impatience, but it was directed at himself rather than his friend and boss. It had taken him nearly two years to regain his former weight and strength after he'd been released from the brutal prisoner of war camp. However, despite his left hand looking normal, whenever he was distressed, it would tremble like an old man's. He hated what he'd become.

"If it does, I'll quit," he replied flatly.

Andrew narrowed his eyes.

"So what's her name?" Although curious about the new gal, Slater was more interested in changing the subject.

"Miss Glory."

Slater barked a laugh. "With a name like that, she's no blushing virgin."

"I'd bet my last dollar she's not a sporting woman. She talks fancy, like she's been to school."

"Must be down on her luck. That's why women end up in a place like this. And sooner or later, they all end up whores."

Andrew glared at him. "It's not like I force them to prostitute themselves."

Slater lifted his hands, palms out. "I never said you did. But there's a reason the good women steer clear of this side of town."

"Well, if she sings half as good as she looks, she won't have to sell herself." Andrew shook his head and shrugged. "She'll start dancing tomorrow night. Since Frannie quit last week, I've been making less money on drinks. It'll be good to have another girl working again."

"I never thought I'd see the day when you were more businessman than gambler."

"And I never figured you'd come back to gambling after you ran off to join the Pinkertons."

Slater rubbed his jaw, already feeling the rasp of whiskers despite having shaved less than four hours earlier. He remembered how he hadn't been able to shave at Andersonville, and how one morning he'd awakened to find a spider had taken up residence in his beard. And then there were the nits . . . . He'd shave again before he started dealing, just as he did every evening. "Yeah, well, that makes two of us."

Andrew laid his forearms on the table and leaned forward. "When I took in that skinny sixteen-year-old kid and taught him how to play poker, I knew he'd be better than me someday. You were good, Slater. Damned good. But for you, gambling was only a way to make some money, not a way of life. When that Pinkerton agent asked you to join, I could see that was something you really wanted to do." Andrew paused to study Slater. "Why did you leave the agency?"

When Slater had come looking for a job from his mentor three months ago, he'd told Andrew only the facts: that he'd been at Andersonville and he'd quit the Pinkertons. Being a gambler made Andrew more observant than Slater would've liked, and the older man had filled in some of the blanks himself. Of course, Slater had neither denied nor confirmed Andrew's assumptions.

Slater shrugged insolently. "I got tired of having them tell me what to do."

"There's more to it than that."

Andrew wasn't going to settle for anything less than the truth this time, and Slater wasn't about to spill his guts. Not to anyone, not even the man who saved his life.

The saloon doors burst open and two drunken cowboys stumbled in, cussing and shoving one another, and giving Slater an excuse to ignore his friend's prying.

"It's too early for this," Andrew muttered.

"Not when they're moving cattle through, and they only have a day or two to blow off steam."

Oaktree was beginning to grow because of the cattlemen and the herds coming out of Texas. Slater suspected it was only a matter of time before Oaktree and other towns like it would be booming because of the cattle and the coming of the railroad. Andrew Kearny had been shrewd to set up his place here, but with more business came more opportunities for dangerous gunplay among drunken men.

With spurs ringing, the new arrivals strode to the bar.

"What can I obtain for you gentlemen?" Dante asked courteously.

"Two whiskeys, little man," one of the young cowboys ordered.

Slater gritted his teeth, angered by the slur against the dwarf even though Dante had once told him only smaller men than him resorted to insults.

Dante poured two shots from a brown bottle. "That will be fifty cents." He paused. "Two bits each."

Grumbling, the boys slapped down their coins and swallowed the rotgut without flinching. They turned to look around the saloon, and their lecherous eyes lit on Molly, who was trying to drum up some upstairs business. The smirking boys ambled over to her, their path not quite straight, and the shorter one tugged her off the man's lap.

"What's goin'—"

"There's two of us and only one of you," the larger of the cowboys interrupted the man who'd been holding Molly.

The man stood, his stance none too steady. "She's mine." He tugged her back against his side.

"Now hold on, boys. Y'all are jest gonna have to take turns," Molly said with a slow drawl and a coquettish smile.

"We don't wanna wait. Been a long time since I done dipped my wick," the smaller and more belligerent cowboy said. He grabbed hold of Molly's wrist and jerked her against him.

"Now just take it easy, fellas," Molly said, trying to defuse the explosive situation. "You hurt me, and I ain't gonna be able to do anything with any of you." Her voice trembled beneath the bravado.

Slater's cards lay forgotten on the table as his hands clenched in his lap. He couldn't abide a woman, even one like Molly who knew the ropes, being manhandled.

The short, wiry cowboy kissed her and held her struggling body in a punishing hold while her former "suitor" was held in place by the cowboy's friend.

Before he could stop himself, Slater stood. "I don't think the lady appreciates your attention."

The cowboy lifted his head and wrapped an arm around Molly's neck, shifting her around so her back was pressed against his chest. "Sure she does." He brought his mouth close to her ear. "Don't ya?"

Her face red, Molly nodded and spoke to Slater. "I'm all right."

Although she seemed to be fine, Slater didn't like the way the cowboy's arm tightened around her neck. Ensuring his sleeve gun was in place, Slater took a step toward them. "Let her go."

The cowboy squeezed Molly's breast and she gasped in pain. "Not until me and her take care of business."

"You're hurting her."

"Why do you care? She's just a whore."

Slater shook his head, keeping his anger tamped down. "It's not right to hurt a woman, *any* woman."

"You ain't gonna stop me, mister." The cowboy started dragging Molly toward the stairs, moving closer to Slater as he did.

Slater shot out a hand and grabbed the younger man, who released Molly as he struggled to escape. With his other hand, Slater punched the cowboy, dropping him to the floor like a sack of flour.

"I wouldn't," Dante said.

Slater jerked his head up to see the diminutive bartender aiming a sawed-off shotgun at the other cowboy, whose hand hovered near his revolver.

Andrew stepped forward. "Get yourself and your friend

out of here. I don't want to see either one of you in my place again."

Without argument, the larger cowboy pulled his friend to his feet, then half dragged him out of the saloon. The few other patrons turned back to their drinks as if nothing had happened.

"Thanks, Slater," Molly said, her face pale except for two splotches of rouge on her cheeks. She readjusted her breasts within her dress. "I'm not usually afraid of liquored-up cowboys, but they were mean ones." She tilted her head to the side, her demeanor turning seductive. "You have to let me thank you proper sometime."

Slater merely smiled and returned to his chair as Molly rejoined the man who'd been fondling her earlier. After a few whispered words, she escorted her customer up the stairs.

Slater reached for the cards, but his left hand betrayed him. Instead, he picked up his coffee cup in his right hand while settling his left in his lap.

"It's nice to know some things haven't changed," Andrew commented, taking his previous place at Slater's table.

Slater feigned ignorance. "I don't know what you're talking about."

"Lady Jane."

Slater kept his expression bland, although his memory supplied him with a picture of the young prostitute who'd nearly been killed by a knife-wielding customer. Slater had been passing by her room and had taken care of the perverted bastard.

Maybe defending others was Slater's way of trying to make up for not protecting a boy a long time ago. A boy who died because Slater was too frightened to help him.

Two

REBECCA threw open the single window in room number three, and although the late afternoon air was cool, it was infinitely better than the mustiness that permeated the enclosed area. She sniffed, already noticing a difference in the moving current. Even as a child she'd never been able to abide stale air, and would crack her window open at night after her parents had kissed her good night.

Tears burned her eyes, as abrupt as the invasion of the bittersweet memory. How she'd fallen these past two years, from a canopied bed with frills and ruffles in an elegant home to a single mattress with coarse bedclothes above a saloon. Of course, that loss was inconsequential to losing her mother and father in one cruel instant. She drew out of the past, afraid to tarry long, or she might lose what will she'd been forced to gain this past year.

Rebecca removed her bonnet and coat, and draped them on a wall hook. Crossing her arms, she inspected her new home and was pleasantly surprised to find it clean and cozy, better than many of the boardinghouses and hotels she'd stayed in on her journey.

Someone knocked on the door, and she cracked it open.

The woman's bright red dress caught her eye immediately, and she reacted with a downturn of her lips. However, the realization that she was now one of *them* softened her mouth. And her condemnation.

Rebecca swung open the door and greeted her visitor in her best hostess voice. "Hello."

The dark-haired woman's gaze swept Rebecca's figure, making her feel like a mare on the auction block. "So you're the new girl." She sallied into the room, forcing Rebecca to step back.

She closed the door and faced the painted woman, noticing the wrinkles at the corners of her eyes and the creases beside her mouth. However, she suspected the woman was only a few years older than her own twenty-two. "Miss Glory Bowen," Rebecca said. "And you are?"

"Cassie. We don't go by long, fancy names around here," she said, her scorn obvious. "I'm in charge of the girls here at the Garter." She lifted her chin as if expecting Rebecca to challenge her sovereignty.

Both annoyed and uneasy in the woman's company, Rebecca realized she couldn't afford to get on her bad side, and forced a smile. "It's nice to meet you, Cassie. I was hoping someone would stop by so I could ask some questions."

Cassie shrugged as if she didn't care one way or other what Rebecca hoped. "Andrew said you might need some help." She snorted. "He didn't say anything about you being a schoolmaid."

Rebecca bristled at the description. "And he didn't say anything about you at all."

Cassie's flinch turned to a scowl. "He's a busy man." She glanced around, then went to the window and slammed it shut. Placing a foot on Rebecca's bed, the woman raised the hem of her knee-length dress.

Rebecca tensed, suddenly aware she was ignorant in this world of saloons and easy pleasures. Cassie withdrew a cheroot from her garter and placed it between her red lips. Shocked, Rebecca watched her lean over to light it with the lamp's flame, then exhale a long stream of smoke.

"Never seen a woman smoke, have you?" Cassie asked, leaning back against the window frame.

Cassie's amused tone swept aside Rebecca's distaste, and she met Cassie's mocking eyes. "As a matter of fact, I have." She didn't add that it had been a newspaper picture of an infamous madam in St. Louis.

Cassie studied her a moment. "You said you had some questions."

Regaining her composure, Rebecca nodded. "Mr. Kearny said there would be dresses to wear. Can you tell me where I can find them?"

"At the end of the hall there's a room without a number. It's got dresses and some other things you might be needing. You take what you want and return it to the room when you're done."

"So everyone wears the same dresses?" Although the idea appalled her, she was in no position to criticize.

"Every Sunday all the dresses are taken to the Chinese laundry and last week's brought back."

At least they were washed once a week.

"What time do we start, uh, working in the evenings?"

"'Bout three on Saturdays and Sundays. Five the other days. If you want to make some extra money by selling yourself, you can go down earlier. At night you work until there aren't any more men to dance with or they're all too drunk to stand up."

Rebecca reeled. "What of days off?"

Cassie held her cheroot between two fingers and laughed scornfully. "You need a day off, you ask me. I ask Andrew." Her expression turned more thoughtful, less cynical. "Lucky for us, he's not crazy or mean like a lot of 'em."

A shiver slid down Rebecca's spine. What had she gotten herself into?

"Look, I don't know why you want to work here, but I do know you ain't got a chance if you're going to act all prissy like some snooty-nosed lady." Cassie paused, then added with more understanding than Rebecca expected, "This is your life now, Glory, and you'd best get used to it."

Her matter-of-fact tone strengthened Rebecca's flagging resolve. "You're right. I'm sorry. It's just all so different."

Cassie's time-hardened expression lost some of its cynicism. "You'll get used to it soon enough. Let's go to the dress room and I'll pick you out something to wear. When it's time to go downstairs later, I'll walk with you."

Panic clawed at Rebecca's chest. "Mr. Kearny said I'd start tomorrow night."

Cassie shrugged. "That's fine, but I thought you might want to spend an evening watching to see how it's done."

In spite of Rebecca's plan to stay in her room that night, the woman's suggestion made sense. "That might be a good idea."

Cassie's smile was almost friendly. "Let's find you a dress before the best ones are taken."

Rebecca followed Cassie down the hall, aware of the contrast between them. Cassie with her shockingly short red dress and she with her proper drab-colored dress. Yet Rebecca was about to become Miss Glory, a woman with more similarities to than differences from Cassie.

The older woman, still smoking her cheroot, opened the door at the end of the hall and allowed Rebecca to precede her in. A variety of colors hanging from hooks on the walls caught her eye, and she stared in consternation at the dresses with far too little material around the bosom and hem.

Cassie critically studied Rebecca for a moment, then retrieved a sky blue dress with yellow piping along the hem and neckline. She held it up against her. "This should fit, and the color will look good with your hair and eyes. Try it on."

"Now?" Rebecca squeaked.

"You afraid someone might see your fancy drawers?" Cassie snorted. "There ain't nobody here at the Scarlet Garter who ain't seen a woman's legs." She winked. "And more."

Her face flaming yet again, Rebecca removed her dress and petticoats. She pulled the blue dress over her head and tugged it down as far as she could without pulling it off her breasts. The hem came to a couple inches below the knees, longer than Cassie's, but it still revealed her ankles and most of her calves.

Cassie fussed with her neckline, drawing it this way and that until she was satisfied. Rebecca glanced down to see fleshy slopes leading to the shadowed crevasse between her breasts and nipples straining to pop out. She flattened her palms over her exposed chest. "I can't wear this."

Cassie merely took a last puff of her cheroot and ground the end out on the window sill. "You'll wear it or you're back on the street. Your choice, Glory."

For the first time, Rebecca truly understood the ramifications of her decision to work at the Scarlet Garter. Hadn't she told herself it didn't matter what she had to do, that she would do it without question? There was someone more important than her reputation, and even her life.

Squaring her shoulders, she nodded brusquely. "What time should we go down?"

"Quarter of five."

Rebecca's stomach growled, reminding her she'd eaten only a piece of bread for breakfast and nothing for dinner. "What about meals?"

"Tent next door serves dinner and supper. Tell them you work here and they'll put your meals on Mr. Kearny's bill, just like the rest of us." Cassie opened a drawer of a scarred dresser and pulled out a red garter. She handed it to Rebecca. "If it breaks, don't worry. Mr. Kearny always makes sure we got enough. You got black stockings and fancy shoes?"

Rebecca nodded.

"Make sure your shoes fit good, or you ain't going to be working long," Cassie advised. "Go on back to your room for now. Any time you want supper, go ahead and eat. But be ready to go downstairs when I come get you."

As Cassie brushed past her, Rebecca touched her arm, halting her. "Thank you."

Cassie squeezed her cool hand, then quickly released it and hurried out, as if she were embarrassed by her action.

Her head swirling with too much information, Rebecca grabbed her discarded dress and petticoats and hastened down the hall to her room. It stank of cheroot smoke, and she threw open the window. In a flurry of motion, she removed the blue dress and replaced it with her staid one, yet it did little to calm her nerves.

Digging into her carpetbag, she pulled out a tiny swatch of white material. She pressed the pristine christening gown to her cheek and sank to the floor by the window.

I'm coming back to get you, Daniel. I promise.

TOO embarrassed to wear her working dress to the dining tent next door, Rebecca went to eat supper soon after Cassie had left. The other women in the tent were attired in clothing more suited for saloons and brothels than dining. Rebecca felt their curious gazes on her, but couldn't meet their eyes. Although starving earlier, she could barely force down the venison and potatoes that were surprisingly tasty. When she was done, she scurried back to her room.

Keeping her mind blank, she dressed in her new "uniform" and brushed her hair, then gathered it into a bun at the back of her neck. Looking at her face in the small mirror, Rebecca could almost convince herself that she remained respectable. However, one glance downward disposed of that notion. Once she descended the stairs, her fate was cast. No more afternoon soirees with the crème de la crème of society; no more waltzing in a ballroom beneath shimmering chandeliers; no more hat tips from gentlemen.

Her lower lip trembled, and she caught it between her teeth. What did any of those gentilities mean if she broke her promise? Besides, she was already ruined in the eyes of her former acquaintances.

A rap on her door dispelled her bitter memories, and she opened the door to Cassie, still in her red gown.

"I thought I told you to be ready when I came," Cassie said.

Rebecca lifted her outspread arms. "I'm ready."

Cassie shook her head in disgust, spun Rebecca around, and plucked the pins from her hair. The long, silky waves spilled across Rebecca's shoulders and down her back. Before she could object, Rebecca found herself being tugged by her wrist down the hall. Cassie ushered her into a room much like Rebecca's, but heavy with cheroot smoke and perfume. Underclothing was thrown across the dresser and bed.

Cassie pressed her down on the unmade bed. "Sit. You need color in your face."

Horrified, but recognizing Cassie's expertise, Rebecca nodded numbly. Keeping her spine stiff, she closed her eyes. Soft bristles brushed against her cheeks, then rouge was painted on her lips.

"Done," Cassie said.

Rebecca opened her eyes and Cassie led her to the dresser's mirror. The woman who stared back at Rebecca had familiar golden-brown eyes, but everything else bespoke a stranger—the flowing hair, pink cheeks, and sinfully full red lips.

"What do you think?" Cassie asked.

I don't know who I am.

"I'm, uh, different."

Cassie shrugged. "You're Miss Glory."

Hearing the name she'd chosen to use, Rebecca nodded at her reflection. No longer was she the daughter of the St. Louis Bowens. "Yes, I am."

She followed Cassie down the front stairs, the ones leading into the saloon. Unaccustomed to cool air eddying around her exposed calves, Rebecca shivered and the tips of her breasts hardened. She was afraid to look down, afraid to see the stark outline of her nipples beneath the blue material.

Kearny met them at the bottom of the steps and Rebecca kept her gaze on him, although she was aware of the leers directed her way.

Her employer's gaze swept across her, pausing on her chest. "You're a vision of beauty, Miss Glory," he said gallantly.

Despite the heat that blossomed in her cheeks, she met his gaze. "Thank you, Mr. Kearny." She lowered her voice. "Thank you for giving me a chance."

Kearny shrugged. "If you do half as well as I think you will, I'll be the one thanking you."

Listening to Kearny's cultured drawl, Rebecca could

almost imagine she was in a drawing room in St. Louis. But the gruff laughter and smell of sawdust and stale alcohol dispelled the image.

"You want me to take her around, Mr. Kearny?" Cassie asked.

He shook his head. "I'll do it."

Kearny threaded her hand through the crook of his arm, and Rebecca felt a wave of déjà vu of her former life. However, as he introduced her to some of the customers, the reality of her position mocked those memories. As the men made a show of touching the brims of their hats, their gazes latched onto her chest, and she had the urge to wave her hands and shout, "I'm up here." But other than their ogling, she found them to be unlike the groping rabble she'd expected, and some of the tension eased from her muscles.

However, she felt a prickle of unease as Kearny led her to a table in the far corner. She recognized the man who'd been shuffling cards earlier that day when she'd come looking for a job. She watched his well-formed hands and agile fingers manipulate the cards with amazing dexterity. A fleeting memory of Benjamin doing the same flickered through her mind.

"Miss Glory Bowen, Mr. Slater Forrester," Kearny said by way of introduction.

His motions unhurried, Forrester gathered the cards and lifted his head. Extraordinary blue eyes and hair the color of a raven's wing made Rebecca's breath catch in her throat. She'd met her share of handsome men, but not even Benjamin had made her feel as if her corset was too tight.

"Miss Glory," he said with a lazy drawl.

"Slater is one of the house dealers. That means—"

"He works for the gambling establishment and the largest percentage of his winnings are the property of the establishment," Rebecca finished.

"That's correct," Kearny said, obviously surprised by her knowledge.

She glanced down, wishing she'd kept silent.

"You've worked in a gambling establishment," Forrester said, his expression giving away nothing of his thoughts.

"No," she replied but didn't offer an explanation.

She was relieved when Kearny smoothed over the awkward silence. "Miss Glory will be singing a few nights a week."

"Can you sing?" Forrester asked.

"Slater!" Kearny reprimanded.

He shrugged indifferently.

Rebecca started to cross her arms but realized it would only maximize her cleavage. She settled on a glare at the dealer. "You can be the judge tomorrow night."

Forrester inclined his head. "I'll do that."

Kearny withdrew his timepiece from his vest pocket and glanced at it. "Slater, would you mind introducing Miss Glory to Simon? I'm expecting a wagonload of supplies any time now."

Rebecca didn't miss the annoyance flash across Forrester's face and opened her mouth to tell him she could introduce herself. But Forrester spoke up first.

"It'd be my pleasure," he said to Kearny, but his eyes were on her.

"Thanks." Kearny turned to Rebecca. "He'll take care of you."

Rebecca gritted her teeth, holding back her retort, as Kearny traversed the saloon, then disappeared into the back.

Forrester rose, smoothed a hand over his tailored suit, and held out his arm. He gazed at her, and she noted that his gaze remained on her face and didn't dip down to her chest. Oddly reassured, she linked her arm with his and rested her fingers on his firm forearm. The smell of soap and the faint aroma of peppermint, scents much more palatable than what permeated the saloon, wafted from him.

As they neared the piano, the player stood and turned around. Rebecca had to tip back her head to see his face. But it wasn't his size that appalled her. It was his color. He was a Negro.

Growing up in St. Louis, she had seen her share of slaves but had little to do with them. Her parents didn't own any, but they did not speak out against the practice of slavery.

"Miss Glory Bowen, I'd like you to meet Simon Richards. Simon, this is the singer Andrew hired," Forrester said.

Simon smiled broadly, and his brown eyes twinkled with pleasure behind his round spectacles. "Pleased to meet ya, Miss Glory."

Rebecca clamped down on her outrage and managed a brittle smile. "Mr. Richards."

"Call me Simon. Ev'rybody does."

"Of course."

Frowning, Forrester said, "I believe Miss Glory needs a drink before discussing a selection of songs." He led her to the bar, where Dante was working. "Bring Miss Glory a special."

Rebecca drew away from him. "I don't want a drink."

"You'll have one any way." Forrester's eyes glittered with anger.

As she glowered at the gambler, Dante returned with a shot glass filled with amber liquid.

"Drink it," Forrester ordered her.

Rebecca debated defying him, but the furious glint in his eyes stopped her. Bracing for the harsh burn of liquor, she was startled to find it was cold, weak tea. She set the empty glass on the bar but didn't meet Forrester's gaze.

"What was that about?" Forrester demanded in a hushed voice.

Rebecca didn't pretend to misunderstand him. "He's a Negro."

"He's a free man. And if you want to work here, you'll give Simon the same consideration you give Mr. Kearny and everyone else in this saloon."

"Including you?"

Forrester leaned close, and his peppermint breath washed across her. "Yes."

"You're not my employer."

Abruptly, Forrester smiled, but the expression was grim and forbidding. "No, but Andrew and I have known each other a long time."

Her thoughts raced with long-held beliefs, her reaction to Simon, and Forrester's threat. If what he said was true, she couldn't afford to antagonize him. "I've never talked to a black person," she admitted.

"Other than their skin color, there's no difference between them and us." Forrester paused. "If you can't get past your narrow-mindedness, you need to find a job elsewhere."

Rebecca quaked inwardly. It had taken every ounce of will she possessed to get this job. Besides, the other saloons she'd seen while searching for Benjamin were far less clean and their clientele coarser.

"It's your decision, Miss Glory," Forrester said.

And with that, the gambler strode away. She watched him in the mirror as he returned to his table and picked up his cards. If she hadn't known how angry he was, she wouldn't have guessed from the bland expression he now held.

"Another?" Dante asked, holding up a bottle labeled Champagne.

"No, thank you."

Dante shrugged and set the bottle aside. He picked up a towel and wiped the bartop. "Slater is correct."

Rebecca's head recognized the truth of Dante's words, but she couldn't change the way she felt. "Where I grew up, Negroes were not recognized as equals."

"Eastern Missouri."

"How did you know?"

Gentle understanding filled Dante's expression. "Your accent, my dear. It's charming, but indicative of your origins."

Disturbed by his perceptiveness, Rebecca asked sarcastically, "And what else do you know about me?"

Dante didn't seem bothered by her tone. "You were raised in relative wealth and received the finest education, wrought with upper-class ideals and mores. However, because of some folly on your part you lost both your wealth and your family, which brought you here, to the Scarlet Garter."

Rebecca looked away as her eyes burned, and she blinked rapidly, so tears wouldn't form. "You're half right, Dante," she said hoarsely. She took a deep breath and turned her head to gaze at Simon. Could she work with him?

" 'No passion so effectually robs the mind of all its powers of acting and reasoning as fear,' " Dante quoted.

Rebecca searched her memory. "Edmund Burke."

Dante smiled, pleased. "It's a gift to have an educated person such as yourself grace our presence."

Rebecca couldn't help but laugh at his overstated gallantry, and some of the ice in her stomach thawed. She considered Dante's borrowed words. Was she afraid of Simon? Is that why she acted so horribly toward him?

Impulsively, she clasped the bartender's small hand and squeezed it. "Thank you, Dante."

Taking a deep, steadying breath, but not so deep as to expel her breasts from her dress, Rebecca rejoined Simon, who sat by the piano, sheets of music in his large hands. She looked over his exceedingly broad shoulders and recognized the top sheet. " 'No Home, No Home.' That seems appropriate to start with," she said.

Simon turned to give her a puzzled look. "Miss Glory?"

She forced herself to pat his shoulder and found the contact wasn't nearly as frightening as she expected. A genuine smile lifted her lips. "Someday I'll tell you a story, but for now, we have a repertoire to arrange."

$\mathcal{T}$HREE

IF Simon suspected Rebecca's discomfort around him, he didn't show it. He treated her with courtesy and friendliness as he spoke in a rich baritone that she found soothing to listen to.

"Do you sing, Simon?" she asked curiously.

He chuckled, a deep rumbling sound. "No, ma'am. I tried one time, but even the chickens squawked."

Rebecca laughed. "Whoever said chickens have an ear for music?"

"They was right, ma'am. I can't hold a tune at'll, but I can make this piano sing." He ran a big hand across the wood, his affection for the instrument obvious.

"Hopefully, between the two of us, we can keep the chickens from squawking too much." Rebecca shuffled through the music they'd chosen. "Mr. Kearny wants me to start singing tomorrow night. Would you be able to practice with me tomorrow, before the saloon gets busy?"

"Tomorrow's Saturday, so men'll be coming in by noon. We'll have to practice early."

"What time will the saloon close tonight?"

Simon shook his head. "Depends on how many folks is in

here. Sometimes Mr. Kearny locks the doors at midnight, sometimes not 'til three or four in the morning."

Rebecca's feet ached just thinking about dancing until the early morning hours. She gnawed her lower lip, tasted the paint, and grimaced. "I hate to ask you to practice after only a few hours of sleep."

"Don't you worry about me, Miss Glory. I can get by on three, four hours of sleep."

"I'm not sure I can," she murmured then asked more clearly. "How about eight A.M.?"

"I'll be here," Simon promised.

The sound of women's voices caught Rebecca's attention, and she spotted two saloon ladies coming down the stairs. Her face heated as she recognized the one who was being fondled earlier in the day, but the other one surprised her in the same way Simon had. However, where Simon's skin was nearly coal black, the woman's complexion reminded Rebecca of rich caramel. Having become more comfortable around Simon as they talked together, Rebecca wasn't nearly as shocked by the Negro woman's appearance.

"She's got it," the black-haired woman said, and charged toward Rebecca. "You're wearin' my dress."

Rebecca stiffened and glanced down at the clothing in question. "I was under the belief that the dresses were shared by us all."

The woman's dark complexion took on a dusky hue. "That's the one I always wear. Everybody knows that."

Rebecca noticed Cassie, smirking, standing back with the men who were watching the proceedings with eager anticipation. Obviously Cassie had known what would happen when she'd chosen the dress.

"I'm sorry. I didn't know." Rebecca managed the apology in spite of her anger and humiliation.

The woman made a grab for Rebecca, and Simon insinuated himself between them.

"Now hold on there, Miss Georgia. Miss Glory's new here, and you ain't giving her a very nice welcome," he said.

Georgia scowled at the tall Negro. "Don't you be taking her side, Simon."

"I ain't taking anyone's side. It's just that Miss Glory didn't know any better." He paused. "You was new here once, too."

Some of Georgia's wrath faded in the face of Simon's quiet voice. "I guess it's all right just this once." She shook a finger at Rebecca. "Just you remember next time."

Unable to speak, Rebecca nodded.

Cassie joined them and glanced around meaningfully at the disappointed men who'd been hoping to see a hair-pulling, fingernail-scratching brawl. "Let's get their minds on drinking and dancing."

Simon sat down and launched into a lively tune. Georgia and the other lady were jerked into the arms of two men and pulled onto the floor.

Humiliated, but knowing she couldn't back down, Rebecca stepped closer to Cassie in order to be heard above the piano's tune. "Did I pass the test?" she asked, her voice rife with sarcasm.

"I don't know what you mean," Cassie said, her expression saying the opposite.

Rebecca smiled with an edge of warning. "I won't be scared off."

Cassie's feigned ignorance melted away. "I don't want no simpering lady upsetting the other girls. I want to make sure you got some backbone so you can do your share of work around here."

Twenty-four hours ago Rebecca would've been pushed to tears by Cassie's callous words, but she'd undergone a transformation. Miss Glory wasn't about to sob like a schoolgirl. She lifted her chin. "I'll do my share, and I'll expect you to treat me just like anybody else who works here."

"You prove to me tomorrow night you can do your job; then I'll start treating you like the other girls."

"Fair enough."

Cassie flounced away, to be caught by a burly man who spun her onto the floor.

Red garters flashed and the women's high-pitched giggles mixed with low laughter as the men spun the girls around in a dizzying parody of a jig. Tomorrow Rebecca would be among them, and although she remained anxious, she also felt a flutter of excitement.

"THAT'S it. I'm out." The cattleman tossed his cards to the middle of the table and shoved back his chair.

The other two men shook their heads, finished their beer, and ambled out of the saloon.

Alone, Slater shrugged and gathered the deck in his skilled hands. The pile of coins in front of him didn't add up to much, but for a Friday evening, it wasn't bad. Rubbing his nose against the stench of tobacco smoke, Slater glanced over at the cleared area that served as a dance floor. The saloon gals were being swung around by men with more enthusiasm than skill. However, the girls didn't seem to mind. He figured it was a lot like dealing cards, in that it was simply a job.

His gaze strayed to the piano, where Simon's fingers flew across the keys. Somewhat hidden beside the piano Miss Glory watched, just as she'd done most of the evening. A couple of men had asked her to dance earlier, but she'd smiled and shaken her head. Fortunately, the men didn't press the issue. Dante's efficiency with the sawed-off shotgun behind the bar was well-known.

With no players in sight and his mouth dry, Slater sauntered up to the bar. Dante brought him a cup of coffee without prompting.

"Thanks." Slater took a sip. "Quiet night."

"Everyone is preparing for tomorrow night's debauchery," Dante said.

Slater smiled crookedly, appreciating the diminutive man's wit. "How's Miss Glory doing?"

Dante glanced over at her and smiled. "She and Simon are getting along splendidly. And I believe she passed her first test."

"Yeah, I noticed she was wearing Georgia's usual dress. I expected a cat fight."

Dante's smile faded. "Miss Glory's not your characteristic daughter of joy."

"If you're trying to tell me she isn't a whore, I'm withholding judgment."

Dante eyed Slater closely. "You're a cynical man, Slater Forrester."

"I've been called worse."

Dante's gaze softened. "Yes, I suppose you have."

The bartender's comment sounded too much like pity, and Slater's irritation made him curt. "Think she'll work out?"

Dante accepted the change of subject gracefully. "I don't believe she has any other options."

Most of the women who worked in places like the Scarlet Garter did so because they didn't have a choice. However, Slater had known a few who preferred that type of life rather than being bound by society's stringent rules or dominated by a husband. He couldn't blame them. He, too, preferred to remain free.

Miss Glory glided away from the piano and joined them, but she kept her gaze on the bartender. "Could I please have a special, Dante?" she asked, her cultured voice both annoying and alluring.

"One special coming right up, Miss Glory."

She accepted the weak tea with a tired smile. "Thank you."

With a flourish, Dante bowed at the waist, then was called to the end of the bar, leaving Slater alone with Glory. He deliberately stared at her, but she continued to ignore him. However, the pulse in her slender neck betrayed her awareness of his scrutiny.

Slater waited with the patience he'd been forced to learn. Finally he was rewarded, and she turned toward him, her eyes flashing.

"Is it me or my breasts that you find so fascinating?" A charming red flush covered her face and spread down her neck and chest.

Slater let his gaze linger on her breasts, wondering if the rosiness colored them, too. He raised his head and smiled lazily. "Both."

Although her blush deepened to scarlet, she didn't look away. "Look all you want. Why should you be any different from the rest of them?" She waved an arm, encompassing the saloon's occupants.

For some reason it bothered Slater that she thought he was no better than the men who were so starved for female company that they bought overpriced drinks to dance with them. "Is that what you think?"

She propped a hand on a deliciously rounded hip. "What else should I think?"

He kept his features bland even as his blood heated. Although he made it a rule not to bed the women he worked with, he was tempted to make an exception with Glory. "I don't need to buy time with a lady."

"You have an inflated opinion of yourself."

"Maybe I deserve it."

Her lips twitched. "You obviously think so."

Slater took a sip of coffee to hide his unexpected amusement. "What about you? Are you too good to be dancing with them?"

Melancholy seized her features, and he saw the effort it took her to force a laugh. "Not anymore, Mr. Forrester."

Her bitter reply made him study her, this time without any preconceptions. Even if Dante was right in his assessment of her, Miss Glory had chosen to work in this place. However, his conscience reminded him that oftentimes a person didn't have a choice in this life.

Andrew strolled out of the back office and came to stand beside Glory. "Have you and Simon worked out some songs?"

"After they worked out their differences," Slater remarked.

Glory shot him a glare. Andrew, confused by their byplay, arched a brow at Slater. However, Slater merely shrugged a shoulder. If Glory couldn't work with Simon, Andrew would know soon enough.

"Simon and I have picked out some songs. He said we could practice tomorrow morning," Glory answered Andrew. "Is that all right with you, Mr. Kearny?"

Slater gnashed his teeth. With Andrew her voice was honey sweet, but with him she buzzed like an angry bee.

"That would be fine, Glory." He rubbed his brow.

"Have you been working on the accounts again?" Slater asked.

Andrew nodded wryly. "When I started this place, I never expected to spend most of my time in the back with those damned books."

"I might be able to help you," Glory said.

Andrew chuckled. "This isn't simple addition and subtraction."

Glory's eyes narrowed. "I realize that. I've worked on account books."

"Where was that?" Andrew asked.

Curious in spite of himself, Slater wanted to hear her answer, too.

Her gaze skittered away. "St. Louis."

"Is there someone I can contact who can give me a reference for your work?" Andrew asked.

Glory shook her head too quickly. "No. Please forget that I even mentioned it."

Slater wanted to push her, but Andrew was more sympathetic. "Perhaps I'll take you up on your offer one of these days," the older man said. "Why don't you get some sleep, Glory? It's already midnight, and if you plan to practice in the morning, you need your rest."

"Thank you," she said in obvious relief. "It's been a long day."

"They'll get longer," Slater said.

She flashed him an irritated look, then took Andrew's suggestion and climbed the stairs to retire for the night. As he watched the gentle sway of her backside, he noticed Andrew, too, was eyeing the new girl.

"Do you think she really knows how to keep accounting books?" Slater asked. An illogical sense of possessiveness wanted Andrew's attention diverted from Glory's figure.

Andrew reluctantly drew his gaze away from her. "It's possible. She's definitely had an education."

"Because she talks fancy?"

Andrew chuckled. "We both know a whore can learn how

to talk like a lady. No, I knew Glory was the real thing when she first came in here looking for some fella named Colfax."

Slater turned Andrew's words over in his head. "It could have been her intended who left her at the altar."

"She didn't say, and I didn't ask. I figured it was her business."

"So why'd she decide to get a job here if she's trying to find this Colfax?"

"I got the impression she was low on funds."

"Like all of 'em."

Andrew turned to face Slater and rested his forearm on the bar. "Do you have something against Glory? You're usually more sympathetic to the women."

Outwardly, Slater remained dispassionate, but inside, an unaccustomed uncertainty seethed. "Maybe I just can't stomach a woman who feels that anyone working in an establishment like this is below her station."

"Has she given anyone problems?"

Slater thought of her reaction to Simon, but he couldn't honestly say she'd treated him badly. Not after he gave her her options. He shook his head. "Not that I know of. Did you notice what she was wearing?"

Andrew thought for a moment, then chuckled. "I'm surprised Georgia didn't make a scene."

Slater grinned. "Oh, she did, but Simon stopped her before it got bad."

"How'd Glory handle it?"

Slater shrugged. "I saw her say something to Cassie afterward. Cassie didn't like whatever she said."

"I'm staying out of the middle. Cassie knows her job, and Glory has a lot to learn. But Glory's smart and she's got spirit. She'll do all right."

Slater lifted his coffee cup, but before taking a sip, he silently toasted Miss Glory.

THE moment the door closed behind her, Rebecca tore off the indecent blue dress and threw it on her bed. Georgia could have the blamed thing with her blessing. Even if all the other dresses were just as short and just as plunging in the front, Rebecca would choose one with a more subdued color, something that would be less noticeable.

She tugged on her wrapper and belted it around her waist, then removed her red garter, stockings, and shoes. Using the cool basin water, she washed the paint from her face. She brushed her hair, and by the hundredth stroke, the tobacco taint had faded to a slight irritant.

She pressed her ear to the door but didn't hear anyone in the hallway, so she slipped out to return the blue dress to its former hook. Back in her tiny room, Rebecca allowed herself to sink into the only chair. She pulled her bare feet up and wrapped her arms around her drawn-up legs. Propping her chin on her knees, she gazed unseeingly at the thin shade over the lone window.

The events of the evening whirled through her thoughts. She'd walked through a den of iniquity wearing a harlot's costume while men ogled her legs and chest. She'd talked with a man of color and apologized to a Negro woman. In the world where she was raised, there were firm, but invisible, lines drawn between whites and Negroes. She'd never questioned them. Until tonight.

She'd also asked a man if he liked looking at her breasts. Dear God, what had ever possessed her to ask such a question? Merely thinking about it, she burned with mortification. Yet Slater Forrester seemed to bring out the worst in her. Those cool blue eyes and dark-winged brows could almost make her believe he was the devil incarnate. Of course, that would explain why she felt so off-balance around him.

The fact that Benjamin was a gambler, too, might have some bearing on her mixed emotions. She'd observed Forrester throughout the evening and couldn't help but compare the two men. Although she'd never seen Benjamin play poker, he'd practiced in their home, and both he and Forrester were as slick as grease with a deck of cards. Even their expressions, pleasant but giving away nothing, were similar. However, Benjamin was blonde and hazel-eyed with a slender frame. Forrester's wider shoulders and more muscular body told Rebecca he wasn't unaccustomed to physical labor. Oddly enough, that softened her opinion of the dealer. Despite his wealth, Rebecca's father had never scorned physical labor like so many of his social class.

Rebecca closed her eyes and pictured her mother and father, laughing and dancing to the tune of a music box in the parlor. That they loved one another was obvious in every look and every touch they exchanged. She'd even caught them kissing on occasion, and although she'd been embarrassed, it had also opened a yearning deep inside her.

When she met Benjamin, she believed she'd found what her parents had shared. Over a year later, Rebecca knew the difference between infatuation and love, and she was still paying for her hard-learned education.

However, she had no choice. She had to find Benjamin and tell him about Daniel. Surely a father would want to raise his son. She clung to that belief, for without it, she had nothing left.

$\mathscr{F}$OUR

"*SHALL we never more behold thee; never hear thy winning voice again when the spring time comes, gentle Annie, when the wild flowers are scattered o'er the plain?*"

Slater opened his eyes, expecting the song to disappear along with his slumber, but as he lay there, the soft strains continued to float up through the floorboards.

"*We have roamed and loved 'mid the bowers when thy downy cheeks were in their bloom; now I stand alone 'mid the flowers while they mingle their perfumes o'er thy tomb.*"

The last vestiges of sleep faded away, and he remembered that Miss Glory and Simon had planned to rehearse this morning. Even as he cursed the early hour, he couldn't help but appreciate Glory's melodic voice. He'd heard famous songstresses perform, and Glory's talent equaled most, and exceeded some of them.

The song ended and the low rumbling of a conversation followed. Even though it wasn't even nine o'clock yet, curiosity drew Slater out of bed. He completed his morning ablutions while Simon and Glory struck up a spirited song, dispelling the melancholy the previous one had evoked. After he was shaved and dressed, Slater took the back stairs and was surprised to find Andrew already drinking coffee behind the bar. It was rare when the older man was up before ten.

Slater crossed to the stove to pour a cup of hot, strong brew for himself. Joining Andrew, he leaned against the bar. Miss Glory's back was to them as she stood beside the seated Simon. Instead of a shorter work dress, she wore a decidedly somber skirt and blouse that covered every inch of skin which had been exposed last night. However, Slater didn't let the proper clothing deter him from appreciating the feminine lines of her back and the slender waist and hips that curved enough to give a man indecent thoughts.

The song ended, and Andrew applauded. He went to Glory and took her hands in his, kissing the back of one, then the other. "That was beautiful, Glory. When you said you sang, I didn't expect a voice to rival Jenny Lind's."

Slater refrained from rolling his eyes at the blatant exaggeration, even if he had been thinking along those lines earlier.

Glory blushed. "Thank you, Mr. Kearny. I'm glad you approve."

"I most definitely approve. And please call me Andrew."

Slater recognized Andrew's charismatic smile. He'd seen it aimed more than once at women Andrew was determined to take to his bed. Not a single woman had denied him. It had never bothered Slater before, but this time he gnashed his teeth to hold back a rise of irritation.

Glory inclined her head but her smile dimmed slightly. "Andrew." She picked up the broadsheets and riffled through them. "I thought a mixture of ballads and lively songs would work well."

"That's fine." Andrew clapped the freed slave's shoulder. "Your playing is, as usual, beyond compare, Simon. Please, continue."

Glory glanced at Slater, and he nodded his head in sardonic acknowledgment. "Pretend I'm not here," he said.

Her distinctive eyes flashed with amber lightning, and the corners of her bow-shaped lips turned downward. She didn't speak and deliberately turned away, but Slater fancied he could hear her less than charitable retort.

Andrew returned to the bar while Glory and Simon conferred on the next song.

"So, do you think she can sing now?" Andrew asked, his tone smug.

Slater couldn't help but chuckle. "You win. But you better make sure she doesn't depress the customers too much with those weepy ballads."

"Don't worry. I expect they'll all be so busy looking at her, they won't even hear the words."

Though he hated to admit it, Slater recognized the truth of Kearny's words.

"I'd like to talk with you," Andrew said, his amusement gone.

Frowning at the uncharacteristic gravity in his friend's tone, Slater followed Andrew to his usual corner table. Glory's dulcet tones remained as background sound, and they could speak with relative ease.

"Did you hear about Victor Stroman?" Andrew asked.

"The owner of the Tin Bucket?" Andrew nodded. "No. What about him?"

"Last night after he closed, someone came in and broke up the place. Not a single table or chair left in one piece."

Slater shrugged and leaned back in his chair. His gaze strayed to Glory, who crooned another sad song. "Maybe someone caught on to his crooked games."

"Just because one of his dealers was dirty doesn't mean they all are. Besides, Victor fired him as soon as he knew about it."

"To protect himself and the rest of the sharps on his payroll."

"You're a suspicious son of a bitch." Andrew shook his head. "No, this was something else."

"What?" Slater asked idly, not really interested.

Andrew leaned forward. "I think someone is trying to take over this side of town. The owner of the saloon either pays up or something happens to his place."

Slater drew his gaze away from Glory and peered at Andrew. He knew things like that happened in sections of bigger cities, like New Orleans, St. Louis, and San Antonio, but not in a bump like Oaktree. "I think you've been to one of the Chinese opium dens."

Andrew sent him a disgusted look. "You know me better than that."

Chastened, Slater realized he did owe him more than a flippant comment even if he didn't buy his theory. "Why do you think it's an extortion scheme instead of a customer who thought he was cheated?"

Andrew propped his elbows on the chair arms and steepled his fingers. "There have been other incidents. A beat-up dealer, a barrel of whiskey disappears, shots fired into a saloon. Taken separately, it's the risks of the business, but together, it smells pretty damned rotten to me."

"All right, say I agree with you. What can we do? The only law in town is a sheriff who wears a badge so he can get free drinks and meals."

An inscrutable expression stole across Andrew's face, warning Slater that he wouldn't like what was coming next.

"You used to be an investigator. You can—"

"No. I don't do that anymore."

"Why not?"

Slater glared at him. "You know why."

"It's been nearly three years now."

The stench of rotting flesh, unwashed bodies, and human excrement nearly overwhelmed Slater, and he fought the memory. His left hand trembled as darkness closed in around him.

"It's only memories, Slater." The soothing voice and the touch on his arm gave him something else to focus on.

The sensory images receded, leaving Slater feeling sick to his stomach.

"I'm sorry," Andrew said with genuine apology. "I shouldn't have pushed you."

Slater scrubbed his face with his hands, using the motion to regain the rest of his composure. He hadn't felt the past so keenly for weeks, and he cursed his weakness for allowing it to engulf him again. "Not your fault," Slater ground out bitterly. "But you see why I can't do it."

Andrew nodded. "I wish you'd talk about what happened during the war."

"What good would that do, besides make you feel sorry for me?" The words came out angrier than Slater intended.

"I wouldn't do that. I wish there was some way I could help."

Slater withdrew a deck of cards from his jacket pocket and shuffled them, the familiar motion calming him as it usually did. "You helped me. You gave me a job."

"Hell, you were doing me a favor. I needed a dealer I could trust."

Slater lifted a sardonic brow. "So you've forgiven me for cleaning you out ten years ago?"

Andrew chortled. "I had only myself to blame, since I was the one who taught you the tricks of the trade."

Slater paused and stared into the distance. "Those were good days, Andrew." He blinked and focused on his friend. "You never told me why you took a chance on a sixteen-year-old thief."

Andrew gazed at him fondly. "I saw something in that ragged kid."

"What was that?"

"Myself." Before Slater could recover from the unexpected answer, Andrew stood. "Those accounts aren't going to take care of themselves."

Slater leaned back in his chair, and his gaze followed his mentor. For the first time Slater noticed Andrew's hair was all gray and that he didn't walk with the same fluid grace he'd possessed when Slater had met him a lifetime ago in the streets of Houston. The years hadn't been kind to Slater, but neither had Andrew come through unscathed.

Troubled, Slater turned his attention to Miss Glory, who now faced the empty saloon as she sang, her eyes closed and her lips moving with the lyrics.

"Now we grieve and then we're gay, yet our joys are quickly flown and the heart droops alone. All our hopes are drap'd in sadness when dear friends are gone." Glory's chin dropped to her chest as the last sorrowful note faded.

A shiver, like a dark foreboding, swept through Slater. He told himself it was simply a combination of the haunting song and the memories that had visited him minutes earlier.

He snapped up his cards and shoved back his chair. As he headed out of the saloon into the morning sunshine, Glory started into another dirge. Didn't she know anything except those godawful sad songs?

REBECCA finished with Stephen Foster's popular and rollicking "Susanna," and grinned when Simon performed a flourish of chords that seemed to hang in the air after the last note died.

She clapped. "That was wonderful, Simon. Wherever did you learn to play like that?"

Simon shrugged nonchalantly but his diffident smile told her he was pleased with her praise. "I always had an ear for music, ever since I was a young'un. My pa made me a recorder, and I used to play it ev'ry chance I could. The master's wife heard me one time and let me inside to try their piano." He paused. "It was like me and them piano keys were old friends. I don't know how, but I could hear a song, then coax the tune out of the piano."

Astounded, Rebecca realized she'd never even considered that a Negro could possess such musical talent. It was another erroneous belief she had to purge from her way of thinking.

"What about you, Miss Glory? I heard lotsa singers, but you're better'n all of them," Simon said.

Homesickness struck without warning, and she struggled to hold a smile. "I have to thank my parents. They would sing songs together when I was a child, and when I was old enough, I joined them."

"That's real nice, Miss Glory. I'm sure they're right proud of you."

Rebecca swallowed the block in her throat. "I'm sure they are."

Simon stood and stretched, and Rebecca was again struck by his size. He towered over her by a foot, and probably weighed twice her weight, yet after her initial shock, she didn't feel intimidated.

"I'd best get some sleep so I can be back here later." He smiled down at her. "I'm lookin' forward to tonight."

"Me, too, Simon."

Once he was gone, the saloon felt cavernous and lonely. Rebecca's gaze strayed to the corner where Slater Forrester had been until he'd marched out of the saloon like he couldn't stand to listen a moment longer. She told herself it was simply her pride that stung, but the disappointment went deeper.

Seeing him come downstairs earlier had jolted her. His black suit followed the contours of his broad shoulders and draped down to hug slim hips. The white shirt offset the dark jacket and deepened his complexion to golden brown, which highlighted his sky blue eyes. His wavy hair was damp, and she'd fisted her hands to fight the urge to run her fingers through the tamed strands. Flustered by her reaction to the gambler, she'd turned away from him, but couldn't banish him from her thoughts. Even an hour later, she could clearly envision him.

Rebecca shoved aside her unexpected and unwelcome attraction to Forrester. She had more important things to worry about, like her debut as a saloon singer. Tonight the bar would be filled with rough men looking for a good time. Her job was to provide the good time.

After a night of watching the goings-on, she knew what to expect. That knowledge was enough to calm the butterflies in her belly, yet her stomach didn't stop churning altogether. For a moment she wished she was brave enough to try a shot of whiskey.

The office door opened and Andrew swept out, his expression one of annoyance. However, when he spotted Rebecca, his face brightened into a handsome smile.

"Are you ready?" he asked.

Rebecca managed a smile. "As ready as I can be."

"You'll do fine."

"Do you expect me to sing all night?"

He came around the bar and leaned against it, crossing his arms. "That was something I wanted to discuss with you."

Rebecca tensed, recognizing Andrew's switch to employer. "Yes?"

"What I'd like you to do is sing for approximately thirty

minutes, then dance with the men for another half hour. Every one of them will want a chance to dance with Miss Glory, sweet songbird of the Scarlet Garter." Andrew winked.

Cringing inside, Rebecca nodded. "Whatever you'd like Mr. Kearny."

"Now what did I tell you to call me?"

She battled the surge of irritation at his scolding tone. "Andrew."

He grinned. "Now that wasn't so hard, was it?"

Rebecca shook her head.

"There's something else we need to discuss," Andrew continued. "I don't run a brothel, but I also don't discourage my girls from making extra money upstairs. However, if they do, my share is twenty-five percent, which is more than fair compared to the other establishments in town."

"I—I don't do that." Rebecca drew back her shoulders and gathered her dignity. "Circumstances beyond my control forced me to take a position in a place I would never have even walked past, had not my station changed. Despite what I now do so I don't starve, I draw the line at selling my body. If you find that unacceptable, then I shall be gone today." With her heart thundering and her breath fast and shallow, Rebecca waited. She hated the helpless feeling of having her fate in the hands of a man. It felt too much like being married.

Andrew's expression remained composed, but a hint of admiration glinted in his eyes. "I thought that might be the case, but recall that I said I don't force my employees to sell themselves. You were hired to sing and dance, and that hasn't changed, unless you feel that you can't work in a place that allows fornication."

Rebecca stiffened, but her tolerance of unacceptable social terms was increasing—she barely felt a flush of embarrassment. "I've come to realize that there's often little choice when it comes to what must be done to survive."

Andrew tipped his head to the side. "What is your story, Miss Glory Bowen?"

Rebecca gazed past him, to a shaft of sunlight filtering through the dirty glass. Dust motes floated through the light, illuminated for only a minute before disappearing into the gloom once more. Was her previous life like one of those dust particles, shining only for a short time before dropping into darkness?

She drew her attention back to Andrew. "May I have a cup of coffee?"

Andrew arched a brow and nodded. "Certainly." He retrieved a cup from behind the bar and handed it to her.

Too aware of his eyes on her back, she walked as she'd been taught all those years ago, shoulders back, spine straight, and head held high. She poured her coffee and was surprised to find Andrew standing beside her, holding up an empty cup. She filled his, too, then allowed him to guide her to a nearby table.

Taking time to make her decision and gather her thoughts, Rebecca sipped the hot coffee. She was grateful Andrew didn't push her, but sat patiently, waiting. He reminded her of one of her father's friends who had bounced her on his knee when she was a child.

"I was born in St. Louis, where my parents were perhaps not wealthy, but well-to-do. They gave me the best education possible, everything from deportment to reading to numbers to riding. Since I was their only child, my father also taught me how to keep the accounts for the house and property."

"That explains how you know how to do bookkeeping," Andrew commented.

Rebecca nodded.

"So why are you here in the middle of nowhere if you're the only child of a family of means?" he asked.

Overwhelming sorrow and fierce regrets swamped her, and she had to look away to regain her poise. "My parents were killed in a carriage accident two years ago. In my grief, I made a very foolish mistake."

Andrew eyed her shrewdly. "This mistake wouldn't be named Benjamin Colfax, would it?"

"How—" she broke off, remembering she'd shown him the picture of Benjamin when she'd first arrived in Oaktree. Andrew Kearny was a very perceptive man. She nodded. "Yes. He gambled away everything I owned."

"How could he do that? He didn't have any legal . . ." Comprehension widened his eyes. "You were married to him."

"I still am."

Rebecca expected him to be shocked, but Andrew merely shrugged. "I've known other married women whose husbands deserted them."

Curious in spite of herself, she asked, "What did they do?"

"Most became prostitutes. They figured it was better to be paid for lying with a stranger than giving it to a husband for free and being left with nothing when he got tired of them."

Aghast at his matter-of-fact tone, Rebecca shook her head. "I could never do that."

Andrew leaned forward, his expression intense. "Never say never, Glory. I would be willing to bet the Scarlet Garter that five years ago you would've said you'd never work in a saloon either."

Ice water moved through her veins. He was right. What if the customers didn't like her singing and Andrew fired her? What if she had to work in a place that demanded that its employees sell their bodies? "Maybe. But for right now I hope to escape that plight."

"That's fine. Can I ask you one more question?"

Although reluctant to bare her soul any further, she nodded.

"What will you do a year from now when you're still working here because you don't have enough money to continue your search for your husband?"

Angry that he made her think about things she didn't wish to contemplate, Rebecca fought down a sharp response. Instead, she answered honestly. "I don't know."

"How long do you think you can sleep in a cold, empty bed after you've known passion in a man's arms?"

Unable to curb her tongue this time, she retorted, "Are you offering to keep my bed warm?"

He leaned back in his chair, his pose nonchalant. "Actually, I'm offering you a place in *my* bed."

She froze, then managed to push herself upright. "If you'll excuse me, I need to pack my things."

As she moved around him, he clasped her wrist. In spite of the fear that coursed through her, she glared at him.

"Calm down, Glory. Your job isn't contingent on you bedding me," Andrew said with a lazy smile.

Her heart thundered in her chest and she fought for air in her tight lungs. "Then why did you suggest it?"

He tugged her back to her chair and released her. "You're the first woman to catch my eye since I opened this place."

"But what about Cassie? I had the impression you and she were, um, close."

He shrugged. "We've shared a bed a few times, but Cassie knows it's nothing serious."

"But you and I would be serious?"

Andrew threw back his head and laughed. "Of course not, but I wouldn't tire of you as quickly."

Rebecca wasn't certain if she should be insulted or indignant. Or simply appalled that she was even having this conversation. "If that's supposed to be reassuring, I can assure you it isn't." She took a deep breath. "I will sing and dance in your gambling establishment, but that is the extent of my responsibilities to you. Is that sufficient?"

"Yes, but I'd be lying if I said I wasn't disappointed. You're the first woman to turn me down."

"Your pride will survive."

He grinned boyishly. "Even if slightly scarred." He glanced at his pocket watch and frowned. "I'll have to open the doors soon, and I wanted to get some more bookkeeping done."

"Would you be willing to pay me to do your bookkeeping?" she asked without thinking.

He narrowed his eyes. "When would you do it?"

She clamped down on the slender string of hope. "During the day, before the saloon opens."

"How can I be certain you'll do a good job?"

"Sit beside me the first time. If I'm doing it wrong, you'll know. If not, you can be assured I'll do a good job." He continued to appear skeptical. "Don't pay me until I've proven myself," she added, upping the ante.

After a minute of thoughtful silence, he nodded. "I'll give you a chance. If you work out, it'll save me time and headaches. When would you like to begin?"

Excitement raced through her. "Today?"

"As good a time as any."

She'd gone from nearly quitting to getting a third job. An-other job meant more money, which meant she could continue her search for her deceitful husband. She couldn't stop until she found him.

Because without him she had no chance of getting Daniel back.

$\mathcal{F}$IVE

SLATER resisted the urge to rub his brow and concentrated on his opponents' facial expressions and body language. The pot in the middle of the table was the richest of the night, and he intended to win it. If only his head would cooperate and stop throbbing.

Although he'd been weaned on faro, often holding the position of Andrew's lookout and case keeper, it was poker that he preferred. Faro tended to be a game of chance unless the dealer used one of the tools of the cheating trade. Poker, however, was far more complicated and required more skill than luck, as well as control of body motions and facial expressions. Slater had learned to spot the nuances of other players, to know when they were bluffing or how good their cards really were. He'd also worked steadily on keeping his own tells hidden and his expression dispassionate. Andrew had taught him how to stack the odds in his favor, but his mentor had also taught him that knowledge should be used to spot a cheater, not become one.

The player to Slater's right swore and threw his cards face-down on the table. Slater glanced across the table at the one man remaining in the game. For the last month, Bill Chambers had played at Slater's table when he was in the Scarlet Garter. He often lost, so it was a good thing the man owned a ranch and nearly a thousand head of cattle.

"You gonna play or fold, Forrester?" the rancher asked in a gravelly voice.

Slater studied Chambers, noting the way his right pinkie moved ever so slightly across the cards, back and forth. It was the same every time. If Chambers was bluffing, that small finger would brush the cards, back and forth. Slater had picked up on his tell the first night they'd played.

Slater narrowed his eyes and his lips curled up deliberately. "I think you're bluffing, and I'll raise you ten."

Chambers's nostrils flared, but Slater had to give him credit for not giving away more. "Fine. Ten, and raise you ten more."

The three men who'd fallen out of the game watched in silence, their eyes darting between the stack of chips on the table and the remaining players' faces.

Slater restrained a sigh as well as the urge to roll his eyes. He swept his own chips into the center. "Call."

He could almost see the expectancy hanging above the table, a dark cloud of tension. Chambers lifted his chin and laid his five cards down. A single pair. Just as Slater had suspected.

He laid down his own hand. "Flush beats a pair."

Chambers's face reddened, but he laughed. "Damn, Forrester! I thought I had you this time. What gave me away?"

Slater grinned crookedly. "You don't expect me to give away my secrets, do you?"

"Well, I know you ain't a cheat. I seen enough of them to know." He shook his head. "I'll figure it out someday." The stocky rancher rose. "But I've lost enough for tonight."

After Chambers left, the other players gave their excuses and went to lean against the crowded bar to drink.

Slater glanced at his pocket watch. 1:45 A.M. Although it was late, the saloon remained crowded. His gaze searched the drunken dancers, and he spotted Glory amid the group. Her partner had his arms around her, his hands roaming up and down her back, and his blunt fingers curving around her backside. Glory grabbed his hands and lifted them up higher, but they soon returned to her shapely ass.

Irritation sizzled in Slater. The man was taking advantage of Glory's inexperience. The customers knew the rules—no inappropriate touching on the dance floor. That stuff was confined to the upstairs rooms, if the women chose to go there.

He swept the poker chips into a bag and sauntered to the bar, where he handed his winnings to Dante.

"You must have had a providential evening," Dante said after setting the bag under the counter.

Slater shrugged, his gaze glued to Glory. "It wasn't bad."

"Perhaps you should reacquaint the gentleman with the rules of the house," Dante said.

Slater turned to him, schooling his face to blandness.

"You, my friend, are skillful at hiding your thoughts at the poker table, but when gazing upon a fair maiden, your eyes speak eloquently," Dante said.

Slater knew better than to deny it. Dante was as good at reading people at his bar as Slater was at reading players at his table. "I doubt she's a fair maiden," he said dryly.

"Perhaps not in the physical sense, but in the spiritual . . ." The music ended, and the girls hauled their partners to the bar to buy them a special. Dante shrugged apologetically and was soon caught up in serving drinks.

Glory's partner dragged her over to the bar, his stout arm around her waist and holding her flush against his side. Glory glanced at Slater and her expression reminded him of a lost kid.

Despite Slater's personal rule of not getting involved, he shifted down the bar, closer to Glory's possessive partner. He'd seen the man before, with his drooping moustache damp with liquor and chewing tobacco. By his smell Slater doubted he took a bath or washed his clothes more than once a month.

"Remove your hand from the lady," Slater said. *Or I'll rip it off.*

The man glared at him, his eyes bloodshot. "I'm buyin' her a drink, so she's mine." His breath stank of tobacco, beer and rotting teeth.

"You know the rules. No inappropriate touching," Slater said, anger simmering below his calm surface.

Rebecca cringed as her dance partner's arm tightened around her waist. She wanted to turn her head away from his ugly face and uglier breath, but if she did that, she wouldn't be able to see Slater, who was the last person she expected to come to her assistance.

"You don't tell me what to do. I bought her a drink and I get her comp'ny while she drinks it. Them's the rules." Belligerence poured off him. Although he was a few inches shorter than Slater, he was wider—and it was muscle, not fat, below the filthy clothes.

"The rules also state that the women are to be treated with respect." Slater deliberately glared at his arm, which was pressed against the underside of her breasts.

Despite the wiry strength Slater's suits couldn't conceal, Rebecca was afraid he'd be no match for the man with his huge hands and barrel chest.

"I can take care of myself," Rebecca said as she struggled past the man's stench to bring air into her agonized lungs.

Slater's blue eyes pinned her, and the heat within them would've made her gasp, if she'd been able to pull in a sharp breath. Instead, languorous heat flowed through her limbs, making her skin tingle and her insides throb.

"I don't doubt that, Miss Glory, but the house rules are clear on touching a woman inappropriately." Although he kept his gaze on her, Slater's words were obviously meant for her dance partner.

"Is there a problem here?" Andrew's authoritative voice severed their eye contact.

"Nothing I can't handle," Slater said, his voice a low growl.

Rebecca's dance partner eased his hold around her waist. "No, sir, Mr. Kearny. No problem at all."

Andrew scrutinized the man but spoke to her. "Glory, finish your drink. It's time for another round of songs."

She nodded, both embarrassed and relieved, and swallowed the weak tea. "Thank you for the dance and drink," Rebecca said through clenched teeth.

The grimy man gave her a curt nod and, after one last glare at Slater, drifted away.

"What was that about?" Andrew demanded of Slater.

"Nothing," he replied, like a boy caught peeking in a bedroom window.

Not understanding Slater's reluctance, Rebecca said, "My partner was a bit presumptuous and Slater tried to get him to behave more like a gentleman." *As if any of the clientele in this den of iniquity were gentlemen.*

"Cassie did explain the rules, didn't she?" Andrew asked.

Rebecca frowned. "No. I didn't think a place like this had rules." Her face flamed with embarrassment. "I don't mean—"

"I understood what you meant," Andrew said smoothly. "But yes, the men know they are to treat their dancing partners courteously. If they don't, they're kicked out." He turned to Slater. "So you were saving Miss Glory?"

Slater scowled. "I was making sure he knew the rules."

Andrew's keen gaze probed Slater as Rebecca looked from one man to the other. It was clear they'd known one another for some time. Was it simply because they were both gamblers? Or was there some other history between them?

"Glory, time to sing," Andrew reminded her not unkindly.

Startled out of her musings, she nodded. Smoothing her dress front with a nervous hand, she joined Simon by the piano and went through the song list while Simon finished playing a lively jig.

"How about this one?" Rebecca asked Simon.

He glanced at it and shot her an uncertain look. "You sure, Miz Glory?"

She shrugged, hiding her own uncertainty and sudden homesickness. "Maybe it'll calm the wild beasts in here."

Simon's eyes twinkled, and as Rebecca began to sing to his accompaniment, the room quieted. Hardened men who drank and swore like there was no tomorrow stopped and turned toward her as cards, drinks, and even women were abandoned for the music.

"Dream of my mother and my home. My mother, my mother. How old-time memories will come, dream of my dear and gentle mother, I dream of my mother and my home." Rebecca's own memories added emotion to the stirring words.

She continued singing the familiar song and allowed her gaze to roam across the scarred and grizzled faces of the men. It was strange to see these hard-edged men become wistful, their thoughts miles from this reeking, sin-filled saloon. But then, all of them had a mother, someone who'd loved them and taken care of them, before they'd become what they were. For many of them, their mother might be the only woman they truly respected.

Thoughts of mother and child carried her to Daniel, and her voice faltered. Despair clogged her throat, and the words were lost as she struggled to hold back tears.

She managed to whisper-sing the last line of Stephen Foster's heartrending song. "How old time memories will come, dream of my dear and gentle mother, I dream of my mother and my home."

Simon's fingers came to rest on the keys and he lifted compassionate brown eyes. "Are you all right, Miz Glory?" he asked in a low, rumbling voice.

She shook her head. "I'm s-suddenly not feeling well."

Andrew was suddenly at her side. "What's wrong?"

"Miz Glory don't feel good," Simon said before Rebecca could.

Andrew placed a gentle hand on her shoulder. "It has been a long night. Maybe you should go upstairs to your room."

Fearful that he might fire her for not being able to shoulder her share, she shook her head. "I can keep working."

Her employer smiled. "It's almost two o'clock, nearly time to start closing the place down. You won't be missed."

"But—"

"No buts. Go on. Besides, you've got most of those big bad men crying in their beer."

She smiled in spite of herself. "Thank you, Andrew. I'll do better next time."

"You did just fine, Glory. Go on up the back stairs so the men won't see you leave."

He kissed her brow as her father had done when she was a child, and moisture gathered in her eyes. Before she completely embarrassed herself, she nodded her thanks and hurried through the back door leading to the hidden stairs. However, she couldn't help but pause in the doorway to find Slater, who'd come to her rescue.

As if he could feel her scrutiny, he raised his head and unerringly met her gaze. He lifted his coffee cup to her in a salute, and in his eyes she saw something hotter, more dangerous than anything she'd seen in her numerous dance partners—admiration and attraction simmering in a molten pool of lust.

Before she could be scalded, Rebecca spun around and ran up the stairs. Her heartbeat pulsed in her head, and her shaky knees barely held her weight.

Once in her room, she slammed the door and grabbed the straight-backed chair. She braced it against the doorknob but still didn't feel safe. Simon's piano music resounded through the floorboards, along with hoots and hollers of the carousing men. It didn't take them long to forget about their mothers and return to their uncouth behavior.

She paced the room, but it was too small for her to work up a satisfying momentum. Although she'd warned herself, she'd been appalled by some of her dance partners—lacking the most basic hygiene and civility. The last one had been the worst, with his ungodly stench and wandering hands.

When she'd seen Slater Forrester wearing his pressed suit and spotless white shirt, he'd been a sanctuary among a sty of pigs. She didn't know why he came to rescue her, but the gesture was as surprising as it was appreciated. Perhaps he was simply enforcing the rules. Or maybe there was more to it.

Recalling the heat in Slater's eyes sent her heart scampering. However, the almost forgotten tension in her belly frightened her. Having been married, she'd learned the strength of desire. And her attraction to Slater was both frightening and exhilarating. Yet nothing could be allowed to come of it. She was a married woman and she took her vows seriously, even if Benjamin hadn't.

Suddenly aware of her aching feet, Rebecca dropped onto her bed and removed her shoes. She hissed at the blisters on her heels and near her big toes. How was she going to dance again tomorrow night? How did the other girls do it?

Closing her eyes to stave off her growing panic, she breathed deeply and felt the pull of her snug dress against her breasts. Frustrated, she removed the offensive garment that smelled of smoke and tobacco and things she didn't want to think about, and tossed it on a hook. At least the dress she'd worn tonight hadn't gotten any of the other girls angry with her. Georgia had worn the blue one that had nearly caused the catfight this evening, and Rebecca had to admit the color was striking with her darker skin. Besides, Rebecca preferred the more muted colors although it hadn't stopped the men from gathering around her like flies around spoiled fruit.

What am I doing here?

Alone and more miserable than she'd ever been in her life, Rebecca blindly sought the cherished cloth where she'd hidden it. She pressed the white gown against her face and sniffed, but only the faint scent of Daniel remained. Choked sobs filled her throat.

As soon as I find your father, I'll return. I promise.

SLATER watched as Andrew ushered the last two drunks out and locked the doors behind them. Andrew's shoulders slumped, and his stride became more of a shuffle as he crossed the dirty sawdust.

"Business was better than usual," Slater commented.

Andrew raked a hand through his hair. "Word of Miss Glory spread fast."

Slater watched as Frank, the burly bouncer, picked up an armload of empty glasses and carried them to the back, where fourteen-year-old Toby washed and dried them. The boy worked only on the busiest nights, and Andrew always made certain someone walked him home after he was done.

"I don't think I've ever seen so many grown men so close to bawling like babies as during her last song," Slater commented wryly.

Andrew shrugged. "Everyone has a soft spot in their heart for their mother, even cussing, drinking, whoring men."

Uncomfortable with memories of his own mother, Slater said, "If you ask me, she shouldn't sing that one again. Seemed to bother her as much as it did everyone else."

Andrew glanced away, and Slater had the distinct impression his friend was hiding something from him. "She had a mother, too."

Had. Past tense.

"So her mother is dead. What about her father?"

"Dead." Andrew cocked his head. "You've never been curious about any of the other girls. Why the interest in Miss Glory?"

It was Slater's turn to look away. "Like you said, she's different." He risked a glance at his friend and grimaced when he saw the knowing smile on his face. "Don't be reading any more into it, Andrew. You know I'm not the type to get tied down with a woman, especially not a saloon gal."

"Not all working girls are like Lydia."

The bad thing about working with someone who knew him well was having past mistakes brought up when they were best left buried. "You're right about that. But Lydia did teach me a lesson I'm not likely to forget."

"What's that?"

"Always make sure the woman doesn't have a husband looking for her."

Andrew shrugged. "From the sounds of it, Lydia had good reason to get away from him."

"Maybe, but she should've told me."

"So you wouldn't have lost your heart?"

Slater glared at him. "I wasn't in love with her."

Andrew laughed. "You were only twenty-one, Slater. Of course you were in love with her."

"How many times have you fallen in love?"

"Too many to count."

Slater chuckled, the tension that had wrapped around him easing with the familiar banter. Although it wasn't his job, Slater always helped clean up the bar after closing.

"I see you brought in a nice bundle tonight," Andrew remarked as he placed a chair on a table.

"Bill Chambers. One of these days he'll figure out how I know he's bluffing."

"Don't hold your breath. Chambers is stubborn enough to believe he doesn't have a tell." Andrew placed his palms at the base of his back and stretched. "Did I tell you Glory's going to be doing the account books from now on?"

Slater set the last chair up on a table. "How'd that come about?"

"She asked me to give her a chance. I'm glad I did. She's better at it than I am."

"She's bitten off a big chunk with dancing, singing, and keeping the accounts."

Andrew shrugged. "She needs the money."

"For what?"

"That's not for me to say. If she wants you to know, she'll tell you."

The fact that Andrew knew something about Glory that he didn't was like salt rubbed in an open wound. He had seen the kiss Andrew had given her before sending her upstairs, and he suspected she'd fallen for his charms, just like all the others before her.

Andrew poured them each a cup of dark sludgy coffee, and added a generous shot of his private stock to each.

"Thanks," Slater said tightly, accepting a cup. He took a sip, savoring the first taste of alcohol he'd had all night. It burned away some of his irritation, but an ember continued to smolder in his gut.

They drank in silence, listening to the fading sounds of the town's revelers. Another hour, and it would be dead quiet.

Andrew set his empty cup on the bar. "You might be better off staying away from Miss Glory."

The unexpected remark rankled Slater. Andrew had never warned him away from any of his previous paramours. "Why's that?"

"Just take my word on this."

Slater narrowed his eyes, and the embers flared to life as

red-hot jealousy slid through his veins, igniting his temper. "So you've already gotten her into your bed."

Andrew laughed, startling Slater. "No. She turned me down flat."

Slater was surprised by the depth of his relief. When had he ever cared who Andrew sweet talked into sleeping with him?

"You don't have to look so happy about it," Andrew groused.

Suddenly feeling generous, Slater slapped his friend's back. "I guess I'm just shocked one lady was able to resist your charm."

"And make no mistake, she *is* a lady." Andrew's voice was uncharacteristically serious.

Despite his earlier judgment, Slater was beginning to believe it. Her plea for help at the bar had sparked some buried sense of protectiveness he hadn't felt in years.

His mood took a downturn. He'd never felt that way about a woman before, not even Lydia, and he didn't need the aggravation. Suddenly, all he wanted was room to move. He grabbed his jacket from the bar and shrugged into it. "I'm going for a walk."

Andrew nodded in resignation.

Slater burst out of the saloon into the nearly deserted street. It wouldn't be long before the town would be cloaked in darkness.

Slater strode down the narrow street, avoiding the patient horses tied to hitching posts. His breath misted in the cool evening but he wasn't cold.

The face of his little brother Rye haunted him. The last time he'd seen him was twenty-five years ago, his tear-streaked face pressed to the orphanage window as Slater was taken away by his new family. He'd made a promise to Rye, that he'd return and rescue him from the cold, sterile place. It was a promise Slater had broken.

Maybe it was a Forrester brother trait. Creede had promised to come back after he exacted vengeance for their mother's death, but Slater had never seen him again. Then Slater hadn't returned to fulfill his promise to Rye.

And now Slater was feeling the same protectiveness toward a woman he hardly knew. But he was older and wiser now. He didn't make promises anymore, and he didn't trust anyone who did.

He emptied his mind as he'd taught himself to do during those long, torturous hours at Andersonville, and walked and walked. No wire or sentries stopped him, and finally the demons were cast out until the next time.

$\mathcal{S}$IX

AFTER Slater fled into the night, Andrew sighed and scrubbed his face with his palms. It was times like this that he couldn't help but wonder what terrors Slater had survived during his incarceration at Andersonville. Just like everybody else after the war, he'd heard about the atrocious conditions at the Confederate prisoner of war camp, but at the time he hadn't known Slater had been confined there.

Soon after the Scarlet Garter had opened, Slater arrived in Oaktree. Andrew immediately knew something wasn't right with his friend. Instead of questioning and pushing, Slater merely accepted whatever was handed to him. Also, the easy smile that used to light his eyes was gone. In its place was a somber look more fitting for a much older man.

Sick with dread for the man who was the closest thing to a son Andrew would ever have, he'd immediately hired Slater. He'd managed to bring back some of the man he'd known, but Slater's bitterness bothered him. Then there were times, like tonight, when Slater's past returned to haunt him, and Andrew could do nothing but let him go to exorcise the nightmares in his own way.

Toby and Dante came out from the back area.

"We got everything washed up, Mr. Kearny," Toby said.

Andrew smiled at the freckle-faced boy, who reminded him too much of another boy. "Thanks, Toby. I appreciate it." He turned to Dante. "Any trouble I need to know about?"

Dante shook his head. "No unanticipated disturbances except for the one you witnessed and mediated."

"Slater and Miss Glory's dance partner," Andrew murmured.

Dante glanced around. "Where is Slater?"

"Out."

The small man nodded. Although he didn't know the particulars, Dante was perceptive enough to pick up on Slater's troubled past. "I shall see you at two P.M."

"Goodnight," Andrew said absently.

"'Bye, Mr. Kearny," Toby said.

After they'd gone, Frank finished sweeping up the old sawdust and laid a new layer down. When he left, Andrew locked the door behind him, then extinguished the lamps in the saloon. A lantern in the back was his only illumination as he carried the profits from the night to the office. He locked the safe with the money inside it and rose. Then, he heard a soft click, and tensed. He hadn't locked the back door. Intent on getting to the shotgun behind the bar, he started to the doorway.

A dark figure materialized in front of him, and Andrew stepped back involuntarily, his heart thundering.

"Evenin', Mr. Kearny," the man said with a drawl and a false smile.

Coolness replaced Andrew's momentary surprise, and he smiled back, the expression just as insincere as the stranger's. "You're a little late. Bar's closed."

The thin-faced man wound his fingers around his low-slung gun belt. "Actually, I'm right on time. I'm here to make you a proposition."

"Not interested."

The man frowned in mock disappointment. "You haven't even heard it."

"Still not interested."

"Oh, I think you are." He glanced around, admiration lighting his angled features. "You got a nice place here. I'm sure you'd hate to have somethin' happen to it, like maybe a fire."

Andrew crossed his arms, anger making him tremble. "Are you threatening me?"

The hired gun lifted his hands, palms out. "I'm merely presentin' a business deal. It just so happens the man I work for can insure your place so it isn't destroyed by fire, or perhaps encumbered by accidents."

"Like the unfortunate accident at the Tin Bucket when all the tables and chairs were broken?" Andrew had suspected such a scheme, and now he knew for certain.

The man's face brightened like Andrew was his prize pupil. "Exactly. Now you wouldn't want somethin' like that to happen here, would you?"

Andrew gnashed his teeth. "And how much would this insurance cost me?"

"My employer believes a hundred dollars a month is a fair askin' price."

"And if I don't believe it's a fair price?"

"Then you'll be takin' chances with your livelihood and you'll have only yourself to blame if somethin' happens."

Andrew fought the impulse to tell him to go to hell. He understood how the game worked; he had seen it happen in other places. But he'd be damned if he'd pay someone not to damage or destroy the Scarlet Garter. He affected a thoughtful pose. "I'd like to think about it."

The man narrowed his mud-brown eyes. "You wouldn't want to take too long to make your decision. You never know what might happen." He stared at Andrew, who refused to look away. "I tell you what, my employer is a reasonable man. I'll be back later this week for your decision. And your one hundred dollars."

Andrew was afraid to speak, afraid his temper would make him say or do something he'd regret. He nodded once.

The hired gun mockingly touched the brim of his hat and strolled out the way he'd come in.

Once Andrew gained control of his temper, he followed in the man's wake and locked the door. Not that it would do much good against men like him if they were determined to get in, but it made him feel better.

He leaned against the door and wiped the dampness from his brow. If the bastards thought he was going to pay to keep them from busting up his place, they had another thing coming. The first thing he had to do was talk with Victor Stroman at the Tin Bucket. Maybe he could help him figure out who was behind the intimidation.

Andrew Kearny had paid his dues tenfold in his life. He wasn't about to pay any more.

REBECCA awoke to a single church bell pealing on the other side of town. The sun shone through her window, telling her it was midmorning. Although she would've preferred covering up her head and sleeping another few hours, she had promised Andrew she'd work on the accounts this morning.

She rose and quickly took care of her morning toilette. After donning a dark skirt and white blouse that buttoned high on her neck, she put her hair up in a bun and checked her image in the mirror. There was the Rebecca she knew, not the painted harlot from last night. She doubted if any of the men she'd danced with last night would recognize her right now. She hoped not.

As she went downstairs, the heavenly scent of coffee struck her nose. Not seeing anyone in the saloon despite the hot stove and freshly made coffee, Rebecca found a cup behind the bar and poured herself some.

She took a moment to look around the deserted bar, noting how different it appeared in the light of day, without the rough men filling it. Although she could still smell stale beer, the aroma of fresh sawdust nearly covered it. Chairs were piled on the tables, just as they'd been yesterday when she and Simon had practiced. Had it been only a day?

"Good morning."

Startled, she spun around, managing not to spill her coffee. Andrew stood in the back doorway, looking as if he'd slept for twenty-four hours. For a moment, feminine vanity took over, and she hoped he didn't notice the dark crescents beneath her eyes. "Good morning, Mr.—Andrew."

"I thought you'd sleep later," he commented.

"I wanted to work on your accounting books."

He crossed to join her by the stove and refilled his cup. Standing so close to him, she spotted bloodshot lines in his eyes that made him appear more tired than she'd originally thought. "What time did you go to bed?"

He shrugged. "My usual. Are you hungry?"

She shook her head. "I can wait until lunch."

"Why don't you come on back, and I'll help you get started, then?"

She followed the older man, wondering if he was upset with her for quitting early last night. Although he seemed friendly, there was a distance to his manner that hadn't been there previously.

Andrew went to his safe and spun the dial around a few times, then flipped it open. As he pulled out the ledgers, Rebecca spotted some piles of money. If only she had some of that, she could go back to St. Louis without finding Benjamin, and provide for Daniel herself. Suddenly ashamed of her dishonest thoughts, she turned away from temptation.

And her gaze collided with a more powerful form of temptation.

"Morning, Miss Glory," Slater Forrester said, his voice low and rough.

Rebecca's heart slid into her throat. Instead of his usual suit, Slater wore snug brown trousers, a tan shirt, and a black vest. In his hands he held a wide-brimmed hat that had seen more than its share of sun and rain.

"Good morning, Mr. Forrester." She blamed her husky voice on the lack of sleep.

"Must be the morning for early risers," Andrew commented. "Where are you headed?"

Slater turned his penetrating blue eyes to him. "I'm taking the day off."

"Want to tell me why?"

"I'm going for a ride."

"Anywhere in particular?"

Slater shrugged. "Not really. I figured I've been ignoring Paroli for too long."

A corner of Andrew's lips lifted in amusement. "Are you going to deal tonight?"

"No."

"All right." Slater turned to leave, and Andrew added, "Be careful. Rattlesnakes come in all sizes and shapes."

Slater's eyes narrowed, but after a moment, he left.

Rebecca stared at the door after he'd gone. "Where does Paroli live?"

Confusion clouded Andrew's face for a moment, then he chuckled. "Paroli is his horse. It means parlay."

Although shockingly relieved he wasn't going to see a woman, Rebecca frowned in bewilderment. She'd heard Benjamin use the word on more than one occasion. "What does it mean?"

"It's a faro term. Means to stack your original bet and its winnings on the next turn of the card."

"I should've known it had something to do with gambling." She couldn't hide her bitterness.

"Of course. Slater and I are gamblers." Andrew's small smile didn't touch his eyes. "Well, shall we?" He motioned to the doorway.

Rebecca led the way back into the saloon, and Andrew righted three chairs stacked on a table. He held one for Rebecca and she sat, letting herself believe she was still a lady for a few moments.

After Andrew got her started, she concentrated on the figures, pushing back thoughts of both Benjamin and Daniel. And the handsome puzzle that was Slater Forrester.

A knock on Rebecca's door startled her. "Who's there?"

"Georgia."

Rebecca frowned. The Negro saloon gal was the last person she expected at her door. She adjusted her dancing dress and opened the door. "What is it?" Cringing inwardly at her curt tone, she forced herself to soften her expression. "I'm sorry. I was just getting ready to go downstairs."

Georgia, wearing her favorite blue dress, lifted her chin, but there was uncertainty in her eyes. "I just wanted to tell you I'm sorry about the other night. Simon was right—you didn't know no better."

As apologies went, it was a double-edged blade, but it was sincere. "That's all right." Rebecca swallowed her pride. "This is all new to me, and I'm just learning how things are."

"I know that now." Georgia glanced down, her fingers lacing and unlacing. "You have a real purty voice." She met Rebecca's gaze and said almost shyly, "I always wished I could sing."

Rebecca relaxed tense muscles. "Have you tried?"

"Oh, yeah. One night after ev'rybody was gone, Simon, he played a song and I tried singing." She laughed. "Poor Simon didn't know what to say. He didn't want to hurt my feelin's."

Realization brought a genuine smile to Rebecca. Georgia obviously liked Simon. She wondered if the feeling was mutual. "Simon is a nice person."

"He's about the nicest man I ever met," Georgia said, as if daring Rebecca to disagree. "And the way he plays the piano . . ." She sighed.

Rebecca leaned against the door frame. "Have you told him how you feel about him?"

Georgia straightened, and her dark complexion turned dusky. "I'm a whore, Glory. Simon deserves a whole lot better than the likes of me."

"Have you asked him what he thinks?"

Georgia's lips pressed together in a thin line, and her eyes snapped with impatience. "No, and I ain't about to. He's a good man." She turned as if to leave, then paused. "You ready to go down?"

Rebecca glanced down at her sore feet. "I am, but my feet aren't. How do you manage to dance every night?"

Georgia smiled, softening her features. "Tonight, after we're done, I'll show you somethin' that'll help. All us girls do it on Sunday nights."

Warmed by Georgia's overture of friendship, Rebecca nodded. "I'll look forward to it."

Rebecca stepped into the hall and closed the door behind her. Men's voices already rumbled downstairs, telling her that few of the rough cowboys observed the Sabbath. She thought of the high-ceilinged church she used to attend with her parents. When she was a child, she searched for reasons to get out of going. But at this moment, Rebecca would trade almost anything to be there, with her mother and father.

Georgia hooked her arm around Rebecca's. "Get rid of that frown, Glory, and let's show them big ol' boys a good time."

Although Rebecca had a difficult time seeing those boys as anything other than vulgar men, she pasted on a smile. As they descended the stairs, her gaze automatically searched for Slater. Then she remembered he wouldn't be in tonight. Disappointment and a flash of panic caught her unaware.

"You all right, Glory?" Georgia asked.

Rebecca shoved down the momentary alarm and nodded. "Just a little nervous," she lied.

"No need. Hell, if truth be told, most of them are more nervous than us. You can tell by their wet, slimy hands."

Despite herself, Rebecca laughed at Georgia's description and she squeezed the girl's arm. "Thank you."

Georgia seemed embarrassed by her gratitude. "C'mon."

Cassie, Molly, and the youngest girl, Rose, were already downstairs and paired up. As Rebecca and Georgia stepped off the last step, they were immediately snatched up by two enthusiastic but less-than-skilled dancers. Rebecca smiled at her partner and narrowly avoided getting her foot stomped on.

It was going to be a long night.

REBECCA managed to last the entire night—it ended earlier than the previous one. By one A.M. the last of the revelers were gone and Frank locked the front door. Rebecca joined her fellow hurdy-gurdy girls for a final drink. A moment before the glass rim touched her lips, she detected the strong scent of whiskey. But she was too late and the liquor burned her throat, sending her into a coughing fit.

Someone pounded on her back. "You okay, Glory?"

Through tearing eyes she saw Cassie looking at her, a glint of mischief in her eyes. "You knew," Rebecca said, her voice hoarse.

Cassie shrugged and exchanged glances with the other girls. "It's a weekly tradition."

Rebecca turned to Dante, expecting him to come to her defense. Instead, he shrugged and smiled. "Perhaps we should have warned you, but one must be initiated into the sisterhood."

The girls giggled, and Rebecca's irritation bled away. She grinned and wiped the tears from her cheeks. "Did I pass?"

Georgia put an arm around her shoulders. "You done good, Miss Glory."

"I hope that whiskey doesn't hurt her singing voice," Andrew said as he waltzed in through the back door.

Flustered and worried, Rebecca assured him, "It didn't." It was suddenly important to her to fit into this group whom she never would have associated with a month ago.

Andrew filled a shot glass with whiskey and downed it. "Any problems tonight?"

"No, sir," Frank replied.

"Nothing we couldn't handle," Dante added with a wink.

"Did Malcolm and Richard show up to deal tonight?" Andrew asked.

"Malcolm was tardy, but he did well. Richard directed the faro table, and I believe the house managed to stay ahead."

Rebecca had steered clear of them, unwilling to befriend any more gamblers. Besides, between her singing and dancing, she didn't have time to visit with the other employees.

"Thanks," Andrew said absently. "Let's get the chairs up."

Andrew, Frank, and Simon immediately began to lift chairs onto tables as Dante cleaned up behind the bar. Rebecca glanced at Georgia, noticing how her gaze followed the flexing of Simon's muscles as he worked. Georgia definitely had it bad for the piano player.

"Your water's ready in the back, girls, and Toby took the tub up earlier," Dante said.

Rebecca was caught in the group of women as they formed

a line to the back and picked up pails filled with steaming water. Carrying one, Rebecca followed them upstairs, where they went into what she thought of as the dress room. In the middle of the floor was a large, round metal tub, and the hot water was poured into it.

"Take off your shoes and stockings, Glory," Georgia said.

Although reluctant, Rebecca followed her example. Then chairs were pulled around the tub, dress hems lifted to expose red garters, and feet stuck into the hot water. Keeping her gaze lowered, she raised her hem to above her knees and daintily placed her feet in the tub. The heat stung for a moment, but was immediately followed by soothing bliss.

"Damn, this is better than having one of those orgasms," Cassie said with a heavy sigh.

"Oh, yeah," Molly murmured.

Her face hot with embarrassment, Rebecca tried to find something proper to focus on, other than bare legs and feet.

Everyone remained silent for a few minutes, simply relieved to be off their feet.

Cassie lit a cheroot, exhaled a stream of smoke upward, and broke the silence. "I lost count at thirty-nine."

"I only had twelve tonight. I think it's my lowest ever," Molly said.

"Twenty-eight for me," Georgia said.

"Sixteen here," Rose said. She rolled her eyes. "I wonder how they'd feel if it happened to them that often."

Rebecca's eyes widened. They couldn't possibly be talking about. . . . Not in one night. Was it even possible?

"How about you, Glory?" Cassie asked.

"Uh, none," Rebecca said, afraid to look anyone in the eye.

She felt their astonished gazes on her.

"Not a single one?" Molly asked, aghast.

She shook her head, surprised she hadn't burst into flames from the heat of her embarrassment.

"You're really lucky," Georgia said. "I'd like just one night where I didn't have none."

Silence surrounded them once more, and Rebecca finally gained the courage to raise her head. Her experience was limited to her short marriage, and it had been rare for her to have an . . . orgasm when she and Benjamin . . . . She couldn't even finish the thought. How often had she wished she could ask someone questions about sexual intercourse? Who would be better to ask than women who did it as a job?

"Um, is it normal for, um, that to happen so often?" There, she'd asked, and no one seemed shocked or insulted.

Molly shrugged. "Sure. Why do you think we soak our feet afterward?"

Rebecca stared at her, confused. "What do you mean? How does it, um, help that part of you?"

Cassie leaned forward and tipped her head to the side. "What do you think we're talking about, Glory?"

Could she even say it? She worked up some saliva in her dry mouth. "Orgasms."

Mouths dropped, and suddenly Rebecca was surrounded by laughter. Fighting tears, she pulled her feet out of the water, intent on escaping their ridicule.

Georgia grabbed her wrist. "Now don't go runnin' off, Glory."

She knew her cheeks were beet red with humiliation. "I'm tired."

"Bullshit," Cassie said. She waved at Rebecca's abandoned chair. "Sit down, honey. We weren't laughing at you. Well, maybe we were, but it was funny."

"I don't understand," Rebecca said, wishing the earth would swallow her.

"We were talking about how many times our feet got stepped on tonight," Rose said, taking pity on her. "Not orgasms." She giggled. "Goodness, if I had sixteen in one night, I wouldn't move for three days."

Molly snorted. "Yeah. We're lucky if we get one a week."

Georgia sniffed. "And that's usually not any man's doing."

The girls broke into another round of laughter, leaving Rebecca totally confused. "I still don't—"

"Sit down, honey, and we'll explain everything. Believe me, between us, we've done it all and seen it all," Cassie said.

Torn between running away and never returning, and finally having her curiosity appeased, Rebecca lowered herself to her chair. She placed her feet in the tub and sighed in contentment. Where did she start?

She turned to Georgia. "What did you mean when you said it's usually not a man's doing?"

SEVEN

EXHAUSTED, Slater used his key to enter the back door of the Scarlet Garter. He'd ridden farther than planned, and thus had taken longer to return than expected. But the long ride had sent the nightmares back into the locked room in his mind. He knew they'd escape again—they always did—but for now, he felt a measure of peace.

Hearing laughter as he climbed the back stairs, Slater paused in front of the room where the women's dancing dresses were kept. He knew the girls got together Sunday nights to soak their feet and do what women did when they gathered—gossip.

Hearing the seasoned whores giggling like young girls, Slater allowed a slight smile. It wasn't that he disliked the prostitutes—hell, some of his most pleasurable memories included a bed and a saloon gal. But over the past few years he'd come to realize they were as much prisoners of their lives as he'd been in Andersonville, and he'd lost his enjoyment in lying with one. Not that he could avoid them completely; when his urges became too strong, he sought out a woman from one of the other saloons, and never the same one twice. It made it easier to live with his conscience when he didn't have to see her every day.

However, Glory tempted him like none of the others. Even Molly, who tried her best to entice him to her bed.

Another spate of laughter caught his attention, and he wondered if Glory was with them. He leaned close to the door.

"I can't imagine doing that," Glory was saying, her tone horrified.

Giggles followed, and Slater frowned, wishing he knew what she referred to.

"The first time was the worst. I damn near bit it off," Molly said.

"I did bite the first time. He hit me. I was always careful with my teeth after that."

Slater cringed after Rose's confession, suddenly realizing what they were talking about. He considered himself experienced, but women talking about sucking—and biting—a man's privates wasn't something he expected to overhear. Flinching at the image, he backed away from the door and tiptoed to his room at the opposite end of the hall, hoping like hell none of the women came out until he was safely inside.

Closing the door behind him, he breathed a sigh of relief. Moments later, he heard the girls returning to their rooms. He'd escaped in the nick of time.

Although he tried to forget their conversation, he kept recalling Glory's comment. It sounded as if she'd never used her mouth on a man. That was possible only if she wasn't a whore, which meant this was probably her first time working in a saloon. So why was a woman like Glory Bowen singing in a place like this instead of the church on the other side of town?

Uncomfortable with the fact that Glory was alone and desperate, Slater impatiently tossed his hat on the bed. Hell, she wasn't his problem, so why was he letting her situation bother him?

Because he saw something in her eyes, something that remained innocent and gentle when she was surrounded by vice and callousness.

Or maybe you're only seeing something you want to see.

Angry with himself, Slater hastily removed his clothes, leaving on his drawers. He caught a glimpse of his back in the mirror and stopped to stare at the scars that striped his back. The oldest had been inflicted almost twenty-five years ago; the newest, three years ago.

It was strange how the visible scars were the least painful.

LAUGHTER greeted Slater when he came downstairs the next morning. Only this time it was a man's and a woman's laughter.

Andrew and Glory were seated at a table close to the stove's warmth, the accounts book and receipts spread out around them. Andrew's head was near Glory's cornsilk one as they conversed easily.

Jealousy punched him in the gut, expelling the air in his lungs. Shocked by the unexpected reaction, Slater had to focus on schooling his features to display indifference. He finished his descent and strolled to the stove.

"Morning," he said as they finally noticed him.

"You got in late," Andrew said with a slight frown.

Impatience swelled through Slater. "What are you, my father?" Hurt flashed in his friend's eyes, and Slater cringed inwardly. He had no right taking out his frustration on Andrew. "Sorry. Just a little tired this morning."

The older man shrugged it off. "Why don't you join us?"

Slater knew he should say no, but found himself sitting next to Glory. "How's it coming?"

She gave him a cool look. "Fine. Andrew was just telling me some stories about his years as a riverboat gambler."

"Slater, here, did the same," Andrew said with a fond smile. "Taught him everything he knows."

A smile tugged at Slater's mouth, and he winked at Glory. "Not quite everything."

Her cheeks pinkened, something a whore's rarely did, and her lips pursed. Remembering what she'd confessed to the women last night, Slater found himself imagining those full, luscious lips wrapped around him. Thinking of being her first only made him harder. He shifted in his chair and caught Andrew's smirk, as if the older man knew.

"Are you working tonight?" Andrew asked him.

Slater tore his gaze from Glory's attractive profile to focus on Andrew. "I'll be here. Everything all right last night?"

Andrew shrugged. "I guess so. I went to see Stroman."

Alarm sharpened Slater's voice. "Why?"

"I wanted to find out more about what happened to his place the other night."

Irritation slid through Slater, but curiosity overrode it. "So?"

Andrew's mouth pressed to a grim line. "It's like I thought. Pay up or risk the consequences." He glanced at Glory, whose intelligent gaze moved between them, then shifted his attention back to Slater. "Someone was here Saturday night after we closed. He gave me the same options that Victor was given."

Fury scalded Slater, but it was accompanied by an icy tendril of fear. He forced himself to loosen his grip on his coffee cup. "What did you tell him?"

"That I wanted to think about it." Andrew slapped the tabletop, startling Slater and causing Glory to draw back in surprise. His expression hardened. "They can go hang. I'm not going to pay them a red cent."

Apprehension dulled Slater's anger. "You do that, and you're liable to end up with a busted-up place, too."

"I know." Andrew's face was grim. "But I'll be damned if I let them extort my money."

"What are you talking about?" Glory asked.

Andrew smiled and patted the back of her hand like she was a little girl. "Nothing you have to worry about."

Temper flared in her amber eyes, but she kept silent. Slater admired her restraint. However, it didn't stop him from voicing his concerns.

"If you don't pay, it'll be the worry of everyone who works here. They have a right to know," Slater said.

"They haven't hurt anyone, just busted up some things."

"But they could. We've seen it happen in other places."

Andrew leveled a hard gaze on him. "Find out who's behind it, get me proof, and then we'll call in the law."

Slater forced a laugh. "And you expect Sheriff Ryder to do something about them?"

"No. I expect the state to come in and clean the varmints out. But I can't contact them until I have solid evidence." Andrew paused. "You could get it, Slater."

Slater's left hand began to tremble, and he quickly drew it off the table and placed the fisted hand on his thigh. His action wasn't lost on either Andrew or Glory.

Andrew, his expression contrite, shook his head. "I'm sorry, Slater. You already gave me your answer."

Slater couldn't bring himself to look at Glory. Embarrassment made him curt. "Pay the man so you don't lose this place."

"I'll think about it."

But Slater saw the obstinacy in Andrew's eyes and knew his friend wasn't about to bend to intimidation.

Damn him!

"When is the collector coming back?" Slater asked.

Andrew shrugged and glanced away. "He didn't say."

Although Andrew was a consummate bluffer at the gambling tables, he couldn't hide a lie from Slater. And the fact that he did lie to him made Slater feel both anger and guilt.

"Why won't the sheriff do anything?" Glory asked.

Slater barked a humorless laugh. "He took the badge because he knew he could get free liquor, food, and whores."

Glory's mouth gaped. "He's supposed to be upholding the law."

"Time to come out of your house on the hill, Glory, and join the rest of us down here," Slater said, unable to curb his sarcasm.

Blotches of red stained her cheeks. "My house on the hill is long gone, Mr. Forrester. And if you haven't noticed, I've already joined you in this den of iniquity."

Slater fought back a grin. "Hear that, Andrew? She thinks your pride and joy is a den of iniquity."

"Slater," Andrew growled in warning.

He shrugged, suddenly feeling reckless. "What? Are you

afraid I'm going to upset Miss Glory's sensibilities? It's not like she hasn't already been shocked all the way down to her prim drawers just by working among us sinners."

"Maybe you should take another ride, Slater," Andrew said firmly. "Clear your head."

Slater gnashed his teeth, knowing he was behaving like an ass, but unable to stop himself. He shoved back his chair, knocking it to the floor, and smiled coolly. "I think I will. I need some fresh air."

He strode out of the saloon, hoping to escape the voice in his head that called him a coward. The same voice that told him Andrew was right to refuse to pay extortion.

Slater had done the right thing when he'd joined the Pinkerton Agency and become a spy for the North during the war. He'd saved lives with his work, yet in the end he was beaten and nearly starved to death in a hellhole. It had taken him three years to regain his life, and he'd decided doing the right thing was only for heroes and fools. And Slater was neither. Not anymore.

ANDREW stood and righted Slater's chair, then smiled apologetically. "I'm sorry you were witness to one of his tantrums," he said.

More curious than uncomfortable at Slater's abrupt departure, Rebecca shrugged. "You shouldn't apologize. It wasn't your fault."

Regret shadowed Andrew's eyes. "Yes, it was. I knew he'd get upset if I pushed him."

Andrew retrieved the coffee pot and refilled his and Rebecca's cups, and carried Slater's empty one to the bar. He returned to the table and sat down, but the easy companionship Rebecca had felt earlier was gone.

She fiddled with the pen. "Can I ask you a question?"

Andrew's smile was a ghost of his usual one. "I won't guarantee I'll answer it."

She smiled slightly in acknowledgment. "How long have you known Sla—Mr. Forrester?"

Andrew's gaze fell to the tabletop. "Over twenty years

now. He tried to pick my pocket in Houston." He chuckled. "Skinny kid, more desperate than anything. I made him an offer. He could have what was in my wallet, or I'd teach him how to gamble." Pride filled his eyes. "He chose gambling."

"Why?"

"He was smart enough to realize once the money in my wallet was gone, he'd have to steal again. But if he learned how to gamble, he could make his own money."

And swindle unsuspecting women.

However, she doubted Andrew or Slater had ever done what Benjamin did to her. But then, how would she know? She hadn't realized Benjamin's true character until everything was gone. She cleared her throat. "So you taught him."

Andrew nodded, and a paternal smile graced his lips. "He was an excellent student, a natural with cards. But Slater had something I didn't."

"A temper?"

He laughed. "He does have that, but I've also been known to lose mine a time or two. No, after Slater didn't have to fight every day to survive, he discovered this streak of righteousness inside him."

Rebecca remembered how he'd come to her rescue Saturday night and how she'd thought it odd. But if Andrew was right, then it was perfectly in character for Slater to have done such a thing.

"And that got him into more trouble than he ever expected. It changed him." Andrew's gaze grew distant. "He's still the best man I know, but now he's afraid."

Rebecca snorted in disbelief. "Slater Forrester, afraid? I find that hard to believe."

Andrew's smile held shadows. "Most people say the same." He blinked aside the melancholy and motioned to the papers across the table. "Do you think you can handle this yourself?"

"I think so."

"Then I'll leave so you can get started. Dante will be here around two to open up the place, so you should have everything picked up by then."

Rebecca nodded. "What about you?"

"I'm going to visit some of my fellow business owners."

Rebecca frowned, sensing his visits had something to do with what he and Slater had been discussing earlier.

Andrew gave her shoulder a gentle squeeze. "Don't look so worried, Glory. I'll be back later." He turned to leave, then paused. "If Slater comes back, don't be too hard on him. He's a good man, but he's had some hard times."

Rebecca listened to her boss leave as she pondered his parting words. The fact that she was attracted to Slater made her want to believe Andrew, but trust was difficult to find after Benjamin's betrayal. Yet here she was, searching for the man who left her penniless. However, she had no choice. Once Benjamin learned he had a son, he'd return to St. Louis with her and give the boy what he needed—a home and a family.

What if he doesn't care?

Rebecca refused to acknowledge her doubts. If she did, she'd have nothing left. She'd already lost both her former life and her respectability to search for Benjamin. Because only if she found him could she keep her promise to Daniel.

However, Slater Forrester wasn't dismissed so easily from her thoughts. To deny her attraction to him was foolish, but to acknowledge it was equally foolhardy. If for no other reason than the fact that she was married, she couldn't allow herself to be drawn to him. Yet Andrew's obvious affection for him and her own curiosity made it especially hard to resist.

Realizing she was woolgathering when she should be working, Rebecca picked up the first receipt on the pile. Finding the correct column, she neatly wrote in the amount, then picked up the next receipt.

If only her life was as easily categorized as bills of sale.

THAT night Rebecca wasn't nearly as nervous as she'd been the previous two nights. She didn't sing because Andrew wanted to save that for the busiest times, so she only danced. However, there were fewer customers, which meant more competition among the girls. On the rare occasions when one of the other women took a man upstairs, Rebecca didn't lack for dance partners. But even though she got paid a nickel for every special a man bought her, Rebecca didn't mind sitting out some of the dances.

Having soaked her feet with the women last night, Rebecca was now accepted into their "sisterhood." Although she still blushed when she thought about all they'd talked about, Rebecca was grateful for their knowledge. Not that she ever planned to try any of those numerous ways to please a man—and herself—but at least she no longer felt so naive.

Only two dealers worked that evening—Slater, who played poker, and Malcolm, who ran the faro table. There was always a handful of men playing faro, but Slater, who occupied his normal back table, sat alone more often than not. When she wasn't dancing, Rebecca watched him shuffle cards and lay them out, either in a solitaire game or just fanning them to keep his fingers nimble.

One time her eyes met his, and lightning sizzled through her. Then he casually looked away, and Rebecca couldn't help wondering if the heated look they'd exchanged had been her imagination.

However, as the week progressed and she and Slater exchanged only a handful of words, Rebecca decided she'd read more into the accidental look than was actually there. She worked on the bookkeeping in the mornings and grew more comfortable in her hurdy-gurdy job at night.

Despite Rebecca's newfound and surprising camaraderie with the other girls, as well as with Dante and Simon, she never lost sight of her purpose for being there. The Scarlet Garter was one of the fanciest gambling, drinking, and dancing establishments in Oaktree, and she knew her husband well enough to know he would search out the nicest place in town. She was confident that if he was in Oaktree, he'd find the Scarlet Garter.

He'd also find his wife, whether he wanted to or not.

$\mathcal{E}$IGHT

AFTER a busy and late night, Rebecca was surprised to hear women's voices in the hallway before noon on Saturday morning. Shoving back the loose hair from her face, she rose from her narrow bed and drew on her wrapper. She cracked open the door and saw Cassie and Rose, wearing relatively conservative dresses and hats, standing in the hallway.

Rose waved at her. "Are you coming with us, Glory?"

She opened the door wider. "Where are you going?"

"We get paid today." The girl's cheeks were naturally bright, lacking the usual paint. "We're going shopping."

Although Rebecca was saving her money, the thought of actually getting out of the saloon and browsing through a store brought a flutter of excitement.

"I can be ready in ten minutes."

Rose clapped her hands in delight. "Oh, good. We're waiting for Molly and Georgia, too."

Cassie rolled her eyes and smiled indulgently at the younger woman. "No need to rush, Glory. Molly takes forever."

Grinning, Rebecca ducked back into her room and quickly shed her wrapper and gown. She donned a rust-colored dress with a pattern of tiny yellow and blue flowers. To determine what coat to wear, she opened her window and the fresh spring air drifted in around her. Back home there'd have been the scent of lilacs and apple blossoms, and for a moment, she could almost smell them.

The sharp ache of homesickness struck her, and she rubbed her chest, trying to remove the pain. But it was centered deep within her, wrapped in years of happiness with her parents in their grand home. She'd taken it all for granted, never once imagining she'd lose both her parents and her home in the space of two years. And never would she have thought she would lose something even more precious—her child.

Moisture burned her eyes, and she blinked the tears into submission. Fortunately, Daniel wasn't lost to death like her parents, but if she didn't find Benjamin, he might as well be. The boy needed his father, if for no other reason than to provide him a home, food, and clothing.

But what if she could simply earn enough money to do those things herself? She could say her husband was dead, and live the quiet—and respectable—life of a widow and raise her son. Excited by the prospect, she finished readying herself, pinning on a small hat and shrugging into a long cape. Glancing in the mirror, she was pleased with her proper appearance.

By the time she emerged from her room, Georgia had joined Cassie and Rose. Although the clothing her associates wore was more acceptable than the typical dancing dresses, the plunging necklines revealed more of their assets than Rebecca thought appropriate. She opened her mouth to state her opinion, but snapped it shut when Molly sashayed out of her room. Molly's red dress clung to her figure all the way to her knees, where it flared slightly. The tight bodice squeezed her full breasts upward to form plump hillocks with a deep crevasse between them. Surely one wrong move would have her bust tumbling out. Topping her outrageous dress, Molly wore a wide-brimmed hat festooned with feathers, ribbons, and bows.

"Let's go, girls," Cassie said, not even giving Molly a second glance.

Rebecca, feeling like a nun among the flamboyant group, brought up the rear. The women teased each other about their hoped-for purchases, but for the first time since she'd been accepted into their midst, Rebecca felt alienated. Working together, they shared a bond, but beyond the saloon their differences were glaring.

Andrew met them at the bottom of the stairs, his admiring gaze moving across each of them. When his eyes found Rebecca, an amused smile touched his lips, which for some reason irritated her. She lifted her chin and met his gaze, daring him to make a comment. Wisely, Andrew kept silent.

"Cassie, you're first," Andrew said.

Puzzled, Rebecca stayed with the others while Cassie followed Andrew into the back room. She wondered why they simply didn't get paid at the same time, but refrained from asking. Instead, she waited as each woman was called in and came out, tucking away her money.

Finally, Georgia exited the office and Rebecca's name was called. She entered the office and closed the door, just as the other women had done.

Andrew had a paltry pile of paper money and coins lying on the table in front of him. He smiled up at Rebecca. "You did well for your first week." He pushed the money toward her. "Eighteen dollars and five cents."

Rebecca's stomach dropped. After all those hours getting her feet tromped on as she smiled prettily at stinky men, this was all there was? She swallowed hard and asked formally, "May I ask how you arrived at this total?"

Andrew smiled. "I should've known the bookkeeper would ask for an accounting."

Her face heated, hoping he didn't think she was insulting him. However, she couldn't help but feel slighted after she'd worked harder than she ever had in her life. "I'm not suggesting you cheated me, but I had thought . . ."

"Here, I'll go over it with you." Andrew glanced at a paper by his elbow and turned it around to face her. He pointed to numbers scrawled across it. "One hundred and fifty-one specials were bought for you this week. At a nickel a drink, that gives you seven fifty-five. On the nights you sing, you get an extra two dollars. And I'm paying you ten dollars a week to keep my books." He looked up at her. "That brings your total to twenty-one fifty-five, then take off three fifty for your room, and that leaves eighteen dollars and five cents."

Rebecca added and subtracted the numbers in her head and arrived at the same total. She felt sick.

"There's no other job for a woman in this town that'll pay as well," Andrew reminded her.

Even though she recognized the truth of his words, Rebecca inwardly railed at the unfairness of her situation. Disappointed, she nodded and scooped up her money, placing it in her reticule.

Andrew eyed her closely. "There is a way you can make more money."

Hope leapt in her, then she noticed the look in his eyes. "No. I can't," she said firmly.

"It wouldn't be that difficult."

She imagined lying beneath those same men she danced with, and bile rose in her throat. Those men with the grubby hands and bad breath and smelly clothes. "Yes, it would be." She drew back her shoulders. "I have to draw the line somewhere, Andrew. I've already sinned more often in the past week than I have in my entire life. I won't permit myself to sink any lower."

"That's a pity. You could make at least ten dollars more a week."

The thought of getting nearly thirty dollars every week tempted her, but in reality she couldn't bring herself to do it. *Not even for my son?*

Doubt and guilt pounded her conscience, but she wasn't desperate enough to sell her body. She prayed she'd never become that desperate.

"No." Rebecca took a deep breath. "Thank you, Andrew."

"You're welcome, Glory," he said, equally formal. He smiled. "Why don't you go buy yourself something pretty? It'll make you feel better."

As much as she liked Andrew, she found his patronizing attitude insulting. However, she knew better than to anger her boss. She pasted on a smile. "I'll see you this evening."

Joining the other women, Rebecca was swept away in their tide of excitement. The girls sauntered down the street, deftly dodging the numerous horse droppings. Whistles and lewd greetings followed them, but the women only giggled and threw their admirers kisses. Rebecca wanted to run back to her room and hide, but Georgia had a firm hold on her arm.

As they made their way to the general store, Rebecca ignored both the lecherous and the disapproving stares. Instead, she studied the structures that constituted Oaktree. The disreputable side of town was made up largely of canvas tent saloons, with a few a combination of wood and canvas. The Scarlet Garter was one of only four buildings that were built completely of lumber. Once they crossed into the reputable side of town, there were more wood structures, although there were also a surprising number of canvas tents, too. She shuddered to think of the damage a fire would cause with the wood and canvas dwellings packed together so tightly.

Compared to the stately elegance of St. Louis, this burgeoning frontier town was raw and coarse, just like the men who populated it. However, judging by the upright women who made a show of giving a wide berth to Rebecca and her fellow employees, civilization was making inroads in Oaktree. In another life, Rebecca would've been one of those holding herself above women like Cassie and wouldn't have thought twice about her lofty manner. Now she was torn by her warring feelings, knowing she was seen as one of the fallen.

The store was one of those structures built of both lumber and canvas. There was little to entice Rebecca to enter, but she didn't have a choice with Georgia hauling her along. The interior was larger than Rebecca expected, and it was crammed with merchandise ranging from ready-made clothing to canned goods to pots and pans and everything in between. Georgia released her and beelined for a corner where hats, gloves, fancy dresses, and frilly unmentionables were displayed Cassie, Rose, and Molly were already oohing and ahhhing over the items.

Uninterested in the frothy clothing, Rebecca browsed through the rest of the store. She spotted a pile of books half hidden behind a stack of trousers, and her spirits lifted. As she searched the titles, she found a copy of Emily Brontë's *Wuthering Heights*, which she'd read when she was sixteen. Her mother had caught her reading it after her bedtime and had chided her on the late hour before confessing it was one of her favorites. Rebecca swallowed the bittersweet memory but clung to the book. She continued through the titles and discovered a copy of Alexander Dumas's *Le Comte de Monte Cristo*. Was there somebody else in Oaktree who spoke and read French?

The price of the two books was twenty-five cents, an amount Rebecca wouldn't have blinked at a year ago, but now debated on spending.

"I'm surprised women like you know how to read."

Startled, Rebecca glanced up to see a buxom woman wearing a dark-colored proper dress and bonnet glaring at her. "Excuse me?"

The woman stared down her long, pointed nose at her. "Why don't you stay on your side of town, where you belong?"

Rebecca's face grew hot even as she wondered how the matron had known. Surely her own demure dress and hat hadn't given her away. She must've seen her come in with the other girls. Still, it didn't excuse her loathsome manners. "I have just as much right to shop here as you do."

The woman leaned closer, her eyes seething with repugnance. "Your kind doesn't belong around our God-fearing folk."

A lump filled Rebecca's throat and she fought scalding tears, but along with her humiliation came indignation. "I was taught that God loves everyone equally, even sinners." She nodded curtly. "Good day, madam."

Rebecca paid for her books at the counter, and just as she finished, Georgia joined her, her dark eyes shining. She held up a hat the exact color of her favorite dancing dress. Peacock feathers, a stylish bird's nest, and silk ribbons adorned the gaudy hat.

"What do you think, Glory?" Georgia lowered her excited voice. "Do you think Simon would like it?"

Although unwilling to be caught dead in such a garish headpiece, Rebecca didn't want to hurt her new friend's feelings. She smiled and said honestly, "I think if he doesn't notice, he's blind."

Georgia grinned. "I'm going to buy it." She glanced at the wrapped parcel in Rebecca's hands. "What'd you get?"

"Books."

Georgia wrinkled her nose. "Aren't you going to buy something pretty?"

Rebecca shook her head. "I'm going back to the Scarlet Garter."

"You can't do that. We're all going over to the restaurant to have a fancy meal."

Although it sounded heavenly after enduring meals of greasy meat and watery potatoes, Rebecca had already treated herself to the two books. "I have to save my money, Georgia. You all have a nice dinner."

Before Georgia could press her, Rebecca turned and hurried out of the store. She kept her head lowered as she walked down the sunny street, not wishing to see the women's disgusted looks nor the men's too familiar leers. The excitement of being paid and going shopping had worn off, leaving her tired and depressed. However, the prospect of returning to her cramped room at the Scarlet Garter only increased her melancholy.

When she'd arrived in Oaktree by stagecoach, she'd noticed a cottonwood-lined stream just outside of town. Getting her bearings, she headed in that direction. As she passed the livery at the end of town, a man sauntered out and blocked her path.

"Excuse me," she murmured, trying to sidestep him.

The man blocked her path. "You're a long ways from the Garter."

Rebecca brought her head up sharply to study the pock-marked man. He looked vaguely familiar. She might have danced with him, but all the faces blurred together. "Excuse me," she repeated more firmly.

She attempted to go around him again, but he caught her arm in a ham-sized hand. He motioned to the barn behind them. "What do you say you and me get to know each other better?"

Rebecca struggled against the panic rising in her throat. "No, thank you. I'm not working now."

The man grinned, revealing teeth stained by tobacco. "Who said anything about work? This would be pleasure."

Only your *pleasure.* Frustrated and tired of men's advances, she glared at him. "Release me."

He only smirked.

"You heard the lady, mister." Slater Forrester strode up to stand beside Rebecca. "Let her go."

"So you can have her?" The man made a terrible hacking sound and spat a brown mass onto the ground.

Rebecca's stomach churned with revulsion.

"She's not interested, and since she's not working, she has a right to ask you to leave her alone," Slater said, his voice calm and steady. Then his tone hardened. "Let her go."

A cruel smile found the man's thin lips. "I don't think so."

Suddenly he pushed Rebecca aside and swung his fist at Slater. The gambler ducked and grabbed the man's arm, twisting it behind his back.

"Don't ever come to the Scarlet Garter again," Slater said through clenched teeth.

"Or what?"

He increased the pressure on the man's arm. "Or I'll have Dante get out his sawed-off shotgun."

The man tried to glare, but it was more of a grimace. "There's lots more places to drink and whore," he said with false bravado.

"And I'm sure they'll all welcome you." Slater shoved the man.

With one last scowl, the man stumbled away as he rubbed his shoulder.

Slater turned to Rebecca, and there was a hint of concern in his eyes. "Are you all right?"

She nodded even as she realized she was trembling. Something like this never would've happened if she hadn't taken the job at the Scarlet Garter. But then, if she wasn't working there, she could be in more dire straits.

And if I hadn't married Benjamin, I'd still be living in St. Louis, still ignorant of women like Cassie and men like my accoster.

"What're you doing in this part of town by yourself?" Slater demanded.

Although extremely grateful for his timely arrival, she bristled at his high-handed tone. "Is it against the law to take a walk?"

He crossed his arms, the motion drawing her attention to his muscular chest and shoulders beneath the gentleman's jacket. However, no gentleman would've spoken to her so, nor would he have engaged with a ruffian. Of course, if Slater weren't a gentleman, he wouldn't have come to her rescue . . . again.

She sighed. "Thank you for your assistance, Slater. I'm sorry I was so curt with you."

Her apology seemed to unbalance him, and his brow furrowed in puzzlement. "You were lucky I was coming out to check on my horse."

"Paroli is in this livery?" Rebecca asked.

He nodded. "Would you like to meet him?"

Rebecca suspected there weren't many people he asked that of. "I'd love to."

He lightly pressed his palm against her lower back to guide her into the barn. Rebecca tried to ignore the heat of his hand and the proximity of his body. But ever since the moment she'd met him, the awareness of his solid masculinity and his piercing blue eyes brought warmth to the part of her she'd denied since Benjamin left her.

She blinked in the relative darkness of the livery, but her eyes quickly adjusted. He stopped at a stall where a beautiful roan horse stood, its head held high over the gate. The roan snuffled into Slater's palm and the gambler laughed lightly, a pleasant sound that lodged itself in Rebecca's chest, making it hard to breathe.

"Paroli, this is Miss Glory," Slater introduced her.

Rebecca smiled and removed her glove to pat the horse's silky neck. "Hello, Paroli. You're a handsome one, aren't you?"

Paroli threw his head upward and whinnied as if agreeing with her.

"He's a beautiful animal. Where did you get him?" Rebecca asked, rubbing the gelding's forehead.

"I won him in a card game in St. Louis a couple of years ago," he replied.

"You've been to St. Louis?"

He nodded. "Quite a few times."

She hadn't expected Slater Forrester to have been in the city she was born and raised in. But then, St. Louis had a number of gambling houses that he probably frequented. A sudden thought occurred to her—did he know Benjamin? Maybe they'd faced off in one of those establishments. The thought made her belly clench with dread. For some reason, she didn't want Slater to know Benjamin.

"I didn't think you'd be so comfortable around horses," Slater remarked.

"I grew up with them. My father taught me to ride when I was five years old. I used to love racing across the fields." She could almost feel the wind in her face and hear her father's laughter.

"Your family had money."

It wasn't a question nor was it an accusation. It was simply a statement of fact. She sensed he wanted to ask her what had happened that brought her here, but he didn't. Nor did she offer an explanation. The truth was too painful.

"If you'd like, maybe we could take a ride together sometime," Slater suggested.

She turned to gaze at him and saw sincerity in his too appealing blue eyes. "I'd like that."

He didn't look away, and she was compelled to hold his intense gaze. He seemed to peer into her, past the mask she'd been forced to don. What did he see? What did she want him to see?

Slater's gaze slid back to his horse. "What were you doing in this part of town?"

"I remembered a stream being over this way when I first arrived." She shook her head. "I couldn't stand to go back to the Scarlet Garter, not after . . ."

"Being at the store with the other girls," he finished.

"How did you know?"

He shrugged, his attention on Paroli. "Every Saturday after they get paid, they spend their money on silly things they don't need." He turned to her, deliberately eyeing the package in her hand. "But you're not like them, and I don't think that package is a new pair of fancy drawers or stockings."

Although embarrassed by his mention of ladies' unmentionables, Rebecca was strangely pleased that he thought her different from the other women. She smiled wryly. "Two books. They've always been my weakness."

He scrutinized her, his poker face unrevealing of his thoughts. "When you're done with those, I've got a few you can borrow."

"You read?"

He scowled. "You don't have to sound so shocked."

An amused smile twitched her lips at his indignation. "I've just never heard of a gambler who enjoys reading."

He turned to fully face her, his arm resting on the top rail of the stall. "So you know a lot of gamblers?"

Her amusement faded. "No." She gave Paroli one last pat. "If you'll excuse me, I'd like to walk down to the stream."

She started to walk away, but Slater caught her, his fingers encircling her wrist. "You go down there by yourself, and you're asking for trouble."

Slater was a convenient target for her frustration. "I just want to enjoy the sun for a little while. Is that too much to ask?"

He slowly shook his head. "No, but there's more men around like the one who bothered you." He looked past her. "I can escort you and keep watch while you enjoy the sun."

She debated his motives, but if he wanted to bed her himself, he had had numerous chances to do so over the past week. And if he was sincere in his wish to protect her like some knight in rusty armor, she had no reason to argue. "Thank you. I accept your offer."

With as much dignity as she could muster under the circumstances, Rebecca walked out into the sunshine ahead of Slater. He was an enigma. Cool and aloof one minute, defending her the next. She expected him to be made from the same mold as Benjamin, but Slater defied any role in which she tried to cast him.

Grateful he was behind her, she continued in the direction of water gurgling over rocks. A narrow, somewhat steep path led down to the stream's edge, and Slater moved ahead of her. He held out his hand, and after a moment's hesitation, she clasped it in her gloved one. His fingers wrapped strongly around hers, making her feel secure.

Halfway down, her toe hooked her dress hem and she stumbled, falling forward. Slater caught her, his arms winding around her waist, their bodies meshed together. Captured in his grip that felt too much like an embrace, Rebecca could only stare up into his eyes, blue like a placid lake beneath the sun. And just as impenetrable.

His gaze flicked to her mouth and, unable to stop herself, she licked her lips. His lips parted slightly, and for an insane moment, she thought he would kiss her. Suddenly, he released her but clasped her hand and continued to lead her down the trail.

Jagged disappointment cut through Rebecca even as sense returned. She was a married woman, and to allow herself to be attracted to another man, especially another gambler, was foolish and inexcusable.

She would not forget herself again.

NINE

SLATER released Glory's delicate hand as soon as they reached the base of the path. He strode to the edge of the stream and focused on the rill of water and the scent of mud and vegetation to dispel the heat in his loins. Feeling Glory's soft curves against him had banished his characteristic control.

Even now, with his back to her, he was aware of her presence behind him. If he concentrated, he could catch a whiff of her light perfume, and he didn't have to close his eyes to imagine her firm breasts and slender waist—her shapely figure was branded in his mind.

Glory came to stand beside him. "It's so quiet and peaceful, it's hard to believe there's a town two hundred feet away." Her lilting voice blended with nature's melody.

Slater squatted down on his haunches and tossed a pebble into the middle of the stream. The sun glinted off the water's surface, disrupted momentarily by the ripples. "It's not nearly as crowded as town, that's for sure."

He felt her gaze settle on him; then she leaned down and placed her gloves, package, and reticule beside the base of a tree. She picked up a small stone, her long, slender fingers, topped by neatly trimmed nails, rubbing it and turning it over. With a snap of her wrist she sent the stone gliding across the brook to bounce on the opposite shore. Grinning, she propped her hands on her hips. "Three skips." She tilted her head, her eyes twinkling. "See if you can top that."

Slater barely restrained a smile and didn't even try not to answer her challenge. He chose a thin, flat stone that fit easily in his palm. He rose and bent his knees slightly, then let it go.

"Three. A tie," Glory said. She searched the ground around her until she found what she wanted and held it up. "Circular, thin, and smooth. My father would say this was the perfect skipping stone." She pursed her lips, and her brow creased with concentration. Then she released the rock. It skipped five times, before floating to the bottom of the stream.

Slater smiled, feeling more lighthearted than he had in years. He found another flat rock and skipped it across the water. Four times it skimmed over the surface.

He feigned a groan. "You win."

Glory's gaze grew distant, and her expression softened. "My father and I used to sneak off to go riding, and often we'd stop by the stream to water the horses and skip stones."

"I had to share my father with an older and a younger brother, but he had enough love to go around." Suddenly embarrassed, Slater cleared his throat and glanced away. He rarely mentioned his past, and even Andrew knew little about his childhood.

"I thought you were an orphan. Andrew said you met when you tried to pick his pocket," Glory said.

"I was orphaned when I was eleven."

"Andrew taught you how to gamble." She flipped a pebble into the water and it plopped dully, drifting to the bottom. "He said you were smart to choose gambling instead of the money in his wallet."

He shrugged, surprised Andrew had been so free with Glory. He obviously liked and trusted her. Maybe he even admired her for not falling into his bed like all the rest. "It was the right choice at the time."

Glory tipped her head to the side and searched his face. "You don't like gambling?"

"It has its advantages if you understand the strategies."

"What about pleasure and satisfaction?"

Slater's gaze swept across her breasts, hidden beneath drab clothing, then met her eyes. "I get my pleasure and satisfaction in other ways."

Her cheeks flushed with embarrassment, but her next words were unexpected. "You haven't been with any of the other girls."

His composure slipped for a moment. "How do you know?"

A self-conscious smile tugged at her lips. "I've watched you." She shrugged. "You've never shown any interest in any of them."

The fact that she wasn't oblivious to him assuaged Slater's masculine pride, but also touched him on some level he didn't want to examine too closely. "So you've watched me."

Her smile wobbled, and she turned her attention to the rocks scattered along the shore. She picked up another stone and tossed it into the water. The ripples disappeared quickly, lost in the current's drift.

She finally shrugged. "I watch Andrew, Simon, Dante, Frank, and the girls, too."

"Why?"

"The Scarlet Garter is the first saloon I've worked in." She laughed lightly, a self-deprecating sound. "I'd never talked to a dwarf or a black person before. Much less a woman of easy virtue."

He noticed gamblers weren't on her list. "They're people just like you or me."

"I realize that, but years of thinking one way doesn't change overnight."

"Do you still feel uncomfortable?"

Glory turned to him, a thoughtful expression on her sun-brushed face that was free of the paint she wore in the saloon. It gave her an innocence he'd never associated with saloon gals. "Sometimes."

"Like today?"

"Yes." Her gaze strayed to the rippling water. "A year ago

I would've been one of those women sweeping her skirts away from Cassie and the others."

"Hard to do when you're one of them now." Slater gazed at her profile: the elegant sweep of her brow, intelligent eyes, and deceptively dainty chin. She was an attractive woman, but he'd known more beautiful ones. Yet none of them had managed to hold his interest outside of bed.

She stood and picked up her books and reticule.

"What books did you buy?" he asked.

"*Wuthering Heights*." Her rosy cheeks deepened to a red blush. "And *The Count of Monte Cristo* in French."

He wasn't surprised she could read French. "I picked up a few French phrases on the riverboats, but nothing I can use in mixed company."

Glory smiled in amusement. "After this past week, I doubt anything you say would shock me."

Slater wondered if she'd think the same if she knew of his less-than-virtuous thoughts concerning her. Like how he wanted to taste her lips, to learn if they were as delicious as the woman herself.

"Would you like me to read aloud? Maybe you'll recognize some of the French words," she suggested.

Just the thought of the foreign words rolling off her tongue increased his arousal to a near-painful state. God only knew what actually hearing her voice might do to him. "No. I'd best get back to the saloon."

"I'd like to stay here a bit longer," she said.

He opened his mouth to argue, but the determined tilt of her chin told him he'd be wasting his breath. Instead, he nodded. "I'll see you later."

Without waiting for her reply, he strode up the hill. At the top, he leaned against a cottonwood to wait. He'd be damned if he left her alone to be bothered again, but he also didn't want her to know he was there. In his experience, once a woman knew that a man might possibly care for her, she exploited that weakness.

As Slater tried to make himself comfortable, Glory's soft voice drifted up to him. The words didn't make any sense, until he realized she was speaking French. She was reading aloud.

Stifling a groan, he closed his eyes and tried to ignore the seductive draw of her voice. However, the sensual shivers that raced through him to settle in his groin weren't dissuaded. If a woman could make love to a man without touching him, Glory was doing it now.

As much as Slater wanted to drown in her honey-smooth voice, he was afraid. Not of his physical reaction, but of the more dangerous emotional arousal. He'd already made peace with the fact he would never marry and have a family.

But he'd made that vow before he'd met Glory Bowen.

AS Rebecca readied herself for her second Saturday night in the Scarlet Garter, she found her thoughts straying to the time she'd spent with Slater earlier that day. Although he was a gambler like Benjamin, Slater didn't possess the same softness that her husband did. Sitting on her bed, she wrapped her arms around herself, trying to imagine it was Slater holding her and trying to regain the sense of security she'd felt in his hold. But the feeling eluded her as her conscience reminded her she was a married woman.

Simon struck up a tune on the piano, scattering Rebecca's unsettling thoughts. Seeing how little money she'd made last week, she was determined to dance more in between her sets of singing. A nickel a drink didn't add up as fast as she'd hoped, so she had to work harder. It was the only way to increase her income if she was determined to hold on to her last bastion of virtues.

Although she had painted her cheeks, she pinched them to add more color and tugged her bodice down even further on her breasts. If the men wanted to dance with a woman who exposed her bosom, then that's what she had to do. After dancing a few rounds, she'd lose her self-consciousness.

Punching down her unease, Rebecca opened the door and headed for the stairs. Cassie and Rose came out of Rose's room and joined her at the top of the stairs.

"Ready to face the lions?" Cassie asked dryly.

"As long as I don't need a whip," Rebecca said.

"If you do, I've got one you can borrow." Cassie winked at her.

Rebecca's eyes widened, and she was left behind as the two women descended the stairs arm in arm. Snapping her mouth shut, she followed them. She didn't know if Cassie was serious or not.

She paused on the second to the last step, and her gaze automatically went to Slater's usual table. There were already three men sitting at it, and they appeared engrossed in their cards. As if sensing her, Slater lifted his head. The force of his gaze punched the air from her lungs, and she struggled to maintain an air of disinterest. Then he turned his attention back to his cards.

Shaking aside the dizzying warmth from the brief exchange, Rebecca took a deep breath and pasted on a smile. Before her foot hit the saloon floor, she was swept into the arms of an enthusiastic, but less than skilled, dancer. Her tally of stepped-on toes began.

ANDREW Kearny wasn't a man who scared off easily. To survive so many years as a gambler, he hadn't allowed bullies to frighten him. However, whoever was behind the intimidation scheme had a tight rein on his guns for hire. None of the saloon owners who admitted to paying for protection had heard anything about him or his enforcers, so Andrew was no closer to learning who the boss was than he'd been six days ago.

If only Slater had agreed to help him. As a Pinkerton, he'd been trained in investigative techniques, and Andrew wasn't too proud to admit his own shortcomings in that area.

As Andrew walked back to the Scarlet Garter, the back of his neck tingled. He rubbed it, attempting to remove the disquiet that rippled through him. He had been asking a lot of questions, but he doubted he was in any mortal danger. Those people wanted money, and they couldn't get it from a dead man. However, they wouldn't hesitate to break some bones to make their point.

"Kearny."

Andrew froze at the familiar drawl, and his heartbeat stampeded. Keeping a composed mask in place, he turned to face the gunman. "I thought you'd wait until after closing to collect."

He shrugged negligently. "I figured an hour wouldn't make a difference one way or another. What's your decision?"

Andrew glanced around, but saw nobody in the darkened alley. He forced nonchalance into his tone and stance. "I need more time."

The gunman stepped closer, and Andrew felt the reassuring weight of his sleeve gun against his forearm.

"More time to move against us?" The man shook his head slowly. "Pay now, or you'll regret your decision."

"It's time someone stood up to you and your boss." Andrew released the spring lock, and the derringer sprang into his palm. He aimed it at the hired gun. "I think you and I and the sheriff ought to have a little discussion."

The gunman didn't seem shaken as much as disappointed. "The boss was afraid of this."

A soft scrabble was Andrew's only warning before his arms were grabbed by two men. One of them twisted his right wrist, forcing him to drop the derringer. Angered by his overconfidence, Andrew glared at the collector as he approached.

"Usually we start with somethin' like bustin' up a place, maybe an employee has an accident, but in your case, the boss doesn't want to take any chances," the man said in his deceptively soft drawl.

Without warning, he punched Andrew in the gut. Andrew doubled over, and only the two men kept him on his feet.

"You're goin' to be an example to everyone else. If they don't pay, the same thing will happen to them."

The next blow caught Andrew in the jaw, and his head snapped to the side. More blows rained on him, not sparing any part of his body. He tasted blood and felt its warmth trickle down his face. Pain exploded in his groin from a deliberately delivered boot. Agony expanded until it was the only thing that remained.

A flash of silver caught his eye, and horror beyond the beating iced his veins.

SLATER yawned, relieved to be done with gambling for the night. The thrill of pitting his skill against others had lost its appeal. Maybe it was time to quit gambling and move on, but where would he go? What would he do? There was nothing else that interested him. Except Glory.

His lack of concentration tonight couldn't all be blamed on his waning interest in poker. When Glory sang those damned ballads, the naked emotion in her face, along with the feeling in her voice, couldn't help but draw his attention. Fortunately, she had that effect on most of the men, including the other poker players, so he'd managed to stay ahead in the game. Unfortunately, every time she sang, he fought the urge to drag her up to his room, where she would sing for no one but him. Only he would be able to see her expressive mouth move and feel the naked emotion in her tawny gold eyes.

Slater didn't like the possessiveness and the frustration that played tug-of-war inside him. Glory was paid to sing and dance with lovesick men, and he couldn't forget that.

He glanced around, and was surprised Andrew wasn't on the floor, urging the last few drunks out the door so he could lock up. He pulled his pocket watch from his vest and frowned. 2:30 A.M. He pushed himself upright and took a moment to overcome the stiffness from sitting so long. Crossing the nearly deserted floor, he went to the bar.

"Have you seen Andrew lately?" he asked Dante.

The diminutive man shook his head, worry etching his brow. "Not since seven. He said he wished to check out the competition and would return before closing time."

Slater's mind raced. That didn't sound like Andrew. Usually he liked to circulate among the customers, which he told Slater encouraged a sense of loyalty to the Garter. Besides, he usually told Slater if he was leaving during the busy hours.

"Is something wrong?"

Slater glanced up to see Glory standing beside him. "Have you seen Andrew this evening?"

She thought for a moment, then shook her head. "Come to think of it, I haven't. Why?"

Slater's gut clenched with trepidation. "I'm going to go ahead and close up."

He and Frank herded out the remaining four men and Slater locked the front door behind them. As he walked back to the bar, he saw that all the women but Glory were climbing the stairs to retire to their rooms.

"Is it common for Andrew to disappear for an evening?" Glory asked, a small worry crease between her eyebrows.

Slater shook his head. "No. Dante said he went out to check on the competition."

"Why would he do that?"

Although Glory was only expressing his own thoughts aloud, his fear made him irritable. "How should I know?"

"I'll help you look for him," she said, undaunted by his curtness.

"No. I'll find him."

She searched his face. "All right. But I'm going to wait up."

"You don't—"

"I know, but I'm worried, too."

The shadows in her eyes mirrored her words. He took her cool hands in his and squeezed them gently. "He probably got into a poker game and lost track of time."

"I'm sure you're right." Her smile fell flat, but the fact she'd attempted to reassure him brought a lump to his throat.

Reluctantly, Slater released her. "Lock the front door behind me, and if the others leave before I get back, remember to lock it behind them, too."

Glory nodded, and followed him to the door. Outside, he listened as she dropped the bar into place, then took a moment to take stock of the town as it settled for the night. Only a few places remained open, and Slater quickly made his way to the closest.

Half an hour later, frustrated and even more worried, Slater returned to the Garter. He knocked, and saw Glory's dark figure glide to the door to let him in.

"No sign of him," Slater reported, raking his trembling left hand through his hair. He captured the hand in his right, trying to stop the shaking.

Glory clutched at the shawl that she'd donned while he was out. "Does he have a mistress he might've gone to visit?"

"He's never mentioned one, and he would've told me."

In all the years he'd known Andrew, Slater had never fretted over him. Although Andrew was only twelve years Slater's senior, he'd been like a father. He was the only family Slater had known since the day he was separated from his little brother, Rye.

"Is there any other place he might've gone?" Glory asked anxiously.

"No." Slater paced back and forth, his booted feet creating a trail in the sawdust. "This isn't like him."

A muffled sound came from the back.

"Has everybody left for the night?" he asked.

Glory nodded.

Thump.

Slater started to the back, and Glory joined him. "Stay behind me."

She did as he said without argument.

Slater grabbed Dante's sawed-off shotgun from behind the bar and led the way to the back room. Only silence met them.

"Could it have been someone moving around upstairs?" Glory asked in a hushed voice.

Slater shook his head. "I don't think so."

The dull thud sounded again, and it was clear the noise came from the back door.

Glory's startled eyes met his.

"Stay here," he said.

She pressed her lips together and shook her head. "I'm going with you."

Slater cursed under his breath, but didn't want to take the

time to argue. With Glory clutching the back of his jacket, he moved quietly down the hall.

Taking a deep breath, he unlocked the door and jerked it open. No one was there. Then he looked down.

"Andrew," Slater said, his heart pounding in his throat. He knelt beside his friend even as his eyes registered the blood that covered Andrew. The older man's face was barely recognizable beneath the blood and swelling. But it was the deep slice across his belly that nearly caused Slater to vomit.

"Dear God," Glory whispered hoarsely, falling to her knees on the other side of Andrew. "Is he still alive?"

A part of Slater hoped he wasn't. He laid his palm over Andrew's heart and felt the weak beat. "Barely. Get the doctor, Glory."

She stared at him blankly, her face milky white.

Slater grabbed her arms and shook her. "He needs a doctor."

She blinked and charged to her feet, then ran down the alley toward the main thoroughfare. Slater had a moment of misgiving about sending Glory alone, but Andrew's life hung in the balance.

Andrew's battered lips moved, but there was little more than a soft moan.

"Take it easy, Andrew. A doctor's on the way," Slater said, resting a hand on his friend's shoulder.

The eye that wasn't swollen fluttered open and sought Slater. The younger man leaned over Andrew. "I'm right here. You're going to be fine."

"Always c-could . . . bluff, b-but never lie," Andrew managed to say.

Slater swallowed hard, refusing to believe there wasn't a chance. "Who did this?"

"The Garter's . . . yours. My will . . . in the s-safe."

Unaccountable anger raged through Slater. "Don't. You're not going to die, damn it."

Andrew raised a shaking hand, and Slater cradled it in both of his.

"Same m-man who c-came to . . . see me. Told him no." Andrew gasped for air. "Example of me."

Slater caught the gist, and a cold fist settled in his gut. "Who are they, Andrew?"

"Don't know . . . for sure." He gasped for air and closed his good eye tightly as pain ravaged his body.

Slater squeezed Andrew's hand gently. "Damn it, Andrew, don't do this to me."

A smile, made more crooked by his swollen lips, touched Andrew's mouth. "Time to toss in . . . m-my cards. Loved you . . . l-like a son, Slater."

Andrew's breath rattled once, twice, then there was silence.

"No!"

Slater's anguished cry echoed in the dark alley.

$\mathcal{T}$EN

THE doctor shook his head, confirming what Rebecca had known as soon as she'd returned—Andrew was dead. A tear coursed down her cheek, and she wiped it away. Although she'd known the saloon owner for less than two weeks, sorrow washed through her. He'd given her a job, one that enabled her to salvage some of her pride. He'd also been her confidant, the only person who knew why she was here and for whom she searched.

"I'll send the undertaker," the doctor said. "He'll be by shortly to pick up the body."

"Andrew Kearny," Slater said. His dark, furious gaze stabbed the doctor. "The body is Andrew Kearny. Send the sheriff, too."

The doctor scowled, but nodded. Then he was gone.

Rebecca, her arms crossed tightly, stared down at Slater, who continued to kneel beside Andrew. Another tear came, and she swiped it away with her wrist. "Should I get Dante and Simon?"

Slater didn't move, and Rebecca wasn't certain if he'd heard her. "I can get Dante and Simon," she reiterated.

"No. There's nothing they can do." He paused, and his next words were barely audible. "Nothing anybody can do."

Her heart hurting for Slater as much as for Andrew, she knelt beside Slater. She laid a hand on the fist that rested on his thigh. "I'm sorry, Slater. I know Andrew meant a lot to you."

His only reply was a tightening of the clenched hand beneath her palm.

She respected his grief and remained silent, listening as the last patrons from another saloon were ejected onto the street. Their drunken laughter was obscenely loud, and their horses' hooves as they rode away felt like physical blows. Then there was nothing but the sounds of a slumbering town.

Rebecca's legs cramped, but she didn't want to leave Slater alone. He'd shed no tears, and his body was stiff, as if he was trying to contain his misery.

Finally, the silhouette of a man appeared at the alley's mouth. Moonlight glinted off his badge as he approached. "The doc said Kearny was dead," Sheriff Ryder said. "Murdered?"

"Does it look like natural causes?" Slater asked, his voice strained.

Ryder squatted down and whistled low. "Looks like he got someone mad at him. Maybe someone who lost a load of money in the Garter."

"Or maybe someone looking for money."

"Yep, could be. Men who dress like Kearny are askin' for it."

Rebecca sucked in her breath even as she felt Slater's muscles bunch.

"Aren't you even going to check to see if he was robbed?" Slater asked in a chilly tone.

Ryder shrugged. "I s'pose."

"Don't bother. He wasn't. He still has his watch and money in his pockets."

"Then what were they after?"

"Isn't it your job to figure that out?" Slater's cold voice dropped a few more degrees.

The sheriff scowled. "I'll ask around, see if anyone saw or heard anything, but don't get your hopes up."

A horse-drawn wagon appeared at the end of the alley.

Sheriff Ryder rose. "Looks like the undertaker's here."

A large man approached them. "I'm here to pick up the body."

"All yours," Ryder said.

Slater's tension was almost palpable, and Rebecca touched his arm. He relaxed only slightly.

The three men carried Andrew's corpse to the wagon. Rebecca waited by the Garter's back door, her legs tingling from kneeling for so long. She heard them speak in low tones for a few moments, then the undertaker climbed back into the wagon and the sheriff disappeared into the darkness. Slater remained motionless as his gaze followed the wagon.

Finally, Slater's shoulders slumped, and he trudged back to Rebecca.

"I have to take one of Andrew's suits to the undertaker tomorrow," Slater said, his voice gravelly.

With a lump in her throat, Rebecca nodded.

Slater opened the Garter's back door and motioned for Rebecca to go inside. He locked it behind them, then stood there, looking lost, an expression she never expected to see on Slater Forrester's face. Rebecca wanted to offer him comfort, but she wasn't certain Slater would welcome the gesture.

"Go to bed, Glory," he said without inflection.

"What about you?"

"I'm not tired."

Pressing her lips together to hold more tears at bay, she laid her hand on Slater's arm. "Andrew was a good man. He'll be missed by everyone."

The words felt shallow, but she didn't know what else to offer that Slater would accept.

He patted her hand awkwardly. "Go on, Glory. Try to get some sleep."

"You need to sleep, too."

He managed a weak smile that didn't so much reassure as trouble Rebecca. "I will."

Unable to think of anything else to say, Rebecca left him

and climbed the stairs. Once in her room, she lay down on her bed and allowed the tears to fall.

DESPITE the late night during which he slept little, Slater rose at ten but didn't don his usual gambler's suit. Instead, he wore plain brown trousers and a woolen shirt. He'd also strapped on his shoulder holster, a remnant of his days with the Pinkertons. The revolver beneath his arm was a reassuring weight in the event Andrew's killer—or killers—came calling.

As the coffee boiled, he went out the back door into the alley. In the light of day, the dark circle on the ground was stark evidence of Andrew's violent death. Slater squatted down beside it, and his fingertips hovered a hairsbreadth above the dried blood. His left hand began to twitch, and his breath hitched in his throat. Shoving aside his devastating grief, he straightened and searched for Andrew's blood trail. He found it easily and followed it.

Each rust-colored drop was a painful reminder of how much Andrew had endured to return to the Garter. With each step, Slater's resolve grew. Whoever killed his friend had wanted him to suffer. Why else did he slit his belly deep enough to expose his entrails?

The trail led to a scuffed area in an adjacent alley. By the size of the circle of dried blood, Andrew had been beaten and knifed here. Slater set aside his vengeance to study the ground. There were signs of at least three sets of footprints besides Andrew's. By Slater's reckoning, two men had held Andrew while a third beat him.

Swallowing the bile rising in his throat, Slater stood and focused on a distant point.

Andrew had been killed because he refused to surrender to intimidation. Why hadn't Slater looked into the racket, as his friend had asked? Andrew had asked very little of Slater for all the older man had given him. And Slater hadn't been able to give him this one thing. If he had, Andrew would still be alive.

Moisture scalded Slater's eyes, and he rubbed them, refusing to give in to his sorrow. Finding Andrew's killers so they paid for their crime was the best Slater could do now. It wasn't nearly enough, but it was all he had left.

He followed the murderers' boot prints, but they were lost among the numerous tracks on the main street. Disappointed, he started the trek back the way he'd come, then spotted an object under some debris. He bent down to push aside the trash and revealed a shiny derringer. He picked it up and immediately recognized it as Andrew's sleeve gun. His fingers tightened around the small weapon as his mind filled in the blanks.

Andrew was stopped in the alley and was able to release the derringer into his hand. However, the two men who held him must have grabbed him from behind before Andrew could use the derringer.

He searched the ground more closely and found a dirty button. Using his fingers, he rubbed the grime from it and recognized it as a Confederate uniform button with the Georgia state symbol. Even three years after the war, it wasn't uncommon to see men wearing pieces of old uniforms, both Union and Confederate. Was this button from one of the men who killed Andrew? Or had it been in the alley for a longer time? Uncertain if it was a clue, he slipped it and the derringer into his trouser pocket.

Slater returned to the Garter and poured himself a cup of coffee, half expecting Andrew to join him. Last night he'd found his friend's will in his safe, and Andrew's dying words were confirmed in the document. Slater Forrester was to inherit everything, including the Scarlet Garter.

He rubbed his burning eyes, blaming the irritation on his sleepless night rather than the grief that threatened to envelop him.

Light footsteps on the stairs alerted him to Glory's arrival. Although a part of him didn't want anyone to witness his sorrow, he was grateful for her presence. She wore one of her staid outfits, a dark skirt with a white blouse. To Slater her clothing was more alluring than the provocative dresses she wore at night. Her hair was loose and flowed over her shoulders, as if she had simply brushed it before coming downstairs. The strands captured the sunshine coming in the windows, lightening the blonde strands to a golden-white river.

Although he regretted her seeing Andrew in his death, he couldn't regret her steadying presence. Without her, Slater might've torn the idiot lawman's head off. He also might've been paralyzed by his grief, but Glory's touch and soft voice had kept him anchored.

"Good morning," she greeted him quietly.

He nodded. "Morning."

Glory poured coffee and carried it to his table. Her gaze slid across his shoulder holster. He stood and held the chair for her.

She sat down and traced her coffee cup rim with a forefinger. Her face was pale and drawn, and dark smudges shadowed her eyes.

"How did you sleep?" Slater asked after he lowered himself into his chair.

She lifted her gaze and smiled slightly. "Not very well. You?"

"Same." He shrugged. "It's hard to believe he's dead."

She nodded and took a sip of coffee. "Do you have any idea who killed him?"

His muscles tensed, and he focused on a spot over her shoulder. "I'm not sure."

"Could it have been those men he talked about, those who threatened him if he didn't pay them money?"

Slater had forgotten she was there when Andrew had talked about the protection racket. He swore under his breath, wishing she'd remained ignorant. "I doubt it. A dead man can't pay them. It was probably a thief." He didn't like lying to her, but it was better than involving her in a dangerous game.

She frowned. "But you told the sheriff that no one had taken his money or watch."

"Maybe he had some other money on him that I didn't know about."

"Did he often carry large sums of money on him that you weren't aware of?"

He should've known she was too intelligent not to question him. "He didn't tell me everything."

Glory's gaze dropped to the tabletop. "Do you think the sheriff will find his murderer?"

Slater barked a sharp laugh. "He couldn't find his backside with both hands."

"So his killer will get away scot-free."

"Not if I can help it." He noticed her skeptical look. "I used to be a Pinkerton agent," he added reluctantly.

She stared at him, as if trying to reconcile his current vocation with being a Pinkerton. "I thought Allan Pinkerton was against gambling."

"He is, but with my credentials, I could meet people he couldn't get other agents close to."

"You were a spy."

Instead of replying, he stood and refilled his coffee cup. He remained by the stove, trying to chase away the chill that remembering brought to his bones. "I did what I thought was right."

She leaned back in her chair, her arms crossed beneath her breasts. As she looked up at him, Slater was captured by the flecks of brown in her golden eyes.

"You're a surprising man, Slater," she finally said.

He tore his gaze away from her. "I'm no saint, Glory, no matter what you heard about Pinkertons and their high standards of morality." Cynicism liberally laced his voice.

A faint smile brushed her lips. "I never thought you were. But it's still nice to know you're not quite as dissolute as I'd assumed."

He couldn't help but chuckle.

"Where will you start your investigation?" she asked after he rejoined her at the table.

He shrugged, unwilling to involve her any more than necessary. "I'll visit some of the other saloon owners, find out who Andrew talked to and what they talked about."

She lifted worried eyes to him. "Be careful. If you stir up the same hornet's nest Andrew did, you could become another victim."

He should have known she wouldn't accept his claim that

Andrew's death wasn't related to the "insurance" scheme. However, he didn't want her to get caught up in the mess. "I've been taking care of myself for a long time. I'll be fine."

They sat in companionable silence for a few minutes, sipping coffee.

"What's going to happen to the Scarlet Garter?" Glory asked.

He took a deep breath. "Andrew left it to me."

She didn't appear surprised. "What do you plan to do?"

Slater hadn't considered it before, but suddenly he realized that if Andrew was killed by the extortionists, he could use the Scarlet Garter to draw them out. It was the most prosperous place in Oaktree, and they wouldn't want to miss out on their part of the pie. Now, instead of dealing with Andrew, they'd have to deal with him. "For now I'm just going to leave things as they are."

Glory nodded. "Do you want me to continue as your bookkeeper?"

Just thinking about the accounting made Slater's head ache. "Yes, if you don't mind."

"Not at all." She seemed relieved.

A knock on the front door startled them, and Slater rose to open it, admitting a frantic Dante.

"Is it true? Is Andrew dead?" the small man demanded, his face red from either exertion or grief.

The sorrow Slater had managed to forget for a few minutes returned full force. He nodded. "He died in the alley early this morning."

For a moment, Slater thought Dante would cry, but he pulled himself together even though his eyes still glimmered.

"Why would someone murder such an honorable gentleman?" Dante asked.

Slater exchanged a deliberate glance with Glory. "It could've been someone who lost money here in the Garter, or it could've been robbery pure and simple."

Glory remained still, but by the firm set of her lips, he knew his fabrication bothered her.

"Could you bring Simon, Frank, Malcolm, and Richard here?" Slater asked Dante before he could come up with more questions. "I'd like to have a meeting with all the employees."

Dante nodded in resignation. Once he was gone, Slater turned to Glory. "Could you wake the girls and bring them down?"

Fifteen minutes later, all the employees of the Scarlet Garter were gathered around him. The women's tear-streaked faces and the men's dismal expressions told Slater how much Andrew had been liked.

"As you all know, Andrew was killed last night," Slater began.

Georgia sniffed and Simon, standing behind her, squeezed her shoulder comfortingly.

"He left the Garter to me, and for now, I don't plan to change anything. If you don't mind working for me, you can continue doing what you've been doing for the same pay," Slater said. "If you don't, I'll pay you for last night and you can leave. No hard feelings."

He looked around and was relieved nobody seemed to be of a mind to quit.

"The Garter will remained closed today out of respect for Andrew, but I'll still pay each of you for the day. Are there any questions?"

"When's the funeral?" Cassie asked, her eyes red and puffy.

"I'm going to see the undertaker this afternoon, so I'll find out then. But I'm figuring on tomorrow morning."

"Does the sheriff know who killed him?" Malcolm, one of the dealers, asked.

Slater restrained an uncomplimentary remark about the lawman and shook his head. "No. He said he'd look into it."

His gaze caught Glory's, and he knew she was wondering if he'd say anything about investigating Andrew's death himself. But he'd decided to keep that decision between them. In fact, if he had his druthers, Glory wouldn't know either. But that cat was already out of the bag, and wasn't about to be stuffed back inside.

"If nobody has any more questions, you can go back to your own places. And remember, the Garter will be closed tonight."

He leaned against the bar, relieved to be done with the announcement.

Molly shuffled over to join him. "I just can't believe he's gone," she said, spouting tears like a watering pot. She leaned into him, and Slater's arms automatically went around her shoulders. Her breasts, bare beneath her wrapper, flattened against his chest.

"You must feel terrible. You and Andrew were such close friends," Molly said, her voice muffled by Slater's chest.

She fingered his shirt buttons and undid one, slipping a hand beneath the wool to press against his skin. She'd made no secret of her wish to go to bed with him, but he couldn't believe she was using Andrew's death to try to seduce him.

He grasped her upper arms and set her back firmly. "Go on upstairs and get dressed, Molly. Or if you want, go back to bed. Alone. You've got the day off to grieve."

Her lower lip thrust out in a pout, but she left, following Cassie and Rose, who ascended the stairs hand in hand. Only Glory and Dante remained.

"I, for one, could use a libation," Dante said. "Slater?"

A stiff drink did sound good, and he nodded to the bartender.

"I'd like one, too, Dante," Glory said quietly.

Dante poured them each a glass of port from a bottle Andrew had set aside for special occasions. If his death wasn't a special occasion, Slater didn't know what was. Dante carried the port over on a tray and joined Glory at the table. Slater took the chair across from the dwarf.

Dante lifted his glass. " 'When beggars die, there are no comets seen; the heavens themselves blaze forth the death of princes.' May Andrew's death be that of princes."

Slater clinked his glass with Dante's and Glory's, then took a sip of the rich wine, but couldn't swallow until the lump in his throat receded.

"That was a fitting quote, Dante," Glory commented. "You're very well read."

The small man held up his glass and stared at the light through the port. "Although my parents preferred to pretend I didn't exist, I had a teacher who saw something other than my stature. He instilled in me a love of words. I would spend hours poring over volumes of Shakespeare and every tome I was loaned."

"He sounds like he was a good man," Glory said.

"Most people saw me as a freak of nature, but he didn't," Dante began softly. "Neither did Andrew. When I asked him if I could sweep his floors, he offered me the position of bartender."

Glory smiled, but sadness shadowed her eyes. "How did you meet him?" she asked Dante.

The small man drew circles on the table with a stubby finger. "I was seeking my way in the world when our paths crossed in St. Louis. At that time, the Scarlet Garter was simply a dream." Dante raised his head, and his eyes sparkled. "But it was a dream I believed because it was Andrew Kearny who dreamed it."

Slater smiled slightly. "When Andrew wanted something, neither heaven nor hell would stop him from getting it."

Dante smiled. "Yes, a more determined man I've never encountered." He glanced at Slater fondly. "You, of course, being Andrew's protégé, are the second most determined man." Dante grew solemn. "I suspect you plan to investigate his death."

Slater considered denying it, but Dante wouldn't believe him. Instead, he nodded. "I'd like to keep my plans between the three of us."

Dante nodded. "You can be assured I won't tell a soul. Also, I will keep my ears open to any information that might correlate to Andrew's death, and shall pass it on to you."

"Thanks, Dante. I appreciate it." Cold fury filled Slater. "I'm going to find who killed him and make them pay."

Neither Glory nor Dante doubted him.

ELEVEN

WEARING a black dress and black hat with netting obscuring her face, Rebecca followed the undertaker's hearse as it wound through Oaktree. Although she hadn't known Andrew long, the grief she held for him was genuine.

The sun had refused to respect the dead, and shined brightly on the mourners winding their way to the cemetery at the edge of town. Cassie, Molly, Rose, and Georgia wore bright dresses that clashed with Rebecca's dark dress. Cassie had defended their choice of clothing, saying it was their way of showing respect to Andrew. In an odd way, it made sense.

They arrived at the cemetery, where a hole awaited the casket. It took a few minutes for the undertaker to supervise the lowering of Andrew into the cold, dark hole.

Slater moved to the head of the grave, removed his hat, and lowered his head. Rebecca's heart ached as she took in his pale features, which contrasted sharply with his midnight black suit. For all of his aloofness, it was clear he'd cared for Andrew a great deal, and for him this must be akin to what she felt at her parents' funeral.

She hadn't seen Slater that morning until they'd all gathered in the Scarlet Garter and walked to the undertaker's together. It appeared Slater had gotten little sleep again last night, and she was worried about him. Guilt motivated him to look into Andrew's death, but it brought no comfort in the middle of the night.

Slater cleared his throat. "I tried to get the minister to say some words, but he called Andrew a sinner and refused to come." Anger flashed in his eyes. "Andrew Kearny was a decent man and had more charity in him than most so-called God-fearing folks. He had a good heart, and respected and cared for those who worked for him. He didn't cheat and he didn't lie, although he might've stretched the truth now and again."

Rebecca smiled through her grief.

Slater's eyes became unfocused as he stared into the distance. "Twenty years ago a half-starved, desperate boy tried to pick Andrew's pocket. Instead of having him thrown in jail, Andrew fed him and taught him a skill he could use to make a living—an *honest* living. Most people wouldn't have given that kid a second chance, but Andrew wasn't like most people. If he was, I wouldn't be standing here today." His voice wavered, and he lowered his eyes to the hole in front of him. "Thank you, Andrew," he said so softly that Rebecca was the only one who could hear his words.

The mourners began to drift away. The Scarlet Garter's women, starting with Cassie, took a moment at the grave to silently bid Andrew good-bye. Malcolm, Richard, Frank, Simon, and Dante followed. Then they, too, headed back to town.

Finally only Rebecca, Slater, and a middle-aged man remained at the graveside.

"I'm right sorry about Andrew," the man said to Slater. "You're right. He *was* a good man, better'n most."

"Thanks, Victor. Andrew would've been pleased to hear that," Slater said.

The man Glory decided was Victor Stroman fingered the brim of his hat, which he held in his hands. "He came to see me Saturday night."

"I figured he might have. I was planning to come ask you about that, find out what you talked about," Slater said.

There was a long pause, and Rebecca peeked through her eyelashes to see the heavy-jowled man nervously shifting his weight from one foot to the other.

"He was asking questions about how my place got busted up," Stroman finally said.

"What did you tell him?"

"That some fella wanted me to pay him so my place didn't have any 'accidents,' but I laughed at him." Stroman smiled without humor. "I mean, who the hell would want to do anything to it? But the next night someone came and busted it up. The next time the fella showed up, I paid him."

"Did you recognize him?" Slater asked.

"No. Never seen him around, which seemed kinda strange."

"He's probably staying out of sight so no one can figure out who he's working for. What did he look like?"

"Dangerous."

"Tall? Thin? Short? What was the color of his hair and eyes?" Slater asked impatiently.

Stroman shook his head. "I told you enough. I don't want to be the next man gutted."

Rebecca barely restrained a gasp. Slater's fingers curled into his palms. "Do you think his employer is one of the saloon owners?"

The older man shook his head, his clamped jaw a sign of his combined stubbornness and fear. "Don't know, and don't wanna know. I figure that's what got Andrew killed. He was asking too many questions he shouldn't have been askin'."

"He was trying to stop this racket and help everyone by doing it." Slater's mouth pressed into a flat line.

"That may be so, but it don't change the facts. Anyone who tries to go up against them, dies." Victor placed his hat on his thinning hair. "I'm sorry about Andrew, but findin' these men ain't going to bring him back and it'll only get more killed." He strode away.

Instead of watching him leave, Rebecca kept her attention on Slater. He clenched his teeth and a muscle jumped in his cheek.

"He's scared," she said.

Slater looked at her as if he'd forgotten she was there. He

jammed his hat on his thick, dark hair and took her arm, escorting her from the grave. "That's how the extortionists work, through fear and intimidation. I should've known Andrew wouldn't give in to their tactics. He never did like bullies."

"Oaktree isn't that big," Rebecca said as they walked. "It shouldn't be too difficult to figure out who the leader is."

"It's big enough. I'm sure whoever's behind it is sitting back, pretending to pay his share, too."

Rebecca grew warm in the sun's rays, but she didn't complain. At least she was alive to feel the heat. "Did you see anything like this when you were a Pinkerton?"

"Not really. My responsibilities were related to the war." His arm muscles tightened beneath her hand. "But I've seen this thing before." He turned his head to gaze at her. "St. Louis, for example."

She frowned. "I don't remember hearing anything about it."

His smile was laced with amusement. "I'm sure you were more outraged than interested in the machinations of gambling institutions when you lived there."

Her face burned, but not from the sun. "You're right. In the case of righteous judgment, ignorance truly is bliss."

"Now that you've walked on the other side of the street, you know there are more shades of gray," Slater said.

A wry smile tugged at her lips. "It was easier when things were black-and-white."

"It always is."

They arrived at the Scarlet Garter and entered through the back door, which they'd left unlocked.

"Would you mind if I did some bookkeeping?" Rebecca asked.

"I'll get the accounts books out for you."

"I'm going to change, then be back down."

As Rebecca headed to the back stairs, Slater caught her wrist. His fingers moved across the sensitive skin, sending darts of pleasure through her.

"Thank you," he said softly.

She tried to ignore the delightful sensations his gentle voice and gentler touch evoked. "For what?"

He took both of her hands in his. "For helping."

"But I didn't do anything."

His smile was tender and rueful. "You did more than you know." He kissed the back of one hand, the feather-light whisper of his lips across her knuckles nearly buckling her knees. Then he released her. "I'll get the books."

Rebecca fled to her room. Inside, she stripped off her funeral attire and donned a casual skirt and blouse. What was wrong with her? Had working in a saloon destroyed all her morals? She shouldn't be feeling the things she felt for Slater while she was another man's wife. Yet try as she might, she couldn't deny the attraction.

They were strictly business associates, just as she and Andrew were. Now that Slater was her boss, she ought to tell him why she was there and for whom she searched. However, if she did that, she might lose his tender touches and the warmth in his eyes. And, God help her, she wanted whatever crumbs he might toss her. *Pitiful.*

Throwing a shawl over her shoulders, she left her room and started for the stairs. She descended to the main floor, where Slater had set the ledgers on her usual worktable. A fresh pot of coffee bubbled and brewed on the banked stove, and the front door was cracked open to allow fresh spring air in to chase away some of the staleness.

"I hope you don't mind. I figured the saloon could use some airing out," Slater said, coming down the stairs. He'd removed his jacket and tie, but still wore his black trousers, which clung to his long, rangy legs.

She cleared her throat. "Not at all. I always sleep with my window open, even in the winter. I prefer that over still air." She pressed her lips together, realizing her nervousness was making her ramble.

"So do I," Slater said, a slight twinkle in his eyes. The twinkle faded. "I'm not much for closed-in spaces."

Unsure how to take his comment, she motioned to the coffee. "Thanks. I have a feeling I'll need it today."

"If you have any questions, give me a holler. I can't guarantee I'll know the answer, though." He hooked a thumb over his shoulder. "I'll just be in the back, going through the inventory."

Rebecca nodded and poured herself some coffee, then began to work on the numbers.

Some time later, the women trooped down the stairs, wearing coats over their work dresses.

"We're going to get something to eat. Want to come?" Georgia asked.

Although pleased she'd been asked, she didn't want to interrupt her work. "I'd like to finish what I'm doing first."

"Suit yourself," Molly said offhandedly.

Georgia glared at Molly, then gave Rebecca's shoulders a one-armed hug.

Slater came out of the back. "You girls going to lunch?"

"That's right." Molly sidled up to him. "Would you like to join us?"

He smiled and shook his head. "No, thanks. I've got things to do here."

After they were gone, Rebecca sighed.

"You could've gone with them," Slater said.

"To be honest, I prefer not to." She rose and refilled her coffee cup. "Molly doesn't like me."

Slater leaned against the bar and crossed his arms. "Does that bother you?"

She joined him. "Oddly enough, yes." Resting her arms on the bar, she said, "I used to have a lot of friends. I guess I miss having women to talk to."

A sardonic smile captured his mouth. "You're not missing anything with Molly. She'll whisper secrets in your ear one minute and stab you in the back the next."

"Are you speaking from experience?"

He chuckled. "I'm not stupid enough to let her get that close."

"Even though she'd like to."

"You have nothing to be jealous of, Glory."

Rebecca's mouth dropped open. "Why would I be jealous? Who you bed or don't bed is no concern of mine."

Slater smiled, and she noticed for the first time that he

had dimples that added a hint of boyishness to his handsome features. His forefinger caressed her cheek. "Whenever you go all indignant, your language becomes that of a privileged young lady."

He seemed amused, and Rebecca had to bite back her indignation. She had no intention of proving him correct in his assumption.

He dropped his hand away from her cheek. "Pressing your lips together isn't very attractive."

"One doesn't have to be attractive to enter numbers in the correct columns."

Slater grinned. "There you go, all ladylike again."

Rebecca rolled her eyes in exasperation, but she couldn't prevent her lips from twitching with amusement. "How is the organization going?"

Slater's humor faded. "Andrew kept things neat and tidy, so there isn't much organizing to do. It's more a matter of me learning Andrew's filing system, and differentiating between what's important and what isn't." He paused. "I heard the girls come down, so I used that as an excuse to take a break."

Rebecca's stomach took that moment to growl, and she pressed her hand against her abdomen.

"Maybe you should've gone with them," Slater said, one brow arched.

"I didn't feel like their company."

"What about mine?"

She tilted her head questioningly.

"Would you care to join me for lunch at the hotel?" Slater asked.

"The hotel?"

"Sometimes I get tired of Barney's cooking."

Flustered, Rebecca shook her head. "I'm saving my money."

"Who said you had to use your money? The Scarlet Garter pays for your meals, and since I now own the Garter, I'll buy your lunch."

"But it's more expensive at the hotel."

"Are you trying to talk me out of going? Or yourself from accepting?"

Rebecca's stomach growled again, and she replied sheepishly, "I'm not sure it would be appropriate."

"You're not in St. Louis anymore, Glory, and the rules don't apply. Would you like to join me?"

She didn't know which she was more excited about, having an intimate meal with Slater or eating something other than the usual fare. Or maybe she did, but didn't want to acknowledge it. "Yes, I would." She glanced down at her outfit. "I should—"

"You look fine, Glory. All respectable and ladylike."

Startled by his teasing, she only nodded.

"I'll grab my jacket and we'll be on our way."

Rebecca only had time to gather the ledgers and the invoices before Slater returned. He placed them in the safe and escorted Rebecca down the sunny street. Their end of town was quiet, but she knew it would liven up this evening. She expected the Scarlet Garter to be busier than usual tonight since it had been closed yesterday. Many who didn't normally frequent the Garter would come, and when their morbid curiosity was appeased, they'd return to their usual haunts. Even understanding that it was human nature, Rebecca shuddered with distaste.

"Would you like my jacket?" Slater asked.

"I'm not cold." She frowned. "I was just thinking."

"Anything in particular?"

"No." She sighed. "I just find it difficult to understand why people like to talk about others' misfortunes."

Slater shrugged. "Maybe it makes them feel better about themselves, glad that they weren't killed or hurt, or haven't lost their money. Besides, not everyone is like that. Some people feel genuine compassion."

Rebecca remembered her own experience when it became common knowledge she had lost her home, her money, and her husband. There were only two people from her past life who were sympathetic to her plight. Everyone else had abandoned her. "Perhaps, but the majority seem to think misfortune is a disease that can be caught by merely being seen with that person."

"What was your misfortune, Glory?"

She shouldn't have been surprised by his astuteness. "Something too embarrassing to admit."

"Ruined before your wedding?"

Her mouth gaped. "Of course not."

Slater chuckled. "I didn't think so. I just wanted to see your reaction."

Her face warm, Rebecca began to wonder if having an intimate lunch with him was such a good idea. However, before she could bow out, they arrived at the hotel. Slater opened the door and ushered her in ahead of him. The gentlemanly hand against her spine brought a measure of confidence as he guided her through the large room. As they wound between tables, many men greeted Slater with nods. One woman, a brunette with snapping brown eyes and a voluptuous figure, grabbed Slater's arm.

"Hello, handsome," she said in a low-throated voice.

"Delilah." Slater's tone was far less friendly.

"You ain't been around lately."

He shrugged. "I've been busy."

Her expression became overly sympathetic. "I was sorry to hear about Andrew. He'll be missed."

"Yes, he will." Slater's body was taut, like a rope stretched to its limit. He took a deep breath and glanced at Delilah's companion, a dark-haired man with a swarthy complexion and obsidian eyes. "Langley. How're things at the Black Bull?"

Langley smoothed the end of his long mustache with his thumb and forefinger. "Can't complain. I hear you got the Scarlet Garter."

"Andrew left it to me."

"You going to sell it and move on?"

Slater smiled without warmth. "Sorry to disappoint you, but I'm keeping it open. It's the nicest place in town. Besides, we deal honest games and have the prettiest girls."

Langley's gaze roved across Rebecca, and she felt the need to take a bath. "Yeah, Kearny always did have a way of finding the prettiest fillies."

"What about me?" Delilah pouted.

Langley smiled with only his mouth. "With the exception of you, my dear."

Slater glanced around, then asked, "Have you had any trouble at your place lately?"

The Black Bull owner looked away. "No. Why?"

"No reason."

Slater's tone was casual, but Rebecca heard the undertone of skepticism.

"We'll let you get back to your meal," Slater said.

"You come on back any time, Slater, and we'll have us another good time," Delilah said, intentionally leaving no doubt of the history between them.

Slater merely nodded once and led Rebecca to an empty table some distance away. He held her chair, then took his own seat. After they ordered their meals, Slater and Rebecca were left alone.

"Didn't Delilah seduce Samson, then betray him?" Rebecca asked casually.

Slater grinned. "I doubt Dancing Delilah's ever read the Bible."

"She's a dancer?"

"Not like you or the others at the Garter." Slater leaned back in his chair. "She dances on stage in a very short dress."

"Shorter than ours?"

He chuckled. "It barely covers her backside."

Scandalized, Rebecca took a mouthful of coffee and nearly spat out the hot liquid. She managed to swallow, but burned her tongue in the process. Gathering what little composure remained, she sat up and primly rested her hands in her lap. "So that's the type of woman you're attracted to."

"I'm not going to apologize for being a man, Glory." He eyed her closely. "Besides, what business is it of yours who I bed?"

"None at all." The words burned as much as the coffee. Not wanting to imagine Delilah and Slater together, she tried to sidetrack her thoughts. "You didn't believe him, about not having any problems."

"No, I didn't." Slater ran a hand through his thick hair. "I suspect it's a business owner in town who's behind the extortion, probably one of the saloon owners. It could be Langley. Hell, it could be Victor Stroman."

"But his place was wrecked."

Slater shrugged. "No one would suspect him of breaking up his own place."

"I didn't think of that."

"You're not supposed to, Glory. You're not a criminal." He tipped his head to the side. "Unless there's something you haven't told me."

She couldn't hold his gaze. "I haven't broken any laws."

He reached across the table and took her hand in his. "I didn't think so. But you *are* hiding something from me."

Her heart kicked her ribs. "Tell me your secrets first."

"Touché." He sobered. "If there's anything I can do to help you, don't be afraid to ask."

She wished she could trust him.

But she wished she could trust herself more.

$\mathcal{T}$WELVE

ALTHOUGH the meal was a pleasant change, Slater took more enjoyment in Glory's company. Her manners were impeccable and, after their food arrived, she kept the conversation light. She'd clearly attended many fancy dinner parties where social chitchat was a learned skill. So how did a woman of her obvious breeding end up in a saloon in Oaktree, Kansas?

Her outrage at his suggestion that she'd been "loose" struck him as honest, so she hadn't been cast out of society for that reason. He didn't have much contact with the upper crust, so he wasn't certain what other mistakes might be unforgivable. And although he was curious, he respected her right to her past. God knew he didn't want to share his own history.

He paid the bill and they left the dining room, which had far fewer patrons than when they'd arrived. Langley and Delilah had finished their meal and departed. It didn't usually bother Slater to run into a former bed partner in public, but having Glory with him had made it awkward. But then, even if Glory hadn't been with him, he would've discouraged

Delilah since it wasn't his habit to bed a woman more than once.

Giving the woman on his arm a sideways glance, he wondered if he'd be tempted to break his own rule, providing he managed to lure her into his bed the first time. Most of his female friends were fancy ladies, but he'd known some real ladies. Most of those he'd met while working for the Pinkerton Agency. He'd discovered that once a privileged lady was out of her corsets and stays, she was no different from her counterpart who worked in a saloon or dance hall.

But Glory *was* different, and the feelings she engendered in him were nothing like those he'd experienced before—tenderness and protectiveness. She also heated his blood and made him ache to run his hands and lips over every inch of her soft skin.

"Thank you for lunch," Glory said. "I'm glad you invited me."

"You're welcome," he said, pleased she'd enjoyed herself.

"May I ask you a question, Slater?"

"Sure. But I might not answer it."

"Fair enough. How did you become a pickpocket?"

"I practiced."

She made a face. "You know what I mean."

Slater sighed. He had the option not to answer the question, but he hadn't hidden the fact he was an orphan. He simply wouldn't tell her the more sordid details. "My parents died when I was a kid, and my younger brother and I were put in an orphanage while our older brother went looking for the men who killed our mother. Not long afterward, I was adopted. Three years later I ran away, and that's when I learned how to steal. If I hadn't, I would've starved."

"Why did you run away?"

He shut out the memories of those nightmarish years and shrugged. "I never really took to the family who adopted me, and I got tired of working their farm."

"So it was laziness that caused you to run away?"

He could tell she was disappointed, but it was better for her to feel that than for him to be on the receiving end of her pity. "If that's what you want to call it, fine."

The way she looked at him unnerved him. It was as if she didn't believe him, like she didn't merely suspect, but *knew*, he was skating over the truth.

"My brothers used to have a hard time dragging me out of bed in the morning for chores," he added. "A lot of times I conned Creede or Rye into doing my chores for me. I'd make a bet with them, and I'd usually win."

"Did you cheat?"

He chuckled. "No, I was just smarter than they were."

She shook her head, her estimation of him falling to comfortable levels once more. "You're a bewildering man, Slater."

"I've been called worse."

"I wouldn't be surprised." Her golden eyes were filled with teasing laughter.

Returning to the Scarlet Garter, Slater felt a confusing onslaught of emotions: sadness that Andrew was dead, pride that the Garter was now his, and worry that he wouldn't be able to maintain its success.

"I have a couple of hours before I have to get ready for work tonight. If you don't mind, I'll continue what I was working on earlier," Glory said as they strolled to the bar.

"I'll get it out of the safe." Something on the bar caught his attention, and he crossed to it. A piece of paper with a note written in block letters: *Time is up.* "Son of a bitch," Slater swore. He was tempted to ball the paper and throw it away, but the note was a clue, however useless it might be.

Glory joined him, worry evident in her somber expression. "What is it?"

He nodded toward the note. Glory's eyes widened. "He was here while we were all gone."

"He could've damaged the place, but left this instead."

"Why?"

Slater shook his head. "Maybe he figures we'd lose business if we had to shut down for a while, and the bottom line is money. The more we make, the more we pay."

"But you don't plan on paying, do you?"

"If I do, Andrew died for nothing."

"If you don't, you could die."

The worry in her luminous eyes arrowed straight to his

chest and tightened his throat. Nobody, not even Andrew, had ever looked at him with that kind of concern. He turned his head away. "That's a chance I'm willing to take."

"Fine," she said tartly. "It's your life." She stomped up the stairs.

She could think what she wanted, but he had no choice. In order to gain the information and evidence he needed to put them out of business, he had to defy them.

Slater studied the note and wondered why the handwriting looked familiar. He searched his memory, but nothing surfaced. Maybe the block letters simply reminded him of something he'd seen in the past.

He considered taking the note to Sheriff Ryder, but figured it would be a waste of time. The lawman was either lazy or corrupt, or more likely a combination of the two. Slater had known many lawmen like Ryder and, although it was a fact of life in the frontier towns, it never failed to anger him. The badge was a symbol of justice, not power.

Carrying the note to the back, he retrieved the ledgers from the safe, although he wasn't certain Glory would return. Her anger implied she cared, but did she care about him or her job? He scowled to himself, not liking his line of thought.

He heard light footsteps on the back stairs and instinctively knew it was her. Was she coming down to continue working or to continue their argument? Either way, he'd have the indulgence of her company.

"I'll take the books," she said, all businesslike, with no trace of their earlier camaraderie.

She reached for them, but he didn't release them. "I can't let them win, Glory." He didn't know why it was so important that she understand, but her estimation of him mattered despite the fact he rarely did anything because of a person's opinion.

"Even if it means you lose?"

Although her voice was soft, the intensity behind her words was unmistakable. "Don't write me off yet, Glory. I used to be a damned good agent."

" 'Used to be.' " She glanced at his left hand. "I've seen how it shakes, Slater. It tells me something happened to you, something that hurt you, not just your body but your spirit, too." She peered up at him. "What if those scars run too deep?"

It irritated him that she had perceived what only a few closest to him had merely suspected. "You don't know anything about me, Glory, so don't presume that you do." He closed his eyes to stave off his mounting anger, or maybe it was fear hidden behind the fury. When he reopened them, he took a step closer to her and felt reluctant admiration when she didn't retreat but merely tipped her head back to meet his gaze. "Andrew asked for my help, and I refused. Now he's dead. The only thing I can do for him now is bring his killers to justice."

Her eyes flashed. "Be honest, Slater. You're not doing this for Andrew; you're doing this for yourself."

He flung out his arms. "What difference does it make?"

"If you're doing it for yourself, you'll take more risks. If you're doing it for Andrew, you'll be more careful, because you know he wouldn't want you dying for him." She grabbed the account books and stalked away.

Rarely did anyone ever have the last word with Slater, but Glory managed it. She was also forcing him to think.

Damn her!

ANY other saloon owner would have been celebrating the crowd's size, but Slater's mind wasn't on profits. Instead, his gaze roamed the floor, scrutinizing every person who entered. Slater didn't doubt that the killers would be bold enough to enter the Garter with Andrew not even cold in the ground.

His attention shifted to Glory, as it too often had throughout the night. Gone was the proper woman who'd studiously worked numbers into columns. Tonight she wore the customary dancing dress that fell just below her knees. But because of the crowd in the saloon, he caught only occasional glimpses of her shapely ankles and calves. Her smiles directed to her dance partners, however, were clearly visible . . . and damned irritating. Although he could tell they were put-on smiles, they still bothered him.

Because it was a Monday night, she wasn't scheduled to sing. He might've asked her to, since they were so busy, but he figured the customers would be there whether she sang or not. Besides, this way she could dance and tally up the drinks to make some extra money, even if Slater practically growled every time a man put his arms around her.

To take his mind off her, Slater joined Dante behind the bar to help refill empty glasses. He let Dante take care of the dancers and the girls, knowing the small man had his own system to tally the specials the men bought for the girls. He also didn't trust himself to be civil to Glory's dance partners.

Andrew had talked about hiring a waitress or two whose only responsibility would be to serve drinks. On busy nights, such as this, there wouldn't be the deep layers of men at the bar getting beer and whiskey refills. His eyes caught Glory, who was pressing back a man whose hand had wandered too close to her breasts. Jealousy surged in his gut, and he took a step toward her before catching himself. It was Glory's job to stave off advances while remaining friendly, even if Slater didn't like it.

He could offer her the option of being a waitress. She wouldn't have to put up with the pawing—or at least, not as much—and he could ensure her pay would be as much as or more than she'd make dancing.

"Now that you're the boss, that mean you aren't going to be dealing anymore?"

Slater glanced up to see Bill Chambers, the rancher who'd lost more than a little money at his table. "Not when it's this busy. Malcolm and Richard are out there if you're interested in a game."

"Malcolm's working faro, and you know how I feel about the tiger. And Richard's table's been busy all night."

Slater shrugged. "Come on back tomorrow night. If it's quieter, I'll be playing."

Chambers leaned against the bar and sipped his beer. "Ever find who killed Kearny?"

"Sheriff's looking into it."

Chambers snorted. "Like he's worth the piss it takes to put out a match. Damned shame, too. I respected Kearny.

Ran a clean house." He leveled his gaze at Slater. "You plannin' on keeping it clean?"

Slater stiffened with the implied insult, but kept his voice steady. "Andrew taught me everything I know, including the importance of keeping things on the up-and-up." He leaned over the bar, his face only inches from Chambers's. "It's the way I play poker, too."

Chambers flushed slightly but held his ground. "If I didn't think you were square, I wouldn't sit at your table."

Taken aback slightly, Slater straightened and topped the rancher's glass with beer. "On the house."

The man chuckled and took a long swig. "You've got style, Forrester. I like that." He aimed a finger at him. "And one of these days I'm going to best you at poker."

Slater smiled, and saluted him with his coffee cup.

REBECCA grimaced as she came down the stairs the following morning. If it was only the dancing, she wouldn't have been so sore, but the two left feet most of the men owned hadn't missed a single toe on her feet. The fragrance of fresh coffee lightened her mood, and she didn't waste any time pouring a cup.

She looked around, wondering where Slater was. The chairs were still piled on the tables from last night's closing, so he hadn't been sitting here. She walked to the back room and saw his dark head bent over some papers on the desk. An empty coffee cup sat beside an elbow.

It wasn't often she could observe him without his awareness, and she took guilty pleasure in the breadth of his shoulders beneath his woolen shirt, accented by dark blue suspenders. His top two shirt buttons were open, displaying a smooth vee without the hint of hair. As thick and fast-growing as his whiskers were, she was surprised by the lack of hair on his chest. However, his shirtsleeves were rolled up on his forearms, revealing a sprinkling of dark hair.

"Like what you see?" he asked without raising his head.

Her face warmed. "How did you know I was here?"

He lifted his head and his eyes twinkled, appearing even

brighter than usual against the dark morning whiskers that hadn't yet been shaved. "The other women clump down the stairs. You descend them like a lady."

He rose and came around to lean against the desk. His dark blue trousers hugged his hips and thighs unlike the loose suit pants he usually wore. More warmth climbed into her cheeks when she noticed the evidence of his masculinity in the snug pants.

"I'll just have to start tromping down," Rebecca said, going for banter to sidetrack more dangerous thoughts. "What are you working on?"

Melancholy darkened his eyes. "I found notes Andrew made while this place was being built and after it opened. It's interesting reading his thoughts about all this and other things."

"Are there any newer notes about the protection racket?"

"If there are, they aren't with these." He glanced down at the papers. "He'd been saving money for twenty years to build a place like this. He didn't plan on stopping in Oaktree nearly a year ago, but he said he had a feeling about the town." He smiled sadly. "He always did have good instincts."

"Was it what he'd hoped it would be?"

"Better. I've been looking at the bank receipts. He has a gold mine here."

"And now it's yours," she said gently.

His thoughtfulness was replaced by self-disgust. "Not that I did anything to deserve it."

"Obviously Andrew thought you did." She took a deep breath. "Which is why he wouldn't be happy if you got yourself killed."

Slater barely restrained his exasperation. "If you're going to try to talk me out of going after his murderers, you're wasting your breath," he said flatly.

Rebecca crossed her arms beneath her breasts and tipped her head to the side. Her thick silver-gold hair shifted across her shoulders. He gripped the edge of the desk to keep himself from going to her and combing his fingers through hair that begged to be touched.

"I would if I thought I had a chance to get through your

thick skull, but you have your mind made up," she said. "Which gives me only one option. What can I do to help?"

He hadn't expected her to offer help, and didn't want her anywhere near men who wouldn't hesitate to kill. "You stay out of the way."

Her mouth curled into a scowl. "You can't go after them alone."

"I'm not going to endanger anyone else's life."

"Only your own."

His left hand twitched and he fought it, but as usual, no matter what he did, it didn't stop. He curled his fingers into his palm, hoping Glory didn't notice. However, her quick glance at his hand and the deepening of her scowl told him she did. "You want to know what you can do to help?"

She nodded warily.

"If anything does happen to me, sell this place and split the profits with everyone who works here."

Her delicate nostrils flared and he could see her opposition in her rigid spine and the set of her jaw, but she nodded, if somewhat stiffly. "Make it legal, or the sheriff will claim it."

Again she surprised him with her insight. "That's a good idea." He studied her hooded gaze. "Have you had experience with this type of thing?"

Her laughter was surprisingly bitter. "Not exactly." Her resentment gave way to formality. "Please don't ask me any more."

He cocked his head, as if trying to figure her out. She braced herself for an argument.

"Do you enjoy dancing with the men?"

Startled by the unexpected question, Rebecca wasn't certain how to answer it. "It's better than other ways of earning a living."

"That isn't what I asked." He didn't seem angry, merely curious.

"No, I don't," she answered.

His teeth flashed white against the shadow of his morning whiskers. "How would you like to wait tables?"

Trepidation brought dampness to her palms. Was he firing her? "Where?"

"Here. Andrew had been talking about hiring a woman or two simply to take drink orders from the men at the tables. After last night's business, I think it would be a good idea."

"But what about the money I earn from dancing?"

"I'll pay you a straight three dollars a night. Two more on the nights you sing, too. Add that to the ten you make for keeping the books, and you'll have a nice weekly salary."

She added it up in her head. "That's thirty-five dollars a week."

He nodded, his gaze never leaving her face. "And no stepped-on toes."

It sounded too good to be true, and if Rebecca had learned anything, it was that everything had a price. "No intimate relations with the boss?"

His blue eyes grew smoky, and he stepped close to her. Lifting a hand, he cupped her cheek, his thumb brushing the sensitive skin. "Only if she wants to."

Sharp desire dried her mouth, and her stomach did somersaults. "I didn't know he was interested."

"Only if she is."

He was skilled at word games, too, which only made him more dangerous. As if his virility and her attraction to him weren't enough to tempt her. . . .

"Even if she is, it's a recipe for disaster," she said with a husky voice.

"Because we work together?"

"Partly."

He arched a dark eyebrow. "The other part?"

She fought for some order in her chaotic thoughts, but Slater's nearness was making it nearly impossible. Then she thought of Daniel and her mission crystallized. "I'm not that type of woman."

His hand dropped away. "You're the happily-ever-after type."

Although her marriage wasn't exactly so, she couldn't deny the hope that once Benjamin learned he was a father, he would revert back to the man who'd wooed her. "Yes."

He stared at her with mesmerizing eyes and for a moment, she understood how a snake could hypnotize a mouse.

However, Slater was anything but a snake, and she, far from a timid mouse. "Would I wear the same as I've been wearing if I take the position of waitress?"

"You're not going to wear something like that." He motioned to her clothing with a derisive wave. "The men don't want someone dressed like a nun serving them drinks."

She touched the high collar at her throat even as indignation brought heat to her cheeks. "Just because I try to maintain some facade of respectability doesn't mean you have to belittle my attempt."

His jaw tightened. "If you want respectability, find a job on the other side of town."

Fighting abrupt tears, she glared at him. "I'll wear what you insist I wear during work hours, but during my own time, I'll dress as *I* please."

"Fine." He picked up the accounting books and handed them to her, then returned to his desk without looking at her.

Rebecca drew back her shoulders and spun about, leaving in a whirlwind of hurt and anger.

$\mathcal{T}$HIRTEEN

REBECCA'S first night of taking and delivering drink orders for rowdy men proved to be hectic, but not nearly as exhausting as dancing with them. At the start, a few tried to swing her onto the dance floor, but Slater stepped in and explained that wasn't her job anymore. After those incidents it was easier, although she didn't cease to use her newfound skill of eluding wandering hands.

Midnight approached, and since it was the middle of the week, the customers began to filter out. Less than a dozen remained, and Rebecca found a moment to lean against the bar and rest.

Dante poured her a special and slid it over to her. "On the house, my dear."

She smiled and raised the glass to him. "Thank you." Her throat was dry, and she drank the weak tea in two gulps.

Dante refilled her glass. "You appeared to have matters well in hand throughout the evening, and it assisted me greatly."

She chuckled. "I'm glad it looked that way, because most of the time I felt like a chicken running around without its head."

Dante made a face. "A highly unappealing image, and one I cannot possibly ascribe to you."

"Thank you." She paused. "I think."

Dante laughed.

As Rebecca surveyed the remaining patrons at the tables, she tapped her fingers to the lively piano music. Simon had an amazing repertoire and possessed a sense of what the crowd wanted. Tonight, it was upbeat songs to counter the more somber music from the previous night. Although Andrew had died only four days ago, time in a frontier town seemed to move at a faster pace than in civilized places. Perhaps it was the uncertainty of life out here.

Molly sauntered to the bar. "Didn't know you were sleeping with Slater."

"I'm not," Dante said without missing a beat.

Molly glared at him. "I was talking to Miss High and Mighty."

Rebecca knew better than to argue with the hot-tempered woman. "I'm not sharing my bed with Slater, and if I was, it wouldn't be any of your business."

"Then why do you get the easy jobs like doing the books and waiting tables instead of dancing like the rest of us?"

"Perhaps because she has knowledge of accounting," Dante answered.

Molly tossed her head. "I could learn."

"No, you'd be too distracted by the object of your wanton thoughts."

Rebecca hid her amusement with a cough and said to Molly, "I used to do bookkeeping, so I have experience, and I was fortunate to inherit my father's head for figures." She shrugged. "As far as I know, Slater is still available."

Molly studied her like she wasn't certain if she could believe her. "You and him ain't . . ."

Rebecca forced a laugh. "Not even interested."

Before Molly could respond, a man curled his arm around her waist and swung her into a jig.

"She's been attempting to lure Slater into her bed for months, but he is not even remotely interested." Dante scrubbed the bartop. "In fact, I believe you are the first to attract his attention."

"Obviously you don't know about Delilah," Rebecca said dryly.

"She's employed in another establishment."

"What does that have to do with anything?"

Dante ceased his cleaning. "Did you know that a wolf will not soil his cave?"

Not understanding how it related to their conversation, Rebecca shook her head.

"They don't like messes within their own home," Dante added.

Rebecca narrowed her eyes. "So he doesn't like to muddy the home waters."

"A mix of metaphors, but accurate." Dante leaned closer to Rebecca. "It's also rumored that Slater doesn't sleep with a woman more than once."

Shocked that she wasn't shocked, Rebecca considered the tidbit of gossip. "Why?"

Dante shrugged. "To answer that, you must ask Slater."

The diminutive bartender left her to help a customer. Rebecca drifted over to the three occupied tables to ask if they wanted refills. No one did.

As she stood at the end of the bar, she noticed Georgia leaning close to Simon, who played an adagio, a slower piece, as prelude to the saloon's closing. Once he was done, he glanced at Georgia, whose smile was the most genuine Rebecca had seen all evening. However, Simon's expression appeared troubled.

Simon rose and said something to Georgia, who frowned. Tight-lipped, he shook his head, then moved off to help Frank usher the remaining men out of the establishment.

Rebecca joined Georgia and put an arm around her friend. "What's wrong?"

"He's a stubborn ass." Georgia's glare drilled into Simon's back.

"What do you mean?" Simon was even more easygoing than Dante.

"He thinks because I wasn't a slave, he's not good enough for me."

"But he's not a slave either."

"Not anymore. But he was born and raised as one."

"I thought you were, too," Rebecca said lamely, realizing she knew little about slaves and slavery. "Since your name is Georgia, I assumed you came from there."

"My folks was from there, but they were freed when their old master died. I was born in Chicago." Georgia's Southern accent had disappeared. "We weren't slaves, but we were dirt poor, living in a cold, drafty room not much bigger than the one upstairs. I ran away after the war."

"I don't understand. Simon is free; you're free. What difference does it make how or when?"

Georgia crossed her arms. "That's what I told him, but he won't listen. Stubborn fool!" She blinked rapidly. "I'm going to bed."

Georgia ascended the stairs, anger and hurt in every measured step. Rebecca glanced at Simon and noticed he watched Georgia, regret and longing in his face. Why was he being so stubborn?

Trying to understand a man was something Rebecca decided was a waste of time. Sighing, she carried dirty glasses to the back. The door to the office was closed, and she debated whether to bother Slater or not.

"He's not in there," Dante said, coming up behind her.

"Where is he?"

"I believe he said he was going to take a walk." Despite his light tone, Dante's eyes were concerned.

"Of all the idiotic—"

Dante's stubby fingers closed around Rebecca's wrist. "He has to do this."

Rebecca gritted her teeth and counted to ten in French. "I just hope he drew up a will earlier today."

Dante chuckled. "I don't think Slater expects to fail."

She knew too well the cost of failed expectations, but didn't say anything more. Instead, she helped Dante wash and dry the glasses, then carried them back into the saloon.

There were no signs of Frank and Simon, who must've departed for the night.

Rebecca bid Dante good night and locked the door behind him, then blew out all the lamps but the one in the back office. She shivered in the cool air. A jacket hung on a hook in the office, and she donned it. Although it was large, it gave her both warmth and a sense of propriety. It also smelled of Slater.

Sitting down behind the desk, Rebecca waited.

IT had been a long time since Slater spent an evening roving from saloon to saloon. He'd avoided the Black Bull, not wanting to draw Delilah's attention, but he'd managed to visit the other fourteen establishments. He spent only five or ten minutes in most, but in the larger saloons he sipped a beer at the bar while he observed the comings and goings.

The last one he visited was one of the latest ones to open in Oaktree. It was also one of the bigger, with a lumber frame covered by canvas. A thin wooden sign that read The Brass Balls was tacked over the open doorway. The name brought a shiver of remembrance down his spine. He and the other prisoners at Andersonville had often referred to the commander of the camp as having brass balls. He shook the bleak memory aside and walked up to the plank and barrel bar. Five men and a skinny woman wearing a short dress and with feathers in her hair were what remained of the night's business.

"What can I get you, mistah?" The bartender's Southern accent wasn't uncommon in the frontier cattle town.

"Beer." As the bartender filled a mug, Slater asked, "This place been here long?"

"A coupla months now."

Slater made a show of looking around the lantern-lit area filled with smoky shadows. "Looks like the owner is doing pretty well."

"Mr. Gavin does like to do things right."

"That the owner's name—Gavin?"

"Leo Gavin."

"I used to know a Gavin, back in Virginia," Slater lied, fishing for information.

"Can't be him. Mr. Gavin's from Alabama." The bartender frowned. "I heard tell he lost his plantation during the war."

"That's a damned shame." Slater sipped his lukewarm beer. "I hope he does better here."

"Me, too. He's a decent enough man, pays a decent wage, and runs a clean place."

"Has he had any trouble since he got here?" Slater asked, keeping his voice casual.

"Nothing more than the occasional fistfight, usually over one of the ladies."

Slater forced a chuckle. "Typical."

The bartender paused. "Why you askin'?"

"Just curious." Since it was part of the rumor mill, Slater asked, "Did you hear about the fella who was murdered in the alley last Saturday night?"

"Owned the Scarlet Garter."

"He was a friend of mine."

The bartender narrowed his eyes. "You the one who got the place?"

Slater nodded. "That's right. I'm trying to find out who might have had a grudge against Andrew."

"I'm sorry about your friend and wish I could help." The bartender sounded sincere. "But it was more'n likely someone who wanted his money."

"That's what the sheriff said, too." Slater didn't bother to add that the sheriff was wrong. He straightened. "I'd best get back and see to the Garter's closing. Good night."

Sighing at his lack of progress, Slater walked the quieting streets back to the Garter. Like most of the other saloons, the Scarlet Garter was dark and closed up.

Going around to the back door, he felt a frisson of unease in the place where Andrew had died. With more haste than usual he dug the key out of his pocket and unlocked the door. A light from his office lent a welcoming glimmer, and he let out an involuntary sigh of relief.

A figure moved in front of the lamp, spilling a shadow

into the hall. Slater's muscles grew taut and his left hand trembled. "Goddammit, not now," he muttered to his hand. Fortunately it wasn't his gun hand, and he eased his revolver out of its shoulder holster.

A figure stepped into the doorway. *Glory.* Swearing, he shoved his gun back into its holster. "What the hell are you doing up?"

The light behind her formed a silver nimbus around her head and outlined her figure, which was covered by a jacket—*his* jacket.

"Waiting for you," she replied. "Did you learn anything?"

Furious at both himself and Glory, he stalked past her into the office. He poured himself some Scotch from Andrew's personal stock and downed it in one gulp. His right hand trembled almost as much as his left. He glared at her. "I almost shot you."

"You didn't," she said calmly, without a trace of doubt, which only fueled Slater's anger.

"But I might have. I told you to stay out of this."

"If something happens to you, I lose my source of income."

Although her tone was cool and businesslike, he noticed the concern in her expressive eyes. But he wasn't ready to acknowledge it. Not yet. Maybe not ever. "You'll be well taken care of if I die."

Irritation chased away her imperiousness. "So I was right. You're trying to get yourself killed in punishment for not saving Andrew's life."

She could rile him faster than any other woman. He lunged close, and felt a twinge of satisfaction when she cringed. However, she held her ground. "This has nothing to do with him. It's between you and me. You want me to drag you off to my bed."

She moved so fast he didn't have time to catch the hand that slapped his cheek. The crack of skin on skin echoed dully. The blow extinguished the fear that drove his cruel words. "I'm sorry, Glory. You didn't deserve that."

"No, I didn't." She closed her eyes briefly. "Damn it, Slater, I don't want you to die."

The naked anguish in her expression forced Slater to move before his brain caught up. He wrapped his arms around her, drawing her close to his chest, and he rested his cheek on the crown of her head. He could smell a hint of jasmine beneath the typical saloon odors, and he concentrated on the light flowery scent that suited her.

"Thank you for caring, Glory."

"Rebecca," she whispered. She drew back and met his gaze. "My real name is Rebecca."

"Rebecca." The rightness of it rolled through him. "It fits you better than Glory."

"Rebecca Glory Bowen." Her smile faltered, and she rested her forehead against his chest.

He had the impression she wanted to say more, but she remained silent. His embrace, which had begun as comforting, became more. His reaction to her soft curves and sweet scent made itself known, and he couldn't deny his desire.

Slater slid his hands up her back and to either side of her slender neck. His thumbs brushed the soft skin below her ears, and she trembled against him. Her silky hair flowed across the back of his hands like a warm waterfall, and her breath was moist and hot against his chest.

Gently, he tipped her head up and gazed down into her half-lidded golden brown eyes. Her cheeks were flushed and her mouth partially open, breathing more heavily, just as he was. With infinite tenderness, he lowered his head and touched his mouth to hers. Her petal-soft lips unfurled and he tasted her, and she swept her tongue across his. The kiss intensified, growing more heated as passion flared to life.

When they finally separated to breathe in deep gasps, Rebecca pushed away. She turned her back to him, her arms wrapped around her slender waist.

Slater came up behind her and folded his arms around her shoulders. He nuzzled her ear and her breath quickened, but her body didn't relax.

"What is it?" he whispered close to a delicate shell ear.

She shook her head. "This is wrong," she said in a husky voice.

"Why?"

She turned within his embrace and he loosened his hold, yet couldn't release her completely. She clutched the lapels of his jacket that she wore with a white-fingered stranglehold. Her face, too, was pale, except for the paint she wore on her cheekbones.

"There's something you need to know," she began, her voice quivering. She met his eyes with a determined gaze. "I'm married."

He stared at her, unwilling to believe he'd heard her correctly. The shame and embarrassment in her expression and stance, however, told him he hadn't mistaken her words. Equal parts of shock and resentment made him back away from her, all the way out the doorway.

"I'm sorry," she whispered.

Injured pride manifested in furious anger. "Why didn't you say anything earlier? Why did you lead me on?"

Her lips became a red slash across her face. "How dare you! I never did anything improper."

"Then what the hell was that kiss about? I wasn't the only one involved."

Her face flushed scarlet, and she couldn't hold his gaze. Direct hit, yet it didn't make him feel any better.

He stalked back to her and used his height to try to intimidate her. "Did you leave him because he couldn't pleasure you in bed? Or was it simply that he was too tight with the purse strings?"

Red-hot fury blazed in her eyes. "He's a gambler just like you, and he lost everything my parents left me, including my home. Then he left me." Her chest heaved and her arms were stiff at her sides, fisted hands held close to her body. "That's why I'm here, doing things I never in my life dreamed I'd be doing."

She pushed past him and Slater, too startled by her confession, let her go. He slumped into the desk chair and stared at the bottle of Scotch.

Glory—no, Rebecca's—admission explained why a lady of her obvious background worked in a saloon. He should've guessed. The only woman he thought he'd loved had also been married, but she'd been the runaway, not her husband.

What if Rebecca lied to him? Would her husband someday find her and drag her back to their marriage bed?

He smiled, but it was more of a grimace. He'd actually considered a long-term liaison with Rebecca, if she'd wanted him. Oh, and she wanted him, that much he was certain of. No woman could pretend to kiss a man the way Rebecca had kissed him. She was a hot-blooded woman underneath that veneer of respectability. However, she was also a married woman with a husband out there who might or might not be searching for her.

At least she'd confessed her marital status before they'd committed adultery. Not that Slater was religious, but he knew better than to get involved with another man's woman.

He snagged the Scotch bottle by the neck and poured a healthy slug into a glass. He downed it in two swallows and refilled it. It was going to be a long night.

REBECCA'S body throbbed with unfulfilled passion, but that was inconsequential compared to the anguish in her heart. She hadn't realized how much Slater meant to her until she'd been forced to confess her secret. She'd nearly lost herself in the kiss that had started tender and turned into a conflagration of desire.

Despite Slater's disgust, she still wanted him. The strength of his arms, the smoky arousal in his blue eyes, and the burning heat of his muscled body. She also wanted to know him, to learn what drove him. And what caused him to fear so badly that his hand would shake and he would refuse to assist a friend.

How could she continue to work for him when she felt this way? She could find work at another saloon, but to be in the same town as Slater and not see him every day would be another kind of hell. Worse, perhaps, than the one she currently found herself in.

She pushed herself off her bed and removed Slater's jacket. Clutching it between her hands, she brought it to her face and breathed deeply of his comforting scent. She'd place it back where she found it tomorrow. She set it aside reluctantly and removed her work dress. Her motions were mechanical as she tried to keep her mind blank.

After donning her nightgown and brushing her hair, Rebecca opened a dresser drawer and drew out the white christening gown. She dropped onto her bed and held the gown tightly as her memory supplied her with pictures of her son.

Although she'd told Slater about her husband, she'd balked at telling him about Daniel. He was already disgusted enough with her. What would he think if he knew she'd abandoned her child? Yet Daniel was the reason she sought Benjamin. A man should know about his son, and he had an obligation to support his family.

Doubts plagued her. Benjamin had spent every penny she had and disappeared. Would a man like that change his nature for his child?

Rebecca had no other choice but to hope he would. Because if he didn't, she would be forced to admit Daniel was lost to her. And she couldn't accept that. Not now. Not ever.

$\mathcal{F}$OURTEEN

ACROSS the following days, Rebecca grew accustomed to Slater's cool attitude and his obvious absences when she worked on the accounting books. Even as she mourned the loss of his company, she understood why he did it, and at times could almost feel grateful.

He took to spending more time away from the Scarlet Garter, too, and she couldn't help but worry for his safety. If anyone contacted him about extorting money, he didn't tell her. Not that she expected him to, but the rift between them bothered her. Especially in the evenings, when the rare meeting of their eyes resulted in Slater quickly looking away.

Because of Slater's absences, Rebecca found herself learning and taking care of more of the day-to-day business. She counted the money from the night's business and tallied it in the books, and helped Dante with the inventory and ordering of liquor. Since Rebecca was constantly walking around the customers, she could stop a "misunderstanding" before it escalated into fisticuffs. Two free drinks were often preferable to replacing chairs and tables, not to mention glassware and whiskey bottles.

However, Wednesday night brought a different kind of

altercation. With Slater gone, Richard was playing poker for the house, and Rebecca sensed a growing tension at his table.

One of the customers, a cowboy Rebecca recognized as a regular, abruptly shoved back his chair, which toppled to the floor. "Take off your coat and roll up your sleeves," he demanded of Richard.

Rebecca, from a position in the middle of the crowd, caught Dante's eye; he nodded to her as he reached for his sawed-off shotgun. Trembling inwardly, Rebecca continued to the poker table, where Frank stood ready to throw the man out.

"Can I get you another beer?" she asked the man, hoping to defuse the situation.

"You can get rid of this cheat," the cowboy said, his hand hovering by his revolver.

Rebecca was aware of the silence and the attention of everyone in the saloon. She forced a smile. "Let's go to the back office and discuss it."

"I respect you, Miss Glory, but I ain't goin' nowhere. This bastard's been cheatin', and everyone should know."

Her mouth dry, she turned to Richard. Although she hadn't taken to the suave gambler, she didn't think Andrew would've knowingly hired a cardsharp. "Have you been cheating?"

"It's against house rules." His slick smile didn't allay Rebecca's unease. In fact, it did the opposite.

"That wasn't what I asked. Have you been cheating?"

He met her gaze squarely. "No."

Although he didn't bat an eye, he was a skilled poker player, adept at hiding his thoughts. Rebecca's gut told her he was lying, but she didn't know how to prove it. The tension notched higher, and the onlookers grumbled and shifted.

"Take off your coat, Richard."

Startled, Rebecca turned to see Slater striding toward them from the back.

Richard scowled. "I know the rules."

Slater smiled coldly. "Then you won't mind removing your coat and proving it."

Richard's scowl deepened, but he stood and took off his jacket, fastidiously hanging it over the back of his chair.

"Roll up your sleeves," Slater said.

"Now, Slater, you—"

"Do it!"

With every eye in the saloon on him, Richard unbuttoned his left cuff first and raised it. Nothing. His movements were slower, more deliberate, as he undid the right cuff. The tense silence in the saloon grew, pressing down on everyone.

Rebecca held her breath as Richard rolled up the right sleeve. Nothing again. Confused, she glanced at Slater.

"I told you," Richard said, indignation in his tone.

"Hand me his jacket, Glory," Slater said.

Richard tensed, and his gaze flicked to Rebecca. She retrieved the coat and handed it to Slater. Purposefully, he checked the inner lining, then the sleeves. He paused, then brought out three cards from the sleeve opening—the jack, queen, and king of spades.

The cowboy who'd accused Richard of cheating surged toward the gambler. "You son of a—"

Slater grabbed his arm, twisting it behind his back so swiftly, Rebecca couldn't follow his motions. The cowboy stilled.

"You were right," Slater said. "And I want to thank you for pointing it out."

Startled, the cowboy stood stiffly for a moment, then nodded. Slater released him.

Slater threw Richard's jacket at him. "Get out and don't come back."

Rather than being cowed, Richard glared at Slater for a moment before marching out of the Scarlet Garter.

Slater raised his voice. "We run a clean house, and I personally apologize for having a snake in our midst. Everyone gets a drink on the house."

Although Rebecca was suddenly overrun with drink orders, she was aware of Slater dividing the money at the poker table among the players. She knew there was a house stake of twenty dollars there, but that, too, was divided among the four players. It was a good business decision, and she couldn't help but admire Slater's handling of the situation. She didn't dare consider what might have happened had Slater not arrived when he did.

Finally, the rush on the free drinks ended and Rebecca joined Simon. Although it wasn't a night she normally sang, she thought some lively songs would lift the lingering tension.

She glanced at Slater and caught him looking at her with approval. A sliver of warmth slid in where only cold had resided since she'd told him she was married.

The evening continued without any more problems, and Rebecca was glad to see Slater circulating among the customers. She also took personal pleasure in simply watching him, something she'd missed. His lean body moved with a grace and economy of motion few men possessed. Every inch radiated confidence, and he held his head and shoulders straight, meeting the eyes of everyone he spoke with. However, a brief glance at his fisted left hand pressed close to his thigh told her he wasn't as calm as he appeared.

As one A.M. approached, men began to drift out and head home. Rebecca picked up dirty glasses and carried them to the bar. As she gathered some from a deserted table, she dropped one. Sighing tiredly, she leaned over to pick it up. Gunshots exploded, followed by the crash of breaking glass. Men's curses and women's screams filled Rebecca's ears and she knelt on the floor, her torso bent over her knees and her arms covering her head. A body flung itself over her, and she opened her mouth to scream.

"Stay down, Rebecca," Slater said, his breath warming her ear.

She snapped her mouth shut and huddled beneath the protective shell of Slater's body. The barrage seemed to go on forever, although it probably lasted less than a minute.

When the attack ended, Slater raised himself off Rebecca. "Are you all right?"

She was shaking so hard, she had to concentrate to determine if she'd been hurt. "I-I think so."

Slater nodded curtly and jumped to his feet, tearing off his jacket. She turned to see flames spreading across the floor. A bullet must have shattered a lamp.

Without thought, she scrambled up to help him. Five other men had joined in, using jackets and their feet to stamp out the hungry fire. Smoke rose around them, and she coughed as tears streamed down her cheeks. Fortunately, they'd gotten to the fire fast enough, and it was extinguished within minutes.

Slater grabbed her arm and tugged her away from the blackened area. "What the hell were you doing?"

"I was helping put out the damned fire," she cursed back, her temper frayed. A coughing fit caught her, and she bent over at the waist.

A warm hand on her back steadied her and, despite Slater's anger with her, his touch was soothing. Finally, she lifted her head.

"Damn it, Rebecca, you could've been killed." The concern in his eyes didn't match his sharp tone.

She looked around, gaping at the damage. The front windows were literally blown out, and the mirror behind the bar was riddled with bullet holes and cracks.

"Georgia's been shot."

Simon's frantic voice broke through Rebecca's shock, and she turned to see her friend lying on the floor. Georgia's complexion was ashen, and blood covered her right shoulder. Rebecca hurried over and knelt beside her.

"Dante, get a doctor," she heard Slater call out, and was relieved that Dante was unhurt.

Blood oozed from Georgia's bullet wound. Rebecca's head swam with dizziness. What could she do?

"We need to press down on it," Simon said. "Stop the bleedin'." His complexion was almost as gray as Georgia's.

A cloth was thrust at Rebecca, and she glanced up to see Cassie's grim face.

Rebecca laid the cloth on Georgia's shoulder and pressed her palms down on it.

Simon maneuvered around to Rebecca's side. "Let me."

Rebecca relinquished the task to Simon and moved out of the way. She used the bar to pull herself upright. Two injured customers were being helped, but both men were upright, so their wounds couldn't have been too bad. Gunsmoke and the remnants of the fire curled through the saloon, leaving an acrid odor in their wake, mixing with the overpowering stench of whiskey from broken bottles. The unmistakable smell of Georgia's blood wove through the tapestry of devastation.

Rebecca's stomach churned, and she swallowed convulsively to hold the sickness at bay.

Cassie wrapped her arm around Rebecca's shoulders, and on her other side, Molly put an arm around Rebecca's waist. Rose was close to Cassie's other side. Tears rolled down Rose's cheeks, and Molly's breath hitched in her throat. They remained by the bar, out of the way, simply holding one another as they looked out at the wanton destruction.

Rebecca's gaze followed Slater as he moved about the room, talking with the men, who stood in tight circles. His expression was tight and his reassuring smiles didn't touch his eyes. Her heart swelled at his concern and ability to stay calm when chaos surrounded him.

Men gathered outside the Garter, their faces wreathed in shadows but their exclamations clear. It seemed almost everybody left in Oaktree had come to see the shambles.

The doctor arrived quicker than Rebecca expected, but he—and everybody else in town—must've heard the attack. He did cursory checks on the two wounded men; it was obvious they had minor injuries caused by breaking glass. Then the doctor went to Georgia's side and drew the dress down off her shoulder to see her bullet wound more clearly. With Simon's help, he rolled her onto her side and found where the bullet had exited.

"How is she?" Slater demanded, anxiety creasing his brow.

"She's lost a lot of blood, but the bullet passed through. Let's get her to her room; I can clean and bandage the wound there."

"I'll carry her," Simon said. He picked her up as if she weighed nothing, and climbed the stairs.

"We'll bring up hot water and towels," Cassie volunteered, glancing at Rose and Molly.

As they carried out their tasks, Sheriff Ryder strode in and halted just inside the door. He whistled low. "First Kearny, now this. Looks like someone's got a serious grudge against the Garter."

Slater's expression revealed nothing, not even contempt. "Looks that way, or maybe some liquored-up cowboys got a little gun-crazy."

Ryder raised his voice. "Anybody see anything?"

Shaking heads answered his question.

"All right, then, you all head on home now," he said. "Nothing else to see here."

Finally, only Slater, Rebecca, Dante, and Frank were left standing amid the wreckage.

"Frank, Dante, make sure there aren't any embers left that might flare up," Slater said.

The two men went to their task.

"Rebecca, go on upstairs," he said.

She shook her head. "I'll start cleaning."

"No. Tomorrow's soon enough. We're all exhausted."

Rebecca remained rooted in place, unwilling to leave Slater.

"No hot spots, boss," Frank reported.

"Good. Go on home now," Slater said to him and Dante.

"I'll be in at noon to help remove signs of this atrocity," Dante said.

Slater managed a slight but genuine smile of gratitude. "Thanks."

"I'll be here, too," Frank added.

Slater nodded his gratitude. He followed them to the door and locked it behind them.

"They'll just come in through the windows," Rebecca said.

Slater stared at the empty panes. "Those windows were Andrew's pride and joy. They came all the way from St. Louis. Cost him a pretty penny, too, but he was determined to do it right."

Rebecca's throat burned, and it wasn't all from the smoke. "Are you going to replace them?"

"I'll order them tomorrow." He turned to her, every sign of vulnerability gone. "Go to bed, Rebecca."

She knew sleep would be elusive and her mind would replay the attack over and over again. However, they were lucky no one had been killed. If it had been any earlier, there would have been more people in the saloon and more chance of someone dying. She turned away and wiped the bar with a cloth, brushing bits of glass into a box. "Was it them?"

He was silent for a minute. "Probably."

Although Rebecca expected his answer, dread brought dampness to her palms and made her heart beat faster. "Have they contacted you?"

"No, which is why I didn't see this coming." He swore vehemently and raked a hand through his hair. "Damn it, I should've been prepared."

Rebecca resisted the urge to offer him comfort. "You couldn't have stopped it."

Slater didn't argue. Instead, he lifted chairs onto tables. "Georgia shot and the Garter busted up." Suddenly he threw a chair across the room. "Goddammit! How the hell can I catch the murderer if I can't even keep my place—my people— safe?"

Driven by something more than concern, Rebecca crossed to his side and rested her hand on his trembling arm. "It's not your fault."

He stared down at her, his blue eyes full of intensity, rage, and guilt. "That note was my warning, and I ignored it."

"Why would they do something like this before asking you face to face for the money? It doesn't make sense."

"I've been asking a lot of questions around town," he admitted. "I was hoping they'd come after me, not the saloon."

Icy fear clutched Rebecca. "Asking questions is how Andrew got killed."

"I know."

Furious, she wanted to strike him. How dare he hold such little regard for his own life?

Slater sighed and sat down heavily. He planted his elbows on the table and scrubbed his face with his palms. "God, I've tried so hard not to give a damn."

Confusion shoving aside her anger, she cautiously lowered herself to a chair beside him. "What do you mean?"

He lifted his head, and Rebecca nearly gasped at the soul-deep pain that filled his expression. "I failed so many times. I tell them, I'll protect them, and they still die."

His words made no sense. "Who did you fail, Slater?" she asked softly.

Bitter laughter. "Andrew. Tommy. All those men at Andersonville."

"You were at Andersonville?"

He nodded, his eyes bleak. "I told them to hang on, that the Union Army would come soon and we'd all be freed. Some wanted to escape, but I convinced them it was better to wait." His lips curled in self-derision. "Ten months. Ten months of hell before we were liberated. Only a few of us lived, and we were more dead than alive."

Rebecca looked away as she remembered all the stories she'd read and heard about the Andersonville prison camp. There'd even been some pictures of stick-figure men barely able to walk. She pressed a hand to her mouth, imagining Slater as one of those emaciated, tortured men.

She felt Slater move, and his arms wound around her, pulling her close.

"I'm sorry. I shouldn't have told you," he whispered.

Rebecca forced back the images that disturbed her, and composed herself. Slater carried enough guilt. He shouldn't feel bad for confiding in her, especially since she doubted he had anyone else. She lifted her head and met his stormy gaze. "No. I'm glad you did." She managed a smile. "Maybe I'll even have a little more patience with you."

A corner of his lips lifted. "I'm not expecting miracles."

This time her smile was genuine. Their gazes held, and Rebecca felt the change between them, subtle yet unmistakable. Slater's nostrils flared slightly, and his eyes became more black than blue. She remembered too well the hunger of his kiss, and her breath quickened with the memory. Shifting, lifting, and their lips were mere inches apart.

Voices upstairs in the hallway broke the spell, and they moved apart. Rebecca resisted the urge to press a hand to her heart, to slow the rapid beat of desire.

Slater met the doctor at the bottom of the stairs. "How is she?"

The doctor passed a weary hand across his brow. "She's

young and in relatively good health. She should be fine as long as infection doesn't set in."

Rebecca joined them. "What can we do?"

"As I told your piano player, change the dressings twice a day for the next couple of days. And whenever she wakes up, have her drink water. After all the blood she's lost, she'll need plenty of liquids."

"Thanks, Doc. Just send me the bill," Slater said. He walked the white-haired man to the door and saw him out.

"I'm going to see her," Rebecca said, climbing the stairs.

Slater guided her upward, his hand at her back.

She knocked lightly on Georgia's door and entered. Simon sat close to the bed, his big hands clenched together as if he were praying. He might have been.

"We just spoke with the doctor," Slater said. "He thinks she has a good chance."

Simon nodded. "Told me the same, but I've never seen Georgia so quiet before."

Rebecca laid a hand on Simon's muscled shoulder. "I can sit with her tonight."

Simon seemed about to shake his head, then nodded. "All right. But if she takes a turn, have someone come get me."

"I'll get you myself," Slater promised. "Get some rest. I'm going to need your help to put the Scarlet Garter back together."

"Mr. Kearny would be sick about the place if he saw it now," Simon said sadly.

"He'd be even sicker about Georgia getting hurt," Slater said. "Go on, Simon. Rebecca will sit with her."

"Rebecca?"

She smiled. "Consider Miss Glory my stage name."

Although nothing could banish the worry from Simon's face, he smiled. The dark man stood and stared down at Georgia a few more moments, then nodded to Rebecca and Slater.

After Simon left, Slater turned to Rebecca. He reached down and brushed his thumb along her cheek. She wanted to lean into his touch, but her husband stood between them.

Slater held his thumb up, showing the smoky grime he'd

wiped from her face. "Wash up, then change into something warmer. I'll stay with Georgia until you get back."

Flustered, Rebecca did as he said. She scrubbed her face clean, donned an everyday dress, and wrapped a heavy shawl around her shoulders. With the windows out downstairs, it would be a cool night. When she returned to Georgia's room, Slater was laying a damp cloth on the girl's fevered forehead. She couldn't imagine Benjamin ever doing something like that, not even for his wife.

Burying her resentment for her wayward husband, Rebecca traded places with Slater.

"Call me if you need anything or if Georgia worsens," Slater said. "I'll be downstairs."

She caught his arm as he turned away. "Take your own advice, Slater, and get some rest. You're exhausted, too."

He shook his head. "I can't sleep, but I can start putting things to right down there."

"What if he shows up?"

She didn't have to explain who "he" was.

"He won't. They're going to let me stew tonight, thinking I'll only get more scared." A vulnerable smile claimed his lips. "Only I've already gone past scared into mad."

"Are you going to pay them?"

His gaze settled on Georgia. "I don't want anyone else hurt."

Although Rebecca wasn't certain giving in to extortion was right, she was relieved to hear Slater's response.

The dim lamplight reflected in Slater's eyes, transforming them to silvery blue. He opened his mouth as if to speak, then abruptly closed it. He left the room, an uneasy silence in his wake.

Rebecca shivered, but she wasn't cold. Regrets pursued her in the lonely quiet broken only by Georgia's steady breathing and occasional soft cry. Regrets were what had brought her here, to this small town on the edge of the frontier, working in a place like the Scarlet Garter. Yet she couldn't hate this life she'd found, the friends she'd made; and she certainly couldn't hate Slater Forrester, who confounded and enflamed her.

But for all that she'd found here, she couldn't forget her greatest loss—Daniel. Tonight had shown her that her new-found life was dangerous, and if she died here, she would break her promise. Daniel would never know his mother or father.

She took Georgia's cool, limp hand in hers and told her of her son and how she would have to leave and continue her search for Benjamin. And if Rebecca cried over new regrets, there was no one to witness her weakness.

$\mathcal{F}$IFTEEN

REBECCA jerked awake, and it took a few seconds to figure out she was in a chair pulled up to Georgia's bed. She'd dozed off and on through the night, her sleep filled with nightmares gleaned from the sudden violence that had erupted downstairs.

She removed the damp cloth from Georgia's brow and placed the back of her hand against her forehead. Warm, but not as hot as the last time she'd checked. Rebecca rewet the cloth in the basin's cool water and dabbed her friend's brow.

Georgia's eyelids moved, and Rebecca held her breath, hoping she'd awaken.

"Come on, Georgia. Wake up," she urged.

After a few attempts, Georgia finally opened her eyes. Confusion lay in their dark depths.

"You're going to be just fine, Georgia," Rebecca said, leaning close and speaking softly.

Georgia struggled to focus and finally succeeded. "G-Glory?"

"You were hurt last night," Rebecca said. "Do you remember?"

More confusion. "Thirsty."

Rebecca poured water from the pitcher into a glass. She raised Georgia's head as she lifted the glass to her lips. "Drink slow."

Some water dribbled down Georgia's chin, but she managed a few swallows. Rebecca eased her head back down to the pillow and dabbed away the droplets on her friend's chin. "Better?"

Georgia managed a slight nod. "Shot?"

"That's right. Some men shot into the saloon."

Her dark eyes widened. "S-Simon?"

Rebecca clasped Georgia's cool hand between both of hers and smiled in reassurance. "He's fine. In fact, he carried you up here last night and stayed with you until Slater made him go home to get some sleep."

Georgia's eyelids fluttered shut, and a tiny smile lifted the corners of her lips. Her even breathing signaled her glide back into slumber. Optimistic that Georgia would recover, Rebecca tucked her friend's arm under the blankets.

A soft knock sounded, and Rebecca rose to open the door. She wasn't surprised to see Simon standing there, looking as awkward as a schoolboy. His eyes were bloodshot behind his round spectacles, and worry carved grooves in his brow. "How is she?"

Rebecca swung open the door. "See for yourself."

Simon peeked past Rebecca, and she tugged the reluctant man into the room. He stood at the foot of the bed, gazing down at the injured woman. A glimmer of hope eased some of his worry lines. "She looks better."

"She is," Rebecca said. "In fact, she was awake just before you came." She paused. "She asked about you right off." Rebecca thought Simon would be pleased, but if anything, he looked more miserable. "I thought you'd be happy to hear she woke up."

"I'm grateful, and glad my prayers were answered."

"Then what's wrong?"

"Even if I got feelings for her, it doesn't change how it is."

Remembering what Georgia had told her, Rebecca crossed her arms and leveled her gaze on him. "How what is?"

Her tone must have been more critical than she'd intended, because annoyance crossed Simon's usually placid face. "You wouldn't understand, Miss Glory."

"Understand that you don't feel like you're good enough for her? Maybe you *were* born a slave and grew up a slave, but you're free now. You are the only one who still sees yourself as a slave." She glanced at Georgia fondly. "Georgia certainly doesn't."

Simon remained troubled, but Rebecca could tell he was thinking about what she'd said. She pressed her advantage. "If Georgia had died last night, how would you be feeling now? Regrets won't keep you warm at night, and they'll hound you every single day." Rebecca thought of Slater, and her own regrets nearly crushed her.

"I'll think about it," Simon said quietly.

"You do that, and when Georgia is feeling better, you can tell her what you decided."

Simon took one last long look at Georgia, then hurried out.

Cassie entered the room. "How is she?"

"Better," Rebecca said.

Cassie's careworn face smoothed. "Good. Me, Rose, and Molly will take turns sitting with her today so you can get some rest."

A week ago Rebecca would've been startled by the offer, but now she merely nodded gratefully. "She woke up about ten minutes ago and drank some water. If she wakes again, try to get her to drink more. The doctor said she needs the fluids to help build up her blood again."

Rebecca left Cassie sitting by Georgia's bed and went to her room to freshen up and cover her piled-up hair with a scarf. She wouldn't be able to sleep, and would feel better doing something to help. Besides, she needed coffee and could smell the odor of it wafting up.

Descending the stairs, she wasn't surprised to see Simon, Dante, Frank, Toby, and Malcolm working. However, she was puzzled that Slater wasn't among them. She poured herself a cup of coffee, noting that Dante and Malcolm worked behind the bar, cleaning up glass and salvaging what they could. Toby swept while Simon and Frank removed the remaining glass shards from the window panes.

"Where's Slater?" she asked Dante.

"Purchasing lumber to cover the windows, and he also mentioned he would order new glass," the small man replied. He was dressed in overalls that were probably a boy's size.

She finished her coffee and set the empty cup on the bar. Brushing her hands together, she asked, "What can I do?"

"You should be sleeping," Simon said from across the room. "You were up all night with Georgia."

"I'm not tired. I'll get a bucket of hot water and clean the tables and chairs." Before anyone could argue, she went into the back to get what she needed.

Rolling up her sleeves, Rebecca set to work. Tiny bits of glass glittered across the wood surfaces and she was careful to shake out her damp cloth after wiping the tables and chairs. She had finished over half the room when a wagon pulled up front.

"Slater's back with the lumber," Simon announced.

The cleaning was forgotten as the men trooped outside. Rebecca joined them, shading her eyes against the late morning sun. Slater bore little resemblance to the gambler Rebecca had met the day Andrew hired her. The starched shirt and pressed suit that had clothed his lean body were gone, replaced by work trousers with suspenders and a navy blue shirt with its sleeves rolled up to his elbows. He wore tan deerhide gloves that emphasized his golden brown forearms and a red bandanna around his neck that contrasted sharply with dark, grizzled whiskers. Once upon a time Rebecca would've sniffed in distaste at a man's unshaven face, but on Slater she found it darkly attractive.

Her heart fluttered in her breast and she felt a thrumming rise in her belly. She clutched the folds of her skirt, needing something to cling to. She'd been attracted to Benjamin, but what she'd once felt for him paled miserably in the face of the feelings Slater evoked in her.

"Let's get this inside and get those windows covered," Slater said to the men.

Rebecca stepped aside so they could carry the wood planks into the saloon.

"You should be sleeping," Slater said, balancing a board on his shoulder.

She narrowed her eyes. "How much sleep did *you* get last night?"

He scowled. "I can go without sleep longer than you can."

Rebecca couldn't help but laugh. He sounded like a bragging schoolboy. "That might be so, but I'm not tired right now." She shrugged. "I can always catch a nap later."

"Who's with Georgia?"

"Cassie, Rose, and Molly are taking turns sitting with her." She paused. "Her fever was lower, and she woke up for a few minutes this morning."

Slater sagged with relief. "That's good news."

"We're due for some."

Slater's smile disappeared. "That's the truth."

The lumber was quickly transferred into the saloon, and Dante, Malcolm, and Toby took the wagon to the general store to replace glassware that had been broken.

While Rebecca continued washing tabletops and chairs, Slater, Frank, and Simon nailed the boards over the broken windows. As they shut out the sunlight, lanterns were lit. It gave the saloon a dreary, closed-in feeling.

Scrubbing the last table, Rebecca felt a prick in her palm. She lifted her hand to find a small, triangular piece of glass stuck in the center of her palm. Blood oozed out around the glass.

Slater appeared beside her. "What's wrong?"

"It's nothing," she said, embarrassed by his attention.

He gently took her injured hand in his. "Piece of glass?"

She pulled her hand away, cupping it within her other. "I'll take care of it," she said, cursing the huskiness in her voice.

He steered her to the back, holding her shoulders firmly so she couldn't escape. His closeness brought a wave of heat that settled between her thighs.

"I told you I could do it myself," she said, fear and anger vying for supremacy.

"Sit down."

Rebecca wanted to defy his order, but one look at his cool blue eyes made her sink into the chair. She cradled her bleeding hand in her lap and gazed at it rather than Slater. It was infinitely safer.

He dropped to his knees beside her and took hold of her hand. She remained stiff.

"Damn it, Rebecca, let me get the glass out," he said, blue lightning sparking his eyes.

She glared at him and he glared back. It was a silly thing to get so upset over, but it wasn't the wound itself that bothered her. It was Slater's concern and gentleness that were infinitely more distressing. She could understand a little pain from a cut, but not the desire that nearly drowned her when he touched her.

Slater growled and caught her hand. Although his grip was firm, he was careful not to hurt her. However, she couldn't prevent a sharp intake of breath when he removed the splinter.

"Sorry," he murmured. Then he gently washed her palm with a damp cloth.

The sting faded as other feelings pushed it aside. She gave in to the temptation to look down at Slater, who worked diligently to clean away the blood. His dark head was only inches from her, the thick hair beckoning her, daring her to run her fingers through the strands. Her breasts were heavy with arousal, and the slide of her camisole over her sensitive nipples heightened the need that coursed through her body. She resisted the urge to shift on the chair to alleviate some of the ache between her thighs. Besides, she knew only Slater could assuage the growing ache, and she couldn't have him. Not when she belonged to another.

As Slater wrapped her hand, she closed her eyes and thought of Daniel and the home she'd left him in. It was run by nuns on the edge of St. Louis and they'd promised to care for Daniel. But she knew there were few sisters and many children, so the care would be only the basics. Only she could give him the love he needed.

"That should take care of it." Slater stood.

"Thank you," she said, her voice barely above a whisper.

"Have you eaten anything today?" he asked after a moment of awkward silence.

She shook her head. "I'm not hungry."

"You can't go without food and sleep indefinitely. You're bound to pass out." He passed a hand over his hair and closed his eyes. He seemed to sway slightly, but before Rebecca was certain, he steadied. "Stay here. I'll be back in a few minutes."

Before she could ask him what he planned, he was gone. She considered defying him and leaving before he returned, but she was too curious. Less than five minutes later, he returned, carrying two plates heaped with food that had obviously come from the tent next door. He set them on the desk.

"Eat. You'll feel better," he said.

He sat down in the chair behind the desk and dug into his own food. She picked up a fork and put some potatoes into her mouth—and realized she was starving. They cleaned off their plates at the same time.

"Feeling better?" he asked.

Her face warmed. "Much. Thank you." To take her mind off the room's intimacy and Slater's nearness, she asked, "Do you think we can open tonight?"

"I plan on it. If your hand bothers you, take the night off. I have a feeling it won't be that busy."

She flexed the cut hand, and although it stung, it wouldn't keep her from working. "I'm fine. Are you sure it's a good idea to go back to business as usual?"

His lips pressed together in familiar obstinacy. "I have to open. I want them to come to me."

Impatience rose in her. "And what? Beat you up? Kill you like they did Andrew?"

Slater reached across the desk and clasped her hands, remembering to be gentle despite the intensity of his expression. "I want the bastards to pay for what they've done."

Rebecca didn't want to understand, but she did. Andrew murdered; Georgia shot; the Scarlet Garter damaged. "I don't want you to become another victim," she said, meeting his eyes.

His gaze caressed her, lingering on her lips. "I don't want to, either, but someone has to stop them."

Frustration spilled into her tone. "That's the sheriff's job."

He shook his head slowly, his gaze never leaving her face. "You and I both know he's not going to do a thing about any of this. So either I do it or they get away with murder."

She studied their hands, still entwined. His long, blunt-nailed fingers knitted with her shorter, slender ones. A white scar about two inches long on the back of his hand caught her attention, and she traced the thin line with her forefinger. "What happened?"

He shrugged. "A souvenir from the first time I tried to pick a pocket. The man had a knife. I was more careful the next time."

Rebecca's heart went out to the boy that Slater had been—alone, desperate, and frightened. "It's a miracle you survived until Andrew found you."

"Until *I* found *Andrew*," Slater corrected with a crooked grin. His smile faded. "Why did you tell me you were married? Most women in your position wouldn't have confessed."

Startled by the unexpected question, Rebecca struggled to find the answer. "It wouldn't have been fair to you."

"Life isn't fair, Rebecca."

The bitter reality of her own life made her smile grimly. "Tell me something I don't know, Slater."

"Why are you looking for him at all? He robbed you of everything you had, then left you high and dry."

It would be so easy to tell him about Daniel, but it wouldn't change anything. Besides, confessing that she'd abandoned her child in an orphanage was ten times more difficult than telling him of her marriage. Benjamin leaving her was something she had no control over, but what she'd done to her own son had been her decision alone. "I want what he stole from me."

"And you really believe he still has the money?" He shook his head, his lips pursed. "He's a gambler, Rebecca. More likely than not, he's already lost it all—and more."

"He's my husband."

Exasperation snapped in his eyes. "You'll probably never see him again. Are you going to waste the rest of your life pining for him?"

She pulled away and jumped to her feet. "I'm not pining for him."

"Then why?" Slater stood more slowly. "You're a beautiful woman, Rebecca. You deserve more."

Her irritation fled. "What do I deserve, Slater?"

Her soft plea sliced Slater deeply, and he almost pressed a hand to his chest against the pain. "You deserve a man who loves *you*. You deserve a man who'll stay with you, no matter what." He paused, letting his gaze drink in her breasts, slender waist, and full hips. His body responded without conscience, his blood heating and his erection pressing against his trousers. "And you deserve a man who'll touch you and pleasure you, then hold you all night and wake you with more loving."

Her face reddened, but her breath came in shorter gasps, her chest rising and falling in cadence with her breathing. "And what man would want to give that to a woman already tied to another by marriage?"

Keeping his eyes locked with hers, Slater came around the desk to stand directly in front of her. His legs pressed against her skirts, the many layers of cloth doing little to block the heat of her body. He unknotted the ugly scarf that hid her beautiful crown, then removed the pins that imprisoned her hair. The light gold strands flowed across her shoulders, creating a silky curtain.

Then he cupped her face in his hands and brushed her satiny cheeks. "A man who wants the woman so badly he can almost taste her, almost feel her beside him as he lies in his bed alone. A man who's willing to accept whatever the woman can give him."

Her tawny eyes widened even more, and her lips parted with a tiny "Oh."

Unable and unwilling to resist her sweet vulnerability, Slater lowered his mouth to hers. Her lips were softer than he could've imagined and he lingered, running his tongue along her plump lower lip, tasting the coffee she'd drunk earlier. He drew away, moving only a few inches, and stared down at her. Her gaze was unfocused, her mouth already slightly swollen from his tender kiss. The urge to sweep her into his arms and carry her upstairs to his bed made him tremble. She wouldn't fight him, of that he was certain. In fact, he suspected passion burned as hotly in her as it did in him. And, God knew, he wasn't exactly the noblest of men and it had been a long time—if ever—since he had wanted a woman as much as he wanted Rebecca. The fact that she was married should have doused his desire, but he didn't care. The only thing that mattered right now was touching her, kissing her, and losing himself in her tight, damp heat.

She lowered her head, resting her forehead against his chest. "It's a sin, Slater. If we do this, we're committing adultery."

He swallowed hard, forcing his brain to think rather than letting his balls lead him. Although he hadn't stepped into a church since the day he was adopted, Slater recalled the Ten Commandments. "It's also a sin to steal."

"That was his choice, not mine. If we do this, I'm choosing to sin."

Slater wanted to argue, wanted to convince her that it also wasn't her choice to be abandoned by her husband. So if she found what her husband denied her in another man's bed, it wasn't her sin to bear. Or was he simply trying to justify his own actions?

He released her and stepped back. It wasn't merely the chill in the back room that made him tremble. "I want you in my bed, Rebecca, and you want me. Maybe that's a sin." He steadied himself. "You have to decide for yourself. But know this, I care about you. Think about that, then make your decision."

Suddenly exhausted, Slater could barely keep his eyes open. "I'm going to get some sleep before opening this evening. I suggest you do the same."

A visible shudder passed through her, but her voice was even. "That's a good idea."

He guided her toward the door and back into the main area of the saloon. Simon continued to clean up the mess.

"I'm going to get some sleep," Slater told them. "Tell everyone we're going to open as usual this evening."

Simon nodded, approval in his dark face.

"Thanks," Slater said with a faint smile.

He and Rebecca climbed the stairs together.

"I'd like to check on Georgia," she said.

Slater nodded, planning to do the same. He knocked lightly and Rose, looking younger than her nineteen years without face paint, opened Georgia's door.

"How is she doing?" Slater whispered, peering past her to see Georgia sleeping peacefully.

"Woke up an hour ago, and Cassie gave her more water."

"Fever?" Rebecca asked.

Rose shook her head. "No." She glanced at Georgia over her shoulder. "She's doing real well, considering how bad she looked last night."

"I'm going to sleep before we open this evening. If she takes a turn, wake me," Slater said.

"I will, Mr. Forrester." Rose closed the door with a barely audible click.

Too conscious of Rebecca standing beside him, Slater took a step down the hall, in the direction of his room. "Sleep well, Rebecca."

She reached out and clasped his wrist. "I care about you, too, Slater."

Wondering why she was telling him this now, he nodded warily.

She glanced down. "Did you know Simon and Georgia care for each other?"

"I suspected."

"He thinks he's not good enough for her because she was freeborn and he was a slave."

Slater scowled. "Stupid reason."

"That's what I told him." She met his gaze. "I asked him how he'd feel if Georgia would've died last night. Right now I'm asking myself that same question about you. Would I regret what we might've had?"

Still uncertain where she was headed, Slater said, "There are no guarantees in life. I learned that a long time ago."

"Maybe I'm just starting to learn that now." She took a deep breath, and her cheeks blossomed with color. "I want you to touch me and pleasure me, and hold me while we sleep. And I want to do the same to you, but so many things have happened in the past year." She paused. "I promise to think about what you said."

A rush of tenderness and desire stole through Slater, and he smoothed a hand across a dust-smudged cheek. "That's all I ask, Rebecca."

She leaned into his palm that curved her cheek. "I'm glad I told you my real name."

"Why's that?"

"I like how you say it."

"Rebecca," he whispered, his body growing taut.

Her eyelids fluttered shut, and he felt her tremble. She took a step back, and another, then turned and nearly ran to her room.

It took every ounce of will Slater possessed not to follow her.

Sixteen

AS expected, business was off that night. But then, so was everyone who worked at the Scarlet Garter. The boarded-up windows gave the saloon a closed-in and dreary atmosphere, casting a pall over both customers and employees.

The dancing was more restrained than usual, and Georgia's glaring absence merely another reminder of what had happened the night before. Simon's choice of songs began to reflect the mood, and Slater went over to talk to him in a low voice. As Slater returned to his table, Simon played something more reminiscent of a party than a funeral. It sparked some life into the men, but it didn't last.

As Rebecca moved from table to table to deliver drinks, she overheard the patrons discussing Andrew's death and the recent shooting in low voices. Most were of the mind that it was pure bad luck, while others made wild speculations about someone having it in for the Scarlet Garter. However, nobody seemed to tie what had happened there with Victor Stroman's "bad luck" at the Tin Bucket.

Rebecca's body was sluggish and her mind kept wandering. She'd slept little that afternoon, but it wasn't the throbbing in her cut hand that had kept her awake. Instead, she'd tossed and turned as she considered Slater's proposition. He wanted her. She wanted him. It should've been a simple decision.

It's a sin, and I've already sinned plenty. What's one more?

Daniel was reason enough to work in this sinful place and dress in sinful clothing and associate with sinful people, but what reason besides selfishness did she have to commit adultery?

Her gaze caught Slater's, and her exhaustion disappeared as her senses narrowed to his mesmerizing blue eyes. Heat prickled her skin and she flushed, but it wasn't embarrassment that heated her face. Now that they'd admitted their mutual attraction, it gave the sizzling looks more potency. She took an involuntary step toward him and he looked away, releasing her as surely as if she'd been held in his arms.

"Miss Glory," a man at a nearby table said.

She pasted on a smile and turned to face him, taking his empty beer glass to get a refill. She carried it to the bar, weaving between tables and evading hands as she smiled good-naturedly at the men. Although she still wasn't totally comfortable among the hard-living men, she'd begun to understand them. Most were simple men starved for a woman's company, but considerate enough to back off if asked. There remained a few, however, who didn't take no for an answer and insisted they could show Rebecca a thing or two. She didn't doubt they could, but what they wanted to show her wasn't what she wanted. At least, not with any of them.

"Another beer, Dante," she said to the small man behind the bar.

"As you wish, my dear," he said, picking up the glass and putting it under the tap in a smooth, practiced motion.

As Rebecca waited, her gaze strayed again to Slater, but this time his focus was on his cards and his opponents. Could she do it? Could she accept Slater's offer to share a bed? Her body had no qualms even now, feeling Slater's allure in the crowded room. But her mind remained mired in indecision.

Dante set the filled glass on the bar in front of her. "You look tired, Glory." Concern etched his brow.

She lifted a shoulder in a half shrug. "No more tired than anyone else working tonight." Picking up the glass, she went to deliver it and collect the two bits.

During the time she'd been getting the refill, some men had left, leaving a table littered with empty glasses. Just as she reached for them, someone fired a gun outside on the street. Rebecca's heart missed a beat, then hammered in her chest, and the blood drained from her face. Her knees felt like porridge and she gripped the back of a chair to remain upright. She breathed deeply to dispel her panic. Nobody was shooting into the saloon. Nobody was shouting. Nobody but her had even noticed the gunshot.

A hand touched her shoulder and she jerked away, her eyes wide. Then she recognized Slater's worried face, and she almost collapsed with relief.

"Are you all right?" he asked, his gaze examining her as if he expected to find a wound.

Although trembling, she nodded. "I heard a gunshot and thought. . . ." She forced a weak laugh. "Stupid of me."

He shook his head slowly. "No, it was understandable. Why don't you take the rest of the night off? It won't be long until we close up."

Only half a dozen men remained in the Garter. Cassie was upstairs sitting with Georgia, and Rose and Molly were leaning against the bar, looking bored. Simon had given up trying to enliven the small group and was helping Dante clean up behind the bar.

"If you don't mind," Rebecca said to Slater.

He smiled tenderly. "I wouldn't have suggested it if I minded."

Her answering smile was tremulous but sincere. "Thank you."

She stopped at the bar to drop off dirty glasses. "I'm going upstairs," she told Dante.

"Get some sleep, Glory," the small man said fondly.

"I'll try."

Simon cleared his throat. "I've a mind to go up and check on Georgia."

"We can check on her together," Rebecca said to him.

They ascended the stairs, Simon staying a few steps behind her. When Cassie let them in, Georgia was awake and aware.

"I'm going back downstairs. You going to sit with her tonight?" Cassie asked.

Although exhaustion dragged Rebecca down, it was her turn. She forced a bright smile. "I will."

"Thanks." Cassie slipped out, her dress rustling in her wake.

Rebecca appropriated the chair by Georgia's bed and sighed inwardly, relieved to be off her feet. "You're looking much better."

"It still hurts some, but nothin' like it done," Georgia said. Her gaze flicked to Simon and back to Rebecca. "Did I miss anything tonight?"

"Not a thing," Rebecca assured her. "In fact, it was pretty quiet."

"Can't blame folks for stayin' away."

Rebecca's stomach twisted with remembered terror, but she kept a smile on her face. "Have you eaten anything?"

"Cassie brought me some soup and lots of water." She wrinkled her nose. "Gonna have to pee."

Rebecca didn't know whether to be amused or shocked. She chose neither, but said matter-of-factly, "There's a chamber pot under the bed you can use."

They talked for a few minutes, and when Georgia's eyes began to close, Rebecca sat in silence until her friend's even breathing signaled her slide back into slumber.

"You can go on to your room," Simon said, startling Rebecca. He'd been so quiet she'd forgotten he was there. "I'll stay with her tonight."

Although she wanted to jump at his offer, her conscience wouldn't allow it. "You're tired, too, Simon. And"—she cleared her throat, embarrassed—"what if she needs to relieve herself?"

Simon shrugged. "It ain't like I never took care of sick folks before. Besides, like you said, me and her have some talking to do."

Georgia might be embarrassed to have Simon help her,

but he was right. They needed to talk. Hoping her two friends could work out their differences, Rebecca rose. "Thank you. If you need any help or have any questions, I'm in room three."

Simon nodded. "Goodnight, Miss Glory."

"Goodnight, Simon."

There was only a murmuring of voices downstairs as Rebecca walked to her room. She changed into her nightgown without lighting a lamp and slid between the cool sheets. Though it felt heavenly to lie down, there was a dull ache in her chest. Usually thinking of Daniel made it bearable, but tonight she wanted something more. She wanted Slater.

And she couldn't have him.

SLATER locked the saloon door behind Dante and slumped against it. One lamp lit the saloon, creating deep pockets of grotesque shadows and giving only enough illumination so that he didn't fall over anything on his way to the stairs. For a moment, panic swelled as he imagined the walls closing in on him.

Slater savagely tugged at his tie and unbuttoned his top two shirt buttons. He breathed easier without the constriction around his neck, although the panic still lingered at the edges of his shaky composure. He reached for the better whiskey hidden beneath the bar with his right hand and for a glass with his trembling left one. The glass slipped from his shaking hand but landed upright on the bar, and Slater poured himself a generous shot. He had every intention of downing the burning liquid in a quick swallow, but only sipped it.

Would the fear always be with him, lurking like a thief waiting for the right moment to strike? The cabin where he'd spent the first eleven years of his life had been small, but he'd never felt the strangling panic there. Even as he wondered, he knew the answer . . . and refused to acknowledge it. He refused to believe he'd forever be frightened of bogeymen.

His gaze drifted to the back door and a shiver slithered

down his spine. Andrew's bloody handprints remained on the door, the last thing he'd left behind. Would his killer show up tonight to get from Slater what he hadn't gotten from Andrew?

The town grew silent around him and he continued to stand there listening, waiting. He sipped his Scotch and ignored his left hand's twitching, the only visible evidence of the nightmares that plagued him.

What if the collector came tonight? Dying had lost its ability to frighten him. While in the prison camp, he'd learned there were worse things than death, and Slater had survived them. But had he done so simply to surrender life now?

Rebecca's words resounded in his head. Was he after vengeance for himself or Andrew? Did it make a difference?

"If you're doing it for yourself, you'll take more risks. If you're doing it for Andrew, you'll be more careful because you know he wouldn't want you dying for him."

She was right. Andrew wouldn't want him to die avenging his death. He'd done everything in his power to keep Slater alive ever since Slater was sixteen years old. To throw away what Andrew fought so hard for would only make his mentor angry. And he didn't want a furious Andrew Kearny to meet him in the afterlife.

Slater finished the whiskey and blew out the lamp. Each stair was a challenge as he used the rail to pull himself up. Glancing down the hall at Rebecca's room, he felt an almost desperate ache simply to see her. He walked on the balls of his feet to her room but, embarrassed by his weakness, he paused. When did Slater Forrester start needing a woman for something other than physical release?

When that woman is Rebecca.

Suddenly anxious, he eased her door open . . . and met her startled gaze as she lay in bed.

"I didn't mean to wake you," Slater said, his voice husky.

She sat up, and the moonlight gilded her hair, transforming it to liquid silver. "You didn't. Why are you here?"

He couldn't answer what he didn't understand. "Sorry for bothering you."

"Don't go," she cried out, reaching toward him.

Taking a deep breath to compose himself against the too-tempting vision, he met her eyes. "Why?"

"Because," she whispered, increasing his arousal . . . and frustration.

"That's not good enough." He began to leave again.

"Wait."

Didn't she understand how difficult it was to see her like this and not make love with her?

"If you want me to stay, then you'd better be prepared for the consequences," he warned, his voice a growl.

She met his gaze squarely. "I'm tired but I can't sleep. Every time I close my eyes, I see you. I see you kissing me, touching me." She paused, and her eyes were nearly swallowed in black. "Pleasuring me."

Slater's erection pressed painfully against his trouser buttons. "Damn it, Rebecca. You said you'd made your decision."

"No, I didn't. At least not until this moment." She scooted to the far side of her narrow bed and flipped back the covers. The pale sheets taunted him.

Slater fought the impulse to immediately accept her invitation. "You said it was a sin."

"It is, but it's *my* sin to bear."

"Why?" He couldn't understand what had changed.

She stared at him, her expression sad but resolute. "I'm weak and I'm selfish."

He stepped toward her but stopped shy of touching her, afraid once he started, he wouldn't be able to stop. Clenching his hands, he held them close to his sides. "You're not either of those. Give me another reason."

His voice was so certain, so sure, that Rebecca was robbed of her hard-won calmness. She'd made her decision, why couldn't he simply accept it? Why did he want more? "It's enough."

He shook his head, his face limned in shadows and his eyes glinting like blue steel. "It's not enough."

Moisture gathered on her eyelashes and a tear escaped to roll down her cheek, leaving a silvery trail. "I'm a married woman, Slater. I can't give you anything more even if I wanted to."

Tenderness, more powerful than lust, slammed through him. He sat on the exposed sheets and gathered her in his arms but she remained stiff. He shouldn't want her, a married woman, the type of woman he'd sworn to avoid. But she hadn't tried to deceive him, hadn't lied to him. And what he felt for her was too damned powerful to deny.

"I know, Rebecca. I shouldn't have asked. I'm sorry." He brushed her long hair with his hand, over and over, whispering his apology again and again. Calming. Soothing.

She finally relaxed against him, her face resting on his chest and her arms wound around his waist. He felt the shudder of silent sobs and the damp warmth of her tears through his shirt. He'd never been comfortable around crying women, but he had no intention of leaving Rebecca to lose her sorrow alone. Did she cry for the loss of her husband? Or was it for herself, for the loss of something more valuable—the loss of innocence?

Her sobs trailed away and she brushed ineffectually at his wet shirt.

He captured her hand in his and held it against his chest. "Don't worry about it."

She lifted her head, her eyes glimmering with moisture and her face tear-stained. But the lift of her chin and her direct gaze told him her pride remained. "I'm sorry, Slater. I didn't want to do this."

Slater's gut clenched. "It's all right, Rebecca." He drew in a breath, hoping to cool the desire that flowed through his veins. "I shouldn't have made you decide."

Her eyes widened, but then she smiled and shook her head. "I didn't mean that. I meant crying." She glanced away, her smile disappearing. "I don't like to cry in front of anyone."

Did that mean she never sought comfort from another person? That she kept everything inside until she was alone and could shed her tears in solitude? She'd probably cried herself to sleep often after her husband left. He reined in his fury at the bastard who'd deserted her, even as the selfish part of him thanked him. If her husband hadn't left, Rebecca wouldn't be here.

His hold on her hand changed to a caress. "You don't have to hide from me," he said softly.

Her gaze slid away, and he had an uncomfortable feeling she had another secret. But he wouldn't press her. It was her choice as to how much she shared.

Rebecca shifted, and her thigh pressed against his. The blankets had fallen away and only the thin material of her gown covered her body. His arousal, which had fled in the face of compassion, returned with an indrawn breath.

With her head bowed, Slater pushed the strands of hair that obscured her face behind her ear. He held on to a tendril, rolling the silkiness between his fingertips. Lowering his face, he smelled the flowery scent that followed her, left a trail of sweetness. He could pick out her scent in the saloon, when it was busy, over the stink of men's sweat and stale liquor and sawdust.

He kissed the curve of her ear, flicked his tongue across it, and tasted her unique scent. Following her slender neck, he nibbled and tasted the soft skin, pausing at the indent at the juncture of her neck and shoulder.

She trembled, and he felt the blood pumping beneath her skin, warm and vital. He bit lightly, then soothed it with his tongue, some primal imperative urging him to mark her as his.

Her hard nipples and the dusky skin surrounding them were obvious through her gown's filmy material. Unable to resist, Slater cupped the underside of a plump breast and swept his thumb across the peak.

Rebecca moaned. "Slater." She arched, pressing into his hand.

He treated her other breast to the same, squeezing and rolling the nipple between his thumb and forefinger. "Is this what you wanted, Rebecca? Is this what you thought about when you lay in bed alone?"

"Yes." Her voice was hoarse, barely audible. "You, Slater, you doing this. I wanted you the moment I first saw you, but I didn't know, didn't understand . . . ."

Slater dropped small kisses along her jawline. "Didn't know what?"

"Didn't know what I wanted. Not then."

"But you do now?"

"Yes." She caught his head between her hands and her eyes were fever-bright. "I want you, Slater."

"I told myself you weren't any different from the other saloon women. I told myself that so I wouldn't want you." He chuckled, the sound rough with arousal. "It didn't work."

He slanted his lips across hers, sliding over them, just as he'd imagined when he should've been paying attention to his cards and late at night, alone in his bed. As Slater kissed her, he struggled to remove his jacket but got it only halfway off his arms when it defeated him. Then Rebecca's hands were there, tugging it off and tossing it aside.

She drew away from his mouth. "Let me."

He forced himself to sit still and watch her agile fingers, made less nimble by her haste, unbutton his shirt and remove it, along with the tie. Then her hands were at his pants and those were gone, as well as his boots and socks, added to the growing pile at the foot of the bed.

His erection tented his drawers, and the hot look in Rebecca's eyes as she stared at him made him throb. She hooked her hands in the waistband and tugged them down, leaving him exposed to her.

"What about you?" he asked, almost not recognizing his husky voice. Before she could answer, he knelt in front of her in the middle of the bed.

Also kneeling, Rebecca tried to halt the desperation that shivered through her, that made her want to climb into this man's arms and never come out. He fumbled with the hem of her gown, then jerked it off over her head, flinging it aside. His hungry gaze slid over her, and gooseflesh rose on her arms and legs, pebbled her nipples. The old Rebecca would've been mortified to be so exposed to a man, but the woman she was now knew what she wanted, and what she wanted was Slater. Although he wasn't even touching her, the intensity of his gaze increased the wetness between her thighs. She could smell her own arousal and her face heated, but one look at Slater's erection replaced her embarrassment with overwhelming need.

She laced her hands together behind his head and pulled him down to her breast, no longer shocked by her wantonness. He sucked her nipple into his hot mouth, and she bent over his shoulder as the sensation shot straight to her wet heat. She burrowed her fingers in his thick hair as he switched to her other breast.

"Lie down," he murmured.

She allowed Slater to help her onto her back. He grasped her wrists and raised her hands over her head as he straddled her body. His erection left a trail of dampness across her belly.

His lips brushed the corner of her mouth. "You don't know how often I wanted to drag you up here, away from all those men who stared at you, imagined lying with you." He sprinkled a line of kisses down her throat, her chest, and to her bellybutton, until she felt his hot breath between her thighs, tightening her core. "You're mine, Rebecca. They can't have you."

She whimpered at his possessive tone and gave herself over to him, forgetting everything else.

He released her wrists and cupped her buttocks, then lowered his head to the core of her heat. The moment he touched her with his tongue, Rebecca clamped down on a scream. Her body convulsed and she gripped Slater's shoulders to keep from losing herself in the intensity. He continued to lick her, until the pleasure became too much, almost painful, and her body convulsed with her release.

He lifted his head and shifted up, along her body, until his erection rested at her entrance. Unable to stop herself, she wrapped her fingers around his silky hardness and fitted him into her. She groaned, the aftershocks giving her a sensitivity she'd never known before. She could feel every delicious inch of Slater as he entered her slowly, carefully . . . lovingly.

Rebecca wrapped her legs around him, pulling him in until he could go no further. Slater gazed down at her, his eyes heavy-lidded with passion. Their mouths met and she tasted herself on his lips, the flavor odd but shockingly erotic. One hand settled on her breast while the other was flat on the mattress beside her shoulder.

He drew back, nearly out of her, then thrust back in. Rebecca gasped and the upward spiral started again. She slid her hands up and down his sides, feeling the glide of muscles flex and relax beneath his burning skin. She matched his movements, arching and meeting, drawing back and coming together.

Slater balanced himself on hands flattened on the bed, his belly brushing hers with every thrust and parry. The feel of him on her, around her, inside her was too little and too much. His movements grew more frenzied and his lips possessed hers, his tongue mirroring the motions of his body, and suddenly she shattered once more, her scream captured by his mouth.

He froze, and Rebecca gripped his buttocks as she felt his hot release fill her emptiness. Another wave of pleasure pulsed through her and she floated on the crest, aware of Slater's labored breaths falling into rhythm with her own.

He sagged and his kiss turned gentle, calming rather than inflaming. She welcomed and returned the slow, lazy kiss.

Slater drew away, but a tender smile claimed those same lips that had possessed her. "Rebecca." Her whispered name was filled with a wealth of emotions, too many for her to separate and identify. But it warmed her, lightened her heart, as nothing had done in a very long time.

Slater shifted to lie beside her and propped his head on his hand to gaze down at her. He didn't speak, but played with her hair, pressing it back behind her ears, then drawing the strands forward to drape over her breasts.

She searched for something to say, some words to communicate how wonderful their lovemaking had been, but the only thing that came to mind was the thing she dared not speak aloud.

I love you.

$\mathcal{S}$EVENTEEN

REBECCA awakened to the predawn glow that filtered in her window. A warmth along her back and an arm around her waist, as well as the satisfying ache between her thighs and her relaxed muscles, reminded her of the night spent making love. She turned her head slightly, careful not to wake Slater, and gazed at his sleep-lax face. His dark hair hung across his brow like a boy who'd been playing outside, but morning whiskers that heavily shaded his lower face dispensed with the boyish image.

He shifted slightly, his arm tightening around her, and he pressed his nose closer to her nape. Despite having made love twice overnight, she felt arousal curl anew in her belly. Her breath stammered in her throat and she stopped breathing for seconds to regain her composure. That she desired him was undeniable, but the depth of her emotions haunted her. She hadn't meant to fall in love with him.

While waiting for Daniel to be born, Rebecca had had weeks to contemplate what had gone wrong with Benjamin. She'd determined that she'd fallen for his chivalrous manners. She'd never loved Benjamin; she'd loved how he'd treated her. With Slater, the love was born of her feelings for him, not empty charm or false fawning. She'd seen past Slater's rudeness to the man he was, and had found someone to respect and love. If she'd been as perceptive with Benjamin, she never would have married him.

And her road wouldn't have led her to Oaktree and Slater Forrester.

Her feelings for Slater complicated matters. For months all she'd imagined was finding Benjamin and telling him of his son, then their going back to St. Louis together and getting Daniel out of the orphanage. But how could she live with Benjamin when her heart was filled with Slater?

What would Slater say when he learned she had a son? Cold invaded her. If he wanted only her and not Daniel, there would be nothing to think about, no choice to make. Her child would always be first in her heart.

A tear trickled into her hair. If finding and staying with Benjamin was the only way to get back her son, then that's what she had to do. No sacrifice was too great for Daniel.

A soft knock on the door startled her and she felt Slater come awake beside her.

"Who's there?" Rebecca called out.

"It's Simon, Miss Glory. Georgia wants you."

"We'll be right out," Slater said.

There was a long moment of silence, then Simon spoke again. "All right."

His footsteps receded. Rebecca turned to Slater, not sure if she should be upset. "Why did you let him know you were with me?"

Slater shrugged. "Does it matter? Sooner or later, everyone will know we're sleeping together."

Rebecca worried her lower lip between her teeth, then caught the impact of his words. "We're going to do this again?"

Slater rose, and Rebecca's gaze settled on his dimpled backside and the flexing muscles as he gathered his clothing. "Get dressed, Rebecca."

Although irritated that he didn't answer her question, she didn't want to keep Georgia waiting. In spite of Slater's seeing—and tasting—every inch of her last night, she felt shy dressing in front of him. However, he kept his gaze averted, concentrating on donning his own clothing.

Rebecca pulled on one of her modest dresses and slipped on her shoes. A few strokes of the brush tamed her tangled hair.

Still silent, Slater guided her out of her room into the darkened hallway. Rebecca hurried to Georgia's door, knocked once, and entered. Georgia was glaring at Simon, who had his arms crossed over his massive chest as he stared at her with matching stubbornness.

"What's going on?" Rebecca asked, sitting on the bed beside the injured woman. "Is your wound paining you?"

Georgia, her dark eyes sparking with anger, pointed at Simon. "Get him out of here."

"What—"

"Get him out!"

Rebecca exchanged a look with Slater, who took hold of Simon's arm and urged him out of the room. Once the two men were gone, the tension in the room evaporated, along with Georgia's fury.

"What happened?" Rebecca asked softly. She had a strong hunch that Simon, despite his seeming change of heart, had returned to his original argument.

Georgia folded her arms on the blankets. "He wants me to marry him."

That wasn't what Rebecca had expected to hear. She scrambled to wrap her mind around the odd turn of events. "But isn't that what you wanted?"

Georgia looked at her like she was a toddling child. "I want Simon, but I don't want to get hitched."

Still reeling, Rebecca didn't understand. "But if you both love each other. . . ."

"He didn't say nothing about love. He said that me almost dying got him to thinking. Said if we were married, I wouldn't be working here and I wouldn't have been hurt."

"That means he cares about you. Surely he loves you, too."

Georgia grunted in exasperation. "Means he wants to control me, and I ain't ever going to let a man do that."

"But Simon doesn't seem like that type of man. I'm sure he wouldn't have asked you to marry him if he didn't love you."

"You don't know much about men, do you, Glory?"

Rebecca couldn't hold Georgia's gaze as she shook her head. "No."

Georgia clasped her hand. "Most men are scared of love. They only want one thing from a woman, a hot hole so they can prove they's a big man."

Rebecca gasped at her coarse language. "Georgia!"

"It's true, honey. I've been around long enough to know."

"So you think Simon only wants a . . ." She couldn't finish.

Georgia's expression lost its harshness. "No, I don't, but that's what makes it so hard. He thinks he's doing the right thing by marrying me and wants to be a big man by takin' care of me."

"Is that such a bad thing, to want a man to take care of you?"

"It is if he don't love you."

"So if he said he loved you, you'd marry him?"

Georgia grinned. "Faster'n you could say wedding."

Rebecca was certain Simon loved Georgia, and if she could convince him to tell her . . .

Georgia squeezed her hand. "And he can't have no help from you. He's got to tell me on his own."

Chagrined, Rebecca nodded. "And if he doesn't?"

"Then nothing changes." Although Georgia's voice was flippant, her eyes held sadness.

Rebecca considered telling Simon anyhow, since she didn't promise she wouldn't. However, when she put herself in Georgia's position and thought of Slater, she knew she couldn't interfere. It seemed she and Georgia were in the same position, loving men who couldn't admit to loving them. There was one glaring difference, however. Georgia was free to marry Simon.

"Looks like you and Slater finally stopped dancin' around each other," Georgia said, eyeing Rebecca's neck.

Her hand flew to the bruise and she scrambled to button the remaining buttons of her blouse. "How do you know it was Slater?" she asked, hoping to sound aloof.

Georgia giggled. "It's barely morning, and you two come in here together. It didn't take much to figure out."

Rebecca's face flamed. "It was only one night."

"Whatever you say, Glory." Georgia obviously didn't believe her.

She grimaced, and Rebecca forgot her embarrassment. "Do you need anything?"

"I'll be fine. Just sore, is all." Georgia closed her eyes. "I'm going to rest now."

Rebecca soothed back her friend's hair from her brow. "You do that."

It was only a minute or two before Georgia's steady breathing told Rebecca she'd fallen asleep. She rose, her muscles twinging, and left the room.

Slater straightened from his slouch against the wall. "How is she?"

"Where's Simon?"

"When I tried to find out what was going on, he stomped off. Probably went home." Slater motioned to the door. "Georgia asleep?"

Rebecca crossed her arms and nodded. "Simon asked her to marry him."

Slater's eyes widened in surprise. "I thought she'd be happy."

"If he'd said three words in addition to the proposal, she would be." She met his gaze. "He didn't tell her he loved her."

Confusion lit his features. "He wouldn't have asked her to marry him if he didn't at least care for her."

Rebecca tilted her head to study him. "So you think he doesn't love her?"

"It's not easy for a man to admit it."

"Why?"

Slater seemed taken aback and answered awkwardly, "Men don't like to talk about that kind of thing."

Rebecca considered Benjamin and how often he'd told her he loved her. By saying the words, he'd convinced naive Rebecca he was a lovesick fool. Yet she knew now that he'd only said what she wanted to hear. *She* had been the fool.

"Sometimes a woman needs to hear the words, if only once, and only if he really means them," she said quietly.

Slater placed his crooked finger beneath her chin and raised her head. Her heart thundered in her chest. Was he about to confess his love for her?

"I'll talk to Simon," he said.

Torn between disappointment and relief, Rebecca nodded. "Georgia doesn't want me to talk to him, but she didn't say anything about you not doing it."

"It's still early. We can go back to bed."

The heat in Slater's eyes told her they wouldn't spend their time sleeping. As much as she wanted to, she shook her head. "I should sit with Georgia. I don't want her to wake up alone. She might try to get out of bed."

Slater continued to gaze at her, his eyes becoming more tender than passionate. "That's a good idea. I think I'll see if I can find Simon, then there are some things I should do downstairs. Will you have time to work on the account books today?"

"When Cassie and the other girls get up and take over sitting with Georgia, I'll be down."

He leaned forward and kissed her, his lips butterfly-light against hers. "I'll see you later, then."

Bemused, Rebecca waited until he entered his room to return to Georgia's side.

SLATER rubbed his throbbing brow as he studied the not-so-neat numbers that Andrew had entered into the account books last month, before Rebecca had taken over the task. He was still trying to get an idea of the amount of money that flowed in and out of the Scarlet Garter. The in columns were fairly self-explanatory, but the outgoing categories were more confusing. There were payments to the food tent for the meals served to Garter employees, to the liquor suppliers, to a dressmaker for the women's dancing costumes, to the supplier of wood for the stoves, and the salaries to each of the employees. There were smaller expenditures, too, that only increased Slater's headache.

"Are you trying to memorize it?"

Rebecca's familiar voice brought a smile and indescribable warmth. "No, just understand it."

Carrying a steaming cup of coffee, she sat down beside him. Only yesterday she would've been more reserved, but not after last night. Merely thinking about the way she moaned his name and sought his touch brought a stirring to Slater's groin.

"What's not to understand?" she asked, her coffee-scented breath wafting across him.

"There are hundreds of entries I'm not sure of, and I have to keep track of everything I need to keep the business running."

"Point some out to me."

He picked out one and jabbed it. "What's this?"

Rebecca leaned closer to read the small writing, and the soft fleshiness of her breast pressed against his arm. Her floral scent enticed him to bury his nose in the thick hair at her nape, but he forced himself to focus. If he allowed himself to be distracted, it would be easier the next time, and even easier the next. Pretty soon, nothing would get done because he'd have Rebecca in his bed all day long.

"The sawdust. Every two weeks it's delivered and payment is due upon receipt," she said.

That made sense. It wasn't like Frank went out to find clean sawdust to put on the floor.

"Most of the payments are scheduled ones," Rebecca said. "Whiskey and beer delivery on Tuesdays and Fridays. Wood delivery on Wednesdays. And on Saturdays, it's payday, but if you should forget, I'm sure someone will remind you." Her eyes danced with mischief.

When Rebecca went over things, it seemed so much simpler. No wonder Andrew had disliked taking care of the accounts. "Who writes the drafts?" he asked.

"Andrew did, so I guess it's you who gets to do it now."

"I want you to be able to sign drafts for the Garter, too, just in case I'm not around when a delivery is made."

"Are you sure? I've only been here three weeks, less time than anyone else."

Although she was the newest employee, she was the only other person who understood the business. If something happened to him, he wanted to ensure that the Garter would continue under someone he trusted. And he did trust Rebecca, far more than time warranted, and it wasn't because they shared a bed. Sex didn't forge trust; gut instinct and getting to know a person did.

"I trust you, Rebecca."

She lowered her head. "Thank you. That means more than you know. But I won't be staying much longer. I took the job here only to earn money to continue my search for my husband."

He flinched, as if a knife had sliced him, and he covered his hurt with anger. "He left you, Rebecca. Why do you want to find him?"

"As long as I'm married to him, I'm tied to him."

"Only if you want to be." She closed her eyes, and he immediately felt sorry for his attack. He continued in a milder voice. "You're not the only woman on the frontier who's either been abandoned by her husband or ran away from him. They don't worry about being tied to their husbands."

Her eyes flashed with impatience. "Maybe I have a little more integrity than they do." She clutched his arm with a cold hand. "If I had a choice, I'd stay here with you, Slater. But I don't."

He opened his mouth to argue, but saw the anguish in her eyes. For whatever reason, she didn't believe she had a choice. "What will you do after you find him?"

She looked away. "Go back to St. Louis."

Slater slammed his fist on the table, making her jump, but he didn't care. The thought of her in another man's—even her husband's—arms brought a searing bolt of jealousy. "Damn it, Rebecca, he left you. Get a divorce."

She shivered. Divorce was another black mark among society's elite, and she'd obviously been steeped in society's values. "It's not that easy," she said. "It costs money."

"I've got money."

She brought her head up sharply, her eyes wide. "You'd do that for me?"

Her incredulous question forced Slater to sit back and think about his impetuous offer. Would he be willing to pay for a divorce for her? It wasn't that he didn't have the money, but it was something he'd never even considered suggesting. However, he'd never cared for another woman as he did Rebecca. He met her hopeful expression. "If you were serious about divorcing him and starting over, I'd give you the money."

Her eyes filled with moisture and she blinked it back. "Thank you," she said in a husky voice. She cleared her throat. "I'll think about it."

"How long will you look for him?"

"As long as it takes."

Irritation spiked in Slater again. "Until you're killed in some saloon in the middle of nowhere?"

She glared at him, her own temper rising. "It's my life."

The thought of her dying alone in some godforsaken town chilled Slater. There was a reason he didn't allow himself to get too close to anyone—losing them hurt too damned much.

Beside him, Rebecca inhaled deeply and let her breath out slowly. "Did you talk to Simon this morning?"

It was obvious she didn't want to talk about her husband anymore.

"I couldn't find him. I went to his room, but he wasn't there. Have you talked to Georgia again?"

She grimaced and shook her head. "She's got her mind made up."

"Maybe we should just stay out of the middle," Slater said after a few moments. "Let them work it out."

Rebecca slumped. "You're probably right, but they're both so stubborn."

Slater bit the inside of his cheek to keep from commenting on Rebecca's own obstinacy.

The unmistakable creak of the back door alerted him to someone entering. He hadn't heard anyone come downstairs and go outside to use the necessary, but maybe he'd missed it while he'd been arguing with Rebecca.

He stood to check it out but was halted by a stranger filling the doorway. The man smiled coldly. "Now isn't this cozy? The new owner with his woman."

Slater felt Rebecca stiffen beside him and he held out his hand to her. She must have understood, because she remained silent.

"Who are you?" Slater asked, although he already knew the answer.

"Names aren't important. I'm here to continue a business arrangement I had with the late owner."

"What arrangement is that?" Slater asked, keeping his voice calm and steady.

"An insurance policy. The first month's payment is due."

"Andrew never mentioned anything about insurance," Slater lied. He hoped Rebecca had the ability to maintain a poker face.

The mustached man shrugged. "It was a recent transaction."

Slater's chest tightened as he struggled to restrain his fury. "As the new owner, I'm going to turn down the insurance."

"That wouldn't be a good idea." The man hooked his thumbs in his gun belt. "You don't want another 'accident' like befell you a couple nights ago, do you?"

"Are you threatening me?"

"I'm just pointing out one of the advantages of my company's policy." The gunman's cold gaze settled on Rebecca. "It would be a shame if she was killed by some accident."

Fear coupled with anger, and Slater's left hand began to tremble. He closed it into a fist to hide its shaking. "The sheriff might be interested in your so-called insurance policy."

The man laughed. "Go ahead. Tell him."

It was as Slater suspected—Sheriff Ryder was paid to look the other way.

The dangerous-looking man's expression hardened. "Don't be stupid like the former owner. Just pay, and nothing will change."

The man as much as admitted to killing Andrew, but Slater needed more. He wanted the person behind the racket. "If I decide to do this, how much will I owe?"

"A fancy place like this can easily afford a hundred dollars."

"That's robbery."

"That's business."

The gunman stepped closer to Rebecca, and Slater tensed. Although he wanted the man behind Andrew's death, he wouldn't sacrifice Rebecca. The man lifted his hand as if to touch her hair and she jerked away from him, equal parts fear and anger in her face.

"Your business is with me, not her," Slater said, putting himself between the collector and Rebecca.

"I'll be back for the money two nights from now. If you don't have it . . ." His meaning was clear.

After a deliberate and lingering look at Rebecca, he strode out. The back door creaked open, then shut behind him.

"He'll do it, too," Rebecca said quietly.

Slater didn't pretend to misunderstand. "He won't hurt you as long as I'm alive."

Her eyes sparked. "Which won't be long if you don't intend to pay him."

Slater clenched his teeth. "And if I pay him, he'll just continue extorting money. It's robbery, plain and simple."

"And you're going to stop him all by yourself?" Rebecca jumped to her feet. "The sheriff won't do anything to help. Do you think the other saloon owners will risk their lives to help you?"

"I have to convince them."

"How? These people killed Andrew, and they could've killed Georgia. They don't care who dies, as long as they get their money." Rebecca was practically yelling.

Slater grabbed her arms and shook her. "Damn it, Rebecca, I won't let them continue terrorizing the town. It has to be stopped."

"Why does it have to be you?"

"Because no one else will stop them."

Her wrath visibly drained away, leaving her limp in his arms. "I don't want to lose you," she whispered in a tear-roughened voice.

His throat constricted and he pulled her against his chest, wrapping his arms around her. Resting his cheek on the crown of her head, he said softly, "I have to do this, Rebecca. I can't let them hurt anyone else."

Especially not you.

He didn't understand it himself, except that it went against everything he believed to let one person hold another's life or death in his hands. It was wrong. And he wasn't going to accept it, even if it meant taking them on alone.

EIGHTEEN

THE sun shined down upon Rebecca as she walked beside Slater, but its warmth couldn't penetrate the chill that settled deep in her bones. She tugged her shawl more snugly about her shoulders and concentrated on the comforting feel of Slater's hand at her waist.

In the end, he decided to pay the extortion money, which would give him more time to determine the person in charge. But even when Slater discovered who it was—and Rebecca had no doubt he would—she feared he'd be able to do little against him. With men like the one who'd visited them earlier that morning surrounding the leader, Slater would be committing suicide by trying to arrest him.

In St. Louis, Rebecca had taken law enforcement and justice for granted, not once imagining places like Oaktree, where the law was corrupt and criminals literally got away with murder, existed. The possibility she might end up in such a place had never occurred to her. All her focus had been on finding Benjamin and getting her child back. Now that she was entangled in such a lawless place, she didn't know what to do. If she hadn't fallen in love with Slater, the answer would've been easy—leave Oaktree and continue her search. She had forty-one dollars hidden in her room, enough to take her away from this place. But it wasn't that simple anymore.

They arrived at the bank and Slater stopped her. She looked up into his somber blue eyes questioningly.

"Are you sure you want to do this?" he asked.

Rebecca managed a shaky smile. "No, but I will."

His expression became even graver. "If you want to leave town now, I wouldn't blame you. Hell, it'd be safer if you did."

She smiled, but there was no joy in it. "Will you leave with me?"

His lips turned downward. "I can't."

She shrugged. "Then I can't leave either, not knowing what'll happen to you."

"I thought you wanted to find your husband."

Rebecca flinched. The words and tone were cruel and she opened her mouth to respond in kind, but abruptly closed it at the veiled concern in his eyes. He was intentionally trying to anger her. "It won't work, Slater. I'm not leaving. Not yet."

He huffed in exasperation. "I could fire you."

"If you were going to do that, you would've done it before we came here." She motioned to the bank entrance. "Let's get this over with. I have work to do."

Although she knew he was annoyed, she also sensed his relief. He didn't want her to leave, but his protective streak wouldn't let him admit it.

Someone came out of the bank and Rebecca slipped inside, followed by Slater. It took only a few minutes for them to be seated in the manager's office. Slater showed him Andrew's will and explained what he wanted done. Thirty minutes later, the papers were all signed and Rebecca was listed as co-signer for Scarlet Garter drafts.

When they came out of the bank, Slater insisted on taking her to the restaurant where they'd eaten before. Rebecca was relieved that his former paramour Delilah was nowhere in sight this time, and she relaxed during the meal. She conversed with Slater, keeping the subject away from the unpleasantries they faced. However, the minute they returned to the Scarlet Garter, Rebecca felt apprehension settle upon her once more.

Slater retrieved the account books and handed them to her in the office. "Work in here this afternoon," he said.

"Where will you be?"

"I'm going to talk with some of the other saloon owners again and see if I can learn anything new."

A chill swept through Rebecca, but she knew it was useless to argue. "I'll see you later tonight, then."

He cupped the side of her face and she leaned into his palm. The iciness was replaced by a heated yearning.

"I'll be back." His gaze caressed her, then he lowered his head and kissed her.

It was meant to be a gentle kiss, but Rebecca didn't want gentle. She wanted the brand of his lips on hers, the promise of his safe return and the giving of her own promise to be here, waiting for him. Wrapping her hands around the back of his neck, she drew him closer, and the kiss turned possessive. Tongues dueled and the hunger, never far from the surface, erupted. Shuddering with the intensity of her desire, she checked to ensure the office door was closed, then reason deserted her.

She grappled with Slater's shirt buttons, releasing only half of them before pressing her hands inside, spreading her fingers over his smooth chest. Heat radiated from his skin, fueling the fire that raged between her thighs. Frantic, she arched against him.

"Rebecca," he said, his low voice rolling across her.

"Now, Slater. I need you now."

He groaned and laid her back on the desk, his hands cupping the back of her head, ensuring she didn't bump it against the surface in her haste. His mouth followed hers. Gathering her cumbersome skirt and petticoat, he shoved them upward, liberating her shapely legs. She wrapped them around his hips and he could smell her musk, hot and ripe. His erection strained against his buttons, and using only one hand, he tried to free himself. His impatience made him clumsy.

"Let me," Rebecca said between furious kisses.

She sat up and with a few flicks of her fingers, his pants were open. Rebecca's soft hand grazed his hardness and he threw back his head, almost losing control with that single touch. She curled her fingers around him.

"No," he ground out, barely holding back. He wanted to be inside her.

He forced her to lie back on the desk again and she went willingly, desperately, winding her legs around him and drawing him close. Awkwardly, he found the opening in her drawers and pressed forward. Staring down into Rebecca's face, he watched her mouth open in a soundless cry as he sank into her. She was wet, hot, and more than ready for him.

"Slater!" Yearning, lust, and desire jumbled in his whispered name.

Slater lost whatever restraint he'd managed to cling to. He thrust into her and withdrew, watching her, taking masculine satisfaction in the ecstasy and desperate need in her beautiful face. She lifted her hips, meeting him with each stroke. He couldn't last, not with Rebecca gasping his name between mewls of pleasure. Angling his thrusts, he felt Rebecca's walls tighten around him. Another stroke, and she stiffened as she cried out. She pulsed around him and his release followed, so powerful that it bordered on pain.

He sank down on her, and even through the barrier of clothing, felt her heart beat wildly against him. Her panting breaths matched his as they struggled to gather air into starved lungs.

Her arms came around his back, held him as he slipped free of her. "That was . . ." Rebecca shook her head, unable to articulate her emotions.

Slater raised his head and smiled gently. "It was." He brushed back a strand of hair from her damp brow.

A tiny voice wanted him to ask her if it had been that perfect with her husband, but he couldn't squeeze the words out of his suddenly aching throat. It wasn't any of his business, yet he hated that the man had seen her in the throes of passion, too. Slater didn't want to share her, and it burned him to know that another man had a legal right to her.

Rebecca swept her fingers across his brow. "Stop thinking," she said softly.

He glanced away. "I wish I could."

He felt the distance spring up between them, even though he still lay upon her. Disgusted and angered by his preoccupation, Slater rose. He tucked himself into his trousers and gave his attention to buttoning his pants and shirt as Rebecca stood and shook down her skirts.

Finally, he raised his head and met her steady gaze. "I have to go."

"I know." She smoothed the front of his shirt. "Be careful."

Two days ago Slater would've let her warning roll off him, but now he had more to lose. She'd become too important to him too quickly. No other woman had burrowed under his skin like Rebecca. And it was just his luck she was bound to another.

"I will," Slater said. He tucked a strand of light golden hair behind her ear. "I'll see you later."

She nodded and crossed her arms, the self-protective gesture more telling than words.

Before he lost his resolve, he left the office. He made a stop in his room, strapping on his shoulder holster and checking his revolver before slipping it into the holster. He pulled on a coat, covering the weapon from casual onlookers. Donning his black wide-brimmed hat, he walked into the hallway.

Molly, wearing a nearly transparent camisole and drawers, exited her room at the same moment. He touched his hat brim with his thumb and forefinger. "Afternoon, Molly."

She propped a hand on her hip and thrust out her breasts. The tan surrounding her hard nipples was obvious beneath the filmy material but he barely noticed.

"You're up early, Slater," she said.

He gave her a halfhearted smile. "It's after two o'clock. Besides, I have more to do now that I own the Garter."

She sauntered toward him, swinging her hips, and stepped up to him. Fingering his jacket lapels, she said, "Even the boss has to take time off for a little . . . diversion."

After his ardent lovemaking with Rebecca, Molly's seductive pose and throaty tone did nothing but annoy him. He grasped her wrists and lowered her hands. "I wasn't interested before, and I'm not interested now, so don't play games with me, Molly."

"Andrew liked my games."

"I'm not Andrew." He eyed her. "Besides, you only warmed his bed for one night. He got tired of your games, too."

Her eyes narrowed and anger flickered in them. "She's a little inexperienced for your tastes, isn't she?"

Slater feigned ignorance. "Who?"

"Glory."

Slater sighed and rubbed his brow. "Are you unhappy working here, Molly?"

She blinked, obviously startled by his unexpected question. "I like it well enough."

"I'm glad. You'd be hard to replace."

Molly preened under the compliment and Slater was reminded that most saloon women were like insecure young girls. Maybe that was why Rebecca attracted him so strongly—she was intelligent and talented and didn't need a man's constant attention. And she had the ability to arouse him faster than any other woman.

"Forget about you and me, Molly. It's not going to happen," Slater said gently.

Molly took a deep breath, then exhaled noisily, her shoulders slumping. "You can't blame a woman for trying."

Slater chuckled, relieved to see the return of her dry humor. "No, you can't." He paused. "How's Georgia?"

Molly shrugged. "I was just getting ready to take over for Cassie."

Slater smiled in sincere gratitude. "I appreciate what you and the other women are doing for her."

Molly shrugged, but her cheeks colored slightly. "She's our friend."

Molly's heart was in the right place, despite her cat-in-heat behavior. "I've got to go," he said. "If you or any of the others need anything, check with Re—Glory. She's working on the books in the office."

Only a tinge of annoyance flashed across Molly's face. "All right."

Slater descended the stairs and headed out. Hoping his old Pinkerton investigative skills remained, he entered the first saloon.

BY nightfall, Slater had visited many of the drinking and gambling establishments in Oaktree. Out of the twelve owners he'd spoken to, only five had admitted to paying "insurance." Slater's gambling skills at reading people, combined with his Pinkerton experience, told him the seven others were too scared to talk. All of them had offered him condolences for Andrew's death, but they didn't ask any questions, as if they knew who had killed him and why. And Slater didn't doubt they linked his death to the bogus insurance scheme.

Slater entered the Brass Balls, where lit lanterns hung from wooden crosspieces that framed the canvas. He strode to the bar. "I'd like to talk to the owner."

The bartender studied him a moment. "You were in the other night. You own the Scarlet Garter."

"That's right."

"Mr. Gavin ain't here. Went to Junction City to pick up some things." The man ran a hand over his sandy, thinning hair. "Should be back in a day or two."

Slater sighed. "Maybe you can help me."

"What're you lookin' for?"

"Information. I'm trying to find out who killed Andrew Kearny, the original owner of the Garter."

"Heard it was thieves."

"Nothing was taken. I think he was murdered because he figured out who was behind an extortion operation that's started up in town."

"A what?"

"Do you know if your boss, Gavin, paid out a fairly large sum of money to anyone in the past couple of weeks?"

"I dunno. He takes care of the money. I just serve drinks."

Slater restrained an impatient sigh. "Have you seen a man

around here, either late at night or early in the morning, talking to Gavin?"

"Lots of men talk to him."

"This one wears a two-gun rig, has a dark mustache, is a little shorter than me, but heavier."

The bartender thought for a moment. "Not that I can recall. But then, I don't see everyone who comes and goes in here." He shrugged. "You'll have to ask Mr. Gavin."

Resigned, Slater nodded. "I'll stop back in a couple of days, then. Thanks."

The bartender's answers were basically the same ones he'd received from the saloon owners. Sighing, he continued to the next place. He steeled himself in case he spotted Delilah and stepped into the Black Bull. At one table, four men were playing a low-stakes game of poker. Three men stood by the bar, drinking whiskey and beer. At a front table John Langley played solitaire as Delilah watched with a bored expression. However, she lit up the moment she saw Slater and jumped up to launch herself into his arms.

"I knew you wouldn't be able to stay away," she exclaimed.

Slater pried her thin arms from around his neck. "I'm not here to see you, Delilah." He gestured with his chin toward Langley. "I came to talk to your boss."

With a cool smile on his lips, Langley motioned for Slater to take a seat. Delilah started to join him, but Langley said, "Get us some coffee, darlin'."

She scowled but didn't argue and left them alone.

"So what can I do for you, Forrester?" Langley asked.

Slater tossed his hat on the table and dragged a hand through his hair. "I'm trying to find out who killed Andrew. You have any ideas?"

The man's hawk features didn't change. "Probably the same people who are demanding money for insurance."

Surprised that Langley didn't skirt the issue like everyone else, Slater said, "That's what I figured, too. Problem is, I had a visit from the bill collector this morning, but I don't know who's pulling his strings." He described the man who'd threatened him.

Langley nodded. "That's the same man who came here last

week, demanding money. I considered not paying, but after what happened to Andrew, I figured a few dollars wasn't worth dying for."

"How much is a few dollars?"

Langley's shoulders rose and fell beneath his black suit. "Thirty a week. A bit steep, but it's better than being murdered in an alley."

Slater's fingernails dug into his palms. "Andrew was trying to stop them. That would've helped everyone."

Langley's mouth pressed into a thin line. "I know he was your friend, but he was a fool. And you're a fool, too, if you plan on going up against them." He paused, his eyes hooded. "I heard about the shooting up of your place the other night, how one of your girls was hurt. Tell me, Forrester, is it worth it?"

Slater studied the man. Was Langley behind the racket? If so, he was covering his own ass by pretending to pay, too. He surveyed the saloon, which was slightly smaller than the Scarlet Garter. How did Langley afford it? Yet the insurance problems had started up only a month ago, and Langley had arrived in town around the same time as Andrew. Of course, it would make sense to wait until the town had enough saloons to make it a profitable arrangement.

"For your information, I'm going to pay, too," Slater said. "You're right about lives being more valuable than some money."

If Langley was involved, maybe he'd think Slater was surrendering to the extortionists. However, that was the last thing Slater intended to do.

Delilah returned with two mugs of coffee and set one by each man, sloshing liquid onto the table. "Here's your coffee," she said ungraciously. "You want anything else, your majesty?"

Slater hid a grin behind his hand.

Langley grabbed Delilah around the waist and hauled her onto his lap. "Only you, darlin'."

She giggled and Slater rolled his eyes, wondering what in hell he'd seen in her that he'd taken her to bed. After taking one sip of the charred coffee, he rose. "I'd best get going."

"No need to hurry off. We could play a game of blackjack to see who gets Delilah tonight," Langley said, a sneer on his face.

Knowing who'd be in his bed tonight, Slater shook his head. "Not interested."

Delilah pouted, but Slater knew she'd end up with Langley and not even miss him. Strange how he used to think one night with a woman was enough. But Rebecca was in his blood, with her teasing smile, her twinkling eyes, and her alluring mix of experience and innocence. His groin stirred as he remembered their impromptu lovemaking in the office.

He still had a few saloons to visit and he'd promised Rebecca he'd return before closing. The thought of her waiting for him was incentive enough to increase his pace.

NINETEEN

EVERY time the Scarlet Garter's door opened, Rebecca's gaze flew to the entrance, and every time she was disappointed when it wasn't Slater's familiar figure. She reminded herself that instead of Slater, she should be watching for Benjamin. She tried to picture her husband, but his features blurred in her memory and she was shocked to discover she didn't care. But then she thought of Daniel with his little pug nose, bright brown eyes, and puckered mouth, and guilt seized her conscience. If only she could have both Daniel and Slater.

With an artificial smile in place, she carried two beers to a table and took the men's money. Glancing at Simon, she caught his eye and he nodded. It was time to sing again. Absently sweeping back her hair, she joined him beside the piano. His large but amazingly limber fingers flew over the keys in a familiar tune and Rebecca's voice picked up the rollicking chorus. Cassie, Rose, and Molly were quickly tugged out to dance, and their red garters flashed as they were spun around.

Rebecca swayed to the tune and lost herself in the piano's notes and her own fluid voice. She concentrated on the set of songs she and Simon performed, thinking only of the music as it flowed through her.

In the middle of a ballad, Slater descended the stairs. His face was freshly shaven and a dark suit had taken the place of his earlier casual trousers and shirt. Her voice faltered slightly and she had to look away to hold the melody. Although she kept her gaze on the crowd, she was aware of Slater's eyes upon her. She focused on the verse, which was about a young man saying good-bye to his sweetheart before leaving to fight in the war. His promise of returning, building a home, and raising a family was never fulfilled as he fell to cannon fire on the battleground.

She ended the song with a slowly fading voice, and silence held in the saloon for long seconds. A smattering of applause followed, which Simon overwhelmed as he launched into the lively "Camptown Races." Rebecca grinned with pleasure as she flung out the lyrics. The somber atmosphere created by the previous song disappeared. Rose, Molly, and Cassie were once again twirled onto the saloon's open floor to dance with abandon. Men clapped and shouted.

Rebecca risked a glance at Slater and warm approval glowed in his eyes. His crooked smile arrowed straight to her chest and settled there. She finished the song with a flourish and moved to the bar amid loud hoots and hollers. Dante handed her a small towel and she dabbed her perspiring brow. As she did so, men came up to buy her a special, which wasn't uncommon after she finished singing. She accepted the drinks with practiced courtesy, but couldn't help casting glances at Slater, who was at the other end of the bar. However, his attention was now on Bill Chambers, who'd probably been waiting for Slater to sit down at his regular table.

When she finished her last drink, she returned to circulating among the customers, retrieving refills and bantering with the rough men. Nobody attempted to grab her derriere or "accidentally" brush her breasts tonight, which both surprised and pleased her. Once she'd gotten past her sense of outrage, she actually liked her work, especially during nights like this.

Finally, the saloon emptied and Slater locked the front door. Everyone fell into the routine cleanup that followed a typical Friday night. Rebecca followed the other women up the stairs, but her gaze caught Slater's. There was only coolness in his eyes and she looked away, troubled. Where had the tender warmth gone?

The only time Rebecca had spoken with Slater that evening was when she'd gotten him a cup of coffee while he played poker. She thought his eyes had softened slightly when their gazes met, but though she loved him, she hadn't yet learned how to read his nuances.

Had she been too forward in the office?

Exhausted by the events of the past week, she didn't try to puzzle out their relationship. Instead, she stopped at Georgia's room and knocked softly, not wanting to wake her friend if she was sleeping.

"Come in."

Rebecca opened the door and stepped inside. A lamp glowed dimly on the nightstand, illuminating Georgia's dark complexion and reflecting in her brown eyes. She'd insisted that she was better and no one needed to sit with her that night.

"Hello, Georgia," Rebecca said, pleased to see her friend looking so well.

Georgia patted the side of the bed. "Sit down, Glory, and talk to me." She rolled her eyes. "I'm goin' crazy just lying here with nothing to do."

"You're supposed to be healing," Rebecca reprimanded gently.

Georgia made a face. "You sound just like the doctor who comes by. Rest, rest, rest. That's all he says."

Rebecca lowered herself to the edge of the mattress. "Smart man. You ought to listen to him."

"You ain't the one tied to this bed."

Rebecca chuckled. "If you can grumble this much, you're obviously feeling better."

Georgia smiled sheepishly. "How was business tonight?"

"Back to the usual crowd. The shooting didn't stop them for long," Rebecca said dryly.

"That's because they all knew you'd be singin'. All them big, strong men gettin' weepy when you sing those sad songs. You even had me teary-eyed up here."

"Sorry," Rebecca said without remorse. "Crying's good for a person, and sometimes they just need a little push to get the tears going."

Georgia snorted. "All it does is ruin the paint on my face."

"Luckily most of those men don't wear face paint."

Georgia giggled. "That's the truth of it." She sobered and glanced away. "Simon sounded mighty good on the piano."

"Have you seen him today?"

"No."

Slater had said he was going to talk with him. She wondered if he'd done so. "Men are stubborn fools," Rebecca said. "Once they get something in their heads, dynamite can't shake it loose."

"I thought Simon was different."

Rebecca laid her hand on Georgia's. "He'll come around. You just wait and see."

She could tell Georgia wasn't convinced, but Rebecca didn't know what else she could say or do without outright lying.

"So, tell me about you and Slater," Georgia said, brightening.

Rebecca glanced away, uncertain how to explain. "He's a good man, gentle, kind, thoughtful."

Georgia rolled her eyes. "But how is he in bed?"

Rebecca's face flamed.

"Did he make you scream?"

"Georgia!"

"Oooh, he does." Georgia smiled smugly. "I knew he'd know how to please a woman."

Despite herself, Rebecca asked, "And how did you know that?"

"Watchin' his hands when he plays cards. He strokes them cards like they was a woman's soft breast." Georgia lowered her voice and her eyes twinkled. "Did he touch you in that secret place?"

Recalling the previous night, Rebecca felt a twitch between her thighs. "That's none of your business," she said primly. She stood and tucked Georgia's blankets around her. "Is there anything you need?"

"Yes, but he won't come up here."

"I'm sorry," Rebecca said softly, wishing she could make everything right between her two friends. But then, she couldn't even straighten out her own life. How did she expect to help others? "If you need anything, just holler. Someone will hear you."

"As long as no one else is hollering." Georgia's mischievous grin followed an embarrassed Rebecca out of the room.

Rebecca stood in the hallway, gazing at Slater's door. Did he plan to come to her room again? Or did he expect her to be in his room? Or maybe he didn't want her at all. Angry at herself for doubting, she went to her room and changed into her gown and robe. Cracking open the door, she peered down the hall; nobody was in sight. On bare feet, she scurried to Slater's room and let herself in. The door closed with a soft *snick* and Rebecca leaned against it to catch her breath.

She looked around his room and wasn't surprised to find it neat and tidy. He struck her as the type of man who didn't like messy, whether it was his appearance, his room, or his affairs. Curious, she walked around the room. A dozen books were piled on the nightstand and she examined them. He hadn't been lying when he'd told her he enjoyed reading.

She opened the armoire. In it were three suits, five white shirts, some vests, and two pairs of plain trousers and three everyday shirts. A pair of scuffed brown boots and a shiny pair of black ones sat on its floor. She drew out one of the suits and ran her fingers along the lapel. By the cut and fabric of the suits, none were more than a year or two old.

The dresser dared her to search its drawers, but Rebecca couldn't bring herself to invade his privacy any further. She leaned over and smoothed the quilt across his bed, and her body began to hum.

Turning away, she caught her reflection in the dresser's

mirror. Rebecca stared at the woman who peered back at her. She touched her mouth and the stranger did the same. Her feet carried her to the dresser and she reached out, pressing her fingertips against the image in the mirror. It was her, yet it wasn't the her she'd been one year ago, not even a month ago.

Suddenly the door opened and she turned her head. Slater froze in the doorway, then relaxed when he recognized her. He closed the door. "I didn't know if you'd come."

Her heart beat a harsh staccato. "I didn't know if you still wanted me."

He studied her as he studied his poker opponents. "After what we did in the office, you didn't know?"

She flushed. "I'm sorry. I've never had an affair before."

"Neither have I, at least knowingly," he said dryly. "Do you regret it?"

Rebecca turned back to her reflection and the woman was perhaps a little more familiar. "I thought I might. But I don't."

"I'm glad." Slater came up behind her, turned her, and angled her face between his palms to kiss her.

Rebecca sighed into his mouth and didn't look in the mirror again.

SLATER gathered Rebecca close in his mussed bed and she laid her head on his shoulder, one warm hand splayed across his chest. He teased a strand of her light golden hair between his fingers.

"Did you find out anything?" she asked, her voice low and intimate.

He sighed, not wanting to discuss the troubles after making love, but she deserved to know. "Nothing new. I think most, if not all, the saloon owners are paying."

She raised her head, laid a hand on his shoulder and settled her chin on it so she could see him. "If that's the case then the person behind it isn't one of the owners."

He brushed the cascading hair back from her face, then ran his fingertips down her spine. "Not necessarily. He might be pretending to pay so suspicion doesn't fall on him."

A furrow appeared between her eyebrows and he tried to erase it with a gentle finger. It remained.

"What does your intuition tell you?" she asked.

He couldn't resist a smile. "Intuition?"

"What do you call it?"

"Gut feeling." He shrugged, his amusement fading. "Remember John Langley?"

The little crease deepened between her brows, and even in the dim light he saw her cheeks pinken. "He was at the restaurant with your friend Delilah."

Slater couldn't resist a thrill of satisfaction at the jealousy in her tone, but he didn't tease her. "He owns the Black Bull. It's the second biggest gaming and drinking establishment in town."

She nodded. "I've seen it. It's a wood structure like the Garter. There aren't many on this side of Oaktree."

"Not yet. Give it another year and most of the places will be wood, not canvas." He absently played with her hair and a tendril curled across his knuckles, as if it were alive. "If he's behind it, it would explain how he can afford such a nice place."

"But if he gets so much business, why would he risk losing it by doing something illegal?"

"Greed. Some people never have enough."

She gazed down at him. "I'd be happy to have enough money to go back to St. Louis."

Pain angled through Slater, surprising him at its fierceness. "What about finding your husband?"

She turned her head to gaze out the window. "I don't love him. I don't know if I ever really did. But I have to go back to St. Louis." She took a deep breath, her breasts pressing more firmly against his side, and she looked at him. "There's someone there waiting for me."

Her voice trembled, which told Slater this person in St. Louis was even more important than her husband. More important than him.

"Who?" He wasn't certain he wanted to hear the answer.

She shook her head and rested her forehead on his shoulder, hiding her expression.

Frustrated and confused, Slater smoothed his hand up and down her side, feeling the indent of her waist and the flare of her hips. He also felt small lines around her waist, marks that he'd briefly noticed while they'd made love. A memory tickled his consciousness and he recalled where he'd seen those marks before—on another woman he'd taken to his bed years ago. Recognition punched the air from his lungs.

"You have a child," he said, his voice barely above a whisper.

She stiffened in his arms, and although she didn't confirm or deny it, he knew he'd guessed correctly.

He sat up, drawing her with him, and lifted her chin so he could peer into her face. "Why didn't you tell me?"

"Would it have made a difference?" she asked, a hint of defiance in her tone.

He thought about that a moment and shook his head. "No, it wouldn't have changed what happened between us."

"Then why should I have told you?"

Slater considered his own childhood, his fond memories of his mother, father, and brothers, then how everything had been lost. Basically sold into child slavery, Slater knew that an orphan didn't have any voice in what happened to him or her. But Rebecca's child wasn't an orphan. Not yet.

"Is it a boy or a girl?" Slater asked.

Her features softened. "Boy. Daniel. He's only six months old, Slater. I had to leave him. I couldn't afford a proper place to raise him. I thought if I could find Benjamin, we could go back together and get him out of the children's home."

Fury filled Slater. "I can't believe a man would abandon his own son."

Her lashes grazed her cheeks as she closed her eyes. "Benjamin doesn't know about him," she said hoarsely. "I didn't realize I was with child until after he left."

Slater's stomach churned. "That's why you have to find him and why you won't divorce him."

"I don't have a choice."

"Yes, you do. I can give you the money to go back to St. Louis."

"What good would that do? I still don't have any way of providing for him. Of course, with my recent work experience, I could probably find a job in a saloon back there." She laughed, a caustic sound. "Just another thing I never imagined I'd do—raise my child in a saloon."

"At least he'd have his mother," Slater said, his tone sharper than he'd intended.

However, Rebecca didn't seem irritated, only resigned. "I may yet have to do that if I can't find Benjamin." She snuggled down beside him, her head nestled beneath his chin. "How did things get so messed up, Slater?"

A lump filled his throat and he wrapped both arms around her, holding her close. He kissed her crown gently because he didn't have an answer to her question.

He held her as he considered her predicament. He could get used to having her with him every night, but the thought of marrying her and raising a child scared the hell out of him. He'd made his decision years ago that he'd never get hitched, and he sure as hell didn't have any plans to be a father.

But his quandary was a moot point. Rebecca was a married woman who might never find her husband, so she'd never be more than his mistress. However, her child was in St. Louis and she would return to him. As much as her leaving would hurt him, he would never try to come between a mother and her child. If finding her husband was what she needed to get her son back, then Slater wouldn't stop her. She deserved the chance to regain her family.

"Rebecca," he said softly, knowing she was still awake.

"Hmmm?"

"I might be able to help you find your husband." He could barely squeeze the words out.

Guarded excitement made her tense. "How?"

"I have a friend at the Pinkerton Agency. If I ask him to find your husband, he'd try."

"I don't have any money—"

"You wouldn't have to pay anything." He tried to work up some saliva in his dry mouth. "I'd like to do this for you."

She stared at him, her expression teetering between hope

and misery. "If they find him, I'll have to leave." Her voice was a husky whisper.

Slater forced himself to nod. "I know, but you'll end up leaving anyhow, someday."

"Why would you help me?" The simple question held a wealth of confusion and grief.

"He's your son. Yours and"—he looked away—"your husband's. If I had a child, I'd want to know."

"But you never would've gambled away my inheritance or left me."

No, he wouldn't have, but that was neither here nor there. "Once he learns he has a son, he'll do the right thing." Slater didn't know if he believed his assurance or not, but the son of a bitch had to be given the opportunity to redeem himself. For his son's sake.

Rebecca remained silent, her gaze aimed at his chest but unseeing and distant. Finally she spoke, but it was in a voice so small he had to lean forward to hear it. "Contact your Pinkerton friend. Ask him to find Benjamin Colfax."

An empty ache settled in his gut, but he nodded. "I'll send him a telegram tomorrow."

Grief placed an impenetrable wall between them, unseen but no less real than the air around them. However, just because he would ask his friend to find her husband didn't mean he'd be able to accomplish it. And even if he was successful, it wouldn't happen overnight.

By offering, Slater had both bound him and Rebecca together and torn them apart. She wouldn't leave until his friend either found Colfax or gave up the search. Either way, she would stay, but their days together were now tainted with waiting.

Rebecca raised her head and moisture glimmered in her eyes, but her cheeks were dry. She leaned forward and kissed him fiercely.

Slater met her kiss with equal desperation.

TWENTY

REBECCA awakened, confused and disoriented, but it took only moments to recognize the comforting weight of Slater's arm around her. Dawn's first hints showed through the window's smoky glass. Still early. She closed her eyes to catch some more sleep, but low moans behind her and the twitching of Slater's body brought total wakefulness.

Lying there, she listened to panicked words that she couldn't understand. However, the pain behind them was distinct and heartrending. She rolled onto her back, thinking her movement would wake Slater. Instead, it increased his thrashing and the horrible moans.

"Let him go . . . no . . . take me . . . my fault."

Alarmed by the guilt and pleading in his tone, Rebecca laid a hand on his chest, hoping to wake him. Her wrist was snatched with a crushing grip. She felt the bones grind together and bit back a cry of pain.

"Slater, wake up," she said through thinned lips. "You're hurting me, Slater."

He released her as swiftly as he'd grabbed her and sat up, gasping. Rebecca rubbed her wrist, but the discomfort seemed insignificant compared to Slater's lost, fear-filled features.

"Slater, are you awake?" she asked softly.

He swiveled his gaze to her and she was startled by the desperation in his eyes that reminded her of a wild animal caught in a trap. However, before she could do or say anything more, recognition flowed back into them.

"Rebecca," he said quietly. "What is it?"

"You were having a nightmare," she replied, searching his expression. "Do you remember what it was about?"

He shook his head, wiped his damp brow with a trembling hand, and turned away—but not before Rebecca caught the lie in his eyes. He knew but he didn't trust her enough to tell her. Hurt, but not angry, she smoothed a hand up and down his upper arm. "Sometimes it helps to talk about it."

His laugh was a bitter sound. "It won't help. Take my word for that, Rebecca."

She looked down to see his left hand shaking uncontrollably, like it had palsy. Wrapping both her hands around his trembling one, she held it, kissed each knuckle. "When I was nine years old, a friend spent the night. In the middle of the night, I woke up to her screaming. I ran down the hall to her room. My mother was already with her, trying to calm her. Mother saw me and told me to go back to bed. I did as she said because it scared me that Alice, my friend, would make such a terrible sound."

Rebecca rubbed his hand between hers. "The next day, after Alice's parents had taken her home, I asked Mother why Alice had been so scared. She said it was a nightmare from the time Alice had been trapped in a closet for hours. I didn't understand. Mother said that even if we don't want to think about bad things that happened to us, our minds will remind us of them when we sleep."

She lifted her gaze to meet Slater's guarded expression. Finally, his features eased. "Your mother was an intelligent woman."

Rebecca nodded and was gratified that his left hand stopped spasming.

Slater drew his right hand down his face, as if wiping away the residual horror of his nightmare. "I'm sorry I woke you." Suddenly, his brow furrowed. "You said I was hurting you." His gaze traveled over her anxiously.

"I'm all right," she reassured him.

"I'm sorry."

"It wasn't your fault." She paused. "Do you have nightmares often?"

He shrugged. "Not often, and it's usually the same one."

She waited, hoping he'd tell her, but he remained stubbornly silent. Sighing, she released Slater's hand. "We can probably sleep for another two hours," she said.

"Sleep?"

She looked up to find him eyeing her bare breasts. Her nipples pebbled under his hot gaze and, despite having made love twice earlier that night, she felt desire heat her blood once more. She was slightly sore from their second frenetic coupling, but her body and heart combined forces to overcome the discomfort.

Rebecca surrendered without hesitation.

A pounding brought Rebecca awake, and this time bright sunlight streamed in Slater's room.

"What do you want?" Slater shouted, his morning voice gravelly.

"It's payday," Cassie replied.

"What time is it?"

"Noon."

"Shit," Slater swore. "I'll be down in a few minutes."

"Tell Glory if she dresses fast, she can have dinner with us."

Rebecca's face flamed and she resisted the urge to cover her head with the blankets.

"She heard you," Slater called out, mischief dancing in his blue eyes.

The women's giggles filled the hallway.

"You didn't have to say that," Rebecca said, more amused than upset.

"They already know," Slater said with a grin that crinkled

the corners of his eyes. He kissed the tip of her nose and threw back the covers. "Besides, why else would we be in bed so late?"

She harrumphed, but her sated body couldn't put any annoyance into it. She brought her knees to her chest, wrapped her arms around them, and rested her chin on them to watch Slater. Her gaze traveled to his dimpled backside and down his muscular legs. Despite having made love three times, she felt the familiar stirrings of desire. She shifted her attention to his back and frowned. Faint white lines marred the smooth skin. "What happened to your back?" she asked.

He stiffened. "It was a long time ago."

Rebecca shoved off the covers and rose to her knees at the edge of the bed. She traced a line with her fingertip and he flinched. Her stomach churned as she recognized the scars. "Someone hit you with a whip or a belt."

"Like I said, it was a long time ago." He deliberately moved away from her and donned a shirt.

Rebecca shivered and tugged on her camisole and drawers as Slater washed his face, using the basin. He didn't shave and his whiskers were dark against his face. On any other man the unshaven look would've made him appear a ruffian, but on Slater it only enhanced his already ruggedly handsome features.

Slater wiped his face, then turned to Rebecca. His poker expression was back. "I'll see you downstairs."

She grabbed his arm before he could escape. "I won't ask again, but if you ever want to talk about either your nightmare or those scars, I'm a pretty good listener." She smiled gently.

His gaze searched her face and his expression lost much of its detachment. He laid his hand against the side of her neck but didn't say anything. He didn't need to. Rebecca understood.

Then he spun around and left. The room suddenly felt very cold and empty.

SLATER pressed his fingertips to his brow, which pounded with an all too familiar headache. He'd thought that Rebecca in his bed might avert the usual result of his nightmare—but her presence hadn't prevented the nightmare in the first place, either.

Sighing, he gathered the papers he'd used to figure the women's pay and slid them into the accounts book. Rebecca would put the numbers in the correct columns the next time she did the bookkeeping. He'd told her to take the afternoon off and have dinner with her friends. She hadn't wanted to, but Slater threatened to give her money for the meal, so she gave in but refused to take his money. The woman had too damned much pride. If he read her correctly—and he believed he did—she would stay in a loveless marriage for her son's sake.

His headache throbbed and he debated having some whiskey to dull it, but decided against it. He had too many things to accomplish today and he needed a clear head to do them.

"Afternoon."

Slater jerked his head up to see the hired gunman leaning against the door frame. He hadn't even heard the man enter. Although his heart pounded like racing horse hooves, he managed to keep his voice steady. "I didn't expect you until this evening."

The man shrugged. "You've already had more than enough time. One hundred dollars."

Resistance flared and Slater was tempted to deny the collector the money. However, as much as it galled him to pay, he dared not take the risk of Rebecca or anyone else at the Garter being hurt like Georgia had been.

"It's in the safe."

The man smirked, as if he knew what raced through Slater's mind. "Go ahead."

The hair on Slater's nape stood on end as he turned his back to the gunman and hunkered down to open the safe. He pulled out the envelope of cash he'd set aside for the payment and relocked the safe. He straightened and found the gunman hadn't moved.

Slater tossed him the envelope, and the man caught it and tucked it into his shirt pocket.

"Aren't you going to count it?" Slater asked.

"Nope. I figure you learned your lesson."

Slater hated that the man was right. "Get the hell out of my place."

"Until next week."

"What're you talking about? I already paid you."

The gunman's laughter was like glass on a blackboard. "That was just the starter fee. From now on, it's thirty dollars a week. I'm sure that won't be a problem for you."

Rage clouded Slater's mind but he managed to rein it in. "That's robbery."

"Call it what you will." The gunman started to turn away, then paused, his motions deliberate. "By the way, the boss doesn't like your continued investigation into his business affairs. Stop asking questions or even the money won't buy you protection."

"Another threat?" Slater ground out.

The gunman shrugged nonchalantly. "A promise." Then he strode away, and the back door opened and closed behind him.

Reacting without thought, Slater grabbed his hat and went after him. He cracked open the back door. The man sauntered down the alley. When he turned a corner, Slater dashed outside and ran after him. He peered around the corner to see him go onto the main street. Slater followed, glancing around warily before stepping out. Since it was Saturday, it was busier than usual. Slater was thankful there were people enough to hide behind.

The gunman turned into another alley. Slater paused at the corner and was met by a revolver's barrel.

"Looking for someone?" the collector asked, his tone low but deadly.

Slater remained silent.

"What did I say about sticking your nose into things you shouldn't?"

When Slater didn't reply, the man shoved the barrel into his gut, nearly driving the air from Slater's lungs. Obviously, it wasn't a rhetorical question.

"You told me to stop asking questions." Slater smiled coolly. "You didn't say anything about not following you."

The gunman laughed. "You got balls, Forrester, but they won't do you any good if you're dead." He tipped his revolver upward, then tucked it into his holster. "No more tricks. You'd hate for that little singer of yours to lose her pretty voice."

Cold sweat trickled down Slater's spine. "Your business is with me, not the people who work for me."

"That's right. It's business, Forrester. Just think of our insurance as a business expense and everything will be fine."

Slater's fingernails cut into his palms. It wasn't that the Garter couldn't afford the "payments," even thirty a week, but paying somebody so they wouldn't hurt anyone or damage the saloon was wrong, pure and simple. But he didn't argue.

The gunman touched the brim of his hat. "See you next week, Forrester. Let's hope the boss doesn't decide your little stunt will cost you even more."

Shaking with rage that he didn't dare let loose, Slater watched the man disappear into the labyrinth of buildings and tents.

"Slater?"

He turned to see Rebecca, along with Cassie, Rose, and Molly, staring at him. "Afternoon, ladies." He forced a smile. "Did you buy out the mercantile?"

Molly, wearing an emerald green dress that clung to her generous curves, stepped forward and pulled a silky camisole from her bag. "I found this." She held it against her expansive cleavage. "Do you like it?"

"It's nice," he replied absently.

With a put-upon pout, Molly stuffed it back in her bag.

"Have you had dinner yet?" Slater asked, more to break the awkward silence than out of real curiosity.

"We were just headed there," Cassie said. "Would you like to join us?"

"Sorry. I've got some errands to take care of, but you all enjoy yourselves."

"We will," Rose assured him.

Aware of Rebecca's quizzical and concerned expression, Slater tipped his hat to the women. "I'll see you later at the Garter." He hurried off, not in any mood to answer questions, no matter how well-meaning.

With his efforts to follow the gunman thwarted, he recalled his promise to Rebecca. He went into the telegraph office and composed his message. After paying for it and watching the telegraph operator send it, Slater told him that when a reply came, it was to be delivered immediately. The man promised to do so.

As he walked back to the Garter, he passed the Black Bull, which was open for business. The gunman was headed in the direction of the Black Bull before he'd caught Slater following him. Of course, there were a half dozen other saloons in the same direction. Before he could talk himself out of it, he entered the place. John Langley himself was working behind the bar.

"Two days in less than a week," Langley said. "What's the occasion?"

Slater shrugged, ignoring the dull ache in his head. "I was just passing by and figured I'd stop in."

"Bullshit. You're still looking for whoever is in charge of the damned insurance racket." Langley didn't beat around the bush.

"You're right. I paid this morning and tried following the hired gun. He was headed in this direction when he caught me on his tail," Slater admitted, observing Langley closely.

The suited man tipped his head to the side. "If you're asking if he came in here, he didn't. I would've noticed him."

Slater glanced down. "Figured as much."

The silence stretched taut between them until Langley broke it. "You're thinking I'm the one behind it, aren't you?"

Slater raised his head and met the man's eyes. He tried to read the truth in them, but the man was a gambler and damned good at it. Almost as good as Slater. "The thought crossed my mind."

Langley laughed. "If I was hauling in as much money as what they're doing, I wouldn't be working behind my own bar."

"Or maybe you would, just to throw everyone off."

Langley stared at Slater. "Think what you want. Nothing I say will change your mind."

He was right, which only further puzzled Slater.

"Thirty a week," Slater said. "That's what I have to pay to keep them from busting up my place or hurting my people."

"Same here. If we had a sheriff worth a damn, he might be able to stop them."

"Maybe, or maybe they'd just get rid of him in an 'accident.' What we need is a federal marshal, but he won't come unless we have solid proof."

Langley narrowed his eyes. "You sound like you've been a lawman yourself."

"Not officially." Slater didn't expand. He took a deep breath and let it out slowly. "I'd best go open up my own place." The corners of his lips lifted in a caricature of a smile. "If I'm going to afford the payments, I'd best make some money."

Slater turned to leave but Langley's voice stopped him.

"Don't get yourself killed like Andrew did."

Slater glanced at him over his shoulder. "I don't intend to."

He returned to the Garter and went upstairs to shave and change into a suit. Rebecca's room door opened as he reached the top of the stairs.

"I thought you were having dinner with the others," Slater said.

"I brought something back for Georgia."

"How is she?"

"The doctor was here not fifteen minutes ago. He said she's healing fine and made a sling for her arm. She can start moving around tomorrow, as long as someone is with her."

Relief spread through Slater. "That's good news."

Rebecca approached him and lowered her voice. "What happened?"

"What're you talking about?"

Her eyes snapped with temper. "I thought you had more respect for me than that."

His defensiveness fled. "I do. It's just that I don't want

you any more involved than you already are." He paused and used the ace up his sleeve. "You have a son waiting for you. You can't take any chances that something might happen to you."

She snorted in an unladylike manner. "Don't patronize me. A stagecoach I'm riding in could tip over and I could be killed. I could be run down in the streets here. Or I could drown in the river."

"That creek is hardly deep enough that you'd get your knees wet," he said wryly.

She glared at him. "You know what I mean."

Slater sighed. "He collected the hundred dollars this morning and raised it to thirty dollars a week."

Rebecca's eyes rounded. "Are you going to pay it?"

"I don't know."

He expected her to argue, but she merely worried her lower lip between her teeth.

"I tried to follow him," Slater admitted. "He caught me. He threatened you specifically."

Her face paled and he hated himself for telling her, but she needed to know.

"Go back to St. Louis, Rebecca," he said softly. "You'll be safe there and your little boy will have his mother."

He expected her to use the same arguments she'd used last night. However, the indecision in her eyes told him he'd finally frightened her. He gnashed his teeth as he held himself back from comforting her. He couldn't promise to protect her. He'd learned from his mistakes.

"I'll think about it," she said in a small voice he hardly recognized as hers. She met his gaze and despair darkened her eyes. "If I die, Daniel won't have anyone."

And if she left, Slater would have no one.

THE gunman tossed the envelope onto the table. "Here's the latest payment."

The suited man opened the envelope and long, slender fingers brought out the bills. He counted them. "One hundred dollars. From the Scarlet Garter?" His Southern drawl was heavy.

The hired man nodded. "Getting rid of Kearny and shooting up the Scarlet Garter took care of it."

He smiled in cold satisfaction. "I thought it might." His smile faded. "What's bothering you?"

"The new owner is as bad as Kearny—talking to the other saloon owners. He tried following me back here after I got the money."

"You didn't lead him here, did you?"

"I'm not stupid. I caught him, warned him off."

"Will he listen?"

"I don't know. Maybe not."

The slender, suited man tapped his fingertips on the tabletop. "What's his name?"

"Forrester, Slater Forrester."

His eyes widened, then narrowed. "Are you certain?"

"Yes. Do you know him?"

"Perhaps."

"Do you want me and the boys to get rid of him, too?"

"Not yet."

The gunman shrugged. "Are you going to need me in the next few days? Since you don't want me showing my face around this town, thought I'd ride over to Ellerson and have a drink and find a willing woman."

"Be back Thursday. I'll let you know about Forrester then."

The hired man left after a nod of acquiescence.

The suited man swore softly. He'd hoped Kansas was far enough away that he wouldn't run into any problems. Most probably he wouldn't recognize him, but Forrester had been sharp. He'd also managed to survive.

Damn him!

TWENTY-ONE

THE following days passed without incident and Rebecca was spared having to make a decision. When the threat had been against the Scarlet Garter, it was easy to convince herself she wasn't in danger. However, now that the threat had been aimed at her, it had become personal.

She didn't want to leave Slater, but was terrified of leaving Daniel an orphan. Daniel would never know to what lengths his mother had gone to give him the family he deserved. But did her son deserve someone like Benjamin for a father?

Rebecca brushed her hair as she sat in front of the mirror. Her bed was neat and tidy behind her, not having been slept in since the first night she'd gone to Slater's room. Her hand slowed and stilled, and she set the brush aside.

Although she knew it wrong, Rebecca couldn't give up Slater. When they made love, he instinctively knew when she wanted him slow and gentle and when she wanted him with a ferocity that would have shocked her not very long ago. But no matter the pace of their lovemaking, he always made her cry out in ecstasy. And later, after they were both sated and boneless, Slater held her in his arms as they slept.

She couldn't imagine sleeping without him, yet she knew the time would come when she'd have to leave.

She pressed her fist between her breasts, fighting the raw pain that shredded her lungs. It took a few minutes before she could walk to her dresser and pull out Daniel's christening gown. She held it in her hands, visualizing how small her son had been, swathed in the soft material. Only she and two of the nuns from the children's home had witnessed her son's baptism. Daniel had shrieked his displeasure when the water flowed over his tiny head.

She shoved the gown back in the drawer and slammed it shut. Adultery and divorce were against her religion, and they were sins rarely forgiven by society, with the blame often falling on the woman. But a future without Slater was almost as unimaginable as a future without her son.

Stop feeling sorry for yourself.

She'd made a mistake marrying Benjamin, and it was up to her to try to make the best of a deplorable situation. Drawing back her shoulders, she bound her hair in a loose ponytail. She placed a bonnet on her head and tied the ribbons beneath her chin. She had to walk to the store and buy another pair of stockings before going to work on the bookkeeping. After smoothing her blouse and skirt, she left her room.

It didn't surprise her to find the saloon empty. Slater was probably in the back checking the liquor inventory, and it was too early for the other women to be up or the men to come in to work. She crossed to the front door, still framed by the broken windows that had boards nailed over them.

"Going someplace?"

Startled, she turned to see Slater by the bar and her heart fluttered in her breast. His hair was tousled and the top two buttons of his shirt were undone, revealing a vee of smooth skin she'd often caressed with her lips. "I have to pick up an item at the store," she replied, her voice husky.

"I'll go with you."

"You don't have—"

"Wait here. I'll get my hat."

Puzzled by his grave demeanor, Rebecca tapped her toes

on the floor as she waited for him to return. He guided her out the door and down the street, keeping her out of the wagon and horse traffic.

"You didn't have to accompany me," Rebecca said when Slater's intensity became unnerving.

"Yes, I did."

She glanced up at his grim face and noticed how his shadowed gaze kept darting about. "What are you looking for?"

"Who," Slater corrected her.

Rebecca stumbled slightly and Slater caught her arm. "You don't think they'd be stupid enough to try something in broad daylight?"

"I think they're *arrogant* enough to try anything they damn well please." He finally looked at her. "And I'm not going to take a chance with your life."

Although his concern warmed her, she hated feeling like a helpless prisoner. "You can't go everywhere with me."

A corner of his lips lifted. "I'm already with you most of the time. The saloon, my bed."

Rebecca's cheeks heated, but no one was close enough to overhear his quiet words. Slater was right. This was the first time she'd left the Scarlet Garter since the day Slater had received the threat against her.

They entered the store and Rebecca veered to the female unmentionables. She was grateful Slater didn't follow, but was aware of his watchful gaze on her. Quickly, she chose a pair of black stockings and new garters for good measure. She carried them to the counter, trying to shield them from Slater. However, the twinkle in his eyes told her he saw them.

Laughing inwardly at her embarrassment—after all, Slater had seen her stark naked—she paid for the items and accepted the bag that hid them from view.

"Will I get a private showing of your new stockings tonight?" Slater asked, his head close to hers as they strolled back to the Scarlet Garter.

Rebecca giggled, then rolled her eyes at her own girlishness. Slater Forrester had a knack for bringing out the younger, carefree Rebecca. "If you're a good boy, I might."

"You tell me I'm good all the time."

His breath tickled her neck and she shuddered. They'd been sleeping together for over a week now and her desire for him had only increased. One of these days he would simply look at her with his smoky blue eyes and she'd drag him upstairs to his room. The image brought a smile, but before she could share it, Slater jerked her toward him. She cried out as she stumbled, and Slater cushioned her fall with his own body. Hooves and wooden wheels missed them by inches.

Slater, his face red with fury, jumped to his feet and swore at the driver, who didn't even look back. He leaned over Rebecca. "Are you all right?" he asked, concern replacing his anger.

"I-I think so."

Slater drew her to her feet and steadied her with an arm around her waist, then leaned down to pick up his hat. As he slapped it against his thigh to rid it of dust, he glared at the bystanders who'd stopped to gawk, and they fled.

"What happened?" Rebecca asked in a tremulous voice.

He clapped the hat on his dark hair, shading his granite features. "He was driving too fast and nearly ran us down."

"It wasn't . . ."

"No." The single word held a wealth of disgust. He picked up the bag with her purchases and handed it to her.

Rebecca laughed weakly. "Like I said, I have more of a chance dying in an accident than being killed."

Slater's jaw muscle bunched and his eyes were blue diamonds. "You're not going to die."

She almost told him he couldn't make that promise, but his stony expression halted her. "Let's get back to the saloon," she said.

Nodding, Slater took her arm and escorted her home.

Rebecca took her purchases to her room and removed her bonnet. She brushed the dust from her blouse and skirt, not wanting to think how close she'd come to being killed in a stupid accident. However, her knees began to tremble and she dropped onto the edge of her bed.

I almost died.

Despite not having enough money to support and raise Daniel, Rebecca was seized with a powerful urge to see and hold him again. Leaving St. Louis had been naive. She'd allowed her wounded pride to dictate to her instead of asking her friends for help. Surely they wouldn't all turn her away.

For Daniel's and her own sakes she had to swallow her pride and return. She had enough money to travel back to St. Louis. She'd leave after payday, which was only two days away.

Her stomach burned and tears blurred her vision. How could she leave Slater?

How could she stay without Daniel?

SLATER paced the saloon floor, his boots creating a furrowed trail in the sawdust. He'd been having so much fun teasing Rebecca that he'd almost missed the recklessly driven wagon. What if the danger had come from a hired killer? He might have succeeded with Slater's attention focused on Rebecca rather than looking for danger. His fisted left hand trembled uncontrollably and he held it in his other hand, damning the tremor he'd gained in Andersonville.

He was going to lose Rebecca one way or another. Either she'd return to St. Louis with or without her husband, or she'd die. The mere thought of her death cramped his gut and tightened his lungs. Although sending her away was nearly as painful, at least she'd be alive and her son would have his mother.

A loud pounding on the front door brought Slater's head up sharply. It was too early for the men to be coming in to work. Besides, they usually used the back door. Withdrawing his revolver from its shoulder holster, he crossed the floor. He cursed the lack of windows that made him unable to see who was outside.

"Who's there?" he called out.

"Message from the telegraph office," a boy responded.

Slater stuffed the gun back in its holster and opened the door. A boy maybe nine or ten years old held up an envelope, an expectant look on his freckled face. Stifling a smile,

Slater took the envelope and ripped it open. He pulled out the paper and unfolded it.

Colfax seen in St. Joe three days ago. Headed east. Continue looking? BC

Brent Chiles, his Pinkerton friend, had come through.

Slater patted his pockets and came up with a pencil. He turned the paper over and wrote one word. *Yes.* He refolded the note, handed it to the kid, and dug around in his pockets. He handed the boy some coins.

"Ten cents for you and two bits for the operator to send my answer. Got it?" Slater asked.

The kid nodded. "Got it. Thanks, mister." He dashed off with the money and Slater's reply.

Once Slater was certain the kid was headed to the telegraph office, he closed the door. So Rebecca's husband was headed back east. He'd bet a month's take that his destination was St. Louis, but whether he was returning because of Rebecca or because of the plethora of gambling establishments, he didn't know.

He heard a door close upstairs, followed by a flurry of skirts. Even before seeing her, he knew it was Rebecca. She paused momentarily on the stairs when she caught sight of him, then continued down.

"Who was here?" she asked after she'd descended.

Slater stuck his hands in his trouser pockets. "Kid with a telegram." He met her curious eyes. "It was from my Pinkerton friend. Colfax was seen in St. Joseph three days ago. He's headed east."

Although Rebecca only blinked, Slater saw the color leach from her face. She crossed her arms and looked past him. "He's going back to St. Louis."

Slater shrugged. "There are a lot of gambling halls there."

"And his son."

"Whom he doesn't know about."

She cringed and Slater was angry with himself for speaking so callously. But despite his worries about her safety, he didn't want her to go.

She lifted her chin, familiar obstinacy glowing in her eyes. "I have to go back there and find him."

Slater's stomach twisted into a painful knot. "I want to go with you." He blinked, as startled as Rebecca by his admission.

"You have a saloon to run."

He strode over to her and clasped her arms. "It's not as important as you."

There was a momentary glimpse of hope in her eyes that was quickly overshadowed by sadness. "Andrew died for the Scarlet Garter. It meant everything to him. You can't simply walk away from it."

What she didn't say was that he was responsible for Andrew's death and Slater had vowed to bring his killers to justice. Yet the thought of Rebecca traveling to St. Louis alone to find her husband, a man Slater detested despite never having met him, rankled him. And made him jealous as hell.

"When will you leave?" he finally asked in a low voice.

"I'll wait until payday," she replied.

His heart lifted slightly to have her with him a little longer. However, he knew she was anxious to return to her son. "If it's a matter of money, I'll pay you now for the week so you can leave tomorrow."

Hurt flashed through her expression. "Are you trying to get rid of me, Slater?"

"No," he replied unhesitantly, shocked she'd even think that. "I just want to help."

Her expression eased into gentle melancholy and she laid her palms against his chest. "You have, more than you know."

The heat of her hands and the warmth of her body so close to his made his heart pound, sending his blood to his groin. Passion coiled in his belly and hot need rushed through his veins. "Not enough," he whispered. He brought his lips down to hers, eased them open, and delved his tongue into her mouth. She tasted of coffee and sweetness that was pure Rebecca. A tiny moan escaped her as she mated her tongue with his.

He drew back before all reason deserted him and rested his forehead against hers. "I don't want you to leave, Rebecca. Not tomorrow or the next day or ever, but you have a son and as long as you're"—he forced the word out—"married, there's no place for me."

She drew away and panicky eyes met his. "Please don't say that, Slater."

He hated being ruthless, but his own anguish forced him. "It's true, Rebecca. You know it as well as I do." He took a deep breath. "Find your husband and do what you have to do. I won't come between a woman and her child."

"But you will between a woman and her husband." The words were bittersweet.

Angry disappointment coursed through him. "Only when her husband is a son of a bitch who ought to be horse-whipped."

"I'm sorry," she whispered. "That was unfair of me."

"Yes, it was." He peered into her eyes, his ire evaporating. "I don't make a habit of bedding married women." *At least, not knowingly.*

"Then why?"

Slater considered her plaintive question, wondering the same thing himself. "Why are two people ever attracted to one another?"

He sensed Rebecca's disappointment in his lukewarm reply, but he wasn't ready to examine his own heart too closely.

"Why indeed?" She took a step back. "I know you mean well, but I prefer waiting until Saturday. That way I won't be indebted to you."

He resisted the urge to grab her and shake some sense into her prideful head. "Suit yourself."

"You're angry."

"Maybe, but it's my problem, not yours." He managed a smile. "You have enough on your mind."

Her eyes glistened as they filled with moisture, but she held the tears back. "I—" She glanced away and pressed her lips together. After clearing her throat, she tried again. "I'll work on the bookkeeping. I want to have the accounts current when I leave."

He nodded, afraid to speak.

She turned around and nearly ran to the back room, where he suspected she'd hide until it was time to work that evening.

He clenched his hands into fists at his sides and sent his

gaze around the saloon. Although grateful Andrew had left him the place, he couldn't help but feel trapped. If he didn't own the damn saloon, he could accompany Rebecca back to St. Louis. He trusted Dante and Simon to keep an eye on the place, but he couldn't leave them with the shadow of the insurance racket hanging over it. Besides, revenge still burned in his gut. Andrew's killers had to be caught and punished.

Last week he'd spoken to all the saloon owners and nobody had been able to help him. However, there had been one owner he hadn't seen. The Brass Balls owner had been out of town. Although it was a long shot, Slater had nowhere else to turn.

He left the saloon and went to Simon's place. The piano player quickly agreed to watch the women at the Scarlet Garter while Slater went to speak with Gavin.

Slater paused at the tent saloon and stared at the Brass Balls sign. Hideous memories of Andersonville bombarded him and bitter bile rose in his throat. Pictures and names swirled through his mind—dead men, men who died slowly through disease, thirst, and starvation, and those lucky bastards who'd been killed outright while trying to escape. Slater had been told he'd been one of the fortunate ones, but the platitude been hard to stomach with the stench of waste, death, and decay still fresh in his nostrils.

The war was three years past and Andersonville was only a blot in history. Forcing himself to ignore the sign, he ducked into the canvas and wood building and stood for a moment to let his eyes adjust to the relative dimness.

He recognized the bartender as the same one he'd talked to the past two times he'd been there. "I'd like to talk to the owner."

The bartender motioned to a bearded man sitting alone at a corner table. "Mr. Gavin's over there."

Slater nodded his thanks and crossed to Gavin's table. The man looked up from a game of solitaire. "Can I help you?" Like the bartender, he had a Southern drawl.

"Are you the owner of this place?"

Gavin made a motion with his hand, encompassing the tent. "Yes, such as it is."

"I'm Slater Forrester. I own the Scarlet Garter. Mind if I sit down?"

"Be my guest."

Slater pulled out a chair and lowered himself to it. He glanced at the solitaire game and tapped the jack of hearts, then the queen of spades on another stack.

Gavin arched a brow and moved the jack. "Thanks."

Slater shrugged and studied the man, who was probably close to Andrew's age. However, where Andrew's thick hair had been gray, Gavin's was still blond but thinning on the top.

"So what can I do for you, Mr. Forrester?" Gavin asked as he continued to play his card game.

"I've been asking all the other owners around town if they've been approached by a man demanding money for protection," Slater began.

Gavin moved the seven of clubs to the eight of diamonds. "And if I have, what would you do about it?"

"I'd ask for your help to stop whoever's extorting our money."

Gavin paused and lifted his pale blue gaze to Slater. "What if I'm behind it?"

Slater frowned, uncertain how to read the man. "Are you?"

Gavin suddenly laughed. "If I were, I wouldn't be sitting in this tent playing solitaire."

"So you've paid?"

"Yes. After one owner was killed, I thought it would be in my best interests to do so." Gavin studied Slater. "You said the Scarlet Garter?"

Slater nodded, his mouth dry.

"Wasn't the man who was killed the previous owner?"

"That's right. Andrew Kearny." Slater tipped his head to the side. "He was trying to put a stop to their operation. They didn't like it."

"He should've left well enough alone."

Indignation made Slater press his fists into his thighs. "He was trying to put a criminal in jail."

"And he was killed for it."

Gavin took three cards from the deck in his smooth hand

and turned them over, running a neatly trimmed fingernail over the top card. "I'm paying because I'm not a fool. I suggest you do the same."

Slater decided he didn't like Gavin. "I did the first time. But I guess I'm a fool, because I'm not giving those bastards any more money. Andrew was right. Someone needs to stop them."

Gavin's attention moved to Slater. "You're playing a dangerous game, Forrester."

Slater heard something almost like a threat in the man's mild tone. "It's not a game when murder is involved." He stood and stared down at Gavin. "Do you know who's involved?"

Gavin held his gaze. "No, but I'll keep my eyes open."

"You do that." Slater nodded once. "Gavin."

"Forrester."

Slater paused at the tent's entrance and glanced back at Gavin one more time. The dim lighting muted the man's features, but his light hair was easily discernible. The feeling that he'd seen him before gnawed at his memory, but he couldn't place him.

Slater stepped out of the Brass Balls and into bright sunshine. Squinting, he replayed his conversation with Gavin, but there was nothing to suggest he was anything but an arrogant ass. In his mind's eye, he saw Gavin run his fingernail over the cards. The gesture stirred some hazy memory, a déjà vu that he couldn't place. He'd seen that tell before, but where?

GAVIN stared at the tent entrance long after Forrester disappeared through it. Clenching his teeth, he gathered his cards and put them in his pocket. He stood and walked past the plank and barrel bar that never failed to make him grimace in disgust. Yet he needed the cover of the saloon to do his business. Just one more month and he'd have enough to move on to a new town where he could build an extravagant gambling establishment, the type he'd dreamed about.

He went out the opening in the back of the saloon and entered a smaller tent that was large enough to hold two cots, a chair, and a stove. Parker lay on a cot, his ankles crossed and his head on his arms. He glanced over at Gavin, his expression questioning.

"Take care of Forrester," Gavin said.

"Same way as Kearny?"

Gavin shook his head. "Make this one look like an accident. A fire, late, after the town is quiet." The man stared past his hired gunman. "I remember him. He was a trouble-maker. It's only a matter of time until he recognizes me, even with the beard."

Parker swung his feet to the ground and sat up. "Been pretty lucky. This is the first one."

"Not many lived to recognize me."

Parker knew what Gavin had been, but he was being paid well for his silence. Besides, Gavin was a stone-cold killer, and wouldn't hesitate to get rid of Parker if he even suspected he'd talked.

Leo Gavin, formerly Confederate Captain Lee Towner, had ordered countless deaths. It had been his job.

$\mathcal{T}$WENTY-TWO

A quiet knock on the door startled Rebecca and she looked up, her eyes crossing for a moment after focusing so intently on the numbers. "Who is it?"

"Simon," came the low-timbered reply.

"Come in."

Simon stepped inside. "You need anything, Miss Glory?"

"Maybe a new pair of eyes." She smiled at his puzzled look and shook her head. "I'm fine. Are you looking for Slater?"

He shook his head. "I wanted to let you know I'll be out in the saloon if you need anything."

Puzzled, she lifted an eyebrow in question.

"Slater asked me to stay here while he done some errand." He shifted his weight from one foot to the other. "Guess he's worried about them men coming back here and doing something."

A frisson of alarm slithered down her spine. "Where did Slater go?"

"Said he wanted to talk to someone. Didn't tell me who."

Rebecca didn't doubt that whoever he went to see was somehow involved in Andrew's death. "All right." She angled a look at the tall black man. "When was the last time you saw Georgia?"

He glanced down, shaking his head.

"She's out of bed and walking around now. In fact, she should be coming downstairs any time."

Panic spread across his face but he covered it quickly. "I'm glad to hear she's up and about."

Frustrated by her own conflicted emotions with Slater, Rebecca was suddenly furious at the stiff-backed piano player. She rose, stalked over to him, and tipped her head back to spear him with her gaze. "She loves you, Simon, and you're throwing that away for no good reason."

He blinked, clearly startled by her vehemence, then his eyes narrowed behind his spectacles. "I asked her to marry me and she said no."

"Do you know why she said no?" Exasperated fury infused Rebecca's voice. "You almost lost Georgia, but you still don't have the courage to tell her you love her." She cursed the tears that burned her eyes. "Damn it, Simon, don't let your pride get in the way of your heart."

His eyes rounded behind his lenses, as if shocked by her impassioned plea or her cussing. Maybe both.

Rebecca heard the stairs creak. She suspected it was Georgia coming down. "I think that's her now. Are you going to be brave enough to take a chance, or are you going to be a coward and let her slip away?"

His nostrils flared and she wondered if she'd pushed him too hard. Without a word, he spun on his heel and left the office. She heard him march into the saloon and then there was silence.

Curious, she tiptoed down the hallway but halted when she heard Georgia's terse voice.

"I didn't expect to see you here this time of day."

"Slater asked me to come in to watch the place." Simon sounded defensive.

Rebecca could almost feel Georgia's disappointment in the silent seconds that followed. Then there was the clump of feet climbing the stairs.

"No, wait," Simon said.

Rebecca held her breath.

"Why should I?" Georgia asked, her pride making her tone contemptuous.

"Because—"

Tell her, Simon.

"If that's all you have to say. . . ." Georgia was definitely irritated and, Rebecca suspected, hurt.

"This ain't easy," Simon grumbled.

"What ain't easy?" Georgia's voice wasn't quite as harsh.

"I was born a slave and was one until we were freed. But you been free all your life."

Rebecca imagined she could hear Georgia's exasperated sigh.

"I barely knew my ma, and my pa was sold when I was a babe," Simon continued. "We didn't talk about love. Don't even know if I believed in it . . . until I met you."

"What're you tryin' to say, Simon?" Georgia asked in a tone Rebecca could barely hear.

"I-I love you, Georgia, and I want to marry you. I want to raise our children together and love them like I never got to be loved by my folks."

"Oh, Simon, I want that, too."

Rebecca heard the tears in Georgia's tone and her own eyes filled with moisture. She had no doubt there'd be a wedding soon.

Rebecca returned to the office to continue working. However, thoughts of Slater haunted her. Although she was thrilled for Simon and Georgia, it reminded her that she and Slater didn't have the option of a happily-ever-after. Despite being tempted to ignore Benjamin's existence, she could never forget Daniel.

She shook the melancholy thoughts aside. In a couple of hours she had to ready herself for work that evening. Only two nights remained before she'd leave Oaktree . . . and Slater's bed.

Even if it was two thousand nights, she knew it would never be enough.

* * *

THE saloon was busy until long past midnight. After Slater ushered the last of the drunken customers out, everyone fell into the closing tasks.

Cassie, Rose, and Molly climbed the stairs with their shoes in hand after the night of dancing. As soon as Simon had the last chair on a table—in record time—he also headed upstairs. Georgia had been down for an hour earlier in the evening. She hadn't been up to dancing, but it had been good to see her talking with the customers. During that hour, Rebecca had noticed missed notes from the piano and couldn't help but grin at Simon's preoccupation. However, she could relate, since her attention was too often drawn to Slater as he played poker.

Dante, having finished his chores, came up beside her. "Good evening, Miss Glory," he said with a slight bow.

She smiled down at the bartender. "Good night, Dante. I'll see you tomorrow."

He returned her smile and left with a lift of his hand. An ache welled in her chest. She hadn't told anyone but Slater of her plan to leave and she dreaded the moment when she made her announcement. Saying good-bye to Dante would be especially difficult; she'd grown fond of the diminutive man.

Frank had left soon after Simon went upstairs, so Rebecca finally found herself alone with Slater. He emptied the money from the box under the bar and put it in an envelope to be counted the next morning, along with the dancers' special drink tallies. Rebecca followed him to the back, where he placed the envelope in the safe and locked it.

"Who did you go see this afternoon?" she asked.

Slater straightened from his position beside the safe. "Leo Gavin, the owner of the Brass Balls. He was the only owner I hadn't met yet."

"Did he know anything?"

Slater's expression darkened. "Not that he admitted to."

"But you think he does?"

Slater crossed his arms over his chest, drawing his white shirt snugly across his shoulders. "I'm not sure. He admitted to paying the extortionists, too, but . . ." He shrugged.

"What?"

"I felt like I knew him from someplace, but I couldn't place him."

"Maybe he reminds you of someone."

His brow creased. "Maybe, but he had this tell—habit—that I've seen before."

"Maybe you played poker with him sometime in the past?"

"It's possible, but I don't think so." He shook his head, as if to clear it. "It'll come to me sooner or later."

Listening to him, Rebecca found herself growing uneasy. Perhaps it was simply Slater's disquiet she was feeling. "What do you say we go to bed?" she asked with forced brightness.

His eyes turned smoky and Rebecca's unease evaporated as another kind of restlessness seized her.

"Or maybe we could just use the desk again." He ran his fingers lightly across the desktop, a dangerously sexy gleam in his eyes.

Liquid heat pooled between Rebecca's thighs and her breasts strained for release, for Slater's touch.

"Am I interrupting anything?"

Rebecca spun around, shocked to see the smirking gunman standing in the doorway with a man on either side of him. The hired gun's revolver was aimed at her and Slater.

"Get over there by him."

Her legs shaking, Rebecca did as the gunman ordered.

"My week isn't up yet," Slater said, his voice conversational in direct contrast to the fury in his eyes.

"There's been a change of plans."

"Why?"

He smiled coldly. "Too many questions. Open the safe."

Slater glared at him. "Go to hell."

The hired gun withdrew a knife from his boot and laid the flat of the blade against Rebecca's cheek. The cold metal made her gasp.

"You don't open it, I start cutting your lady friend," he said. "She won't be very pretty when I'm done."

Rebecca's heart hammered in her chest, making her dizzy with fear.

Hatred blazing in his eyes, Slater opened the safe.

"Give me all the money."

His movements stiff, Slater piled the small stack of bills into his hands and held it up. "This is it."

"Don't forget the envelope with tonight's take."

Slater's jaw muscle jumped but he didn't argue.

"Set it all on the desk."

Slater did so.

The hired gun turned to his underlings. "Tie them up."

"What're you going to do?" Slater demanded.

"Burn the place and you two with it."

Rebecca gasped sharply. "You can't do that. There are other people upstairs. They'll die."

The gunman shrugged. "That's not my problem. The boss wants Forrester out of the way and he wants the Scarlet Garter burned to the ground. A fire takes care of both."

Rebecca's mind raced. She had to warn their friends upstairs. She opened her mouth to scream. One of the men clapped a hand over her mouth, stifling her shout. With her hands held behind her back, all she could do was kick at her captor, but her long skirts prevented her from doing any harm.

"Keep fighting and I'll kill Forrester right now," the leader said, his knife blade against Slater's neck. Blood trickled from a thin cut.

Rebecca's eyes widened and her cries died, as did her struggles.

The leader removed the knife from Slater's throat. "You try that again and he's dead."

Sick with dread and helplessness, Rebecca nodded dully. The man released her and stepped back.

"Before I die, answer me one question," Slater said. "Who's behind all this?"

The collector met his gaze. "Someone you used to know."

Slater frowned.

"Tie them to the chair. Her in it and him on the floor behind it," the leader said. "And gag them."

Rebecca was pressed down into the chair and her wrists were lashed to the chair arms and her ankles to the front legs. Behind her, they pushed Slater to the floor and bound him to the back chair legs. A cloth was pressed between her lips and tied snugly behind her head. It dug into the corners of her mouth painfully.

Once Rebecca and Slater were secured, the hired gun scooped up the money on the desk. "It's too bad you didn't mind your own business."

Although Rebecca couldn't see Slater, she heard his growl.

The gunman laughed, then motioned for his two lackeys to leave the room. He followed after tipping his hat to Rebecca in a parody of courteousness, and closed the door behind him.

When Slater heard the door shut, he struggled against his bonds but only succeeded in abrading his wrists. The men had done their job well. The chair moved slightly as Rebecca, too, attempted to pull free.

Slater searched for something to use to cut the rope but there was nothing in sight, much less anything close enough to reach. A wave of panic swept through him. Although he'd often worked in the cramped office with the door closed, he'd known all he had to do was stand up, open the door, and walk out. But this time he was trapped.

His breath caught in his throat and his heart hammered against his chest. The gag made it harder to breathe and his panic notched upward. He closed his eyes and pictured a wide, open vista with knee-length grass bending in a fresh breeze. However, the image wavered and the horrific memories returned with a vengeance.

Pitch darkness and the stench of rotting food, piss, and body waste made his stomach turn inside out. Remembered groans and sobs of hopelessness and despair filled his ears. Nausea ripped through him and he fought to hold back the caustic bile.

Slater focused on Rebecca, on her breathing; her scent; the warmth where they touched. Although it didn't vanquish the too-real flashbacks completely, the panic lessened to a tolerable level.

"I got my gag off, but the rope is too tight to slip out." Despite the quaver in Rebecca's voice, Slater had never heard anything more beautiful.

He closed his eyes and tipped his head back. Straining against the rope brought pain, but it was a physical ache he could deal with, unlike the mental anguish of his bleak memories that felt too damned real.

Breaking glass sounded.

"What're they doing?" she asked.

Slater grunted, unable to answer because of his gag. However, he knew what the sound was—breaking liquor bottles. Alcohol would spread the fire faster. He doubled his efforts to escape but only succeeded in deepening the cuts around his wrists. Blood trickled down his hands.

His left hand shook violently. The flashbacks clawed their talons into Slater's mind, forcing him to witness Tommy's beaten and bloody body as if he were lying in front of him. Then the darkness swept through him again. He fought for air in his tortured lungs even though there was no hint of smoke yet.

"Slater, we have to get out of here," Rebecca shouted.

Her frantic voice momentarily chased the demons away. Her face was pale as she looked down at him over her shoulder.

"Slater, try to get loose."

Her stern voice gave him an anchor and he used every ounce of mental strength to press the blackness aside. His muscles strained and he grunted as he attempted to pull his wrists apart, but the rope merely cut deeper into his flesh.

An animal-like sound of frustration escaped him.

"Listen to me, Slater. We have to get loose or we'll die." Rebecca's voice was quiet and steady, soothing.

How often had Slater hoped death would take him in Andersonville? Even as a boy, locked in the small shed overnight with the other child laborers, who were treated less humanely than the man's cows and horses, he'd thought about death as his only way out.

But no longer did he want death for himself, and definitely not for Rebecca. She had to live for her son. And he wanted to live for her.

He renewed his struggles and blood made his wrists slippery. Tugging his right hand upward, he grimaced but could feel some movement. Abruptly his right hand slipped free of the rope and he jerked the cloth off his mouth.

"We have to tip over the chair," Slater said. "Then I can slip my arms free."

"Okay."

"To your right on the count of three. One, two"—Slater paused to rally his strength—"three."

Between the two of them, they toppled the chair. Rebecca cried out softly as they hit the floor. They lay awkwardly for a long moment, catching their breaths. Slater wriggled down the chair legs until his arms were free. His left hand shook badly and it took him a frustratingly long time to untie his ankles. He pushed himself to his feet, swayed, and had to wait for the dizziness to pass.

"Slater?" Rebecca asked. His name was filled with a wealth of concern.

"I'm fine," Slater automatically replied. As he worked on Rebecca's bindings, his left hand lost its shaking and his nightmares faded. Once she was free, he helped her to stand. Her face was wan, but her expression was resolute.

"They haven't started the fire yet," Slater said.

"What're they waiting for?"

"They probably want to make sure everyone's asleep so the fire isn't noticed too soon."

Slater tried the door, half expecting it to be locked or barricaded, but it came open easily.

"What're we going to do?" Rebecca asked, her lips close to his ear.

"You're going to sneak up the back stairs and get everyone out."

She eyed him warily. "You can't take on three armed men by yourself."

Feeling the confidence he used to possess before Andersonville had stripped it all away, Slater grinned. "I wouldn't bet on that." Then he sobered. "Stay behind me until I tell you to run for the stairs."

She removed her shoes, holding on to Slater to keep her balance. He gazed down at the top of her head as she bent over and his heart constricted with the intensity of his emotions. "Rebecca."

She looked up and met his gaze. "Yes?"

He continued to stare at her, to glut himself on her determined eyes, winged brows, delicate nose, stubborn chin, and bow-shaped lips. Abruptly, he wrapped his arms around her and tugged her close, pressing his mouth against hers. If he didn't survive this night, he'd tasted heaven one last time.

Releasing her, he stepped back. Her mouth was slightly swollen from his possession and her eyes were wide. With difficulty, he shifted his attention to the danger surrounding them.

He peeked around the door, at the hallway leading to the saloon. Clear. "Go."

After a slight hesitation, Rebecca slipped out behind him and her bare feet whispered across the floor. Once she was on the back staircase, she could no longer be seen by anyone who happened to look down the hall. She was safe for the moment.

Ensuring the path was still clear, Slater crept down the hall in the opposite direction, toward the bar. He kept his back pressed to the wall. As he neared the doorway into the saloon, the stench of spilled whiskey struck his nose and he choked down the impulse to cough. He heard low voices and the rough chuckles of two different men, but neither one was the leader. He must have left his cronies to burn the Scarlet Garter.

Over my dead body.

Listening for a minute longer to make sure only the two men remained, Slater peeked around the corner. He spotted them standing at the other end of the bar, close to the piano. His luck remained—their backs faced him.

Without a weapon, it would be suicide to confront them. However, the sawed-off shotgun was beneath the bar. If he could just get to it. . . .

He took a deep breath and slipped behind the bar, keeping low. Safe. Scuttling on his hands and knees he reached the shotgun and his fingers closed around the welcome metal. Before he lost his nerve, he cradled the weapon in his hands, and rose. "Hold it."

The two hired killers spun around, their surprised faces almost comical. The one wearing a threadbare gray jacket made a move for his weapon.

"Don't," Slater commanded, his voice steely.

The pasty-faced outlaw moved his hand away from his gun.

Footsteps at the top of the stairs caused Slater to stiffen, but he didn't dare turn away from the two would-be arsonists.

"Looks like you caught a couple of varmints," Simon said as he came down the steps.

Slater's taut muscles relaxed when the ex-slave joined him, a revolver in his big hand. "The women?"

"Miss Glory took them out the back. Said she'd get the sheriff."

Slater grimaced, but didn't comment. The lawman could hardly ignore what these two had done. However, Slater didn't trust him to keep them locked up. But now he had enough to call in a federal lawman.

He and Simon disarmed the men and forced them down into chairs.

"Keep your hands on the table," Slater ordered.

The two men pressed their palms on the tabletop.

"Watch them," Slater said to Simon. "If they move, shoot 'em."

"With pleasure." The ex-slave smiled.

Slater went to the front door and opened it. He stepped out into the moonlit night to see if he could spot Rebecca and the sheriff. Instead, he saw Cassie, Molly, Rose, and Georgia huddled together at the corner of the building.

"C'mon in," he called to them.

They hurried toward him, shivering from the cool air, and Slater ushered them inside. He wished Rebecca was safe with them, but expected her to return any moment with Ryder.

Cassie marched over to the two men. "So that's the low-down bastards who wanted to burn the place with us in it," she said, anger etched in her voice and expression.

"That's them," Slater said.

"Hope they hang," Molly said with a disdainful sniff.

"If they were involved in Andrew's death, they will. If not, they'll spend a long time in prison for attempted murder." Slater's gaze settled on the gray jacket one man wore, and his eyes narrowed. He followed the line of buttons and noticed one was missing. Drawing nearer to the outlaw, he scrutinized the remaining buttons.

Rage filled Slater and he jerked the gray-jacketed man to his feet. "You were there. You were one of those who killed Andrew."

The man's face paled. "Don't know what you're t-talkin' about."

Slater shoved him back down into his chair as he fought the urge to bash his teeth in. "I found your missing button in the alley where Andrew was beaten the night before he died."

"Lotta fellas wear old Confederate coats," the second outlaw said.

"But not many with the Georgia state symbol on it. Tell me who your boss is and maybe you'll be spared from hanging."

The man with the coat glanced at his cohort, his eyes fear-filled. "Maybe—"

"You tell, and the boss'll kill you himself," the other outlaw warned.

Both outlaws clamped their lips together. It seemed they were more afraid of their boss than of Slater.

"What should we do with them?" Simon asked.

"Take them to jail," Slater replied, frustration giving his tone an edge.

They prodded them out the door and down the dark street to the sheriff's office. A lamp glowed in the window and the door opened easily under Slater's hand. The jail was empty.

His worry intensified and he quickly moved the outlaws

into a cell. With Simon watching them, Slater found the keys in the desk and locked the door.

"Maybe they went the back way and we just missed them," Simon said.

"Maybe." But Slater's gut was telling him otherwise.

Something had happened to Rebecca.

TWENTY-THREE

AN arm bent behind her back, Rebecca refused to give Sheriff Ryder the satisfaction of knowing how much his hold pained her. Instead, she stumbled along, trying to stall for time as the lawman hauled her through the dark town. It seemed they were the only two people awake in Oaktree until she spotted a dim glow lighting one of the numerous tent saloons. She considered screaming, but instinctively knew it would result, at the least, in a broken arm.

"Make a noise and you're dead," the lawman said, guessing her thoughts.

Shivering, Rebecca forced her legs to keep moving. Her working dress left her shoulders and lower legs exposed to the cool night air.

When the sheriff propelled her in the direction of the lighted tent, she stiffened. But he didn't stop and she would've fallen if he hadn't been hanging on to her. As it was, her shoulder was nearly torn from its socket and she couldn't help but groan at the stabbing pain.

However, her aches were forgotten as she was shoved into the tent. As she stumbled in, she caught a glimpse of a wooden sign above the door—The Brass Balls.

Appropriate.

She ducked her head and closed her eyes in the sudden brightness.

"She's supposed to be at the Scarlet Garter, tied up with Forrester."

The voice was familiar and she blinked until blurs coalesced into people. The hired gun stood beside a seated man, whose arrogant expression told Rebecca he was the boss, the man who'd ordered Andrew's death and the attack on the Garter that had resulted in Georgia's injury.

"Both she and Forrester escaped," the sheriff reported. "She came to the office to get me."

"I take it the saloon isn't burning," the bearded man said, his voice tempered but his expression furious.

"No," Ryder said.

"I'm sorry, Mr. Gavin. They were tied up. My two men only had to start the fire after the town was quiet," the hired gun said, sweat forming on his upper lip.

"Obviously they failed," the man named Gavin said, fury behind his curt words. "And Forrester is still alive."

Rebecca was surprised to see the hired killer shuffle his feet. Obviously this Gavin was even more ruthless than his hired lackeys.

"I'm sorry, Mr. Gavin."

"As well you should be. You're paid well for your competence, which seems to be lacking this evening." Gavin sighed and gazed up at Rebecca. He smiled and his expression reminded her of a snake eyeing a mouse. "You did the right thing bringing his whore to me." His lecherous eyes roamed across her. "It's a shame you're valuable to Forrester. I could use a woman like you."

Despite her fear, Rebecca scowled. "Nobody uses me."

"Everyone is used by somebody, even if that person is unaware of it."

Rebecca pressed her lips together.

"Is there anything else you want me to do?" Sheriff Ryder asked Gavin.

"Give Forrester a message." Gavin paused. "Tell him I have something he's looking for."

The crooked lawman opened his mouth as if to argue, then closed it abruptly. He gave Gavin a terse nod, released Rebecca, and strode out of the tent.

Rebecca spun around, intent on escape. However, the hired gun moved faster and grabbed her, one arm around her waist and a hand covering her mouth.

Gavin rose and brushed his knuckles against Rebecca's cheek. "I imagine you're quite a hellcat in bed, too."

She glared at him, wishing she could spit in his face.

Gavin only chuckled. "I'd like to tame you for myself, but I'm afraid my time here is limited."

A chill swept down her spine as she looked into his frigid eyes. Gavin was a man who possessed no morality, no sense of right and wrong. A person like him wouldn't care who he had to hurt or kill to get what he wanted.

"I knew Slater Forrester a long time ago." Gavin's eyes took on a distant look. "In another life."

She furrowed her brow. Slater had told her Gavin was familiar, but he hadn't been able to determine where he'd known him. Obviously Gavin had recognized Slater and remembered him.

"I was an officer at Andersonville the last year of the war," Gavin explained.

Shocked, Rebecca stared at him with a mixture of horror and revulsion. Even if the hired gunman's hand wasn't covering her mouth, she couldn't have spoken.

"The majority of the prisoners died, you know. But there were a few, like Forrester, who were too stubborn," he said with grudging admiration. "However, I didn't expect to run into him here. He's put a wrinkle in my plans. But with your help, I'll be rid of him for good this time."

Rebecca flailed her arms and legs, but the hired gun only laughed at her ineffectual struggle. Tears pricked her eyes and she fought to keep them from spilling. Slater was walking into a trap and she was the bait.

ONCE the two outlaws were in the cell, Slater laid a hand on Simon's shoulder. "Stay here and watch them."

"Where you goin'?" Simon asked.

"To see if Rebecca and the sheriff are at the Garter."

Slater hurried out and strode to the saloon, hoping Simon was right and they'd taken the back way. But even as he hoped, he knew she wouldn't be there. Sheriff Ryder was being paid not to interfere, which was why he did nothing about Andrew's death or the shooting up of the Scarlet Garter. Slater had suspected Ryder's guilt, but he'd hoped the sheriff was only incompetent and not corrupt.

The Garter was silent and empty, increasing Slater's fear for Rebecca. Ryder must have taken her to whoever was in charge. Frustration tore at him and he barely restrained the urge to overturn a table.

He'd promised Rebecca he'd protect her, just as he'd made the same promise in the past. And just as in the past, it seemed he was destined to break that promise.

"No," he growled aloud. This time he'd keep his vow.

The Garter was supposed to be burned, and he and everybody inside killed because Slater had been asking too many questions. However, in the past week, Slater had done little investigating. The only person he'd questioned was the owner of the Brass Balls. Leo Gavin.

Slater pictured the familiar man with his cultured drawl and habit of drawing his fingertip down a card face. He knew him. Closing his eyes tightly, he tried to remember.

A fingernail scraping along a jack of spades.

A contemptuous order given with a Southern drawl.

A Confederate coat.

Like the one the hired killer wore with buttons emblazoned with Georgia's symbol.

Andersonville.

Captain Leroy Towner.

Slater steadied himself with one hand on a table. Captain Towner had been one of the cruelest officers at Andersonville. He'd been behind the torturing and killing of many of the prisoners. When the Union forces had freed the camp, most of the Confederate officers had been captured and tried because of the atrocious conditions at the prison camp.

Towner must have escaped and changed his name, as well as his appearance.

Cold determination filled Slater. Towner would pay for all the lives he'd destroyed. And if he hurt Rebecca, the former Confederate officer would never be tried for his crimes—Slater would kill him.

He hurried up to his room and donned his shoulder holster. Stacking the odds, he stuck Andrew's derringer in his boot and tucked another revolver into his belt at his back, hidden by his jacket.

As he strode out of the saloon, he almost plowed into someone.

"Forrester," Sheriff Ryder said.

"Where is she?" Slater demanded.

Ryder seemed taken aback for a moment, then smiled slightly. "Leo Gavin."

Slater wasn't surprised. Ryder, however, wasn't prepared for the fist that caught him squarely on the jaw. The lawman spun around and dropped to the dirt. Torn between getting to Rebecca and tossing Ryder's ass in jail, Slater swore. He leaned over and grunted as he maneuvered the sheriff's limp body over his shoulder. At the jail, he walked past Simon and dumped Ryder in the empty cell. He removed the lawman's revolver from its holster and, after a moment's hesitation, snatched the badge from Ryder's jacket. Slater locked the cell door behind him, leaving the ex-lawman lying in a heap on the dirt floor and the badge on the desk.

"Miss Glory?" Simon asked after catching the key ring Slater tossed to him.

"Gavin has her. I'm going to get her."

Simon wisely kept silent.

"If I don't come back, send a telegram to the nearest fort commander and tell him former Confederate Captain Leroy Towner from Andersonville is here, posing as a gambler named Leo Gavin," Slater instructed Simon.

The ex-slave nodded somberly.

His concentration focused on rescuing Rebecca, Slater once more went out into the night. However, this time he had an objective and a target. Not knowing how many men Towner employed for his dirty work, Slater decided to enter by the most direct route.

Slater pushed aside the canvas and entered the tent saloon. Although he knew Towner was expecting him, he was surprised to find the ex-Confederate officer sitting at a table playing solitaire. In the chair beside him sat Rebecca, her body stiff and her tawny eyes enormous in her too pale face. Slater's relief was tempered by the hired gunman's revolver held inches from her head.

"Are you all right?" Slater asked, keeping his attention divided between her and Towner.

She nodded in a jerky motion. "You shouldn't have come."

He consciously loosened his muscles and shrugged. "I didn't have a choice."

Towner leaned back in his chair, a cold smile on his thin lips. "You never could just stand by and watch, Forrester."

Slater turned his full attention to Towner, not bothering to hide his hatred. "Not when Captain Leroy Towner tortured and killed men not because of his duty, but because he was a vicious son of a bitch."

"So you remember."

"Hard to forget when I can still hear the screams."

"The problem with you, Forrester, is you have a conscience."

"You've never had that problem."

Towner shrugged. "That's why I was so good at my job." He sighed. "I suppose I can't convince you to forget about me."

Slater barked a sharp laugh. "No way in hell."

"Then I'm afraid we'll have to kill you and your courtesan." His expression hardened. "Remove your weapon or I'll have Parker blow the woman's brains out."

A chill swept through Slater. Towner wasn't bluffing. He removed the revolver from his shoulder holster and set it on the table.

Towner arched an eyebrow, his meaning clear.

Slater stared down at the hated officer for a full minute, debating which weapon to sacrifice. He finally reached down and eased up a trouser leg to lift the derringer from his boot. He laid it beside his revolver.

Towner scooped up the derringer and studied it, his expression amused. "A hideout gun. Just what I would expect from a gambler." His amusement fled. "Any other weapons?"

Slater glared down at him, keeping his mind blank and his eyes locked with Towner's. "No."

"You'd better be telling the truth, Forrester, or she dies first, then you."

Slater forced nonchalance in his shrug. "You're going to kill us anyhow."

"But as you very well know, there are many ways to die, some more difficult than others."

Remembering Towner's brutality, Slater flinched inwardly. However, Towner wouldn't win this time. He wouldn't escape justice a second time.

"I had such plans for this town and you disrupted them." Towner paused. "I still like the idea of you and your paramour being burned to death in your saloon, but I don't have the luxury to be so dramatic now. Parker here will have to dispose of you someplace outside of town, the unlucky victims of a robbery gone bad."

Slater shuddered at Towner's matter-of-fact tone. To discuss murder like he was discussing dinner was evidence that the man was insane. Of course, Towner had already proven that at Andersonville.

Parker jerked Rebecca up and wrapped an arm around her neck.

"If you try anything, Parker will snap her neck and shoot you," Towner said.

His blood cold, Slater nodded. Then he caught Rebecca's determined gaze. She opened her mouth slightly and her eyes shifted to the side, toward the hired gunman. Although he didn't understand exactly what message she was trying to impart, he knew she had an idea.

He wanted to shake his head, to tell her not to try anything that might get her killed. She had a son, someone who depended on her. Not like him, who had no one. But before he could get across his warning, she dipped her head and bit Parker's forearm.

The gunman shouted and shoved her aside, grabbing Towner's attention. Slater reacted, reaching for the revolver behind his back and bringing it up to squeeze the trigger. Parker flew backward, a hole in his chest.

Slater swung his gun barrel to Towner, who held the derringer. He fought the urge to squeeze the trigger, to put down the conscienceless killer like he would a rabid skunk.

"Drop it, Towner," Slater ordered.

Towner stared at him, his eyes as flat and devoid of emotion as a rattlesnake's. "If I do that, I'll be tried in a military court and hanged."

"Better than you deserve."

"I was a soldier doing my job."

Slater's finger twitched on the trigger. "You were a monster who enjoyed hurting people."

Anger flashed in Towner's eyes. "Don't tell me you didn't enjoy spying for the Yankees, knowing Rebs would be killed because of the information you passed on."

"That was different."

"Because you didn't have to see those boys killed on the battlefield, their blood soaking into the ground?"

Slater's stomach churned. No, he wasn't like Towner. He did what he had to in order to lessen the number of lives lost in a war that should have never been fought.

Movement from Towner sent Slater throwing himself to the side, firing his revolver as he moved. A burning sensation creased his side but he barely noticed it. A blossom of red appeared on Towner's shoulder and the former Confederate officer slumped in his chair, the derringer slipping from his fingers to drop onto the floor.

"Slater!"

Rebecca rushed toward him and he captured her shoulders. Her dress was dirty and a strap was broken.

"Are you all right?" Slater asked, his heart hammering in his chest.

"I'm fine. But you're bleeding."

He glanced down, surprised to see scarlet blood staining

his white shirt along his left side. Touching it gingerly, he grunted. "It's only a scratch," he assured her. A single tear streaked down Rebecca's cheek and he wiped it away with his fingertip. "I'll be fine. I promise."

She rested her forehead against his chest, her body trembling. He wanted nothing more than to take her back to his room at the Scarlet Garter and simply hold her, but he had a long overdue task to complete first.

Reluctantly, he eased her away and ducked his head so he could see her face. "I have to take care of Towner."

She nodded, compassion and understanding lighting her eyes.

Slater moved over to Towner's side and nudged his injured shoulder. The former Confederate officer groaned but remained unconscious. Slater stared down at the man who'd ordered Andrew's death and who had been the cause of countless other deaths. The ex-Pinkerton spy tipped his head back and closed his eyes, picturing the faces of those men he'd known at Andersonville.

We're finally free.

CAREFUL of his healing side, Slater gingerly sat down behind his desk in the Scarlet Garter. Although he was slightly self-conscious about the badge pinned to his vest, there was a surprising sense of rightness, too. It was similar to the feeling he'd had when he accepted the Pinkerton offer to become a spy for the Union during the war. But then, Andrew had always told him he had too much integrity to become a professional gambler. It seemed his old friend was right.

Those behind the insurance scheme were in custody, awaiting justice. A contingent of six soldiers had arrived yesterday afternoon and had left early this morning to take former Confederate Captain Leroy Towner to the fort's stockade. He'd be tried in a military court of law for his war crimes and would more than likely hang, just as the Confederate officer had predicted. A federal marshal was on his way to take over law enforcement in Oaktree, but until he arrived, Slater had agreed to do the job.

Slater heard light footsteps on the stairs and recognized Rebecca's ladylike tread. The past two nights, since they'd nearly been burned with the Scarlet Garter, Rebecca had slept in her own room. She'd assured him she wasn't angry, but something else was bothering her. He suspected he already knew what it was.

A soft knock sounded on the office door.

"Come in," he called out. He wasn't surprised to see Rebecca, nor was he startled by the rush of heat that flowed through him at her appearance. She wore the same conservative outfit she'd had on the day she'd come into the Scarlet Garter asking Andrew for a job, but it did nothing to lessen her beauty.

"May I speak with you?" Rebecca asked, her tone stiff and formal.

He gestured for her to enter, and she stood awkwardly, her fingers twining and untwining.

"It's payday," she said quietly, her gaze darting to his eyes, then retreating.

Slater's heart sank. "You're leaving."

She lifted her chin. "Yes."

He rose, came around the desk, and perched on a corner. "To get your son or find your husband?"

"Yes."

Her ambiguous answer left him irritated and confused. "What will you do when you find him?"

"He deserves to know he has a son."

"You didn't answer my question."

Uncertainty clouded her expression. "I don't know."

"Why don't you get your son and bring him back here?"

She suddenly laughed, a burst of bitterness. "And raise him here, in a saloon?"

Slater fought down angry hurt. "It would be better than being raised by parents who don't love each other."

Rebecca closed her eyes and her eyelashes brushed her ivory cheeks. When she reopened her eyes, she looked tired. "What would you have me do with Benjamin?"

"Divorce him. You deserve a helluva lot better than someone like him."

"And what man would want a divorced woman who has a child and works in a saloon?"

I would.

She shook her head. "No. I have to give him a chance. He's a father now. That'll make a difference."

She was trying to convince herself, as well as him, that she was doing the right thing.

"Will you wait until the federal marshal gets here?" Slater asked.

"Why?"

"I'll go with you." He clasped her cool hands in his. "I want to make sure you get to St. Louis safely."

Although she seemed pleased, there was a glint of sadness mixed with it. "You have the Scarlet Garter to look after."

"Dante can do that. He'll keep things running smoothly until I return."

She worried her lower lip between her teeth. "When do you expect the marshal to arrive?"

"Any time now."

She stared past him, her expression both thoughtful and hopeful. Finally she focused back on him. "All right. I'll wait for a day or two."

Almost boneless with relief, Slater smiled and cupped her cheek in his palm. "Thank you." He lowered his head, intent on kissing her, but she turned away and his lips brushed her cheek.

Before he could say anything, she stepped away. "I should g-go." Then she whirled around and was gone.

Puzzled, Slater let his hands fall to his sides. If she was angry with him, she wouldn't have agreed to wait for the marshal to arrive so Slater could accompany her. However, it was obvious she no longer wanted his attentions. Did she regret the adulterous affair?

She was everything he wanted in a woman, but she was also married and had a child. What if she divorced her husband? Would he be willing to marry her and accept her son as his own?

Although his mind was troubled by the question, his heart had no qualms.

TWENTY-FOUR

REBECCA sank into the tub and sighed blissfully as the hot water embraced her aching body. After two days of traveling, first by stagecoach and then by train, she and Slater had arrived in St. Louis. Although she'd been raised there, Slater knew more about the accommodations and he chose a respectable, clean, and modestly priced hotel.

She closed her eyes and allowed the water's heat to massage her sore muscles. It was too late in the day to get Daniel from St. Francis' Home for Orphans, but tomorrow morning, she promised herself, she'd have her son in her arms again. And this time she wouldn't let him go.

Her thoughts drifted to Slater and his steadfast presence during the journey. He didn't speak much, as if knowing Rebecca needed time to think and plan, but he was always there to lean on without asking anything in return. She could almost believe he loved her by his actions, but he'd never spoken the words, so she didn't dare confess her own love for him.

And it *was* love, not the infatuation she'd felt for Benjamin. Smooth, suave Benjamin who'd swept a naive, grieving young woman off her feet, then proceeded to steal everything she owned. A tear slid down her cheek and she angrily wiped it away.

A soft knock sounded a moment before the door between her and Slater's adjoining rooms opened. Rebecca crossed her arms over her breasts even as she realized the silliness of her actions. Slater knew her body almost as well as she did.

His eyes widened slightly, but he kept his gaze on her face. "I just wanted to make sure you were all right," he said as he sat in the wingback chair near the tub.

Heat infused Rebecca and her nipples peaked in the warm water. "I'm fine." Her voice came out huskier than she'd intended. "How're you doing?"

"Fine," he replied without inflection.

His eyes drifted down, across the water, and she wondered how much he could see beneath the surface. She resisted the urge to squirm beneath his hot gaze.

Slater cleared his throat and met her eyes. "I'm going out for a little while. I want to see if there's a message from my Pinkerton friend."

His words acted like a bucket of ice water. "Do you think he's heard anything more of Benjamin's whereabouts?"

"Maybe." He paused, as if grappling for words. "I have to be back in Oaktree on Monday."

That was only five days away. "Why?"

He studied his hands. "Being a saloon owner isn't enough. I've agreed to become Oaktree's new sheriff, permanently."

Rebecca stared at him, shocked by his declaration. "I thought . . ."

A sardonic grin played across his lips. "You thought I was content playing poker every night. I was. For a time." He sobered and the dark blue of his eyes was almost eclipsed by the black pupils. "I told you my younger brother, Rye, and I were put in an orphanage when I was eleven. A month later I was adopted. Even though Rye didn't go with me, I was glad to be gone from that place, but it turned out the man was only looking for cheap labor. For over three years I slept in a shed not fit for pigs and worked from sunup to sundown." His gaze took on a distant cast. "I hated that shed.

"There were other children, too. One of them was a boy

who reminded me of Rye. I tried to look out for him, even promised him I'd keep him safe."

Slater's eyes glimmered and he glanced away, but not before Rebecca caught a glimpse of the young boy he'd been. She wanted to comfort him, but that hurt little boy was long gone. "What happened to him?" she asked, although she already suspected.

"Lowell, the man who adopted us, whipped him one day for falling asleep in the field. Tommy never got better and one morning, when I tried to wake him up, he was dead. About a year later, Lowell tried to whip me. I'd gotten big enough by then that I could defend myself. I used the whip on him and ran away. I didn't stay around to find out if I killed him or not."

Sympathy for the boy Slater had been and the scarred man he'd become nearly suffocated her. That someone would have less regard for a child than an animal shocked her, yet she was learning that life outside her cloistered upbringing was harsh and unforgiving. While her childhood had been filled with love, laughter, and nearly anything she wished, Slater had endured cruelty and deprivation. Who was she to judge how he'd stayed alive? He'd done what he could and grown past his degradations into a man who possessed integrity and a strong sense of justice and responsibility.

He took a deep breath. "Andrew caught me picking his pocket about six months later."

"And instead of turning you in, he decided to help you," Rebecca said.

A tiny smile tugged at Slater's lips. "Yes. He taught me everything he knew about gambling so I wouldn't have to steal again."

"How did you get involved with the Pinkertons?"

"At the start of the war, I was a riverboat gambler. I didn't take sides, so both the Union and Confederate soldiers left me alone. One day this man came up to me and made me an offer. The Pinkerton Agency was looking for spies for the Union Army and I was in a unique position. The war had dragged on for two years and it was getting harder and harder for me to stay neutral, so I agreed to work for them.

"For a year I gathered information and passed it on to agents. Everything was going smoothly, too smoothly. Then I went to Atlanta, using my gambler cover to find out what I could about Confederate troop movements. I was sent to Andersonville."

She nodded, remembering the night he'd told her. The night Georgia had been shot.

His expression turned bleak. "They had these boxes, just big enough for a man to fit in but he couldn't stretch out. I spent three days in one. It reminded me of the shed I was locked in at night as a kid, but ten times worse. For a long time after, I couldn't even be in a building without getting the shakes."

She glanced at his left hand, realizing the involuntary trembling was probably a reminder of those dark times. "That night you had the nightmare. You were dreaming about being locked up again."

"Yes." He took a deep breath and met her gaze. "If you hadn't been with me the other night, the Garter would've burned down and we would've died. I panicked but you helped me focus on getting free."

"I'm sorry, Slater. I didn't know."

He smiled tenderly. "Nobody did. Andrew knew some of my past, but you're the first person I've told everything."

Humbled and grateful that he'd trusted her, Rebecca cleared her throat of the lump before she could speak. "What happened to your brother Rye?"

His gaze clouded. "I don't know. I wanted to go back to the orphanage to get him, but I never got there. I had an older brother, too. Creede. He was sixteen, so he didn't have to go into the orphanage like Rye and me." Long-held hurt and anger filled his expression. "I used to dream he'd rescue me from Lowell, but after a year, I gave up. I figured he didn't care about me anymore."

"Or maybe something happened to him and he couldn't come for you," she offered.

"We'll never know," Slater said with a shrug that didn't hide the years-old hurt.

Muffled sounds drifted in from the bustling city but inside

the room, there was only expectant silence. Remembering her first impression of Slater, Rebecca realized his prickly attitude had been a mask to hide his emotional wounds. Ever since Andrew had been murdered, however, Slater had emerged from behind that mask and become the man Rebecca had fallen in love with.

"Oaktree is lucky to get you as sheriff—you're a fair and honest man, Slater Forrester," she said.

His gentle smile settled in her heart. "Thanks, Rebecca. I care about your opinion." He paused and his eyes darkened with passion. "I care about *you*."

Hope quickened her pulse. Did he love her?

Suddenly Slater rose and took two steps toward the door. "I have to leave. Will you be all right?"

Disappointed, she managed a reassuring smile. "Yes. Do what you have to. I'll finish my bath, then go to bed."

Slater gazed at her for a moment longer, then disappeared into his room.

Rebecca settled back in the tub of now-lukewarm water. A part of her wished she'd never find Benjamin. But that wouldn't change the fact that she was a married woman who couldn't give Slater all he deserved.

SLATER expected to find a note waiting for him in St. Louis and he wasn't disappointed. Brent's message had been succinct; Benjamin Colfax had been seen gambling in the higher-class gaming establishments in St. Louis for the past two nights. However, it was the last line of Brent's message that blindsided Slater.

Two men named Forrester living in Texas. Interested?

One night while sharing drinks after an assignment, he'd told Brent about not having seen his brothers since he was a child. Brent, having grown up in a large, devoted family, had been outraged, and since then he'd made it his personal mission to find Slater's brothers. Slater had forgotten all about it. But it seemed Brent might have finally succeeded. Slater sent a reply asking for more information, then instructed the operator to deliver any more messages to the hotel.

Right now, Slater had a more urgent matter to attend to. Trying to put himself in Colfax's shoes, Slater considered where he might be tonight. There were a handful of higher-class gambling houses that came to mind and he headed for the nearest. Rebecca had shown him the photograph of Colfax, so he knew what the man looked like.

Slater wore one of his fancy suits and blended in with the other gamblers as he entered the first establishment. It wasn't the most extravagant in St. Louis, but it made both the Scarlet Garter and John Langley's Black Bull, the two fanciest places in Oaktree, appear shabby. The sounds of men's low voices, cards and coins being slapped on tables, and bottles and glasses clinking were as familiar to Slater as his own voice.

He went to the bar and ordered brandy. While he sipped it, he searched the room for Colfax. Spotting three possibilities, he surreptitiously circled the men. However, on closer inspection none turned out to be Rebecca's husband. He went to the next gambling hall, which was just as crowded. He wandered around the large room as if studying each poker and faro table to determine where he might choose to play.

"You're courting Lady Luck tonight, Colfax."

Slater turned and spotted Rebecca's husband, a man with thick brown hair parted in the middle and a pencil-thin mustache, sitting at a poker table.

Colfax chuckled, an oily sound that made Slater grind his teeth. "Her name isn't Luck, but Elizabeth."

"When's the wedding?" another player asked.

"A week from Saturday."

Slater frowned. How could Benjamin Colfax marry when he was already wedded to Rebecca? Did he think Rebecca was dead? But no, he wouldn't have had time to search for her in the week he'd been in St. Louis. Hell, he shouldn't have had time to find a new wife, either, unless he'd met the woman during a previous trip.

"You'd better enjoy your freedom, Benjamin. I hear marriage is a bit like prison," another man joked. "And the wife holds the key to your cell."

Everyone laughed.

"Not so with my Elizabeth. She understands my nature," Colfax said.

"They always say that in the beginning."

"I'm certain I'll be able to handle my own wife." Colfax's smugness reminded Slater of a fox who'd raided the chicken coop.

Slater already despised the son of a bitch for using up Rebecca's money, then abandoning her—but to commit bigamy . . . .

He fought his murderous urge and forced himself to watch the poker game with a dispassionate expression. When one of the players bowed out, Slater took his place.

Colfax's gaze flickered over Slater, gauging him to determine what kind of player he was. After years under Andrew's tutelage, it was easy for Slater to keep his face from giving away his thoughts.

However, it wasn't as simple to keep his mind on the cards. Instead, he was torn between beating Colfax to a pulp and trying to determine what Rebecca had seen in the dandy. Only when Colfax spoke courteously to the barmaid did Slater figure it out. Colfax's smooth manners would've hidden his true nature from someone as young and innocent as Rebecca. She had been nothing more than a bank to back his gambling. Slater suspected his latest fiancée was just as innocent and comfortably well-off as Rebecca had been.

Slater kept fairly even with his bets, losing some and winning some, but always observing Colfax. Finally, two of the players made their excuses and left. Having lost more than he won, Colfax rose to leave.

Slater followed Colfax out of the gambling hall.

"Been in St. Louis long?" Slater asked as he fell into step beside Colfax on the boardwalk.

Colfax glanced at him. "A week this time. However, I've visited often."

"Did I hear that congratulations are in order?"

"I'm getting married next week."

"First time?" Slater pressed.

"Yes. I never met anyone like Elizabeth before."

Slater ground his teeth. "Not even Rebecca?"

Colfax stumbled slightly. "Who?"

"Rebecca Bowen Colfax. Your wife."

Colfax's mouth gaped and his eyes widened, but Slater knew his reaction was due to being caught in his lie rather than finding out Rebecca was alive. "I thought she was dead."

"Bullshit. Once her money was gone, you left her to find someone else you could swindle." Slater pulled his derringer out of his pocket and pressed it against Colfax's side. "For reasons of her own, Rebecca has been searching for you and I'm going to take you to her."

Colfax tried to resist, but soft living made him no match for Slater. He escorted Colfax to the hotel's back door and upstairs to Rebecca's room. Although he preferred to tar and feather the bastard, Slater cared too much for Rebecca. If she wanted Colfax to know of his son and be given the chance to make amends, Slater would abide by her wishes.

He knocked on Rebecca's door and she opened it, wearing a wrapper around her gown. Her long hair was loose, falling over her shoulders like a silvery white waterfall.

A hand flew to her mouth and the color disappeared from her cheeks. "Benjamin."

Colfax nodded stiffly. "Rebecca. I see you didn't waste any time finding another man."

Slater threw him against the wall and dug the derringer's barrel into his jaw's underside. "You insult her again, and I'll kill you."

Colfax's complexion turned pasty white.

Slater grabbed his arm and shoved him into Rebecca's room. She closed the door behind them.

"I found him playing poker in one of the gambling halls," Slater said to her, then added dryly, "It seems he's engaged to be married."

Rebecca slapped Colfax, snapping his head to the side with the force of the blow. She shook her head, staring at Colfax like he was something unpleasant she'd stepped in. "Why?"

Colfax's nostrils flared and he deliberately straightened his lapels. "Because I need money to gamble, and you, dear Rebecca, had none left."

"Because you stole everything I owned."

Slater remained silent, allowing Rebecca to vent the anger she'd nursed for months.

Colfax narrowed his eyes. "You wanted a gentleman for a husband. I wanted money. It was a simple business arrangement."

Rebecca's eyes filled with moisture, but there was only fury in her expression. "I thought you loved me."

"Come, come, Rebecca. Love is a foolish notion propagated by silly young girls."

Rebecca stood in front of Colfax, her arms folded beneath her breasts. "And you used my naïveté to wed and bed me, then disposed of all my money at the gambling tables." She paused and lifted her chin. "By the way, you have a son."

Colfax blinked, then laughed. "Surely you don't expect me to believe that."

Fury blazed from her eyes. "His name is Daniel."

Colfax made a show of looking around the small hotel room. "Where is he?"

"I had to leave him at an orphanage when I went to look for you. I'm going to get him tomorrow." She swallowed hard and Slater knew much of her pride went with it. "You have an obligation, both moral and financial, to him."

Colfax pressed his lips together. "How do I know he's mine?" He glanced at Slater, his meaning clear.

"You have my word, your *wife's* word," Rebecca replied before Slater could feed Colfax his fist.

Colfax began to laugh. Slater glanced at Rebecca, who frowned in confusion.

"What's so damned funny?" Slater asked.

The man continued his inane laughter.

Colfax had married Rebecca as a business arrangement, and Slater assumed he was marrying the woman named Elizabeth for the same reason. A sick realization dawned. If Colfax married for business reasons, how many of those transactions had he conducted?

"How many wives do you have?" Slater demanded.

Colfax wiped his streaming eyes. "I've lost count."

Rebecca swayed and she cast out a hand to steady herself. "You mean we were never married?" Her voice was faint.

"If Colfax never divorced any of his so-called wives, none of the marriages after the first were legal," Slater explained, a dizzying mix of fury and relief swirling through him. "That means he had no legal right to gamble away your money and property."

With an outraged cry, Rebecca flung herself at Colfax, her fists striking his chest. The fop attempted to protect himself, but humiliation fueled her rage. Slater allowed her to land some solid blows before he pulled her away from him.

Rebecca struggled to escape, but suddenly all the fight left her. She collapsed in Slater's arms and turned to bury her face against his chest.

Colfax adjusted his vest and jacket. "As I have no legal obligation to Rebecca or my so-called son, I shall leave."

"The hell you will," Slater growled. "Polygamy is against the law, as is stealing."

"I'm not a thief."

"You swindled innocent women out of their money and homes, which is even worse than robbing them outright. The only place you're going is prison."

"You have no proof I was married to any other woman than Rebecca."

Slater smiled coldly. "Maybe not yet, but I will." He paused. "My friends at the Pinkerton Agency will be more than willing to help put you away for a long time."

Colfax's bravado melted away. "I won't survive in prison."

"We can only hope." Slater glanced down to see Rebecca gazing up at him, her eyes filled with both embarrassment and gratitude. "I'll be back after I drop him off at the jail."

Rebecca nodded and retreated, wrapping her arms around her waist. Concerned by her silence, Slater didn't want to leave, but Colfax had to be escorted to jail. In fact, it was a task Slater relished.

Slater hauled Colfax away, but it took some time to explain to the St. Louis police why the man needed to be in jail. Although the police were reluctant at first, once Slater informed them of Rebecca's situation and the fact Pinkerton could track down the other so-called wives, they readily agreed to hold Colfax.

As Slater began to leave, Colfax called out, "What about my son?"

Slater stopped and gave him a steady look. "What son?" Then he left, intent on returning to Rebecca.

Standing outside her door, he knocked softly. "Rebecca, it's Slater."

He heard the shuffle of feet.

"I'd like to be alone," came her soft voice through the door.

Although disappointed, Slater respected her need. She was probably embarrassed to find she'd been only one of many women duped by Colfax. "All right, but if you want to talk, you know where I'll be."

"Thank you," she whispered.

Slater trudged to his room and removed his jacket, shirt, and boots. Lying down on the bed in the darkness, he heard Rebecca's muffled sobs.

Sleep was a long time coming.

THE following morning Slater was up early, and he shaved and donned dark trousers, a shirt, and a vest. He didn't want Rebecca to go to the orphanage alone. Besides, he was curious about her son. He hoped the boy had blonde hair like his mother instead of taking after his father.

He stepped into the hallway at the same moment Rebecca's door opened. She appeared startled to see him, but beneath the surprise, there was pleasure.

"Good morning," she greeted him with a tentative smile.

"Morning," he said. "Care to join me for breakfast?"

She shook her head. "I'm too nervous to eat anything, but I would like some coffee."

He extended a crooked arm and she took it. Her palm was warm on his forearm and there was no sign of her restless night in her bright eyes and pink cheeks. The hotel had a decent restaurant, and once seated there, Slater found he wanted only coffee, too.

"Thank you for finding Benjamin," Rebecca began after her first sip of coffee.

"It was what you wanted."

She tipped her head to the side, and with her demure hat and dress there was little resemblance to Miss Glory. "Yes, I did." Her bow-shaped lips tilted upward. " 'Be careful what you wish for' seems apt in this situation."

Slater traced the cup's handle. "Do you regret it?"

"No," she replied without hesitation. "I just never expected to learn I had a child out of wedlock."

"You thought you were man and wife."

"My father used to say ignorance wasn't an excuse."

"No, but it is an explanation. You have nothing to be ashamed of. It was Colfax who was at fault."

She finished her coffee and glanced around at the growing number of customers. "At least I don't have to make the decision whether to divorce him or not."

Slater stiffened, then forced his muscles to relax.

Rebecca leaned forward and placed her hand on his. "I want you to know that on the way to St. Louis, I decided to divorce him and damn the consequences. I didn't want to live with a man I hated for the rest of my life."

Slater's heart lifted and words rose in his throat. However, he didn't dare speak them yet, not until he was certain. "Are you ready to see your son?"

A blindingly bright smile lit her face. "More than ready."

He felt a stab of jealousy for the child that brought Rebecca so much joy.

Slater paid a cab to take them to the orphanage on the other side of town, then asked the driver to wait for them when they arrived.

A somber, black-robed nun answered their summons. She remembered Rebecca, and after a quick appraisal of Slater, the sister went to get Daniel. Slater sat down, but Rebecca paced the office as they waited. Nearly ten minutes passed before he heard the nun's footsteps returning.

He stood as she reentered with a thrashing bundle in her arms. Rebecca froze and Slater pressed his palm against her back to urge her forward. However, he kept his gaze averted from the infant. He moved to the single window and stared out the glass unseeing, listening to Rebecca speak to her son in a soft, loving voice.

He couldn't compete against her child for her affections. Free of Benjamin, she could stay in St. Louis and find a husband more fitting for someone as genteel as herself. Her experience with Colfax would give her the wisdom to choose a man more prudently, a man who could love her and her child.

A touch on his arm startled him out of his thoughts and he turned to find Rebecca gazing up at him, her eyes reflecting uncertainty.

"Slater, I'd like you to meet my son, Daniel," she said.

Against his will, his gaze settled on Daniel and Slater found himself captured by the boy's eyes, which were only a shade darker than Rebecca's. The slight upturn of Daniel's nose and the shape of his chin reminded him of his mother.

"Would you like to hold him?" Rebecca asked.

Before he could retreat in terror, Rebecca was placing Daniel in his arms. The child weighed little but kicked and flailed his legs and arms, making Slater tighten his hold on the boy.

Daniel stopped moving and stared up at Slater with unblinking eyes. The baby seemed to be gauging him, and Slater smiled at his own fanciful thought. Slater brushed the boy's hand with his finger and Daniel captured it in his fist, tugging it toward his mouth.

"He's probably hungry," the nun said. "I'll get a bottle for him." She disappeared, leaving Slater alone with Rebecca and her son.

Slater continued to watch the infant, his unease turning to wonder.

"He's beautiful. He looks like you," Slater said quietly, his gaze remaining on Daniel.

She laughed, her cheeks blossoming with color. "I doubt he'll like being called beautiful when he's older."

"Handsome, then."

Rebecca nodded. "Better." Her face grew soft with fondness as she watched them. "It's hard to believe you don't have a child of your own. You seem comfortable holding a baby."

Slater suddenly realized he wasn't nervous. "I've held one or two before, but never really thought much about them."

"What do you think of Daniel?"

There was an intensity in her tone that implied she was asking more than the obvious. "He's your child, Rebecca."

She glanced down. "And Benjamin's."

"No," Slater said sharply, causing Daniel to fuss. Slater crooned to the boy until he calmed, then spoke to Rebecca in a quieter voice. "Daniel will grow up to be a better man than Colfax could ever hope to be because you're his mother."

Bitterness twisted Rebecca's lips. "Except I have no way to support him."

Slater resisted the urge to embrace her, comfort her. Instead, he gazed down at Daniel's angelic face and the decision that had seemed so difficult suddenly seemed so simple. "Being sheriff will keep me away most of the time," he said, keeping his voice casual. "But since I plan to hold on to the Garter, I'll need someone to manage it for me."

"What about Dante?"

Slater snorted, drawing a soft gurgle from the infant cradled in his arms. "I had to twist Dante's arm to manage the place just for the short time I'm here. He prefers bartending. Besides, he hates bookkeeping."

Rebecca leaned close and her breasts pressed against his arm, sending a rush of blood southward. She brushed a finger across her son's fine-spun hair.

"I might know someone willing to manage the Scarlet Garter and do the bookkeeping," she said, her warm breath fanning across his wrist. "But she has a son and no husband."

Slater squelched a smile. "She wouldn't mind raising her child in a saloon?"

She huffed a gentle laugh. "The only thing she's worried about is Daniel being spoiled by all his aunts and uncles."

Slater's heart slid into his throat and he had to swallow twice before he could speak. "What about a father?"

With Rebecca so close, Slater saw the butterfly pulse quicken in her slender neck. She turned her head slightly, enough that she could meet his gaze. "His mother would have to wed, and Daniel will always be number one in her heart. Not many men would accept second place."

"He'd have to truly love and respect her." Slater cradled Daniel in one arm and cupped the side of her face with his free hand. "I love you, Rebecca Glory Bowen. Will you marry me?"

Rebecca's eyes filled with moisture. "I love you, too, Slater. I have for a long time." She worried her lower lip between her teeth. "But are you sure you want to marry a fallen woman?"

Slater caressed her satin-smooth cheek with his thumb and smiled rakishly. "That's my favorite kind."

$\mathcal{E}$PILOGUE

EIGHTEEN MONTHS LATER

FORTUNATELY the train had taken them most of the distance, but the final thirty miles to Locust, Texas, were spent in a bone-jarring stagecoach. Even Daniel, who saw the entire trip as one big adventure, grew weary of the bumpy ride and finally fell asleep in Slater's lap.

Although it was warm, Slater didn't mind his two-year-old son being draped across him. He'd adopted Daniel a day after he and Rebecca had married, and couldn't have loved a son of his own blood any more than he loved Daniel.

"I hope Dante remembers to order an extra case of whiskey. We were getting lower than usual on it," Rebecca said with a frown.

Rebecca had taken over the management of Miss Glory's Bonanza, formerly the Scarlet Garter, upon their return to Oaktree and she took her responsibilities seriously. Sometimes too seriously. "Don't worry. He'll remember," Slater reassured her.

"You're right. Dante's been tending bar longer than I've been managing," she said with a self-deprecating smile. Her expression dovetailed back to anxious. "Georgia better not go into labor early. I told her I'd be there when their first child was born."

"She's only five months along. You have another four months, three at the earliest." Careful not to jostle and awaken Daniel, Slater brushed her arm with his fingertips. "Calm down."

She glared at him. "Easy for you to say. They're your brothers."

"Whom I haven't seen in nearly thirty years." He took a deep breath to dispel his own nervousness. "Maybe this is a mistake."

Rebecca clasped his hand. "No, this isn't a mistake. They're your brothers. They want to meet you."

It'd been over a year ago that Slater first made contact with Creede and Rye. He'd sent a telegram to them, asking if they had a brother named Slater. Both had immediately replied that they did. It was over a month before Slater sent a letter to them, telling them a little about himself. It wasn't long before they were exchanging letters on a regular basis. Rebecca had talked him into letting his deputy watch over Oaktree while they visited Slater's brothers.

Slater could finally ask Creede face to face why he'd abandoned him, and apologize to Rye for not returning to get him out of the orphanage. Both tasks lay heavily upon Slater, but he knew he had to do them for his own peace of mind.

The stagecoach finally arrived in Locust, which turned out to be smaller than Oaktree but with more families. It made sense, since Oaktree was a cattle town and Locust a farming community.

The stagecoach drew to a halt in front of the only hotel in town. Daniel remained sleeping, so Slater carried him out of the coach after Rebecca was given a hand down by the driver.

A small cluster of people stood nearby—two men, two women, and five children. Despite the many years that had passed, Slater immediately recognized Rye and felt moisture sting his eyes. The last time he'd seen Rye, the six-year-old had his face pressed to the orphanage window, watching him leave.

Slater was barely aware of Rebecca taking Daniel from his arms before he walked over to his little brother. "Rye," he said, his voice breaking.

"Slater." Rye's voice was thick with emotion.

Rye stepped forward and wrapped his arms around Slater. Slater hugged Rye and a tear dampened his cheek as he remembered happier days, when he and Rye would catch frogs in the pond near their family's home.

It was Rye who stepped back first, and Slater reluctantly released him. A man with thick gray hair neared Slater, staring at him as if he were looking at a ghost.

"We thought you were dead," Creede said in a husky tone.

Slater stared at the middle-aged man, wondering where the headstrong sixteen-year-old had gone. "Hello, Creede," he said, sticking out his hand.

Creede gripped the outstretched hand. "You take after Pa."

Slater barely remembered their father, but what he did recall told him Creede was right. "Where'd you go?" Slater had no idea what he'd say until the question came out.

Creede tipped his head to the side, dark blue eyes puzzled. "What do you mean?"

"I thought you'd come back for us after you took care of those men who killed Ma."

Creede shifted his weight from one foot to the other. "I wanted to. I truly did, Slater. But it took me two years to find them, and by then, I wasn't the boy I used to be. I think maybe I was ashamed for you and Rye to see what I'd become."

"And what was that?" Slater demanded.

Creede paused and his gaze went to the handsome woman he'd been standing beside. She nodded gently to him.

"A gun for hire," Creede confessed.

The boy in Slater was shocked, but the man understood.

Rebecca joined him, as if sensing Slater's conflicted emotions, and laid her soft palm on his arm. "It wasn't that he forgot about you. It was that he loved you too much."

The smoldering anger Slater had carried with him for years flickered out. He knew all too well how a man could be haunted and shamed by things he'd done. Glancing at Rye, Slater noticed a shadow in his younger brother's eyes, too. Life's harsher lessons had left marks on each of the Forrester men.

But maybe when it came right down to it, none of that mattered. They were brothers, bound by blood and by early memories that shaped and honed them into the men they'd become.

"Are you all right?" Rebecca whispered, her expression filled with concern and love.

Slater nodded and took their sleepy son from her arms. Holding Daniel with his right arm, he wrapped his left around Rebecca's shoulders and faced his two brothers, his head held high. "Creede, Rye, this is my wife, Rebecca, and our son, Daniel."

As if Slater's words swept away the last vestiges of awkwardness, the Forrester clan surged forward to welcome the last brother home.

TURN THE PAGE FOR A PREVIEW OF THE
EXCITING NEW ROMANTIC SUSPENSE
NOVEL BY MAUREEN MCKADE

Where There's Fire

COMING FALL 2008 FROM BERKLEY SENSATION!

SHONI made a sharp U-turn and braked at the mouth of a shadowed alley. As she jumped out of her car, a young girl raced out of the passageway, her dark eyes huge in the pale oval of her face.

Shoni caught her arms and the girl squirmed and kicked. A toe caught Shoni's shin and she gasped. "Take it easy. It's all right. I won't hurt you." She tried to restrain the kid without hurting her as Shoni evaded thrashing legs and arms.

The girl, who was maybe seven years old, stopped struggling and clutched Shoni's sleeve. Despite the cold evening, she wore only a light jacket over a faded Shrek T-shirt and thin, often-washed jeans. "They're hurting him!"

Shoni dropped to a crouch in front of the girl. "Who?"

"My friend. John."

"How many men are hurting him?"

"Three." The streetlight caught her face, revealing shiny tear tracks trailing down her caramel-colored cheeks.

"Get in my car and lock the doors. Don't open them for anyone but me."

Shoni pressed her toward the car as she drew out her cell

phone and called 911 one-handed. The operator's professional, impersonal voice came on and Shoni quickly gave her the information needed to gain assistance.

Once the girl was safely in the Toyota, Shoni turned and ran into the pitch-black passage. Her nape tingled and she drew her standard-issue Glock 19 out of its holster at her back. A rustle made her freeze and she leveled the pistol in the sound's direction. A cat's glowing eyes stared back at her.

"Damn it!" She tipped up the barrel of her weapon and nearly collapsed in relief. With adrenaline streaming through her veins, she ran deeper into the fetid alley.

Within moments, she picked up the unmistakable sounds of fists against flesh and the occasional moan and grunt. She was almost to the rear of the alley when she spotted shifting shadows. She crept closer, her heart hammering in her chest. Her eyes adjusted until she was able to make out three men surrounding another.

Rage surged through her at the uneven odds and her finger curled around the trigger. A moment later, her brain caught up and she realized the attackers seemed afraid to get too close to the single figure. She eased her finger's pressure and took the proper stance. "Freeze! Police!"

Three heads turned her way, but Shoni was peripherally aware of the victim, who kept his attention on his attackers. Seconds later, the bullies scurried away. One was holding his side and another was limping painfully as they made their escape. Shoni placed her weapon back in its holster.

"John!"

A blur rushed past her and Shoni realized the little girl hadn't followed orders. She ran straight to the man and nearly knocked him down. Her arms wound around his waist and he hugged her, leaning over her.

"Shhh, I'm all right," he murmured soothingly.

The man's low, masculine voice sent a shiver of awareness through Shoni. Ignoring her unexpected reaction, she approached him tentatively and stopped a few feet away. With his head bowed over the girl, Shoni could only see thick, shaggy hair that covered the tops of his ears and brushed his collar. "Are you all right?"

The man straightened his spine, but kept a protective hold on the girl. He looked down a chiseled nose flawed only by a break that had healed with a slight crook. An untrimmed beard and moustache the same gilded gold as his hair covered the lower half of his face, but his direct silvery blue eyes snared her.

He nodded in reply.

Caught by his direct gaze, it took her a moment to realize what his nod meant. She cleared her dry throat and fell back on police procedure. "I'll call an ambulance so you can be checked out at the hospital."

"No! No hospital." His voice was amazingly rich and deep.

Shoni's neck muscles tightened as she searched his expression. Despite her fairly impressive height of five foot ten, she had to tilt her head back to meet and hold his unwavering gaze. "Detective Alexander with Norfolk PD."

The man's lips curled into a sneer. "And I'll bet you even have a shiny gold badge."

Taken aback by his vehemence, Shoni held up her hands. "I've got no beef with you. I was just passing by when I heard a scream." She glanced at the wide-eyed girl, her face blurred in the darkness, as she clung to him. "It was a good thing she yelled." She paused. "Did you recognize the men who attacked you?"

"No."

Shoni knew John hadn't spoken the truth, but she didn't dare call him a liar. His defensiveness was already notched up but everything in her railed against letting the perpetrators get away. "If they're behind bars, they can't hurt anybody."

His expression turned ugly and he shook his head. "They'd be out on bail in less than twenty-four hours."

She didn't bother arguing and said quietly, "I'm trying to help you."

For a long moment, John studied her then nodded as his granite expression eased. It wasn't much, but Shoni figured from this man it was a huge concession. She reached into her pocket and the man tensed once more. "I'm just getting one of my cards," the detective said, keeping her voice calm.

Shoni withdrew one of her business cards and passed it to the man who simply stared at it. She continued to hold it out, willing to give him time to judge her. Like an abused dog, this man didn't trust easily.

Finally, John reached out to accept the card from her grasp. His cool, calloused fingertips brushed her hand and a shock traveled up her arm. A core of restless heat settled in her belly. He stilled, as if he, too, felt it, and allowed the contact to remain for precious seconds longer.

When he drew his hand away, Shoni let out a gust of air and realized she hadn't breathed the entire time their fingers touched. What was wrong with her? Unshaven men who lived on the street weren't usually her type. So why the breathless heroine act?

"If you need help, call me," she said.

"Why?"

She studied him and realized he wanted a real answer, not a canned reply. "I care."

He met her gaze and his distrust remained, but slowly, a sliver of acceptance stole into his icy blue depths. He tucked the card into his jacket pocket.

Shoni noticed how he favored his right arm, but was blocked from getting a closer look by what she suspected was a deliberate shift of his body. "Are you sure you're all right?"

"I'm fine." The distrust was back in full force.

The succinct reply reminded her too much of her own answer to Bob when he'd asked how she was doing. Shoni guessed John, too, was lying.

Restraining a sigh of frustration, she squatted down and spoke to the girl who hadn't relinquished her hold on the man. "My name is Shoni. What's yours?" she asked, using the same soothing voice she used to defuse domestic disturbances and strung out addicts.

"Lainey."

Bright flashing lights invaded the alley and the blaring yowl of a siren filled the narrow passageway. Headlights illuminated the man and the girl, giving Shoni an unhindered view of them. But before she could catalog more than their basic physical characteristics, John scooped Lainey into his arms and loped away, in the opposite direction of the police cruiser. He moved with surprising grace, his stride long and confident. His secondhand jeans and jacket couldn't disguise his impressive body—not muscle-bound, but well-proportioned shoulders that tapered to a narrow waist and nicely rounded backside. In fact, other than his unshorn hair and beard, and his thrift-store clothes, he didn't look like one of the desperate, hungry homeless who populated Norfolk's streets.

Two uniformed cops hurried over to Shoni's side.

"What happened?" one of them asked.

She stared into the blackness that had swallowed up the man and the girl. For a terrifying moment, she wondered if she'd allowed a sexual predator to escape with a child, but remembering the man's obvious protectiveness, she knew her instincts had been right.

"It was only a misunderstanding," she said. "Let's get out of here."

KEEPING up his guard, John guided Lainey through a maze of trash-littered alleys. He moved on the balls of his feet, his footfalls soundless, and the action was familiar in a way he couldn't pinpoint. But then, he didn't remember a whole lot these days. However, caution and wariness were second nature, traits he'd obviously retained even though he'd lost the rest of his identity.

"Are we going to Gram's?" Lainey asked.

John glanced down at the girl. "Yes."

"What about Mom?"

John managed to keep his antagonism hidden. "She shouldn't have taken you with her."

"She needed me."

The girl's defense of her mother made John's throat tighten even as fresh anger surged through him. The only thing Mishon needed was her fix. "Not tonight. She's working."

He wondered how much Lainey understood about what her mother did. Probably everything, which only made him more furious.

Lainey's great-grandmother Estelle lived in a rundown apartment building, less than a block from the waterfront warehouses. It was the only inhabited building in a radius of three blocks. Everything around it had been bought by a developer who planned on creating another trendy, upscale area like the popular Waterside. The developer had tried to have Estelle and the few other stubborn tenants evicted, but had lost the battle due to a technicality.

Despite the fact it was a weekday night, a handful of school-age boys and girls lounged outside on the apartment steps. The pungent and undeniable scent of marijuana tickled John's throat as he and Lainey climbed the warped wooden stairs. The kids watched them with suspicious inky black eyes, the scant light caught by studs and hoops in pierced ears, brows, and lips. Although John wasn't a stranger to them, he wasn't the right color to trust either. However, Lainey was Estelle's great-granddaughter, which was the only reason John wasn't hassled.

The combined odors of urine, stale alcohol, and vomit weren't pleasant, but they were familiar. There were holes in the wall of the stairwell, as well as descriptive—and pornographic—nouns and verbs scrawled across the faded pea green paint. John ignored them and kept his body between the wall and Lainey, even though he knew she'd seen the crude words numerous times, and probably understood them, too.

With a hand on Lainey's skinny shoulder, John steered her down the hallway, lit only by one dim incandescent bulb. He knocked on Estelle's door and listened to the older woman's shuffle as she approached. There was a pause then the chain lock and two bolts were undone. The door was swung open by a leather-faced woman with weary brown eyes and tight gray curls close to her scalp. She was fully a foot shorter than John, but her weight probably equaled, or exceeded, his.

John gave Lainey a gentle shove into the apartment. Once they were inside, the woman wrestled the door locks back in place even though they wouldn't keep out a determined thief. But Estelle had a reputation as a tough bird since she'd lived in this building ever since it was built. Morey, her revolver, hidden close to the door, also served as a deterrent.

Wearing a shift that clung to her rolls of flesh, Estelle propped a fist on a generous hip. "You found her," she said in a sand-over-gravel voice.

John, conscious of the bleeding gash on his arm, held his cuff tight and bent his arm to keep blood from dripping onto the floor. Fortunately, his coat was black so the blood didn't show but he stood angled so Estelle wouldn't see the tear in the sleeve. "She was with Mishon."

Estelle's eyes narrowed, but all she said was, "It's past your bedtime, Lainey."

The girl made a face. "I'm not tired."

"Don't care if you are or you ain't. Off to bed."

With a typical childish pout, Lainey trudged into the tiny bedroom she shared with her mother. She paused in the doorway. "'Night, Gram. 'Night, John." Then she closed the door behind her.

Estelle dropped into her chair that sagged from years of use. Her tiny apartment embodied the definition of clutter. A pile of old magazines and a basket of yarn with knitting needles in the middle of a project lay on either side of her favorite chair. Figurines of cats, dogs, children, pigs—whatever caught Estelle's fancy over the past fifty plus years—covered every available surface.

John picked up a ceramic black and white dog curled up on a pillow. An image flashed through his mind, of a dog with the same colors, jumping to catch a Frisbee in its mouth. In his memory, he heard laughter and turned, but the image disappeared before he could see the girl's face.

"You're gonna bust it." Estelle's voice startled him back to the present.

"What?"

"The way your hand is curled around that dog. Looks like you're trying to crush it."

John immediately uncurled his fingers and set the figurine down.

"You remember somethin', Johnny?" Estelle asked, her gravelly voice almost gentle.

He shook his head. "Not really. Just pictures, pieces of a puzzle."

"It'll come. Don't force it."

The bird clock on the wall chirped twelve times, each chirp a little weaker than the previous.

"So what happened tonight?" Estelle kept her gaze aimed at her knobby arthritic hands.

John considered lying, but the old woman could smell a lie a mile off. "I spotted them on Mishon's usual corner. She'd just scored and there was no way in hell I was going to leave Lainey there." He paused. "On our way here, Mishon's pimp, Jamar, and two of his goons jumped us in an alley."

Estelle's nostrils flared. "Bastards." She paused. "Guess I owe you one."

John smiled at her grudging tone. "Lainey's a good kid. Besides, *I* owe *you*."

Estelle harrumphed. "You don't owe me nothin'. I was just doin' what any decent human being would do."

John's gut told him there weren't very many of those left in the world. At least, not many who would care for a stranger with no name and no past.

"I care." Detective Alexander's soothing, solicitous voice echoed faintly in his mind. He didn't know if he could believe her, but a part of him wanted to . . . badly. However, he didn't dare take the risk.

After glancing into Lainey's darkened room, Estelle said in a low voice, "Jamar likes 'em young. Don't surprise me none that he wants Lainey."

The seven-year-old would bring a good price either in Jamar's stable, or if he sold her to someone looking for a young virgin. Preteen girls were a valued commodity, but they were also high risk. If Jamar was caught pimping a girl like Lainey, he wouldn't last long in prison, provided he even made it that far. John almost wished he'd told the detective the truth. But even if he had, she could only get Jamar for assault, which wouldn't give him what he deserved.

"If Mishon is desperate enough for a fix, she might make a deal with Jamar," John said, the words leaving a foul taste in his mouth.

Estelle glared at him. "No need to be tellin' me what I already know." Her wrinkles deepened. "As long as Lainey's here with me, Jamar knows better than to bother her. And if it comes down to it, I'll call the police."

He shifted his weight and his injuries from the fight throbbed. "You and Lainey going to be all right?"

Estelle snorted. "As long as I got Morey, we'll be fine."

A corner of John's lips lifted in amusement and he stepped toward the door.

"You goin' to that drafty warehouse where you been stayin'?" Estelle asked.

"Home sweet home."

She made a face that didn't leave any doubt what she thought of his comment. "I still think you ought to check with the cops, Johnny. Might be someone's lookin' for you."

A chill chased down his spine, although again he couldn't attribute it to anything specific. However, the scars on his body, the ease with which he defended himself and the violent nightmares that haunted him warned him he was a dangerous man. Maybe someone the police were looking for, but not as a missing person.

"I'll think about it." It was the same answer he gave every time she brought up the subject.

Careful he didn't leave any blood behind, he undid the bolts and chain. "Lock up behind me."

Estelle grumbled and heaved her significant frame to her feet.

John closed the door behind him and waited until he heard the old woman re-bolt the door.

"You can go now," she said, obviously knowing he remained on the other side.

John squelched a grin and walked away.

The front stoop was empty and his shoulders sagged with relief. Although the kids weren't normally a threat, if they were hopped up on meth or heroin, that was another story.

And unpredictability yields the worst possible scenario.

The words drifted from that mysterious cache in his brain that remembered, but guarded its secrets zealously. Out of habit, he took a circuitous route to the warehouse he called home. In actuality it was located less than a block from Estelle's, but he walked four times that far to disguise his path. He didn't know why . . .

With his injured arm, he awkwardly climbed the rusty ladder attached to the side of the warehouse and dropped noiselessly to the flat roof. A cold wind buffeted him and sliced through his clothing. Over two weeks after discovering the roof opening, John followed the familiar path and lifted a maintenance hatch. Another ladder and he was inside the dim warehouse, his entrance sealed from the interior so no one else could access it.

There was an office on the second floor that he'd claimed. The space hadn't been abandoned long since the couch and desk chair showed little sign of rodent activity and the water was still running in the bathroom. The only thing he didn't have was electricity, which would be a problem as winter drew nearer. And by the feel of the north wind tonight, winter was closer than he wanted to consider.

John tossed off his coat and ruined bloody shirt, and shivered in the cold night air. In the bathroom he washed away the dried blood on his bicep, revealing a cut four inches long and half an inch deep. He suspected it could use stitches, but with no insurance—let alone a last name—it would heal on its own. That it would leave a scar was a given—one more for his collection.

But it's the first one I actually know how I received.

John dug around in his frayed backpack, which held all his earthly possessions. The first aid kit, left behind by the former office tenants, yielded a nearly flat tube of antibacterial cream. He slathered it on the cut, ignoring the discomfort. After placing a gauze pad on the wound, he used duct tape to hold it in place. If he was incredibly lucky, he would be current on his tetanus vaccination.

He gazed in the smoky mirror, at the shaggy-haired stranger who stared back at him.

"Who the hell are you?"

But the image didn't answer. Instead, his reflection blurred and he could almost feel a small hand on his cheek.

"Will I have to shave someday, Daddy?"

John whirled around, expecting to see a young girl standing beside him. But he was alone. Did he have a daughter out there . . . missing him?

The thought of a family made his gut twist in a visceral knot. Maybe Estelle was right. Maybe he should visit the local police station and find out if someone was looking for him. It had been three weeks now. Surely if that family existed, they would've filed a missing persons report.

Torn by conflict, John rummaged in his bag and pulled out his only other shirt, a black turtleneck. Grabbing the roll of duct tape again, he returned to the office. Laying out his jacket on the desk, he used the gray tape to mend the tear in his sleeve. When he was finished, the fix wasn't pretty, but it was efficient and that was all that mattered.

He slipped on his jacket and his hands slid into the pockets by habit. His fingers closed on the business card. . . .

Detective Shoni Alexander. Homicide Section.

Despite the detective's tough attitude, he'd sensed a vulnerability in her that triggered some atavistic protectiveness. Ridiculous, considering she was a cop and he didn't even know who the hell *he* was.

"I care." The two words whispered across him once again. From anyone else he would've laughed, but his gut told him Detective Alexander was sincere.

A foreign scuffle from below caught his attention. Too loud for a mouse or rat. Not noisy enough for a dog. Either a clumsy cat or a human being. And, granted, his memory was pretty much Swiss cheese, but he couldn't remember meeting a clumsy cat.

Falling into a stealthy crouch came as naturally as breathing. Although there were no lights in the warehouse, John had memorized the layout between eating at St. Anne's soup kitchen and rummaging in dumpsters.

He glided out of the office, onto the five-foot-wide walkway. He dropped to his knees noiselessly and crept up to the railing to peer through the metal bars and down at the expansive room.

Another foreign sound—tinny, uneven. Then liquid being splashed against a surface.

Frowning, John crab walked to the top of the stairs. A dim motion below caught his eye and he used his peripheral vision to try to determine what it was.

But before he could, the unmistakable scent of gasoline drifted up to him.

What the hell . . .

A soft click and low laughter.

At a primal gut level John recognized the whoosh that followed.

Fire.